BassetBooks

This Time

Joan Szechtman

Published by
Basset Books, LLC
Milford, CT

Copyright © 2009 by Joan Szechtman

Basset Books LLC trade paper first edition 2009.

Basset Books LLC
Collected Stories Bookstore
12 Daniel Street
Milford, CT 06460
bassetpublishing@collectedstoriesbookstore.com

ISBN-13: 978-0-9824493-0-1

With love to my parents, David and Thelma Udell

And to the memory of Beverly "Ginger" Dick

Acknowledgments

It is my pleasure to thank the many people who have helped me with this project. I could not have produced this work without the generous assistance from the members of Critique Circle (www.critiquecircle.com), the award-winning, online workshop for writers. While far more people supported my efforts than I can list here, I am grateful for the exceptional guidance I have received from Beverly "Ginger" Dick, Kelli Gailfus, Fiona McLaren, and Brad Schoenfeld.

Of the many members of the Richard III Society who have helped me, I wish to thank Rollo Crookshank, David Luitweiler, and Brian Wainwright for vetting my historical facts and ensuring that my speculations on the undocumented historical aspects of Richard III and his era were credible:. Any errors that may have crept through after their review are mine.

Many thanks to my dear friend, Ed, whose unflagging support gave me the courage to press forward.

I wish to thank my editor, Janice Hussein, and my agent, Susan Shaw. This book would still be moldering on my computer if not for their support.

I would be remiss if I failed to acknowledge the aid I received from my local library and for the interlibrary loan system that gives me access to public and university libraries throughout the United States.

Part One

ONE

Monday, August 22, 1485
The battle of Bosworth
Bosworth Field, England

King Richard III spurred his steed through Ambion Wood, rejecting the advice of his generals to run from the battle. Two armies, one led by Lord Thomas Stanley and the other by Sir William Stanley, were positioned to support whoever won. Then King Richard broke line, forcing the Stanleys to show their fealty, taking the battle to Henry Tudor—king against usurper.

For a moment his thoughts strayed, and he saw not his select troops by his side or the battle before him, but Anne, his wife, now dead five months.

"Anne," he whispered, reaching for her across the horse's mane, but her image was gone.

He blinked and the battle came back into view. The balance was tipping to his enemy. He swept his gaze past the wood and saw Henry standing among his men. *I will have you or I will be with Anne.*

Sir John Cheyney loomed before him, blocking Richard's charge. He swung his axe and sent this giant of a knight clattering to the ground.

With his select troops by his side, he fought on toward Henry's camp, his blood hot in his veins. The challenger stood but a few feet away, protected by his knights and soldiers. Richard swung his axe savagely and inched forward. A horse screamed as it and its knight thudded to the ground.

The horror rose like bile in his throat as the legs of Sir Percival Thirwall, his standard bearer, were cut off.

Jesú! He still carries my banner.

His pulse hammered, matching the pounding of horses at his rear. Stanley's army bore down and attacked—him.

No…they have turned against me!

Hands grabbed his reins and pulled; his warhorse was mired in thick mud.

"TREASON!" His courser crashed down and he was unhorsed. The mud pulled at him as he staggered to his feet.

Richard smashed his axe into the neck of a soldier. He tasted the man's blood as it splashed through an opening of his visor. "TREASON!" he screamed, advancing through a blood-red rage. A blow crashed against his chest, stealing his wind. His armor pierced, Richard fell to his knees. The last sounds he heard were the shouts of Henry's victory.

Saturday, August 21, 2004
Ambion Technologies
Portland, Oregon

Richard lay with his eyes shut, his body leaden. With the sounds of battle gone, his thoughts turned to his wife.

Anne, at last I have come to join our son and you for…

"Hey Mike, good job!" a man's voice spoke, then some laughter from the same location.

The mirth jarred his senses. *Am I not dead?*

"Thanks, but it's only half, isn't it?" another asked. His voice bespoke of youth.

He heard men's voices but could not interpret the dialect. He sensed their movement, but could not smell their bodies. The odors were strange.

"More than half. I have my grail, thanks to you," the older voice said. "And I know something no one else does, I know exactly where the battle was fought."

"But, don't you need to recover your investment? It still has no commercial viability," the younger voice said.

"Mike, I've every confidence in your abilities. You'll solve it."

"I-I'm not confident, Hosgrove. We are unable to keep anything sent into the past intact beyond thirty seconds."

Richard's body tingled as sensation returned. His head spun. He kept his eyes closed and listened.

"Wow, for such a well-muscled man, he appears positively gaunt," the young man said. "Uh, I see you're using restraints on him. I guess it's a good idea, but won't that start things on the wrong foot?"

"I've given it some thought, and decided that it would be best if we explain things to him first. Then we can release the straps."

"You're the boss."

Where were the sounds of battle, or if done, the groans of the wounded and dying? And why is there no stench of blood and shit and sweat? The language I'm hearing—what is it? Why is it familiar but strange? Where am I? It can no longer be Redemore, can it?

He opened his eyes for but a trice and was so blinded by the bright light; his eyes snapped shut in protest. His heart raced. He forced himself to listen.

"Mike, can we return him if we have to?" the older man asked.

"I don't know. The timing was tricky enough as it was. I'm afraid to go back myself."

"You wouldn't have to go back, Mike, but check into it. Think of it as insurance."

Did the older man call him Mike?

"Yeah, more like short-term insurance," Mike said.

It is English! Why do I not comprehend?

The older man spoke again. "Katarina should have been here by now. She's the only one who has studied Early Modern English to the depth that we'll need."

"When did you call her?" Mike said.

"Um, almost an hour ago. She said she'd leave right away. It would be just like her to get distracted. It's starting to piss me off!"

"I bet she ran into some traffic," Mike said. "It gets pretty busy around this time, even on a Saturday."

Saturday? What was happening? He'd gone into battle on Monday. Had he just lost five days of his life?

As his head cleared, he dared to open his eyes. Prepared as he was, the light still assaulted him. He scanned the chamber. Much of what came into view was unfamiliar, but he could make out a long gray table to his left with six plain gray chairs around it. Overhead, the ceiling was partitioned into rectangles, some of which glared with a bright white light. He tried to sit up.

Jesú! I am tied down. I am a prisoner, but by whom? This chamber is not like any I have seen.

He flexed his hands and feet to test the bonds. He saw the odd attire on the two men, the taller a white-haired, barrel-chested man and the other, a young blond-haired man of slight build. He thought the younger one was Mike. He could not guess their heights while lying on his back, but could tell the older man was taller than the other by a half a head. The air had an odor that was unlike anything he had ever smelled.

"He's awake," Mike said.

"Good," the white-haired man said and walked closer to him. He pulled a chair up and sat down. "You will have to trust that what I am about to say is true, Richard. It will come as a shock, but there is no good way to prepare you."

"Jesú!" Richard exclaimed, straining against the fetters.

"Ah, he -"

The door burst open, interrupting the older man. A tall, slim lad entered the room. His skin was smooth and unshaven.

The older man rose and waved the lad over to his side. "You said you were going to leave immediately."

"I did, Hosgrove," a woman's voice spoke from the lad's lips. "Not only did they raise the bridge, but I'd forgotten about the construction on Burnside."

Hosgrove? Is that his name?

When the new person stepped closer to Richard, he realized the lad was in truth a woman dressed like a man. *Heretic.*

"Why is he tied down?" She reached for the strap.

The scent of lavender clung to her, bringing Anne to mind. Some of the tension left his muscles.

"Hey wait!" Mike said. "You don't know what he'll do."

The woman let go of the strap. "Okay, but we're not going to keep him tied to this table much longer."

Richard struggled to make more sense of the words that were spoken. It seemed the woman was advocating in his behalf. Mayhap he misjudged her.

She patted his hand and spoke slowly in his dialect. "Richard, we mean you no harm. I will prove it by releasing you if you swear that you will not try to harm us."

Her accent was strange, and not all the words were meaningful, but he did understand her more than the others.

"I swear," he said, studying the woman's dark eyes, "I will not harm you." His voice came out in a harsh whisper.

She tipped her head to the two men and they undid the ties. He quickly sat up, but his head spun and he lost his balance. He felt her hand on his arm, preventing him from falling back.

"They gave you something which is causing you to feel this way," the woman said. "It will wear off quickly."

He frowned. *Trapped.* His head pounded. If this were a chamber, it was small and cramped, but extremely bright to his eyes. Where was he? It was too clean for a prison.

His muscles were slow, barely able to heed his commands; he could not do anything to defend himself. They knew his name, but he was used to people knowing who he was. Still he could ask them some questions, and he understood the manly dressed woman.

"Tell me truly, where am I and who are you?"

The woman started to rephrase his query, but Hosgrove waved his hand. "His meaning's plain enough. You just translate my explanation. I'm sure he won't understand anything but a few words from me.

"You were about to be slain on Bosworth Field by Stanley's army. We saved you from that fate." Hosgrove fixed his watery blue eyes on Richard. "Through science and technology, which people of your time would undoubtedly call magic, we have brought you five hundred and nineteen years into the future. It is the twenty-first of August, 2004."

Had he heard correctly? Stunned, he concentrated on the woman's interpretation. *Two-thousand and four? Impossible.* He scanned the chamber again, seeing more of the unfamiliar than in his first survey. He could put none of what he saw into any context that he knew. He moved his hand to grip the dagger on his belt—the dagger and belt were gone. He pinched the bridge of his nose instead.

The man named Mike rounded the table and stood between him and Hosgrove. "Historical records state that you died that day on Bosworth Field," Mike said. "But, we substituted someone who was already dead and pulled you into this time seconds before you would have been slain by Stanley's army." He moved closer.

Richard remained silent, concentrating on the woman's interpretation. When he stood, Mike stepped in and jabbed his right hand at him. Richard hesitated a moment and then yanked Mike's right arm and pulled the man's back to his chest. He immobilized the slightly built man, pinning one arm between them and the other against Mike's ribs.

Hosgrove called out, "Frank! Joe! Get in here NOW!"

"Return me or I will make your demon regret this day," Richard said, injecting as much menace in his voice as he could.

The woman stood frozen by his side. The door banged open, and two men advanced toward him. They were both tall and so muscular that their garments seemed to strain in protest. One had spiky, brown hair that was so short you could see his pale white scalp. The other had a warm, honey-brown complexion, but his cold eyes could freeze a man as easily as the gaze from the gorgon. *Saracen.* Richard tightened his grip.

Mike twisted in Richard's grasp. "Let me go, you're breaking my arm!"

"Release him now," the Saracen said.

By their deportment, Richard knew they were guards, despite their lack of armor and weapons.

The men approached him from either side. He was flanked and without weapons, save for the man he was holding. He saw a blur of motion to his right. Before he could move, the brown-haired man pressed a small, black cylindrical object against his bare arm. The object burned into his skin. He lost his grip on Mike and he fell, his muscles bunching in rapid spasms.

The woman knelt beside him, pleading, "Promise you will not do anything like that again. They have not hurt you. They will tie you up again if you refuse."

"That's ridiculous, Katarina," Hosgrove said. "He lied to us before. Move out of the way so we can restrain him."

The woman stood, and Richard felt something cold and hard against his wrists. The two guards jerked him to his feet and pulled his arms tight behind his body.

As his control returned, the pain in his arm moved from his muscles to the bone, while the stress on his wrists and shoulders served to aggravate it. He twisted his body trying to ease the pain in his shoulders and tugged hard against the restraints on his wrists.

"Richard! Stop struggling. You're hurting yourself," she said.

He stood rigidly still and clenched his jaw. His body ached.

"Get those cuffs off him now, Hosgrove," she said. "I don't understand why you went to all this trouble and expense, only to treat him like this. Maybe he thought he had to defend himself. He probably didn't understand that Mike was only trying to shake his hand."

Hosgrove paused. "Tell him, Katarina, that if he tries anything like that again, we won't be so gentle. We'll do more than stun and cuff him." He turned to the guards standing by. "Return to your posts."

Richard shrugged his shoulders once his hands were free. "What do you want of me? Why am I here?"

"For me, you are the grail, the source," Hosgrove said.

"How can that be?" Richard asked, frowning. "I am not Christ. How dare you blaspheme our Lord and savior?"

"My apologies, I didn't mean it literally," Hosgrove said. "Tudor was the victor at Bosworth. Because of that, history was revised to agree with his version of events. You've been vilified for over five hundred years. You are the only one who knows your thoughts and what really happened. This is why we had to bring you to the future and not someone else. Besides, you'd be dead if we hadn't."

Katarina used the more familiar English to transform Hosgrove's statement, but the similarity between the languages was apparent.

"I am very sorry for what we are putting you through. We have handled this badly." She paused. He let her hold his hand in hers, stroking his bruised wrist. "You don't even know our names. I am Katarina Parvic, the older man is Evan Hosgrove, and he," she pointed to the slight, blond man, "is Michael Fairchild. I know this does not mean anything to you, but at least you now know our names. Please call me Katarina."

"You say this is a future time, and in truth, I see things for which I have no comprehension." He fingered the hem of the shirt they had dressed him in while he was unconscious. "Five hundred years! How can I believe?"

"I know," Michael said, kneading his arm. "We can show you a newspaper. Today's date is printed at the top of each page. You'll be able to tell by the way it's printed and other things about it that we are telling you the truth." He opened the door and left the room.

Michael returned just as Katarina finished translating. "I had a copy of *The Oregonian* at my desk. I figured it would do for starters." He dropped the newspaper on the table, and shuffled through it for a few seconds, setting some pages aside.

"Come with me." She pointed to the table with the paper.

Richard stood and saw she towered over him as much as his brother, Ned, had. He'd ignored her height before, but now, despite his situation, he needed to ask.

"Katarina, how tall are you?"

She laughed. "I'm just over six feet, but I may seem taller because my shoes have a heel." She took her shoes off and stood facing him. "Is this less of a shock to you?" She laughed again.

She exceeded the height of the tallest woman he had known.

Katarina kept her shoes off until they sat down at the table.

The images jumped out at him before he saw the print. These were not the highly decorative illustrations that he remembered in bibles or Psalters. The images were all in color, and the people in them appeared real, not like the portraits he had. He ran his fingers over them, and they were flat. There were no ridges or bumps, other than the texture of the paper. But it was much thinner and more uniform than the paper he had handled. He tore his eyes away from the pictures to the print, and read the large plain type of the twenty-first century date to the left of the banner.

He closed his eyes, willing the images to vanish.

Katarina's fingertips brushed his back. "Are you all right?" she asked.

He opened his eyes. "I am lost."

"Look, Richard," Hosgrove said. "We explained it all to you. You have to give it time. You'll adjust."

Katarina started to translate, but he stopped her. He stood up and placed his fists on the table and leaned over Evan Hosgrove.

"You dare to be familiar?" His voice took on his accustomed authority. "You will call me, Your Grace. You will bow before me."

Michael slunk down in his chair, hugging his arms. Hosgrove glared at Katarina, eyebrows knitting together.

"I think we need to take a break, Hosgrove." Katarina turned to Richard. "Please let me explain some things to you that will help you feel less lost. Will you allow me to do that, Your Grace?" She touched his arm with her hand.

He drew back from Katarina and glowered at Hosgrove. "They must leave, Madam." He saw fear cross Katarina's features to be quickly replaced by a guarded expression. "I swore, Katarina. Do you not trust me?"

"Hosgrove, Michael," Katarina said, nodding to them both. "I'll be all right. It's getting late, and I need to work with him on language. Why don't you two go now and leave me with him?"

"Are you sure?" Michael asked.

"Yes, Michael. Anyway, security's here so don't worry."

"I think you ought to have this," Hosgrove said, holding up the black cylindrical object.

"Are you out of your mind? I think that would be the last thing I should have in my hands," she said.

Hosgrove jammed it back into his pocket and stormed over to the door with Michael two steps behind him. "Don't mess this up Katarina," came Hosgrove's parting shot.

TWO

"Please sit down," Katarina said after the door closed.

"You do trust me?" Richard asked.

Her lips edged up into a wistful smile. "Yes, I do. Will you trust me?"

Richard gazed around the strange room and at the willowy woman sitting in front of him. He felt ashamed that he should have thought to threaten her. He sat sideways in the chair and faced Katarina.

"Yes," he said, keeping his voice soft and low. He had to get her help, her absolute trust.

"Will you allow me to call you Richard?"

"You may, Katarina. I will not seek obeisance from you."

"Thank you. Let me begin by confirming that you have been brought into the future. This is the twenty-first century, and it is a very different world from the one you knew."

"Five hundred years," he whispered, holding her brown eyes with his. "What kind of world is it? You will show me?"

"I'll try," she said. "You need to suspend your disbelief about some of what I say until you see for yourself. You are going to find much that is unimaginable from your time. Please be patient."

"Am I still King?"

"According to history, you are dead. So no, you're not King in this time. In fact, we pulled you into this time a few seconds before you would have been killed. We left a dead corpse in your stead. They mutilated your body, Richard. I'm sorry."

He heard the sincerity in her statement. "Will you return me to Redemore Plain when you are done with me?"

"No! That would be a horrible thing to do!" she said. "Besides, what reason would we have to send you to certain death?"

Richard said nothing. He squeezed his eyes shut and put his head in his hands, elbows on the table. He shrank from her hand when she brushed his back. Why did her touch bother him?

"Richard, I did not mean to offend. Please forgive any transgressions on my part."

He saw concern in her eyes. "I am not offended."

"Before we start with my helping you understand life in the twenty-first century, I would like to understand something about you. I know from what I've read that you were a fair-minded ruler. Why did you allow some enemies to live after you conquered them, but not others?"

"What do you mean, Katarina? The leaders are usually executed for treason. It is customary to spare the subordinates."

"They were only following orders, eh?"

Though baffled by the question, Richard nodded.

"But what about the Stanleys? They were leaders and yet you let them live."

Those traitors! He should have executed the hostage, Lord Strange, Thomas Stanley's son. Why had he allowed Stanley to see through his ruse? Stanley knew he had lost his own son. Had Stanley gambled his son's life, thinking Richard had not the heart to kill another man's son?

But they were all dead now, all his enemies, all his friends— dead. He froze on the thought.

"Richard?"

"I vowed never to give quarter again, had I held the day at Bosworth. The Stanleys betrayed me after I showed leniency. But for them, I would have prevailed at Bosworth."

Katarina's pupils grew large and her lips parted slightly. While Richard would not describe her expression as one of pity, the word that came to mind was in his Latin vocabulary— *misericors*—caring heart.

"Why did you trust Lord Stanley? He was married to Henry Tudor's mother, after all."

"I needed his support and he kept his word. He isolated her from Henry."

"But surely Hastings proved his loyalty by alerting you to Elizabeth's intentions of cutting you off, denying her husband's will. Yet you executed him in great haste."

Loyalty! He averted his eyes, having no wish for Katarina to see the anger that still burned after two years. "I had proof of his treason. It was not something I did lightly. But why should it matter to you? As you have shown, all those events occurred over five hundred years ago. Surely it is no longer of importance."

"Do you really believe that, Richard?"

"I do not know what to believe. Everything I have known and believed has been shattered."

"Please, let me help you pick up the pieces."

"I do not think it possible," he said.

"Give it time." Her voice betrayed her emotion.

Richard stared at Katarina and then down at his hands. He picked up *The Oregonian*. "Help me to understand this first."

"It will be my pleasure," she said spreading the front page out for them to view. "Newspapers are printed on a cheap grade of paper, so we just throw them away."

As Katarina explained how the newspaper was organized, she encouraged him to read random paragraphs to her. He felt embarrassed by his halting speech and her frequent corrections. But he understood her purpose and kept his temper in check.

She put each section aside when they finished reviewing it. The classified ads were spread open, and she stretched, rubbing her eyes. "These are advertisements for jobs, places to rent, and things that people are selling." She folded the last section. "It's getting late. I don't know about you, but I'm really hungry."

"I do feel the need for sustenance," he said.

"I will have to leave your presence to get us supper. Will you be all right being here alone until I get back? It will take about an hour."

"I have need of the privy chamber. Where is it?"

Katarina smiled. "We call it a bathroom now, and it has additional functions. I'll show you what we have, and how to use it. Follow me."

She brought him to a small chamber opposite the main entry that contained several unfamiliar objects; some were white. The first thing Katarina did after she opened the door was to push down on a silver lever that protruded from the squat-shaped white object.

"You eliminate your…"

He jumped away from Katarina and gave a startled yelp when the water rushed through it.

Katarina giggled. "I did not mean to alarm you. This is what we use instead. It's called a toilet. That little lever causes fresh water to flush your waste away."

He pointed to a white roll on the wall next to the toilet. "What is that?"

"Toilet paper, you use it instead of hay." She tore off a piece and handed it to him.

The softness of the paper pleasantly surprised him.

"What do the other objects do?" he asked.

"This is a shower," she said, pausing to open the door. Water sprayed out of a pipe toward the back wall when she turned a knob. "You can take a hot shower as often as you like. You adjust the temperature to what you want with this knob. Here is soap and the shampoo is for hair."

Richard twisted his hand, palm up then palm down, feeling the water beat on him like a summer's rain, but warmer. "How do I stop the water?"

She reached in front of him. "You twist it this way to turn the water off."

He inhaled the scent at the nape of her neck, and he suddenly felt aroused. He wanted to follow his body's desires, but the situation stopped him. He stepped back quickly to put a bit of distance between them.

They returned to the main chamber, and she had him wait by the table before going to the door.

"Joe, I'm picking up dinner for us, can I get you anything?"

"No Ma'am, I've already eaten."

"I'll be back in about an hour," she said and disappeared down a corridor.

Richard watched as the guard closed the door. He was relieved that he was finally alone and able to think, for the moment.

He explored the room for anything he could use for a weapon. The chairs by the table had metal frames, but he could not see how to dismantle one to fashion a pole or a pike. Every other movable object was either too flimsy to be suitable, or too solidly constructed for easy conversion.

If he could open the door, he'd need a way to disable the guard seated outside the only exit.

Katarina appeared to be his only hope of escape. He could not fathom to what or where this escape would lead, but he determined to sway her to his cause.

He picked up a section of the newspaper, and scanned each page. He carefully said the words out loud, trying to remember what they sounded like. He sighed; it seemed he would have to relearn English. At least he found many of the words familiar, if not from the English or spelling he knew, then from the Latin or French. He had learned some new words from the context in which they were printed.

He heard a soft knock at the door.

Katarina walked in and put a large canvas sack on the table. "I hope you don't mind my joining you. I thought this would be a good time for you to ask me questions. I also got some wine so that we could have something besides water."

Remembering the unpleasantness when he grabbed Michael, he asked, "What hath they wrought on me, Katarina? Why did I feel on fire?"

She emptied the contents of the sack while answering, "It's impossible to explain in your terminology, but they used a device called a *stun gun* that prevented you from fighting." She set up two place settings and then set two wineglasses down, uncorked the bottle, and poured them each a glass of the red wine.

Handing a glass to Richard, she said, "A toast to you Richard, I wish you much happiness and prosperity."

Katarina took a sip, but Richard held the glass to his nose and sniffed.

"Is something wrong with the wine?" she asked.

He shook his head. "No, it is different." He took a sip.

"Does it meet with your approval?"

He nodded. "I have never tasted wine like this. What is it called?"

"Shiraz." Katarina put her glass down and doled out the rib steak and roasted root vegetables onto each plate. "I hope the food in this century is acceptable to you."

"Is that beef?"

She nodded.

"Why is it red? Did you not boil it?"

"Boil it?" She frowned. "That would ruin this delicious rib roast."

He pushed away from the table. "Are you trying to sicken me?"

"What?" She cut a small piece of the meat and ate it. "I'm eating it and it's not making me sick."

He sat down, frowning.

"Now what's the matter?" she asked.

"Where are the sops, and why is the meat not cut?"

"We no longer serve sauces with everything, and we cut our food with these." She held a knife and fork up.

He copied her and found the fork awkward in his hand, but it did the job. He glanced up to see her smiling.

"Do you find my eating amusing?"

"No," Katarina said. "It is just that I'm seeing things I took for granted, as if it were the first time, through your eyes. I'm sorry if I made you uncomfortable."

"You are forgiven."

She cast her eyes down and twisted her napkin. "I am sorry."

He put his hand over hers. "I know."

He drank some wine and then pointed to one of the vegetables with his fork asking, "What manner of food is this?"

"It's called a potato, and is native to this continent. You'll discover many new foods."

He ate some. "This is quite good."

"I am going to speak in modern-day English from this point on, until I leave tonight. I will speak slowly. Ask me anything you want, but try to ask it, as best you can, by imitating me.

"Before I switch completely to Modern English, there is one word that you need to know because it is so widely used, and that word is OKAY. Some meanings are: all right, agree, acceptable, and approve. You will have to determine which it is by how it is used." Katarina paused. "Okay?"

Richard smiled for the first time. "Okay."

THREE

Richard watched Katarina leave after they finished eating. The guard was still positioned outside the door of his prison. He waited a few minutes before attempting to open the door. If there was only one guard, perhaps he could overpower him, but then what?

The door did not yield.

He studied the plain chamber; perhaps there was a secret door, a way out. He ran his hands along the smooth wall, but the only breaks he found were obvious to the eye, the opening for the bathroom, and two small chambers where paper and other supplies were stored.

The ceiling over his head was paneled, with regular breaks. It was not that far above his head, perhaps that afforded a way of escape. Richard climbed on a chair and pushed at the panel. It was light and moved easily.

His heart raced. He craned his neck back, peering into a small chamber with a second ceiling not three feet above the first. He lowered the panel and climbed onto the large gray table, pushing a second panel aside. He stood on his toes and stuck his head through the opened ceiling, scanning in every direction. This chamber was not as well lit as the lower, larger one. The gloom was broken by points of light in the same location as the brighter lights below.

He pulled on a thin metal crossbar and it flexed easily. It would not support his weight. Also, it appeared all the dust had accumulated by his head. He sneezed, sending up additional clots of dust. He sneezed again and again, in rapid succession.

"Hey! You okay in there?" a voice called from the other side of the door.

Richard quickly slid the panel back into place and jumped down from the table. "I am okay."

The door opened and the guard filled the doorway, holding the stun gun in one hand and the doorknob in the other. He stared at Richard for a few seconds before speaking.

"Hey buddy, I just thought I'd let you know, the lights will go off at eleven, that's an hour from now." He stepped back into the hallway and shut the door. Richard heard the lock fall into place.

If he could not escape, then he could be clean. He entered the bathroom, disrobed and turned the shower on. He stood in the shower and let the water beat on him. This was pure luxury; it was better than a bath. Yet Katarina had assured him that this was commonplace now.

He knew Anne would have loved this, for even though their servants would prepare their baths, they could not just stand under a spray of hot water.

Richard remained in the shower long enough to scrub every bit of his body several times over. He stayed until it got too cold to be enjoyable. He put the loose garments back on and went to bed.

He fell into a fitful sleep and dreamt of Anne, his son, family, friends and enemies throughout the night. But mostly he dreamt of Anne. While each dream was different, each ended the same. Anne would be tantalizingly close and then vanish.

"Anne, do not abandon me," Richard whispered. Abruptly, she pushed him into a chair, her expression wild, and then fled, disappearing into the bright mist.

This last dream, between sleep and wakefulness, took place in this room. What did it mean?

"Richard," a man's voice called from beyond the door. "It's me, Evan. Are you awake?"

Richard jerked from his sleep, squinting his eyes against the glaring ceiling lights in the windowless room. His head ached and the previous day's loose garments were twisted and bound him uncomfortably. Kicking the tangle of blankets from his feet, he rose to a sitting position.

He rested his feet on the gray carpet, longing to go beyond the locked door, longing to experience the twenty-first century.

"Richard," Evan called again. "I'm coming in."

Richard walked toward the door and watched the knob twist just before the door opened. Evan Hosgrove walked in carrying a small paper sack and some clothes.

"Breakfast," Hosgrove said, holding a brown bag on which were painted brightly colored symbols and letters. "I'll put it down there." He pointed to the large gray-topped table where they had worked yesterday.

Its appearance made him think of stone, but Katarina had called the material plastic. Indeed, it did not feel like stone.

"Why don't you eat first, and then I'll leave you alone so you can take a shower. I understand Katarina showed you how to use it. Here's a change of clothes for you, as well." Hosgrove pointed to the garments.

Richard was not used to eating immediately upon awakening, and he wanted to stand under the shower and feel the water relax him as he had done after Katarina left.

"I will shower now," Richard said slowly, staring Hosgrove down.

"Okay, I'll return in a half hour. Will that give you enough time?" Hosgrove asked. He spoke slowly enunciating each word. He walked out of the room when Richard nodded.

Richard put his ear to the door from which Hosgrove had exited. The only thing he could hear was a soft hum that came from somewhere over his head. He tried to twist the knob but it did not turn, nor did it yield when he pulled on it. He abandoned his efforts and went into the bathroom.

He put the water on as hot as he could stand and stood under the stream for a few minutes thinking. As much as he relished the shower, he knew that he'd go mad if he had to remain forever here.

I am a prisoner.

He scrubbed his body vigorously with the soapy washcloth until his skin felt a bit raw and was blotchy pink. He turned the shower off and toweled down after the water had cooled. The mirror was fogged, reflecting his stubbly chin in a blur. He could not find a shaving blade.

Richard donned the clean garments and found Hosgrove sitting at the table when he entered the main chamber.

"There is no razor and I cannot shave. I would be clean-shaven."

"We don't use cutthroat razors anymore." Hosgrove stood and showed Richard a small object in the palm of his hand. "This is a safety razor, which has two small blades imbedded in the flat part here."

Richard picked up the razor. "It has no substance. How will it cut through my beard?"

"I'll show you."

Richard ran his hand over his face after he finished shaving, liking the smooth feel of his skin. But, he had been stripped of all his weapons, save his mind, and he had hoped to gain at least a knife or razor to defend himself. This razor was useless. He left it on the sink and went into the main room.

"Would you like to eat before the food is completely cold?" Hosgrove asked.

Richard sat down. "I will break my fast." He smelled bacon and eggs, but all he could see was an odd stack of food; the bacon and eggs were packed between a bread-like substance. He stared at it.

"Sorry, Richard. It's a sandwich. You pick it up with your fingers and just bite into it."

After taking a bite, he found the food wasn't as tasty as his usual fare. It was cold, but it would have to do. He searched for some ale to drink, but the only things that appeared drinkable were a glass filled with a yellow-orange liquid and a pot filled with a hot, brown liquid.

"What are you drinking?" he asked, seeing Hosgrove drinking from a mug that he had just filled from the pot.

"It's called coffee. Why don't you try some?" He filled a second mug and handed it to Richard.

Richard took a sip of the black coffee. He liked its bitter taste and nodded approvingly. "What is this yellow liquid?"

"Orange juice."

Richard raised his eyebrows in surprise. Oranges were a rare treat; they had to be imported from Spain or Portugal at great expense. *Are they so common here that they can waste them on juice?* He decided to save it for later and finished his egg sandwich instead.

He had just swallowed the last bite when both Katarina and Michael entered the room. Katarina carried a large book that Richard thought had to weigh half a stone.

"What is that?" He pointed to the book.

She put it down on the table next to him. "This is a dictionary. It has thousands of words that are in use today, their definitions and pronunciation, as well as their correct spelling. I will show you how to use it later."

"I read that your father was killed in battle when you were eight," Hosgrove said, speaking slowly. "What happened to you and what was it like for you?"

"Hosgrove!" Katarina said. "Must you start with that? He's had quite a shock already, and you dive right into the deep end without any preparation. I won't reword that. Think of something else to ask. I'm sure that can wait until tomorrow."

Hosgrove folded his arms and frowned. "Katarina, I am not paying you for your opinion. I am paying you to get around any language barrier that may exist between Modern English and fifteenth century English. And now that I've heard him speak, I find I understand a lot more than I thought I would. In fact, I'm not sure how much longer I'll need your services."

Richard understood Hosgrove's initial question and was about to answer it, not waiting for Katarina to reword it into a fifteenth century form, but she spoke before he could say anything. He even understood the rapid conversation between Katarina and Hosgrove, and he could see Hosgrove was angry and Katarina was upset.

The next words out of his mouth were in French, hoping that Katarina would understand him and Hosgrove would not.

"I do not know if you can understand me. Tell me if you can and I will continue," Richard said, focusing on Katarina.

Hosgrove asked, "What language is that, Katarina? It sounds a little like French."

"It is," Katarina said to Hosgrove in English. She turned to Richard and answered him in a mix of modern and fifteenth century French. "I speak French and Hosgrove does not, as far as I know. I do not know the French of your time as well as I know the English of your time, so you will have to speak plainly."

"I understood his question," Richard continued in French. "And I did not much like it. I see you are upset by what he said."

Hosgrove started to interrupt, but Katarina held up her hand, stopping him.

"I knew he would ask you some difficult questions, but I thought he would give you a chance to become accustomed to us first." Her gaze shifted from her hands to Richard's eyes. "He is going to dismiss me unless he can't understand you. That upset me, too. I don't want to be dismissed."

"I would prefer that you remain," Richard said. "Tell him that I am more comfortable speaking in French as that was the court language for a great part of my life."

"Is that true? I thought your brother changed all that. I think it would be better if you told him you need me to explain those terms whose meanings have reversed and for the more obscure words and pronunciations." Katarina put her hand over Richard's. "You see, I have other obligations, and I cannot be with you for most of tomorrow, and it would be better if you two could talk to each other without me."

Richard frowned at that last bit of news and then nodded in agreement. He turned to Hosgrove and using English said, "I am able to understand much, but there is much that I hath no understanding for. I will need Katarina to be here for those words I mishear and do not know. I need her to stay with me."

"Very well," Hosgrove said. "I will start over. I've read that your brother Edward gave you first command at eighteen years of age at Barnet. It was your first major battle. According to our information, Warwick had the advantage. To what do you attribute your win?"

Mention of that battle brought back bitter memories. He'd been pitted against men he knew, men who were friends—to kill and see them die. Though fourteen years in his past, it still affected him.

"What does it matter? The wheel of fortune turned for Edward that day."

"Do you mean to tell me it was just dumb luck?" Hosgrove's forehead creased.

"The weather was horrible. You could not see ten feet in front, and the lines kept shifting. It was not until after the battle that I learned Hastings' army was broken, and some of his men had fled to London reporting we had been killed in battle."

"The news of your death was greatly exaggerated," Michael said in a flat voice.

Hosgrove scowled at Michael.

"It continues to be," Richard said, matching Michael's tonal quality.

Katarina covered her mouth with her hand and Michael laughed outright.

"The accounts of the number of men that opposed your ten thousand are inaccurate at best. In fact, one account has it that the Lancastrians had three times as many men as Edward," Hosgrove said.

"They had more men, especially after Hastings was broken. But we were not aware of that during battle, and so we kept fighting. I came up on the right and Exeter was to my left, instead of directly in front."

"How did you know to turn?" Hosgrove asked.

"If we kept going straight, we would have headed for the marsh. We could see nothing and hear nothing in that direction. We had to turn or be trapped. I did not know Exeter had swung to the left until after I changed my position and met him in battle."

Hosgrove went to the flip chart, and drew a heavy, black line down the middle of the blank sheet.

"Let's say this is the North Road, and Barnet is at the bottom here." Hosgrove tapped the marker on the line. "Where were you positioned?"

Richard strode to Hosgrove and placed his thumb to the right of the line, about a third of the way up from the bottom of the pad. "Here."

Hosgrove handed the capped end of the marker to Richard. "Mark it up, show me what happened."

Taking the marker with his left hand, Richard began drawing a circle where his thumb had been.

"I didn't know you were a southpaw," Hosgrove said.

"Southpaw?"

"Sorry, that's American slang for left-handed."

Southpaw had a much kinder sound to it than did sinister from the Latin, which came to mean clumsy, or worse, evil, in his time.

Richard continued, "Everything was enshrouded in mist, obscuring the enemy. I had a choice of going straight and being trapped in the marsh, or swinging left. If they were directly in front of the marsh, then I risked exposing my right flank. I judged that was the lesser risk and positioned some lookouts on my perimeter." He drew as he spoke.

"You guessed correctly," Hosgrove said. "But you were still outnumbered. Am I to believe that only the Lancastrians confused the banners and fought each other, thus swinging the odds in your favor?"

"That is what happened," Richard said. "I learned from Edward that Oxford and Montague fought against each other because they mistook Oxford's banner for the York Sunne, and he was where they expected Edward to be. Their artillery hit the wrong army."

"Seems like they shot themselves in the foot," Michael mumbled.

"What?" Richard asked.

"It's just an expression that means even though you have the superior arms, you become your own worst enemy and do the job for him." Michael said, putting one foot up on the table while pointing at it with his hand. "Pow!" he said, underlining his action.

Richard laughed. "That is an apt description, more true perhaps for what happened on Edward's front. He was facing lines that were six deep, backed by cannons and some handheld guns. Again—"

"I didn't realize you had handheld guns then," Katarina said, cringing when both Hosgrove and Michael glared at her.

"I would not use those guns, although my soldiers have. They could blow up on the soldiers who used them, but the guns were fearful to hear. I did not want to be in front of one, for they could kill when they did work. Do they work today?"

"Much too well," Katarina said. "Sorry for the interruption, Richard. You were saying…"

"The darkness and the fog worked in our favor. They were unaware that Edward had been pushed back, replaced by their own. Instead of hitting Edward's force, they shot themselves."

"It still happens today," Hosgrove said. "We call it *friendly fire*. What a load of bullshit that is. I lost five good men in Korea that way. We were pinned down by our own artillery." Hosgrove squeezed his eyes closed for a few seconds. "Sorry, nobody wants to hear about me.

"I would like to move to another subject for the moment, but I do intend to return to this battle in detail later. I've had several of the maps replicated, and I would like you to mark them with the troop movements as best you can," Hosgrove said. "This is in regard to Hastings. At what point did you think he could not be trusted and why?"

Richard could not bring himself to reveal the true depth of Hastings' betrayal, but he would answer the question. "From the beginning, Hastings was Edward's most loyal chamberlain. I thought his loyalty remained unbroken because he notified me of my brother's death and urged me to come to London with all due speed to assume my position as protector, as prescribed in Edward's last will. I did not understand his treachery at the time, but I had my proof by the June thirteenth council meeting."

"Have you reconsidered?" Hosgrove asked. "You said—at the time."

"No!" He stared Hosgrove down, noting with satisfaction that he could still dominate, despite his smaller stature and the intervening gap of five hundred years. *Five hundred years!* His mind was overwhelmed with wonder.

"I did what I had to do, but I have come to understand Hastings' actions. I mistook his loyalty to my brother and the Prince as loyalty to me. However, had he succeeded in suppressing Edward's precontract with Eleanor Butler, he would have allowed a bastard to illegally rule England. He committed high treason."

"Why didn't you arrest Elizabeth? Wasn't she the leader?"

"You would have me put a woman in a position where she might be executed?" Richard asked. "What kind of people are you?"

"Why is one life any more precious than another?" Michael asked.

Richard glared at Michael. "You would have me execute the mother of my brother's children?"

"I'm not saying that women should be executed. Personally, I think capital punishment is an abomination in a civilized society."

"I don't agree, Michael. I can see where execution is justified," Katarina said. "I do think you have to be damn sure you got the right person. My problem is having a double standard based on sex."

"Enough!" Hosgrove said. "You can talk about it over lunch, but not on my dime. And speaking of lunch, I told Frank to order some pizza. He should be bringing it in momentarily. Now might be a good time to take a break."

The three of them stood after Hosgrove left the room.

"We'll be right back, Richard," Katarina said. She followed Michael out of the room.

Richard stood in the empty room and again wondered why they confined him. He would have to solicit Katarina's help. He resolved to somehow induce her to stay with him after Hosgrove and Michael were done with their questions.

Hosgrove returned to the room carrying a small case containing bottles. "I thought you might like to have some ale with your pizza." He put the ale on the table.

Frank came in with the other guard. He held two large square boxes that were about three fingers thick. Michael and Katarina walked in as Frank opened the boxes.

The aroma filled the room. The pizza smelled alien to Richard, but not unpleasant. His mouth watered.

Richard watched as everyone else helped him- or herself. Katarina walked over to him, carrying two paper plates, each holding two slices of pizza.

"Take one of them Richard, you'll have to taste it to see if you like it or not," Katarina said. "You pick it up like this with your fingers and take a bite out of it like this." She demonstrated how to hold the slice and then took a bite.

"Help yourself to some ale if you want. Otherwise, you can have soda." Hosgrove picked up a bottle and twisted the cap off, taking a long draw. "Richard, we don't have any tankards, so you'll have to drink it out of the bottle as I just did. Did you see how I twisted the cap off?"

"Yes." Richard took a bottle and was surprised at how easily the cap came off. He drank a third of it down before he sat back down. "This is ale?" he asked.

"American ale," Michael said. "It's probably more bitter than what you've had. It's because of the hops."

"I like the pizza," Richard said, diplomatically.

He turned his head in Hosgrove's direction and asked, "What battle was Korea? Will you tell me about it?"

Hosgrove arched his eyebrows. "Your memory is good, I only said that in passing. Korea wasn't a battle; it was a war and is a country on the other side of the world, south of China on the Pacific Rim. I'll get an atlas after we finish eating and show you where it is. Anyway, I was stationed there in 1950, just having been promoted to First Lieutenant in the U.S. Army. I was sent out on my first patrol, and we encountered enemy fire. I called for backup, but they screwed up the telemetry and our own artillery was shelling us. We scrambled for shelter, but I had five dead and three wounded before they corrected their error. That was my first week. It went downhill from there."

Richard hoped that on seeing the maps of Hosgrove's battle, he'd better understand what had happened. Then it hit him. *1950! That was more than fifty years ago. How old is Hosgrove?*

Once the lunch debris was removed, Hosgrove got his reproductions of the maps from Richard's battles and spread them out on the table. Barnet was on top. Richard studied the map for a few minutes and then closed his eyes, seeing the battle in clear detail even though fourteen years had passed for him.

"I see some errors on this map. May I mark it up?"

Hosgrove handed Richard a pencil, grinning so hard that his blue eyes became slits. "Please do! I have several copies of each map, too."

Richard set to work. He talked while marking the map. After a few minutes he noticed he'd made an error on one of his lines and started to put hash marks through it.

"Wait a minute," Michael said. "Are you crossing that out?"

"Yes. I was in error."

"You can erase it instead." Michael picked up a squarish white object and rubbed it on the errant line. Only a faint trace of the line remained where the pencil had indented the paper. He handed the eraser to Richard. "This works much better than the bread crumbs you would use, but don't rub too hard or you'll tear the paper."

Toward the end of the day, Richard could barely focus.

"I would rather be fighting than talking about the fighting," he said.

"Aha! Spoken like a true soldier," Hosgrove said. "Anyway, you'll be relieved to know that we're done for the day. We'll see you tomorrow morning. I will be asking some of the more difficult personal questions then and Katarina won't be here."

Richard nodded. He noted that Hosgrove had not offered any additional information about Korea, but he decided against bringing it up at this time.

Richard was glad to see that Katarina made no move to leave when both Michael and Hosgrove did.

"You look exhausted," Katarina said once the door closed. "Do you want me to bring you something to eat and then leave you alone, or would you prefer if I stayed and continued helping you with differences in today's world from what you know?

"Stay," he said, resting his hand on hers. "Am I a prisoner?"

FOUR

Katarina swallowed hard. "You're not a prisoner, but I agree, I think we're treating you like one. I don't have the authority, but Hosgrove does. I'll be right back."

She ran out the door and down the hall to Hosgrove's office. He was gone. The word "Damn," involuntarily escaped her lips. She entered his office and used his phone to call him on the mobile.

"Hosgrove! It's me, Katarina, where are you?" she asked impatiently.

"I was just going to pull out of the parking lot. Why?" he asked.

"I want to take Richard to my home, at least for two or three hours. We shouldn't be treating him like a prisoner."

"Wait right there," Hosgrove said and hung up.

Three minutes later, he marched into his office, shouting, "Katarina! Are you fucking out of your mind? You want to take him, a person who could overpower you in a second, into your home?" Hosgrove shouted and began pacing.

"I trust him. He won't hurt me," Katarina said.

"Well I don't! No, you can't remove him from here." He leaned toward Katarina, glowering.

"Hosgrove," she said. "Do you know what he said? He said he felt like your prisoner."

"Goddamn r-ri-," Hosgrove said. He changed to a more conciliatory tone. "Listen, I've put better than eighty percent of my fortune into this. I've got to protect my investment."

"It's not the money, is it? I know you don't trust him, but you trust me, don't you?" she asked.

Hosgrove spun around at these words and faced her. "I trust you, Katarina, but not him. He's already tried to escape."

"What do you mean, 'escape'? And anyway, wouldn't you in his position?"

"Last night, after you left, he searched for a way out."

"How do you know, were you spying on him?"

Hosgrove stared at the floor and then directly into her eyes. "I'd be a fool not to have him monitored. We activated the surveillance cameras and watched him climb onto the table. He moved a ceiling panel. And then, this morning, he tested the door. It was locked."

Hosgrove did have a point. Still, Richard wouldn't know about cameras, and it was a clear invasion of his privacy. She frowned. "I don't know what to say. You've set up the room so he can't escape, and you still spied on him. That's just not right."

"The point is, he tried to escape twice. Do you still think I should risk setting him loose?"

"Yes, he's smart, and don't you think you'll get better cooperation if you ease up a bit and let him see what the world is like, even if it's only for a few hours?"

"Maybe. How will you guarantee he won't skip out on you?" he asked.

"I think once he sees how different everything is, he might think twice about skipping out as you say. Also, since you're paying for security, why don't you make your rent-a-cops earn their keep, hmm?"

"What do you mean?" he asked.

"Have them follow me to the house and stay close enough by so I can call them if I need them. But, they will not come into my house."

"I don't like it, Katarina."

"But you'll like it less if he refuses to cooperate because he feels imprisoned," she said. "If you thought you were a prisoner, would you cooperate with your captors? Or would you do anything to foil their plans?"

"No. He could hold you hostage or worse. You saw what he did to Michael."

"I don't agree. He's already had enough opportunity to harm me if he had wanted to."

"You had security to protect you here," Hosgrove said. "You'd be much more vulnerable at home."

"What difference does it make if your guards are just outside my home or outside the lab's door?"

"Okay, I'll agree only if you take this." Hosgrove handed her a pager. "Press this button if you feel you need help. They can be in your house in seconds."

Katarina stuffed the pager in her jean's pocket. "How much do you want to bet that I won't be needing this?"

Richard was beginning to think Katarina would not return, when the door opened and both she and Hosgrove entered.

Hosgrove spoke. "Katarina got me to agree to let her take you out of here, but only if you swear that you will not do anything to harm her and do whatever she asks of you."

"I swear," Richard said. "On my grave."

Hosgrove laughed. "Bear in mind that my guards will be there as well. They can and will subdue you in seconds if you try to do anything to make Katarina feel uncomfortable."

"I gave you my word. If that is not worth anything to you, then why did you ask me to give it?"

"Yes, well, you are different from what I had expected," Hosgrove said. "I will hold you to it." He spun on his heels and left the room.

Richard turned toward Katarina. "Thank you for arranging this with Hosgrove."

"There are conditions as you've heard," she said. "I trust you even if Hosgrove doesn't. Well, what are you waiting for? You'll get to ride in my Avalon."

"Avalon?"

"My car." She steered him out the door and into the hallway of Ambion Technologies. The two guards followed.

The area on either side of the corridor they had entered was divided into small cells. He could see over the low walls. "Why do the walls only come up to my shoulder?"

"Those are partitions for the cubicles, uh, work areas."

"I do not see or hear anyone but us. Are the cubicles always empty?" he asked.

"No, it's Sunday and most people don't work on Saturday or Sunday," she said.

He followed Katarina through a double door into an open area. He stopped so abruptly that the two guards nearly ran into him. "What is this chamber made of?" He stared in astonishment. The ceiling was three stories above him, with stairs that he could see through, going to the third floor. A glass wall that was clearer and larger than anything he had ever seen surrounded the chamber. He also did not expect to see trees indoors.

"Richard, our technology allows us to make these large glass walls. Don't you want to leave? I thought you were anxious to get away from here."

"Aye."

She headed for the glass wall and before he could stop her from walking into it, two large panels slid open with a hiss. She grabbed his hand and pulled him through the newly created opening. He staggered under the force of the unexpected heat.

Her mouth quirked up into a smile, "Oh yes, we are having a heat wave and I forgot to mention it. We are able to control the temperature in buildings and cars, but we'll have to allow a few minutes for the car's interior to cool off."

He saw his first car a minute later when they walked to the parking lot. The newspaper photographs did not prepare him for the reality. He expected them to be taller, but he'd have to bend just to get in. How could anyone find comfort folded up?

She had him wait a minute or so before getting in, but the interior was still very hot to the touch. She showed him how to operate the door and window before she got in. "You need to put this seat belt on." Katarina pointed to a strap hanging by the door, and put hers on. "Just slide this metal clip in there."

"It is extremely hot." Richard put his own seat belt on.

"What did you do when it got hot and you were in full armor? I bet it was like this."

"Perhaps it was. I did not notice it so much as I notice this."

"Yes, well, you didn't have air-conditioning. I bet everything was hot."

She moved a couple of levers and they were moving. Before he could say anything, she spoke. "I know you're going to find this all new, so don't hesitate to ask."

He could only nod in assent; this was so overwhelming.

"Good, I'd like to listen to the radio. I'll explain it later. You'll hear voices and music, although the people and instruments are not physically here with us," she said. "I've been listening to Jazz; a form of music which I know is new to you. Just sit back and let it relax you."

The song of a man's love for a woman again brought Anne to Richard's mind. Already in turmoil from the most recent events, his emotions overtook him. Though she predeceased him, he was still in love with her. He quickly turned his head toward the window in an effort to hide his grief.

He sensed Katarina's eyes on him and heard her say, "Richard, I am so sorry. I should have known not to play that album."

Richard wiped his eyes with his hand and saw her reach toward the radio. "No, leave it be," he whispered, his voice cracking.

The music played as they continued to her house. He remained locked in his thoughts, silently observing the strange sights. He was occasionally tempted to ask why she would sometimes stop, and at other times not. He was unable to determine the pattern. He caught her glancing at him, her expression one of bemused concern. He kept silent, thinking that too many questions would make him appear weak and knowing that once he started down that path, he would be unable to stop.

The car had cooled considerably by the time they approached a bridge. He found his voice. "Is this the bridge you mentioned was up yesterday?"

"Yes." Her voice held surprise. "I can't believe you understood me then."

"Not then, but the sign naming the Burnside Bridge brought it to mind."

She shook her head. "You have an excellent memory."

"Aye."

The traffic eased once they crossed the river. She drove to Reed College, but instead of taking a right onto the campus, she turned left and then left again at the end of a wide tree-lined street. Then she turned right onto a small byway that ended at a white house and turned off the car. "This is it, Richard, my home. It's modest, but I love it here."

Ambion's security van pulled up behind them.

Katarina showed Richard around the house. He stopped in front of a cherry-wood sideboard that was cluttered with framed photographs of different sizes.

"Is she your sister?" He picked up a photograph of a pretty, dark-haired young woman who was wearing a cap and gown and holding a sheet of paper with the writing facing him.

"No, that's my daughter, Elaine. She'd just graduated from the university when that photo was taken." She beamed.

He traced Katarina's features with his eyes—her fair skin, smooth brow, clear brown eyes, and full lips. "How old is she?"

"She's twenty-five now, the photo was taken three years ago."

"You appear much younger than thirty-nine or forty."

"Bless you," she said, putting her hand on his arm. "Actually, I'm forty-seven."

"Jesú! I am thirty-two, and I thought you to be younger than I."

She grinned. "I'm often mistaken for someone in her mid-thirties, but you've made me feel even younger."

"Is your husband alive?" he asked.

"Yes, quite alive," Katarina said. "But we're divorced and he's remarried."

"Do you have more children?" Richard asked.

"No, and since our marriage didn't work out, I'm glad we took precautions."

"Precautions?"

"Um, birth control."

"You are able to control when you get pregnant and still perform your wifely duties?" Women had tried to prevent unwanted pregnancies in his time, but his bastards were proof of how unsuccessful those measures were. And yet, as much as he and Anne had tried to have more children, they were unable to have more than one living child.

"Yes," Katarina said. "Enough about me. Why don't you keep me company while I make something to eat, and we can talk about other things."

Richard followed her into the kitchen.

"You can sit here." She pointed to a high stool by a counter. She took vegetables out of a tall white box.

"What is that?" he asked, pointing to it.

"It's called a refrigerator, and it keeps food fresh by keeping it cold. This smaller compartment at the bottom is the freezer, and it keeps food frozen, thus preserving it longer." She pulled out the freezer drawer and removed a small tub as she spoke.

Katarina got a bowl, scooped out a bit of the tub's contents and brought it over to Richard. She handed him a spoon, "Here, try the ice cream. It's really dessert, but a little before dinner won't hurt, and I think this is something that is completely new for you. Just take a little bit and eat it slowly, it's very cold."

He put some in his mouth. "Mmm, what is this made of?"

"Basically, it's frozen cream that is whipped with air and sugar and other flavors. This happens to be plain old vanilla. Do you like it?"

"Aye!" He licked the last of the ice cream on his spoon. "I never really liked sweets, but this is nectar from the gods." He could only smile.

She laughed. "I wouldn't go quite that far. Please put the nectar in the refrigerator while I make dinner."

After he put the ice cream away, he noticed his hands were a little sticky. "My hands are dirty."

"Do you remember where the bathroom is? You can wash them in there."

Except that it lacked a shower, the chamber reminded him of the one at Ambion, the color choice being similar, a light tan. He washed his hands and face half a dozen times, the stickiness long since taken care of. When he returned to the kitchen, he sat back down at the breakfast bar and continued to examine his hands.

Her back was toward him as she was busy preparing dinner. He stared at his hands and then glanced up in her direction.

"Katarina, I just washed my hands over and over, and yet I feel dirty. I understand not."

She turned around from the counter where she was chopping up some vegetables; a small knife in one hand and a carrot in the other. She frowned. "What would make you feel clean?"

"I would like to shower. Cleaning my hands did not cleanse me."

"You have some time now, dinner won't be ready for another fifteen or twenty minutes anyway."

After she told him where to find the towels, he went upstairs to take his second shower of the day.

What is wrong with me? I never felt compelled to clean myself this much before.

He thought he would finish long before dinner would be ready, but found she was placing the utensils on the table when he returned. They both sat down at the table.

Katarina placed her chin on her clasped hands and fixed her eyes on his. "I've been thinking about what you just told me, and I have to ask you something that you might find offensive. It's important that you answer me honestly."

He searched her face. "You cannot offend me."

"You'd be surprised," she muttered. "First, there's something that I must tell you. Often, rape victims complain that they feel dirty despite having scrubbed themselves clean over and over in a short period of time. Now has…"

He slapped his hand on the table, making the fork jump. "I have not been raped!"

"I'm sorry, but please hear me out. This is important."

He sat back and folded his arms against his chest. "I am listening."

"You have said that you're washing more than usual. Your reaction is understandable considering…I mean, it wasn't your idea to be brought five hundred years into the future.

"Then what are you saying? That I have been somehow violated?" He caught his breath. "Is this true, what you say about rape?"

"Yes, Richard, it is."

He remembered how fragile Anne had been after her first husband was killed in battle. Two years earlier, her father had arranged the marriage to Margaret de Anjou's son, Edward, when she was only fourteen. Had Edward forced himself on her or was it because she'd been widowed and was now fearful? Had she given herself to him only out of duty, merely grateful because he'd freed her from his brother's clutches? Surely their childhood friendship had meant more.

He became aware of Katarina's eyes upon him. "I shall think upon it."

"Changing the subject, what do you think of Hosgrove?"

"I respect him," Richard said. "He was a soldier, he knows what it is to lose men. I am also wary of him. I feel he means me harm."

"We should eat. Dinner's getting cold." She cut into the lamb chop and took a bite.

"You say I have been violated and then you speak of Hosgrove, and yet you do not explain."

"I'm not trying to imply he's done anything like that. But I need to put my thoughts in order. Later, okay?"

"Okay." He took a few bites of the lamb and then picked at the salad. He noticed Katarina watching him. "This food needs getting used to."

"I think you already know that there's much that you'll have to get used to. I'd like to help you if you'll let me."

"That would be my preference."

After dinner, she brought him into the living room and caused a device she called a TV to light up. He could not take his eyes off of it.

"What is this marvel? They cannot be real people in there, can they? They look so real, not like puppets at all."

"These are images of real people, not puppets." She handed him a small flat object. "The remote will allow you to change the channel, which will alter what you see, by pressing this button here. You can control the volume by pressing this button if you want it louder, or this one if you want it softer. Why don't you play with this and see what's on the other channels while I fix us some dessert? Unless you don't want any more ice cream."

"I would like more." He began switching channels before Katarina stood up.

He was still using the remote to change channels, when she returned with the ice cream. "I do believe channel-surfing is part of the Y-chromosome," she said, handing him a bowl.

"What?"

"I meant it's something men do," she said. "Please let me have the remote. I want to watch the news."

She selected a channel. "This is CNN and they're covering the situation in Iraq. Right now they're showing some old footage of American soldiers degrading and torturing Iraqi prisoners."

He put down his ice cream and concentrated on the news.

Katarina muted the TV once the commercial came on. "I imagine you have a thousand questions just based on that one news report. So why don't you just ask?"

He did not know where to start, so he picked one at random. "Are the King's subjects allowed to question what he does with his army? And if those people are prisoners, cannot they do anything they want to them? Where is Iraq? What are…"

"Stop! I'll forget them if I don't write your questions down. I'm going to get a globe of the world so I can show you where everything is. This is going to take a while." She stood.

She returned a couple of minutes later carrying a globe of the world, which she put down on the low table in front of them. She jotted down his earlier question while he spun the globe around. "This is new," he said, pointing to a continent.

"This is where we are, too, in Portland, Oregon," she said, resting her finger near the coast. "This whole continent, North and South America, wasn't discovered by Europeans until 1492, by a man named Christopher Columbus." She turned the globe until England faced him. "This is England, your home, or it was five-hundred years ago."

He put his fingers on both places she had indicated and moved the globe slowly back and forth. "How far are we from England?"

"Approximately six thousand miles. The sun rises eight hours earlier in England."

"And where is Korea, where Hosgrove said he was?" Richard asked.

She showed him, and then responded to his earlier questions, starting with Iraq's location. He shook his head in disbelief when she told him that women as well as men enlisted in every branch of the armed services today.

"You know, we even went to the Moon, way back in 1969. We watched man landing on the moon as it was happening. I'll never forget that," she said. "Also, we don't have a monarchy. There is no king in this country."

"Does England still have a king?" he asked.

"Yes, but now England is headed by Queen Elizabeth the second, in fact."

"How do people here become leaders?"

"Everyone is elected, from the lowest office to the president, who is our country's leader. All registered voters are able to choose who'll lead the country once every four years," she said.

"And to answer one other question before you add all the others that I see forming behind your gray eyes, there are rules regarding the treatment of prisoners of war, which if violated, can lead to court martial, prison, and at the least, dishonorable discharge. So you see, there are serious consequences if these rules are broken."

He grimaced, wondering if the ones who gave the orders would be held responsible. "I should not be here. I am more lost than yesterday."

"You'll be fine. You're asking some very good questions. You really do have an ear for language. Based on how today went, and now this, I'm sure you'll be fine without me tomorrow."

"I would prefer not to face Hosgrove without your help. Can you not alter your plans?"

"I'm sorry," she said. "I'm a professor at the college we just passed, and I have meetings all morning."

"Damn!"

"I'm flattered, but I'm sure you understand—duty first. Also, I really should be getting you back to Ambion."

He cringed at her words. He had managed to blot out all thoughts of Ambion Technologies, but now it came rushing back to him. He could not face going back there, not tonight. He took her hands in his and peered into her dark brown eyes. "I should prefer to stay here tonight. They will not be there until the morning."

"Is it that bad? Going back to Ambion Technologies, I mean?"

"Aye."

"I did say I trusted you, and I do believe you are being honest with me. Okay, I'll call Hosgrove. I'll have to talk him into it."

"Do you think you can ask Hosgrove to remove the guards?"

Her eyes narrowed. "Was this your plan, Richard? To get me here alone, with no one to see what you do? I think they will stay."

"No!" He gasped. "I swore I would not harm you. I only thought to get away."

Katarina nodded. "Okay, does that mean you are no longer planning to escape?"

He stood and paced in front of her. "I do not have the means to survive in your time, Katarina. I need your help. I must get away from Ambion." He sat back down and held her hands. "Hosgrove does make my skin prickle. I must get away from him."

"I thought you said you respect him, Richard."

"I do. I respect my enemies."

"I'll help you, but only if you promise to return tomorrow," she said. "And you must convince me why I should help you after we speak to Hosgrove."

"I promise." He shuddered.

"I'll put it on speaker phone so you can hear what we both say." She punched in the number.

Hosgrove exploded when Katarina suggested Richard stay with her until the morning. "You fucking want me to let him do what? You fucking better get him back to Ambion now or I will personally come over to your house and fucking do it myself!"

"You fucking try to do anything to Katarina, and I'll fucking kill you!" Richard roared.

Katarina was waving her hands, and laughing at the same time. "Stop it, stop it, both of you. Hosgrove, I have you on speaker. I think that it will be for the best if he stays here tonight. I'll drop him off first thing tomorrow. Oh, and call your goons off, they're not needed."

"You better have him here in the morning, or I'll…"

"Or you'll what?" she said. "I promise, I'll get him there." She hung up the phone.

"Hmm, I guess I don't have to teach you the most popular word for impolite company in the world today."

"The word sounded different in my time, but everyone knew it. And the meaning is clear." One corner of his mouth crooked up. "Can he do anything to you?"

"No, he's all bluff. I can go to the police and the newspapers if he tries to do anything to me. Are you in danger? You can't go to the police or the newspapers like I can."

"There is something I heard him say to Michael when I first awakened. I did not understand it at the time, but the words have stayed in my mind. He means to return me to Redemore."

"That's horrible!" she said. "I'm surprised that Hosgrove would even consider that, if for no other reason than that he's made a huge investment in this project. But then, that means he'd have to behave rationally, and that may not be one of his strong suits. Are you sure about what you heard?"

"Aye. I have a very good memory and a very good ear for language. He means to return me once he is done with me."

Her eyes widened. "That's right! You remembered my mentioning the drawbridge. Wow! I'll help, you've got my word." She walked over to the window and pulled the curtains aside. "The guards are still here."

He walked up behind her. "Can I not do anything tonight? Will I endanger you?"

"I think you'll be safe for another day with them because they still don't know everything they want to know. Keep some information back, even if you have to pretend you don't understand them," Katarina said. "You don't have to worry about me, I'm safe."

"I want your help, but I am afraid for you, Katarina."

"I have a rough idea of what I can do," she said. "I'll be fine, you'll have to trust me on this."

"Thank you."

"Don't be so quick to thank me. I haven't done anything yet."

"You have. I have tonight's reprieve, and I have hope," he murmured.

They were standing close to each other. At once, her smell, her beauty, her intelligence, and the kindness she had shown overcame him. It had been five months since he had buried his wife and two days since he was catapulted into the twenty-first century. There was so much he had to learn, but all he could think of was Katarina. Heat from desire spread through him and his member stiffened. He turned away from her, his face hot.

She put a hand on his shoulder, stopping him mid-turn, "It's okay, I feel it, too. But you're right, we probably shouldn't act on it."

"Christ." He moaned and turned back to her. "I do desire you."

"Does our age difference bother you?"

"You mean because you are fifteen years my senior?"

"No," she said, "because you're five hundred years my senior!"

They both laughed.

"It's getting late, and we have to be up early. Follow me and I'll set you up in my daughter's old bedroom."

She dashed up the stairs and he fell in behind her, matching her pace. She stopped abruptly at the top of the stairs and snapped her fingers. "Oops, I forgot to…"

His foot hit the top step at that moment and he bumped into her. To his horror, he saw her pitch forward, heading straight for the wall opposite the landing. He caught Katarina by the waist, and pulled her back away from the wall.

"Urk!"

He held onto her. "Are you all right?" He turned her so they were facing each other.

"Yes," she said, her breath hot on his forehead.

The entire length of her body pressed against him. He was immediately and once more aroused.

"Richard," she whispered, "this is wrong." Her body said differently.

She put her hands behind his head and kissed him, her tongue explored his mouth. He pressed her up against the wall while she slid her hands to his shoulders and wrapped her legs around his waist. She traced her tongue along his chin until she got to his ear. "Take me to my bedroom."

A thrill shuddered down as she nibbled his ear and then traced his throat with her tongue. He carried her to the bed and placed her on it. His heart raced.

She rolled away from him just as he was about to get on top of her. "Take your clothes off. I'll be right back." She stepped out of her clothes and hurried to the bathroom.

He groaned at the delay, but quickly stripped.

She returned and stepped up to him, her luminous eyes scanned him. "My God! Haven't you been eating? You're so thin!"

"I lost my appetite after my wife died."

"You ate well tonight and last night."

"I found my appetite."

He stood close to her and cupped his hand over her breast. "You are very beautiful." He breathed into her neck and then licked her ear, tracing his tongue along her jaw until he found her mouth. "Oh God, it has been so long."

She gently pulled away from him. "It's been too long for me, too. But I have to slow you down. You can get deadly diseases from having sex with the wrong person. You are going to have to learn how to use condoms." She showed him one.

"You are not the wrong person. You cannot be."

"No, I'm healthy. But you can't tell by just looking. You have to know how to use them. Besides, they will prevent unwanted pregnancies. I can still get pregnant, and that wouldn't be good at my age."

He sat down on the bed and pulled her next to him. "Show me."

Their lovemaking left Richard feeling more relaxed than when he was brought into this time, and if he were to be honest, for many months before that. Katarina's lips brushed his mouth before she rolled onto her side and snuggled into him spoon fashion. He wrapped his arms around her, and she propped her head on his shoulder.

He whispered into her ear, "I am a stranger to you and yet you trusted me. I do not understand."

She rolled onto her back and turned her head toward him. "I feel as though I've known you for years. I've read so much about you, and I think I've built this impossible idealized image of you in my mind. Now I can touch you and speak to you. It's impossible for me not to trust you."

"I am very glad you did."

"Me too, now go to sleep. We have to be up early tomorrow."

A faint odor penetrated Richard's senses. *Lavender.* Anne stirred. Her silken hair fluttered against his cheek and tickled his nose. He wrapped his arms around her and she tucked her back into his chest.

"Beloved," he softly spoke in the archaic tongue, "I had the strangest dream. I thought..."

A high-pitched sound disturbed their quietude. She stirred to rise but he held her tighter.

"Richard, let go of me. I have to turn the alarm off, and we have to get up," Katarina said.

"Oh God." His voice cracked. "I-I..." He rolled away from her, tears blinding his eyes.

Katarina sat back down on the bed and rested her hand on the back of his shoulder. "I was going to make breakfast for us, but I'll stay here with you if you prefer."

He put his hand over hers and rolled onto his back. With his other hand, he reached up and brushed her straight brown hair behind her ear. "Make breakfast. I forgot where I was."

"Are you sure?"

"Aye." He forced a smile.

"Why don't you shower while I prepare breakfast?" She stood. "A man I used to see left some underwear here. I'll put a pair of them in the bathroom for you."

FIVE

Richard put the razor down and leaned into the sink, staring at his reflection. The face he saw was once considered handsome. But that was before he lost his son and then his wife. He sighed. Now it was thinner than it should be and lined with pain, making him seem older than his thirty-two years.

He eyed the mirror for another few seconds, shook his head and then splashed cold water on his face to break his trance-like state. Running his fingers through the tangle of his curly hair; he appreciated the simplicity of having it short. Even Katarina's was shorter than his.

Unlike adjusting to the shower, the clothes worn today would take some getting used to. He liked the soft undergarments, but found the zipper that closed the britches, hazardous. He wondered just how many injuries resulted from some hasty action. He took elaborate steps to ensure he would not get caught in it. So far, his favorite items were the shoes—Katarina had called them trainers. He liked the bounce they gave to his step and the immediate comfort they afforded. He hurried down the stairs.

At seven o'clock in the morning, the day promised to be very hot. The sun poured into the kitchen, creating a dappled pattern on the breakfast bar where Katarina had set out coffee and a selection of food.

She sprinkled about a half cup of a brown flaky substance into a bowl and added fruit and milk. "Help yourself to the cereal." She poured coffee into both mugs and handed one to him.

He took a sip of his coffee. "Why do you think I was feeling unclean? It would seem impossible that it is related to women who were violated."

"I do think it's related, just not sexual. In a sense, you were violated by being pulled out of your time and not only into this time, but into a very different culture as well."

He rubbed his temples in a deliberate circular motion. "Why am I here in the twenty-first century?"

"I thought Hosgrove explained it to you. There are many mysteries surrounding you that he wants to solve."

"Perhaps, but you said this was done at great expense."

Katarina drank some coffee. "Hosgrove is what we call loaded. He accumulated great wealth, and I guess he chose to spend it before he dies. He's seventy-eight."

"Seventy-eight!" He shook his head. "Why is he threatening to send me back?"

"That is the billion dollar question, Richard. I have no idea." She reached for the coffeepot. "Do you want more coffee?"

"Thank you." He held his mug out to her. "You said you had a lover? Does he live here?" He put some cereal into a bowl and added fruit and milk to it.

"Jeff lives a thousand miles away in Los Angeles," Katarina said between mouthfuls. "He'd fly up once or twice a month, and he liked to travel light. That's why some of his stuff is still here. I doubt he wants it back."

Richard blinked. "He can fly?"

"Everyone can," she said. "All it takes is money. There's an invention called a jet that will fly people thousands of miles in hours. It only took him a couple of hours to get here."

"First newspapers, cars, the TV, and now flying. How am I going to ever learn everything about this time?"

"You do it the way we all do, by living and experiencing life here and now. You don't have to learn it all in one day, you know." She patted his arm.

He put his hand over hers and lightly caressed her fingers. "I do not know if I can learn enough to survive. Everything seems so complicated. I am not made for this time."

"No one is," she said. "But we've all had a lifetime to get accustomed to the way things are now. It won't be easy, but I'll help. You can start today. Just ask when you want to be shown something, anything. I think you're a fast learner, especially with language. You're very observant and will do well if you allow yourself to."

"I am concerned for your safety. I do not want to put you in any danger. I have enough blood on me."

"What do you mean, blood on you?" Her eyes widened in alarm.

How could he tell this gentlewoman of the many deaths he'd had to suffer? Then he had no choice. But now…

"As a general and king, I commanded men to their deaths. As England's constable, I ordered executions. Is that not enough?"

"It is," she said. "But by the way you said it, I thought there was more.

His hand dropped to his belt to rub his fingers over his dagger's carved handle, to be comforted by its touch, but there was no blade, only cloth. In a single motion, he swept his hand upward and pinched the bridge of his nose. "Will your helping me put you in peril now?"

"No. Hosgrove's quick-tempered, and he can be rough, but I'm positive that I'm in no danger. You needn't worry on my account."

"I have misjudged people," Richard said. "George hurt the most—I thought I knew him because we were so close as children. I continued to defend George, despite his treachery. I stopped when I almost lost Anne. Though I no longer trusted him, I could not hate him. His execution did bother me greatly." He frowned, remembering how he had begged for George's life.

"As I understand it, you blamed the Woodvilles. Some reports go so far as to say you were determined to avenge his execution."

"I may have said things in grief and anger, but I did not avenge his death."

"You asked why you were brought here," she said.

"Aye." He coveted that answer, but he wondered how much Katarina was privy to.

"As you've probably guessed by now, it's something every Ricardian since Bosworth has wanted to know with certainty," she said. "Hosgrove wants to solve the mystery of the princes, your nephews."

"What do you mean by mystery?"

"Rumors persist to this day that you had them murdered," she said. "I thought the rumors started when you were king."

"They did." *Why would anyone today be concerned over bastards?* "I did what I could to quell those rumors, but once I got them safely away from their apartments in the Tower, I had to keep their whereabouts hidden."

"What happened? Most historians think they weren't seen at the Tower after October, 1483," Katarina said. "Some have it earlier and some later."

"They would not have been seen in London after September because they were out of the country by then, alive and protected."

"How sure are you?"

"As sure as I can be. I received letters written by their hands. The last letter I received from Richard was signed in May of 1485, and the last one from Edward was signed in June of that year."

"Weren't they together?" she asked.

"No. Edward was in Ireland and Richard was in Portugal."

"Why didn't you send them to your sister in Burgundy?"

"By my reckoning, Burgundy would be the first place my enemies would think of. And, I thought it would be safer for them to be kept apart."

"Your enemies claimed you had them killed to prevent them from rebelling against you."

"That is outrageous," Richard said. "I needed them alive, but in no position to rebel."

"I think Hosgrove is hoping that you will be able to provide incontrovertible proof that you didn't kill them."

"How do I provide proof of something I did not do?"

"Henry Tudor, being the victor at Bosworth, rewrote a good bit of history about you, and would have us believe you were the one to have them executed in order to remove them from succession," Katarina said.

"But Edward's marriage to Elizabeth was not legal. His precontract with Eleanor Butler had been consummated," he said. "The crown was legitimately mine."

"When did Bishop Stillington make this known?" she asked.

"He confirmed my brother's bigamy before the bishops, nobility and aldermen, June the twenty-sixth."

"Did you try to refute it?"

Richard shook his head. "This turn of fortune solved many problems for me. By then, I had reason to be afraid for my life and for my son's life, had Edward succeeded his father."

"So you used that time to strengthen your case," Katarina said. "You must have done a good job, because you did get the crown."

"They agreed that I should be king and not Prince Edward."

"So, not only do you claim your innocence, but you also say that you had no motive to murder them."

"Their murder would have made it seem otherwise, I needed them alive."

"Why?" she asked. "Setting aside they were your nephews for the moment, didn't they pose a threat to your rule? Didn't they supply a reason, if not a basis, by which your enemies could rebel?"

"No. They were hidden from the Woodvilles, but—"

"Elizabeth didn't know where her sons were? That must have been very hard on her."

"It was, but I had no choice."

Katarina jammed her fists on her hips. "I would have stopped at nothing to find my daughter if she had disappeared like that. I think that was a heartless thing to do, not to tell her."

He couldn't believe this accusation. He had ensured their safety. He controlled his anger.

"These were my choices—kill innocent children to guarantee they could not be used to start a rebellion; return them to their mother who I had every reason to believe would start a rebellion as she had already tried; or secrete them out of the country as I did."

She bit her lip. "I'm sorry, it's just that as a mother I felt compassion for what your sister-in-law must have gone through. But I'm curious, why did she agree to let her daughters stay with you?"

"She knew they would be safe with me, and she may have thought they would learn where their brothers had been sent."

"Do you know that despite Henry doing his utmost to make you the villain, he never directly accused you of murdering them."

That was a satisfying bit of news. He had succeeded in securing his nephew's safety and protected them from Henry. He wondered if he'd ever discover what their eventual fates were.

"Then Henry did not know where they were," he said. "They had to be alive and out of Henry's reach, for he would have killed them. They were more a threat to him than to me."

"I'm sure that Hosgrove has been holding off talking about it while I was with you," she said. "He knew I couldn't be there today, and he doesn't want me to learn what he thinks he will discover. He wants to be the one who solves a five-hundred-year-old mystery."

"Does no one today know what happened?" Richard asked. "Are there no records of them past September of 1483?"

"Unfortunately, no." Katarina poked her spoon around her nearly empty bowl of cereal. "And just hearing what you know will not be enough for Hosgrove. He'll want hard evidence they survived you."

"I will provide what I can."

"It's getting late," Katarina said. I promised Hosgrove I'd have you there early. Why don't you finish your breakfast? Then we'd better get going."

SIX

Richard hunkered down in the car, knowing he would have to face Hosgrove without Katarina. "You said that you have a plan to get me away from Ambion Technologies. I would be most interested in learning something about it."

"I bet you're interested." She smiled. "It's going to depend on my friend, Sean. If he can help, I'm going to take you out to dinner tonight. Then you're going to disappear leaving me innocently behind. That's Plan A."

"Is there a Plan B?"

"No."

He shuddered.

"Don't worry, I can rely on Sean. We've been friends for fifteen years, from when I first moved here. Otherwise, I'll just have to come up with a Plan B." Katarina pulled the car into the Ambion lot.

"Are you ready to deal with Hosgrove alone?" Katarina asked as they walked toward the building.

"I will manage. I have had to deal with much worse."

They entered the building together.

It was just after eight-thirty, and Hosgrove was pacing around the atrium. "Where the hell have you been?" He spat the words out the second they entered the building.

"What do you mean?" Katarina asked. "It's only eight-thirty, it's still early."

"Eight-thirty is not early. I've been here since seven."

"I meant for normal people, Evan," Katarina said. "Besides, didn't the guards call and let you know that we were on our way?"

"Yeah, well," Hosgrove said, his color returning to normal. "Are you joining us Katarina, or do you have to be at the university today?"

"What are you doing, Evan, trying to make me feel guilty? You know I have to work. I'll be back around four to pick Richard up. I'm taking him to Morrison's."

"That wasn't part of the plan," Hosgrove said.

"You can't keep him locked up in that room, Evan. Besides, he needs a break from Ambion and I already promised. Don't make me go back on my word."

A shadow crossed Hosgrove's countenance. "All right, but don't push me too far."

"I will need to take Richard shopping first—he can't go to that restaurant dressed like this." She swept her arm past his torso.

Hosgrove nodded. "In that case, why don't Mike and I join you two? I'll pick up the tab, of course."

Katarina spluttered. "I-I..."

Richard stood by Katarina and put his arm around her waist. "We want to be alone. You will have me all day. Please grant us this time together."

"Is something going on?" he asked, shifting his gaze from Richard to Katarina.

She blushed. "What do you mean?"

"I'm not blind." Hosgrove shifted his eyes back to Richard. "You may be able flatter the lady here into doing your bidding, but I won't be tricked. Is that clear?"

Katarina poked at Hosgrove's shoulder. "No. The only thing that is clear to me is that you are being a goddamned prick, and you're insulting both of us. Now why is it so hard for you to understand that after a day of questions, Richard needs a few hours away just to clear his head? It would drive me mad if I had to stay in the same place twenty-four seven. Wouldn't it you? Or are you really keeping him prisoner?" Katarina stared at him. "In fact, why doesn't he stay with me again tonight after dinner is over? I'll bring him back in the morning just like I did today."

Hosgrove frowned. "Security goes with you, just like before. And they go in the restaurant with you, too."

Katarina nodded. "Not the same table though."

Richard watched Katarina leave, wishing he did not have to face Hosgrove without her. He felt Hosgrove's hand on his arm, and he shrugged it off before turning to walk back toward the offices.

"So, what are your thoughts about us now that you've seen something of what things are like in the twenty-first century?" Hosgrove asked.

The question caught Richard off guard. "If I had seen these things in my time, I would have thought that they were put forth by Satan to tempt me from God, or perhaps there were placed before me by God, but unto what purpose I would not know. Katarina explained that the things that are strange to me are things you see every day, and they are neither instruments of the devil nor miracles of God. I have more to learn than I can imagine."

Hosgrove's menacing look dissolved into a genuine smile. "A lot has changed in five hundred years."

He led Richard to a different room from the one they had previously occupied. Michael was seated in a chair opposite the door at a large, slate-gray, oval table. It dominated the room. Hosgrove walked to the head of the table where there were some objects Richard could not identify, and one that he could, a TV. It was next to the table in its own cabinet.

"First, my apologies for giving you such a hard time last night." Hosgrove paused, staring at the floor. "I guess I did it again this morning. Michael talked to me about it this morning before you got here. He thought I was rather harsh with you. Perhaps I was." Hosgrove sat and gestured to the chair to his right, inviting Richard to sit.

Richard grasped the sides of the black-leather chair and pulled hard. It slammed into his gut, knocking out his breath. He staggered back into the wall behind him, hitting it with a thud.

He was still clutching the chair when he pitched forward, causing it to roll back to the table. Hosgrove ran to his side and grabbed his arm, preventing him from falling.

Neither Michael nor Hosgrove suppressed their laughter. "I'm sorry Richard, I don't mean to laugh at you," Michael said. "We should have warned you about the chairs. We just didn't think. We're so used to all these chairs being on rollers."

"Me too," Hosgrove said. "We can get you a chair that doesn't roll around if you'd feel more comfortable."

Richard did not like being the object of their amusement, but held his tongue and accepted both their apologies with grace. He sat down and took care testing the chair. It rolled freely. "I would prefer another chair."

Hosgrove pressed a button on one of the devices and spoke into it. "Linda, have Harry bring one of my armchairs into the executive conference room."

He released the button and a woman's voice said, "Yes, Mr. Hosgrove, I'll send him right over."

"What is that device you just used?" Richard asked.

"This? An intercom. The person I get depends on which button I press. In this case, I paged my secretary."

In his day, secretary was a coveted position. That women were secretaries today did not mean the position was any less desired, but it did surprise him.

Soon the door opened and a man carried a green leather armchair with a wooden frame into the room. "Where do you want it?" the man asked.

"Right there is fine." Hosgrove pointed, dismissing him. He pushed one of the black leather chairs to the side and replaced it with the green one.

"Okay Richard, you know that we want to ask you a few questions regarding things that happened to you, or those close to you, where our information is very limited at best," Hosgrove said. "I'll start with a simple question, but one that is of a personal nature. Please do not take offense."

His manner has become much more conciliatory. Perhaps I have nothing to fear.

"Did Anne consummate her first marriage to Prince Edward?" Hosgrove asked. "Many historians think not."

"It was consummated," he said, struggling to keep his tone even. How he wished he had been gentler with her. It had hurt him that she shrank from his touch when first they married. "Marriages were arranged to increase the family's power and wealth. At fourteen, Anne was told she had to marry him."

"Had she protested the marriage?" Hosgrove asked.

"No. She was an obedient daughter and Edward was young and handsome. She had no objection. It is better now where people are more free today to marry for love and not for estates or title or other political arrangements."

"That may be true, but many marriages today end in divorce," Michael said. "Love may be overrated."

Hosgrove snorted. "I never knew you were a cynic, Mike. It wasn't overrated as far as I'm concerned. The only time my wife and I were separated was when I served in Korea. We were together for forty-three years until she died." Hosgrove paused before murmuring, "May God rest her soul."

For a fleeting moment, Hosgrove showed his true age. Richard felt *misericordis* toward his jailor.

"Well, we are not here to talk about me, or about love and marriage," Hosgrove said. "Maybe we should take a short break. I ordered some bagels and coffee earlier, why don't I see if it's been delivered yet."

Hosgrove buzzed his secretary and had her send in the food. Both Michael and Hosgrove helped themselves to it. "Richard, why don't you try some, especially the lox." Michael took a bite. "Mmm, it's delicious, thanks." He nodded toward Hosgrove.

"What manner of food is this?"

"Basically, it's bread, cheese, and smoked salmon," Michael said.

He fixed a plate as Michael had done and bit into the bagel. "Do you intend to return me to my time once you are done with me?"

Michael drew a quick intake of breath, glanced at Hosgrove, and then concentrated on his bagel.

"Yes... well... I think we should get back to the task at hand, don't you?" Hosgrove said.

Richard studied Michael, then Hosgrove, waiting for one of them to answer him. Neither did. Their lack of response confirmed he should proceed with whatever plans Katarina devised.

"Richard, do you need to use the men's room before we continue?" Michael asked. "I'm headed there myself, and I can show you where it is."

"What is the men's room?"

"Oh sorry, it's where the toilet is for males, and the Ladies room is where the toilet is for females," Michael said.

"Go. I've got to review my notes anyway," Hosgrove said.

Michael signaled Richard to follow him, and they both walked out of the conference room. Michael spoke in a low voice when they turned down a corridor a few feet from the conference room. "Richard, why did you ask that question? Do you want to go back to your own time even if it means certain death?"

"Why are you so sure that I would die?"

"I don't even know if we can do it, but we would have to exchange you for the body we left in your stead. There's a law in physics regarding the conservation of mass and energy. Bottom line, we can't add mass to the fifteenth century and subtract mass from the twenty-first century only. The balance would be thrown off, and I don't know what would happen. Also, if you didn't die when you went back you could change history and that could well mean that the world as we know it today would no longer exist," Michael said as they entered the men's room.

"You can use those if all you need to do is urinate." Michael pointed to the urinals. "Else, use one of the stalls there." He nodded at an open stall before walking up to a urinal.

Michael resumed speaking after they left the men's room. "Listen man, I'd be very careful if I were you, especially if you don't want to go back. Hosgrove's an okay guy, but he's got a temper and he acts on impulse. I don't think this project would exist if he were more cautious, but... well, I'd err on the side of caution if I were you."

"Thank you for the warning," he said. "Yesterday you opined the state should not execute for any crime. How would you maintain order if the state could not exercise its right to execute for certain crimes?"

"I didn't say crimes shouldn't be punished, I just said that the state should not execute for any crime."

Richard arched an eyebrow and shook his head.

"We've been able to prove some people on death row were innocent. Would you have the State execute them?" Michael paused. "Anyway, no one is executed with the speed at which you did in the fifteenth century." He resumed walking to the conference room.

"How long does it take?" Richard asked as they walked into the conference room.

"How long does what take?" Hosgrove asked.

"Richard was asking how long it takes to execute a man if found guilty of a crime."

"It takes years," Hosgrove said.

"Years, Jesú!"

"Unlike your summary execution of Hastings," Michael said. "How sure were you of his guilt, and why didn't you—a man of law and justice—give him due process?"

"You challenge my authority? What evidence have you of Hastings' innocence that my council did not? They were unanimous in the decision to execute him." He turned aside, to signal an end to this line of inquiry. He still regretted the speed with which he had executed Hastings.

"I have some questions regarding your brother's sons," Hosgrove said. "No one knows what happened to them, especially after you left London to go on your progression."

"I kept them under heavy guard in the Royal apartments until September of that year. By then, it was no longer safe for them to remain in London."

"Is that because of Buckingham?" Michael asked.

"Aye." Richard stared at his fists and saw the past. Tyrell stood before him, having just brought word of Buckingham's movements. Buckingham, the man whom he had once trusted, had turned against him.

"Your Grace," Tyrell had said. *"They are no longer safe at the Royal Apartments."*

"Richard?" Hosgrove's gruff voice pulled him back to the present.

"I had written to my mother. She was ready to hide them until they could be safely removed. Then, I arranged with Brampton to hide Richard in Portugal and Tyrell to hide Edward in Ireland."

"How close can you come to the exact dates and times when these events occurred?" Hosgrove asked.

"I can provide certain dates, but not the hours. I was not there. Why did you not use the instruments that brought me here to go back and discover for yourself?"

Hosgrove glared at Richard, but it was Michael who answered. "Until now, we didn't know where and when to discover the events as they actually unfolded. For one, it's not physically possible for objects to exist in both times for more than a total of a half minute."

"How were you able to get me if you could only exist for less than a minute?"

"We carefully planned and rehearsed it in this time before we dared to go back for you," Hosgrove said. "You'd be surprised at how long thirty seconds really is."

Michael continued, "Each time we send something back to the past, it remained in this time simultaneously. Each second an object, living or mechanical, spends in both times causes internal harm that is cumulative. We tried to send cameras back to the past, and at first, we thought we could film events over time. Our first test lasted just over five minutes, and when we concluded, the camera disintegrated and became a pile of ashes, melted metal and plastic. We learned from experimentation that the longest any object could exist in both times without being irreparably damaged was thirty seconds."

"Were the people who brought me here affected in anyway?"

"I went with the team and I don't believe the effects are permanent. I was the smaller knight wearing Stanley's colors," Michael said. "You swung your axe at me."

Richard jumped to his feet and pointed at Michael. "You! What weapon hath you that you felled me?"

"Didn't you see the musket-like gun?" Michael asked. "Only this didn't fire a lump of lead, it fired a tranquilizer dart that was calibrated to pierce the armor and deliver a sedative to you."

"I could not see it through my visor. How did you find me?"

Michael arched his arms over his head. "We had a starting point, but it wasn't easy. The records aren't exact, but once we zeroed in on the troop movements, we were able to predict where the battle had occurred."

"How were you able to locate me if it was so difficult to locate the princes?"

"We had the exact date, approximate time and location, and it was outside, in the open," Michael said.

"Was it because the princes were inside a building? Did that interfere with the camera?"

Michael nodded. "It meant that we couldn't scan wide areas as we did for you. Because we didn't know what had happened to them, we thought they could have been killed or spirited away any time from when you were crowned to after Henry became King. That's close to two years of time we'd have to capture in intervals of thirty seconds each. We don't have the resources to do that. Do you see our problem, Richard?"

He pinched the bridge of his nose. "I will provide the dates and locations to the best of my knowledge. Will that suit your purposes?"

"It'll help," Hosgrove said. "We will need to find some letter or artifact from them that proves they were alive after you went to Bosworth. Perhaps some of the letters they sent to you survived."

"They did not," Richard said. "Parchment was cleaned and reused. The paper was destroyed to prevent it from being used by my enemies."

Hosgrove groaned. "You're telling me that I still won't be able to prove anything now that I know what really happened?"

Richard nodded.

"You don't know that!" Michael said. "You don't know if documents didn't survive in Ireland or Portugal somehow."

"You have indicated none has survived over the centuries. Why would this knowledge change anything?"

"It may not," Hosgrove said. "But it does give us new places to look."

"We have recorded your final battle," Michael said. "Are you interested in seeing it?"

The idea that he could watch his final moments simultaneously excited and terrified him. He gulped, his mouth gone suddenly dry. "Aye," was all that he managed to rasp out.

"Prepare yourself," Michael said. "You will be seeing how you died. This was taken before we substituted the corpse for you."

Despite the warning, the battle affected Richard more than he expected. His heart slammed in his chest when he heard the screams of the wounded, man and horse, and heard himself cry out, "TREASON," until his own voice was stilled.

It was worse to see his friends—his loyal soldiers—die at the hands of the enemy.

Why was I so eager for battle? Why did I choose so poorly? Did I not care for my men and for England, if not for my own life?

SEVEN

Katarina calmed down once she got in her car. While she was angry with Hosgrove, she was angrier with herself for potentially ruining Richard's chances. She hoped Hosgrove had not suspected anything was afoot when she rejected his suggestion that he and Michael join them. She wouldn't know until four, when it was time to collect Richard. She needed the day to make her plan work.

She had gotten to know Hosgrove through her association with the Portland Chapter of the Richard III Society. He had offered her a position as language consultant on this project because of her specialties in Middle and Early Modern English. On learning what they had intended to do, she was extremely skeptical that they could actually go back in time, let alone bring Richard III into this century, intact, as it were. To her astonishment, they had succeeded.

When Richard had said Hosgrove was considering returning him to the fifteenth century, she had believed him. He had been an idealized man, created out of the existing historical records of the non-Shakespearean ilk. Now that he was flesh and blood, she found she liked him on his own terms, and not just because of the intimacy they'd shared.

She felt that it was unlikely to go anywhere. While attracted to him, she had every reason to believe that Richard would want a woman who could have his children, as he so obviously missed his own. At forty-seven, she was too old to consider that.

And Richard was right. Hosgrove had treated him like property. She could see it in how he kept trying to control every aspect of Richard's existence. She was extremely relieved to have secured this second concession.

When she had moved to Portland after her divorce, she'd rented a modest apartment in the Pearl District, and Sean Collins had been the building's superintendent. A few days after moving in, her car had broken down, and without his help, she would have missed an important meeting.

Now, she was a tenured professor and department head at Reed College. Although not associated with Portland State, she had been able to help get him admitted into the university through her professional associations. He needed just a few more credits to get a degree in Computer Science. This was a significant change for the high school dropout who had rebelled against his father and left home.

She called him from a pay phone before her ten o'clock meeting. She heard the answering machine pick up on the second ring. "Hey Sean, pick up if you're there. It's me, Katarina, and I need to talk—"

"Hey! Sorry I couldn't grab the phone in time," Sean said. "How are you?"

"Fine, listen, I'm glad you're there. I need your help tonight. It's really important, but I don't want to discuss it over the phone. Can you meet me at the university library today before two?"

"Yeah, I'm meeting with my adviser at noon. I should be finished by one."

She would have just enough time after the last meeting to cut across Portland to the university campus. "I can be at the library around one."

Katarina arrived at the library a few minutes early. She walked up to the entrance and had her hand on the door handle when she heard Sean.

"Hey, Katarina, I'm right behind you. Wait up."

Grinning, she turned around and walked toward him. "It's good to see you again." She kissed him on the cheek. "Do you mind if we stay outside and walk? I don't want to talk in the library."

"No, sure, that's fine by me," he said, giving her a hug. "Good to see you again, too. I miss my favorite tenant."

They walked side by side; she nearly matched his six foot five inches in her heels. The heat shimmered off the ground giving the landscape a surreal quality—apropos of what she was about to say.

"I need you to suspend your natural skepticism and listen to what I have to tell you. Just take it on faith, okay?"

"Shoot, I'm all ears," Sean said.

"Before I tell you anything, you must promise that you will keep this to yourself," she said, putting her hand on his arm.

He stopped and faced her.

"I promise. So, why are you being so paranoid?"

Katarina frowned. She didn't think she was being paranoid, but it certainly could appear that way to an outsider. "I don't know if you're familiar with the Richard III Society, but I'm a member."

"You mean the dude Shakespeare wrote about—the hunchback who murdered his nephews?"

"Tudor propaganda. He wasn't deformed in body or spirit. The society's mission statement is to restore Richard III's good name and discredit the Shakespearean version."

"Wait a minute," he said, standing with his arms akimbo. "You mean to tell me that all this cloak-and-dagger is about someone who's been dead for a few hundred years?"

"Let me finish." Her voice grew tight with frustration. "Some of the chapter members are quite wealthy, and the richest member, Evan Hosgrove, funded a project where we have been able to pull Richard from just before he was to be killed in battle into this time. He's here in Portland, very much alive."

He put his hand on her forehead. "Well, you're not running a fever." He frowned, shaking his head. "So tell me, are you on drugs? I thought time travel was impossible, except for how we all do it, forward, a nano-second at a time."

Katarina rolled her eyes. "I asked you to suspend your skepticism, and I'm not hallucinating. You've always known me to be pretty levelheaded. Anyway, you'll be able to verify some of the information."

"Okay, spill it."

They turned around and slowly walked back toward the library.

"I was told that this technology has been available for a few years, but it is very limited as to what can be done. Michael, Dr. Fairchild, modified the technology to go back in time," she said.

"What's his doctorate in?"

"He's a quantum physicist." Katarina bit her lip. "At least that's what I remember him saying."

"I have read about a quantum computer. It's supposed to simultaneously affect subatomic spin in two places at once."

She shrugged her shoulders. "My field is linguistics, not quantum mechanics, my friend. Your guess is better than mine."

"Fair enough. So what's going on?"

"I've been led to believe that Hosgrove is thinking of returning Richard to the moment when he was pulled into this time."

"And that's a problem because…?" he asked.

"Because he was brought here seconds before he would have been killed in battle. He'd have to be returned then, else our past is affected. I'm asking for your help in getting him away from Hosgrove. Will you do it?"

Sean stopped and stared at her. "So the real issue is by returning him you risk millions of lives because of the chance that the past will change. That means they'd have to return him dead just in case they can't find the exact moment."

"Oh my God, I never thought of that. I don't know that Hosgrove has thought it through to that extent either." A chill crept up her spine. She couldn't let that happen.

"You bet I'll help. What did you have in mind?" he asked.

"Hosgrove's letting me take Richard out to dinner tonight. I've made reservations at Morrison's—you used to work there, didn't you?"

"Yeah, on and off. So what do you want me to do?"

"He has to vanish. Can you bring him to your apartment? Hosgrove doesn't know of our connection, and I've been calling you from pay phones."

Sean tugged at his mustache. "That was smart. Yeah, I can do that; what's the setup?"

"I took the chance you'd be able to help, so I made a reservation for you at seven-thirty. Our reservation is for eight, which means that you'll already be seated, and I'll be able to point you out to Richard. I've got some money. He needs clothes, the dinner will be expensive, and whatever else." She handed eight hundred dollars to Sean. "Let me know if you need more."

He stuffed the money into his wallet. "I assume someone is going to be watching you."

"Two of Hosgrove's security guards will be watching. Somehow, you're going to have to disguise him, and quickly."

"Leave it to me, I've got friends in low places."

She laughed. "Did I ever tell you how much I love your humor?"

"This guy, you really think he's Richard III?" Sean asked.

"I know he is. He most resembles this portrait." She handed the copy to Sean. "Anyway—he'll be with me."

He folded the copy and put it in his pocket. "What does he sound like? Does he even have an English accent?"

"His voice is deep and unsurprisingly commanding." She planted her hands on her hips and stared at the sidewalk. "His accent is hard to describe. It's similar to someone from Appalachia with overtones of a Scottish burr."

"I think I know what I have to do. I got a friend who's the head dishwasher; I'll stop by and see him this afternoon. Uh, what's his size? I imagine he won't show up for dinner wearing work clothes."

Katarina described Richard as she was now seeing him in her mind's eye. "He's about five foot eight, overly thin but well muscled, and I'd say small- to medium-boned."

"Should I get him a small or medium?"

"I'd get a medium, it'll be a bit loose, but I'd be afraid that the small would be tight on his shoulders." She remembered his shoe size and added, "And he wears a size ten sneaker. He won't be wearing those tonight, so maybe you could pick up a pair."

"Big feet for a little guy, eh?" Sean laughed. "No problemo. I'll wait for about forty minutes after I see you are seated, and then I'll head back to the men's room. Make sure he goes in after me. I'll take it from there."

She squeezed his arm. "I can't thank you enough."

"You already have, Katarina. I'm getting my degree soon, and I'll be able to quit being super in a few months. This is my thanks to you. Besides, you're paying for it."

"Until tonight, then. Thanks again." She walked back to her car.

EIGHT

"I'm taking you shopping first," Katarina said when she walked into the conference room at ten of four. "You can't go to the restaurant dressed like that."

The effect she had on Richard was complete. He had seen her naked, but this short clingy black gown that hugged her every curve was provocative. He couldn't believe that women dressed so suggestively today. Certainly, women in his day wore low-cut gowns as this was, but they didn't show the leg and they didn't show much of the woman's form below the waist. And neither did she compromise on her shoes. They added at least another three inches to her already tall stature.

He liked her hair loose as it now was, forming a rich mahogany-brown frame around her oval face, cut short to curve into her chin. "You are very beautiful," he said.

"Why thank you, Richard. We'd better get going; we'll have to find you some appropriate clothes."

"You can charge his clothes to this Nordstrom's card." Hosgrove handed it to her. "There should be enough money on it to cover a suit, shirt, shoes, and other incidentals. Are you going to the one at Lloyd Center? I think they have a tailor on the premises."

Katarina nodded, slipping the card into her purse.

"Just get him back here the same time tomorrow. You're welcome to join us, if you don't have to be at the college."

"Are the security guards going to be parked in my driveway all night again? Because if they are, I'd prefer that they bring him here. I have to be at the University at eight tomorrow morning."

"I think I can arrange that," Hosgrove said.

Richard and Katarina walked out to the car, trailed by Frank and Joe, the two security guards that were assigned to them. When they got in the car, Katarina kicked off her heels and tossed them behind the front seat. "I hate driving in high heels." She turned left out of the lot. "I think you should go through with it."

"I intend to escape Hosgrove's grasp. I nearly changed my mind this morning because he was so apologetic and did not press or get angry when I could not supply him with proof my nephews survived."

"Don't even consider it. Sean came up with a scenario where Hosgrove would make sure you're dead before sending you back."

"Why would he do that?"

"To ensure the past won't be affected."

Richard shivered. "Michael was able to take me aside and warn me that Hosgrove is considering returning me to the Battle of Bosworth, to undo what he had done. They also showed me the final moments of the battle. I saw how I was slain."

"I'm very sorry they made you watch. It must have been terrible for you to see."

"It was my choice," Richard said. "Seeing myself die was not as hard as witnessing my friends and my loyal followers suffer the same fate. I was the one eager for battle; they advised me not to fight. Their deaths are my doing."

"But, this wasn't the first time you led men into battle who died fighting for you."

He didn't know why it had affected him so deeply this time. Had he ignored the suffering just because he'd been successful? "The other times I won. I was able to reward my men and support the families. Nor did I allow the families of those I defeated to pay for their husbands' treason."

Katarina pulled into a parking lot opposite Lloyd Center. They neared the sidewalk as Joe and Frank entered the lot.

The Ford Escape rolled to a stop, and Frank leaned out the window, his elbow dipped outside the door. "Wait for us."

"I have a better idea," Katarina said. "Meet you at the ice skating rink by Macy's."

Ice-skating. Had he heard correctly?

She tugged his hand. "Come on, we can cross."

He had heard correctly, but seeing ice-skaters in the middle of a building in the August heat was one more miracle he added to the list. He turned from the skaters. This might be the best opportunity to slip away. Katarina put her hand on his arm when he started to back up.

"Now is not the time," she said. "Anyway, our babysitters are here."

"Babysitters?"

"Frank and Joe." She guided him toward them, and they went to Nordstrom's at the far end of the mall, located men's apparel and helped Richard select a wardrobe appropriate for the restaurant. He was outfitted in a pewter-gray suit, white shirt, and crimson tie. The tie color was the only thing that Richard really liked.

He noticed a bookstore on their way out. "I should like to go in there, if we have enough time."

"Sure," Katarina said. "We have about half an hour."

From the outside, the bookstore appeared small, but the interior fanned out to quite a large area that he reckoned held thousands of books. He stopped near the entrance, wondering how he'd be able to choose any book before they'd have to leave. "Where do I start?" He spread his arms to encompass the entire store.

She shrugged. "What books did you like to read?"

"I would read romantic tales for pleasure, but I think history would be more advantageous."

"Uh, I don't think the romance novels of today are quite what you'd expect. I'm sure history is the better choice." She checked the time. "Maybe it would be better if we went to the restaurant a little early."

As much as he wanted to be in the bookstore, leaving early would give them more time to work out the details of his escape. "Perhaps we should."

She used the time getting to Morrison's to detail what she had worked out. "Sean is already at the restaurant. This way, I'll be able to point him out when we enter. He's a tall, slim black man with a shaved head and a moustache. He knows me and I've shown him a copy of your portrait."

"Is he taller than you?"

"Very funny, in fact he is." Katarina frowned. "What was I saying? Shortly after we sit down to eat, but before we order anything, I want you to get up and find the men's room. Wash your hands, and do anything else you need to do, but come back to our table. Make sure you take at least five minutes."

"Ah," he said. "You are setting up a feint."

"Exactly, about halfway through dinner, Sean will go to the men's room. You must follow him soon after he goes in. Do whatever he tells you to do. Joe and Frank will, of course, investigate when you don't come back to the table after five minutes, maybe more.

"I want to say my good-byes now, because once we are in the restaurant, I won't be able to. Also, you can never contact me after this is done. If I think it is safe, I'll contact you," she said turning onto Broadway. "It has been an honor to know you."

"The honor is mine. I am ever in your debt."

"First, let's see if this works."

When they arrived at Morrison's, Katarina drove to the valet parking line and waited for a ticket. They got out of the car and queued up in a small anteroom and waited to be seated. The benches were filled with couples waiting for their tables.

She stood to the side where they could look into the dining area, and nodded in Sean's direction. He was alone at a small table off to the side of the room.

Once they were seated and attended to, Richard asked the waiter where he could find the men's room and excused himself. Frank and Joe were being seated four tables away, and Richard used that diversion to his advantage. He strode past the kitchen to the back of the dining area and ducked into the men's room.

He did not return to the table immediately, but instead watched Katarina from the alcove. She was studying the menu when Joe grabbed her wrist. "Where is he?" Richard heard Joe ask as he leaned toward her.

Katarina jumped in her chair. "Joe! Don't scare me like that. He just went to the men's room. He'll be right back."

"He better be!"

"You're hurting me, let go!"

"Not until Frank—"

Richard clamped his hand on Joe's wrist and pulled his other arm behind him. "Let go of her now," Richard said quietly against the chatter of the diners.

Joe immediately released her. Richard relaxed his grip. "Hey man, take it easy. I just wondered where you went."

"I see," Richard said. "If you touch Katarina again, I will break your arm."

Joe walked back to his table, flexing his hand.

"Did he hurt you?" Richard asked. "I heard you say he did."

"I'm fine. You can't go around threatening people like that. The next man may not back down, and you could end up dead," she said. "Why don't you look at the menu and decide on what you want to eat."

He studied the menu. "I will order the oysters and roast duck."

"Order the chinook salmon and the buccatini pasta for me when the waiter comes to take the order. If you'll excuse me, I'm going to the ladies' room," Katarina said. "Here's the wine list. That local Pinot Noir is good, I've had it before."

They had finished their appetizer and were about five minutes into the entrée, when Katarina said *sotto voce*, "Sean just walked over to the men's room. Eat a couple more bites and then go." She raised her wineglass and smiled.

"They might try to follow me into the men's room again. Delay them if you can, to give me time."

Richard excused himself and walked toward the men's room. He found Sean standing at the end of the hallway marked "Employees Only." He walked up to Sean and entered the small room with him. Sean locked the door behind them. The back wall held two rows of small doors. He pulled some clothes out of a large paper bag he was carrying and placed them on the long bench that was in front of the wall.

"Richard, take your clothes off and put these on. I've arranged for you to be a dishwasher for tonight. I'll take you to my place when the restaurant closes for the night."

He nodded in understanding. "Where will you be?"

"I have to go to work. I already lost a half-day, but I'll be able to complete my shift before I have to pick you up." He handed Richard a small object that fit in the palm of his hand. "Here's a cell phone in case you need to reach me for any reason. Just hit this button and it will call this number." Sean pulled another phone out of his pocket. "Go ahead, try it."

When Richard pushed the button, Sean's phone made a musical noise.

"Okay," Sean said, "put the phone to your ear like I'm doing and talk."

"What should I say?"

Sean spoke softly into the phone. "Can you hear me on the phone and not just in the room?"

His eyes widened. "Aye." He thought of all the times he could have used this technology, of all the times he could not communicate with those he had to and those he wanted to.

"Nobody here says 'aye.' You'd better get used to saying yes or yeah if you want to blend in." Sean demonstrated how to use the phone. "Keep it with you at all times in your pocket where you can reach it quickly. If anything happens and you are afraid to talk, use the phone to call me, I'll know it's you from the number. Just don't end the call. I'll track you down from the phone."

"You can do that?"

"I can't, but the police can."

"What are police?" he asked.

"Law enforcement."

"Would that be the same as a Sheriff?"

"Yeah," Sean said. "And now, whether you like it or not, I have to cut your hair."

"Do what you must." He sat.

Once it was cut, Sean handed him a cap and told him he'd have to wear it at all times in the kitchen, and then added, "I think you'll want to leave it on after you see what I've done to your hair."

Richard gave him a weak smile.

"Wait here, I'm going to get Manny. He'll show you the ropes. I won't be back until much later tonight." Sean collected Richard's clothes on his way out.

"Frank," Katarina said, "do you think asking me the same thing repeatedly will result in a different answer? I don't know what happened to Richard. The last thing he did was to excuse himself to go to the men's room. He should be there."

"We've searched. He isn't."

"Then hadn't you better call Hosgrove?"

Frank held his hands up. "I'm not calling him. You do it."

"I'll call him tomorrow if I have to. Richard said he'd be back, I believe he will. Meanwhile, I'd like to eat without you breathing down my neck. Please go back to your table, or check the men's room again, or go anywhere else. Just not here." She stabbed her fork at him.

Frank went back to Joe, and they both went into the men's room and came out, not seeing Richard. Frank pointed to the right at a door marked "Employees Only." "Whaddya think? Could he have gone in here?"

"Dunno, it's worth a shot," Joe said.

Frank opened the door and they went in. The room was empty, but they could see another door with an exit sign over it on the far wall. "Let's try that door," Frank said.

"Hey, what's that blinking light?" Joe asked, pointing to a panel to the right of the opened door.

Frank shrugged. "There's nothing out there but a couple of dumpsters. I don't think he could of gotten out this way."

"We oughta check behind the dumpsters. Maybe he's hiding back here." Joe switched on a flashlight, and they walked between the dumpsters and searched. "Nothin', let's head back."

As they emerged from between the dumpsters, a floodlight came on, blinding them. "Hey!" Joe shouted, raising his hand to shield his eyes.

"What are you doing here?" a man's voice asked.

"Nothin', we took a wrong turn," Frank said.

"Bring them to my office," the same voice said.

Two large men approached them. Frank held his hands up. "I'm coming. Keep your hands offa me."

"Yeah, me too," Joe said, holding his hands above his head.

They followed the men to the office.

"Tell me why I shouldn't call the police and have you arrested for skipping the bill," the manager said.

They were in the manager's office, flanked by two husky valet parking attendants doubling as security. Joe glanced at Frank and took the lead. "We fully intended to pay, sir. We were looking for a friend and thought we saw him go into the locker room. When we didn't see him there, we decided to try the other door, thinking he went that way."

"Is your friend an employee here?"

"No, sir."

"That door is clearly marked for 'Employees Only' in large black letters," the manager said. "I won't press charges, but you'll have to pay and leave immediately. And I wouldn't hang around if I were you, because then I will call the police. Do you have your car parked here?"

"Yes, but we parked on the street," Frank said.

"Jesse," the manager said to one of the valet attendants, "walk them to their car, and please see to it that they pay and leave."

Katarina watched as Frank and Joe were none too gently escorted out of the restaurant. It didn't appear they noticed her still seated at the table. On impulse, she asked the waiter if she could see the manager. "Bring me my check, too, thank you."

The manager came to her table with the check. "You asked to see me?"

"Yes, I came here with a young man, about five foot eight, with long, dark brown hair, almost black. He disappeared about a half an hour ago, and I just saw two men being escorted out of the restaurant. Now I know it is entirely possible I've been stood up, but as you see, he has not eaten half the food on his plate. I would have thought that if he'd decided to stand me up, he'd have at least waited until dessert."

"So, you're worried that there may have been some foul play involved."

"Yes." She frowned. "I am concerned. Those two men you escorted out just now—they followed my friend immediately before he vanished. Where did you find them?"

"Out back in a little alley where our dumpsters are. Do you want to see it?"

"Yes, please, er, ah… Sorry, I don't know your name."

"It's Ken," he said as they both walked toward the back. "Yours?"

"Katarina."

They continued in silence until they reached the armed door. "You won't hear this in the restaurant, but it lights a panel in my office and in the kitchen if anybody opens it without disarming it like this."

He put the floodlight on, and they both searched behind the dumpsters.

"Could they have put him in the dumpster?" she asked.

"I suppose it's possible, although I didn't think they could have without our seeing them do it," he said. "They wouldn't be able to lift the top of these dumpsters and put anyone in it, so the only place they could have done that is through one of these side doors."

"I don't want to look. Do you mind just telling me what you see?"

He opened one of the side doors that was just big enough to accommodate a large trash bag, and shone the light into the interior. After scanning both dumpsters, he repeated, "Only garbage."

"Thank God," she said.

"I'm sorry your date skipped out on you, Katarina."

"Me too, but I'm quite relieved you didn't find his body instead."

Hosgrove started shouting at Katarina as soon as she said hello. *Frick and Frack must have called.* She held the phone away from her ear, and when he finally quieted she asked, "Are you done?"

"I'm not nearly done!" Hosgrove shouted. "You were supposed to get him to Ambion tomorrow morning. Now how do you propose to do that, Katarina?"

"Will you shut up and listen? I'm as flummoxed as you."

"Go ahead," Hosgrove said.

She swore she could hear him clenching his teeth.

"I spoke to the manager because I was worried Richard may have been the victim of foul play as he left his food half eaten. Anyway, we searched the back of the restaurant and even searched in the dumpsters, but we didn't find him anywhere. I think he must have doubled back from the men's room and left through the regular entrance. My guess is he will probably try to get out into the countryside thinking he might be able to survive there."

"Where are you?"

"Home. I didn't see any point in hanging around."

"Didn't you try to find him?"

Katarina suppressed her anger at Hosgrove and said in a slightly exasperated tone, "Not only did I, but so did Joe and Frank. The manager threw them out because he thought they were trying to stiff the restaurant for the meal, but they parked themselves a block away and searched the neighborhood. When I came out, they grabbed me before I could get my car from

Valet Parking, and we searched together. I don't know how he did it, but he seems to have disappeared."

"That's what they told me, too. I don't know what to do, Katarina. Aside from seeing this enterprise go up in flames, I also don't see how Richard will be able to manage in this twenty-first century society. You know him better than any of us. Where do you think he'll try to go?"

"I already said—the countryside. Or what about Forest Park? That's huge."

Hosgrove's voice brightened. "Wouldn't that be ironic? Does he know Ambion's right at the park's edge?"

"I don't think so. He'd be easy to spot in a business suit and wing tips. I'm tired and it's late. Why don't I stop by tomorrow, and we can review our options."

"Okay Katarina, but I'm going to have my men search for him. Expect a call if they find Richard. I'll want you to come here immediately."

NINE

Richard stood in the locker room feeling very alone. He had just cut himself off from Katarina, the only person who had befriended him in a world that was completely alien to him. The last time he felt this dislocated was when he was seven years old and he was pulled from the only home he had known.

All of England had been at war. It was felt that he and George would not be safe at Fotheringhay Castle. He'd had little or no contact with his parents or older siblings for the first seven years of his life except for his brother, George, and an older sister, Margaret. It was with these two that he formed his earliest bonds. He and George were sent away under the protection of heavy guard, with George as his only companion.

He turned his thoughts to the present and walked down the row of lockers, randomly pulling at the doors. One opened and he was eyeball to breast with a picture of a scantily clad woman. His eyes bulged. "Jesú!"

At that moment he heard a derisive snort. He turned toward the snort, banging the locker door shut. Two men stood opposite him, dressed as he was.

"You Ricky?" a short, thin man asked.

He nearly said "no," but then realized it was a form of his name. "Aye—er—yes."

"Manny," the thin man said pointing to himself. "An' he Tito." Manny aimed his thumb at the other man.

"Yes." He noticed that Tito resembled him, if you didn't check too closely. He at once appreciated Sean's cleverness. People rarely took notice of people of no importance.

"He don' speak good English like me," Manny continued. "You work in kitchen for Tito tonight. Don' talk, jus' do what you're tol'."

The guards were not in view when he exited the locker room. He followed Manny into the kitchen and could see Frank and Joe talking. They stood near Katarina. When Frank moved toward her, Richard was torn between wanting to protect her and knowing he could not. He held his breath when Joe headed in his direction. But Joe walked right by him, as if he were invisible.

Manny pointed to a large, full, black-plastic garbage sack that was nearly filled. "You gunna tie it like this an' throw it in the dumpster."

He hefted the sack, and brought it out to the dumpster. Manny opened the door on the side, and Richard stuffed the bag in. It was heavy, but not as much as the armor and arms he used to haul around for hours at a time.

"You pretty strong. I show you what else you gotta do."

They entered the kitchen from the rear. Manny brought Richard over to a large sink where dirty pots and pans were stacked. "They don' go in the dishwasher, you gotta do by han'."

He eyed a large pot on the floor that was as high as the sink and as big around. He could see the bottom was thickly lined with burnt tomato sauce, tapering as it rose to the top until there were only a few flecks. "How is this cleaned?"

Manny put some powder in the pot and had Richard spray it with hot water until it was about two-thirds filled. It foamed into a white froth that resembled the head on a tankard of ale. It took both their muscle to drag it out of the way while they let it soak to loosen the burnt food.

"That guy there, he head chef. You do whatever he say." Manny waved his hand at a man wearing a white tunic and chef's hat. He seemed to be everywhere, barking orders at the cooks and making sure all the meals were prepared to his standards. The chain of command went down from there, and Richard was at the bottom, a position that he'd never experienced before. After only a few minutes of doing this work, he determined he never wanted to experience it again.

Manny showed Richard how to unload the dishwasher and stack the dishes, and while it was the easiest of his duties, it was also the hottest. The dishes burnt his fingers when he grabbed them as they exited. And he was surrounded by clouds of steam from the hot water puddles that formed at the bottom.

As the senior dishwasher, Manny saved loading the dishwasher for himself. A short time after he and Manny cleaned the large soup pot, he had to scrape the duck he had abandoned earlier into the garbage. The next dishwasher load was ready to be unloaded. His stomach growled in protest.

It wasn't long before he lost his appetite in a haze of cooking odors that mixed fish, meat, cheese, and grease. He frequently had to mop the floor of the grease that made it hazardous for everyone to walk on.

His hands were raw from washing the pots and pans; his muscles ached from bending over, and lugging fifty-gallon soup pots filled with liquid, but mostly because he was on his feet for six hours without break. The one short break he did have was when Manny *helped* him dump the trash shortly after midnight. Manny wanted to have a smoke and dragged Richard away from the dumpster to his secret spot.

Richard went to sit down on a box while Manny lit his cigarette. "Don' sit there," Manny warned, taking a deep drag.

"Why should I not sit down? I have been on my feet for hours." Richard sat.

"Rats, the rats have nests here," Manny said. "Wanna butt?"

He jumped up as quickly as he could. He hated rats. "What is butt?"

"Cigarette. Here take a drag," Manny said, handing Richard the unlit end of his cigarette.

When he sucked on the cigarette, his throat burned and he choked on the smoke. He coughed violently and had to grab onto the chain-link fence they were standing next to in order to remain standing.

Manny snatched the butt and slapped him on the back. "Hey man, you shoulda tol' me you don' smoke. You okay?"

Richard inhaled the air deeply when he stopped coughing. "Yes, I am okay."

"Good, lez go in."

The sweat stung his eyes as he scrubbed the latest load of pots. He thought of how Anne had been disguised as a cook's maid and hidden in an inn in London. She'd had to endure much harsher conditions for weeks before he'd found and rescued her. He needed to last only a few hours. He at once felt ashamed at his own inner complaints and extremely proud of her courage and resolve.

Finally, at two thirty, the restaurant closed, and everyone dragged out to the street. Sean was waiting for him in front of Morrison's, much to his relief. He had sustained himself on blind trust, and for once, his trust was justified.

"Hey man, you look exhausted," Sean said, opening the car door for Richard and then going around to the driver's side. He put the car in drive and pulled out. "There's a sandwich for you in that bag. I figured you'd be hungry after working all night. Go ahead and eat it. I've already had mine."

Richard had not realized just how bone-tired he was until he sat down in the car. "Thank you, but I think I will just close my eyes for the nonce."

"Hey man, wake up! We're here, at my apartment. Wake up." Through a haze of exhausted sleep, Richard felt Sean poke him in the side. "C'mon, I can't carry you. Wake up!"

He opened his eyes and sat staring at Sean.

"We're at my apartment. You can go back to sleep when we're inside."

He got out of the car and followed Sean. He had to lean against the wall to steady himself, while Sean fumbled for his key.

"This is what they call an efficiency," Sean said. I'm afraid you'll have to share it with me—all of one entire room and bathroom. I hope you don't mind sleeping on this cot, it's all I have."

"This is very kind of you, Sean. The cot will serve."

Sean pulled out the sandwich he had offered earlier. "Um, hungry? I can put it in the fridge if you don't want it now."

"I am tired. I would prefer to sleep." Grateful for the respite, he stretched out on the cot feeling utterly alone in an alien world.

TEN

Evan Hosgrove reviewed his options prior to meeting with Ralph Sanders, the hospital administrator where he'd purchased the body Ambion substituted for Richard—the body that was now five-hundred years in the past. Worse, he did not know where to find Richard. He now wished he had opted for buying a skeleton and building an artificial body, but at the time he was convinced it would not be realistic enough even to pass for the mutilated corpse that became Richard's remains.

Sanders had called him first thing to set up an appointment, insisting they meet immediately. Hosgrove knew that could only mean one thing: the deceased's family was pressing for the remains. He didn't know if he could reverse the substitution even if Richard were in his possession, but there was zero possibility he could do it now. How could he have been so stupid as to allow Richard out of his sight? He was lucky once; he should not have counted on a second time.

Joe, Frank, and Katarina had all confirmed that Richard was not to be found in the restaurant itself. How could he have disappeared, seemingly without a trace? Hosgrove couldn't even call the police, because for all practical purposes, Richard did not exist.

His secretary ushered in Ralph Sanders.

"I'll get right to the point, Mr. Hosgrove." Sanders sat down. "The family wants their son's remains—however small—to be returned to them so they may put him to rest."

"And if there are no remains?"

"No remains?" Sanders pulled at his tie. A bead of sweat ran down his neck and trickled under his collar. "They need a copy of your records showing where his remains were interred."

"No, that's company confidential information. If we could have the name of the family, we would be happy to go to them directly."

"And that information is confidential. Not only do we respect their privacy, but legally, we are bound to it."

"Then our hands are tied." This was so frustrating. He should have planned better, but his overwhelming desire to bring Richard into the present had outweighed his better judgment.

Sanders sat back in the chair and rested his elbows on its arms. He formed a steeple with his hands and rested his chin on it. "You have until Friday to produce your records to prove that it was used for medical research or they will be subpoenaed. That is, unless you can return the body. Then we will not pursue the records, and they will remain company confidential. It's your choice."

Hosgrove leaned forward and stared down at Sanders. "Why don't you ask the family if they would be willing to discuss this with us directly? I see that you are caught in the middle of a sticky situation. If you could remove yourself from the picture, then your risk and exposure would be minimized."

Sanders stood up to leave. "I will think about it."

"Just one thing before you go. Why are they asking these questions now? It's been over two months since their son died."

Sanders turned when he got to the door. "It all has to do with those newspaper reports about cadaver misuse and fraud at U.C.L.A. They suddenly got worried that their son was somehow involved in a similar fraud. They're quite serious. You know that several people have been arrested and tried in the U.C.L.A. case."

"But that was over six months ago. Why did they wait until now? Why did they agree to release the body for research in the first place?"

"They didn't say."

Cutting off further inquiries, Sanders left, slamming the door behind him.

Hosgrove called Michael, demanding he report immediately.

Michael appeared in the doorway—it seemed before Hosgrove could return the phone to its cradle.

"Close the door and sit," he said. "Sanders was just here and has demanded the remains or he'll subpoena our records. And that's not the worst piece of news, although it doesn't help. Richard has gone AWOL."

Michael sank slowly into the chair and his face lost all color.

"Mike, are you all right?"

Michael nodded. "I'm stunned by what you've told me, on both counts. Where could he have gone? How can he manage in today's environment?"

"That's a very good question. He's no fool and I doubt that he'd chance it without any help. What do you think?"

"What about Katarina? He was with her, and she's spent a lot of time with him besides," Michael said.

"Exactly! But, she must have gotten someone else to help her because Frank and Joe saw her alone in the restaurant after Richard disappeared, and they watched her leave the restaurant alone later and followed her to the house. He wasn't with her."

"But who?"

"I don't know, Mike, but I plan to find out."

"How are you going to do that?"

"I've got some people tailing Katarina. She might lead us to him, and I have contacts at the phone company…" Hosgrove didn't bother to clarify his thinking further.

"What do you want me to do?" Michael asked.

"You work out how to switch them back."

"But without Richard, what good will it do?"

"He'll be there. All I'm asking is for you do your job, Mike."

"I-I'll do what I can, but I'm not sure there is enough time to do that."

"You heard what I said about the family wanting the body back, either that or share the logs of what was done with the body. We can't share those records, and I will not lose this facility. I will not accept failure," Hosgrove said. "Am I clear?"

Michael gulped. "Yes."

"I have to call Katarina. Please excuse me."

Michael left the office.

"Hello, Katarina? It's me, Evan."

"Hi Evan," Katarina said. "I was just on my way to Ambion Technologies."

"You don't have to come here. I've been thinking about what you said last night, and I'm inclined to think you might be onto something. I, uh, I also want to apologize for shouting at you the way I did. I was upset. Can you forgive me?"

"Of course, I understand. I was just as upset, maybe more than you," Katarina said. "I'm quite worried about him. I mean, how will he get on in the twenty-first century?"

"Maybe he'll try to find you, Katarina. He did seem to trust you more than anybody."

"I hope so. I'll call you if I learn anything. Thanks for letting me off the hook, Evan. I've got a lot to do today and this really helps. Let me know if you hear anything. I've come to like the guy."

"I will certainly call you if I learn anything, Katarina." Hosgrove hung up the phone. He didn't believe her.

ELEVEN

The flush of a toilet brought Richard out of his dreamless sleep. It took a few moments to remember he was in Sean's apartment. The room had three areas: sleeping, eating, and the lounge where Sean had placed the cot. The sleeping area was tucked into the left side of the apartment.

Sean emerged from the bathroom sporting a towel wrapped around his middle. "Glad you're awake. Why don't you take a shower while I make some coffee?" Sean grabbed some clothes from the closet and handed them to him. "You can wear this until we find pants that'll fit. Just roll up the cuffs. Don't worry if they're too big on you. You can cinch the waist in with this belt."

He held them against his waist. Not only were they for a much taller man, but the eight-inch gap in the waist made the pants unwearable. "I believe they would have fit my brother. Do you have anything smaller? I do not think I will be able to keep them from falling down."

Sean walked over to an old oak dresser that was dark from age and stained with fingerprints around the pulls. He opened the bottom drawer and pawed through the clothes. "The only thing I have is my old gym shorts from high school. I've gotten a lot bigger since then." He handed them to Richard.

"They are so short," he said, frowning.

Sean laughed. "No problemo my friend. Everyone wears shorts these days. Just shower and put these clothes on for now. We'll get you something more suitable first thing. I left a fresh towel for you, feel free to use my shampoo."

He stripped and turned the shower on as hot as he could stand. He poured shampoo onto his hair and lathered up. Now that Sean had hacked off most of his hair, the length felt foreign to the touch. It was something else that he would have to get used to.

Once he toweled down, he donned the clothes Sean had provided, glad they were temporary. He wasn't pleased about showing his hairy legs in public. He left the bathroom.

"What shall I do with the dirty clothes?" he asked Sean.

"Just throw them in that sack over there," Sean said, taking a swig of his coffee. "Grab some coffee, I want to show you something."

Sean was seated in front of a screen, similar to Katarina's TV, but flatter, and the images weren't those of people. Richard had seen devices like this one at Ambion Technologies. He tapped the screen. "What is it?"

"My computer," Sean said. "Hey, grab that chair over there and sit down."

He sat and took a sip of coffee. "I am sorry for being so ignorant, but I do not know what computer is."

Sean turned toward him. "Not to worry, man. I'll show you as much as I can about it."

Richard leaned in and studied the screen.

"Good thing you got curly hair. It's hiding my very bad haircut. Anyway, I want you to see this." Sean pointed at some images. "I searched for you on the Internet and found these pictures, which sort of look like you."

Richard studied the portraits painted from the originals that did not survive the centuries. Henry VII probably had the artists copy those fine paintings and coarsen his features to make him appear more villainous. However, they did resemble him. "How does that work?"

"I'll explain as much as I can later. We should get started, there's a lot we have to do today, and then I have to go to work tonight," Sean said.

"Is there anything to eat?" Richard asked. "I am very hungry."

"Oh sorry. I usually don't have breakfast. Tell you what, we can stop by McDonald's and you can get an Egg McMuffin or something while we're on our way to get you some clothes. You can eat it in the car while I drive." Sean stood up and grabbed his keys. "Let's go."

They were in the car, driving to McDonald's when Sean asked, "So, do your friends call you Richard, or something else?"

"I was addressed as 'Your Grace,' but that would not be appropriate today."

Sean laughed. "Which would you prefer, Dick or Rich?"

"Dick."

As Sean pulled into the lot, Richard thought he recognized one of Ambion's security guards walking out, carrying a coffee. He sank down in the seat.

"Problem?"

"I think that is one of the guards from Ambion."

"He's looking this way. Bend down like you're tying your shoelace."

Sean put the car in gear. "I'll go to the drive-through for you. Just keep your head down. I'll let you know when it's okay." Sean waited until they were on the road before handing Richard his breakfast.

He sipped his coffee and noticed a bunch of McDonald wrappers floating around behind the driver's seat, "I see you frequent this establishment."

"Yeah, I've been meaning to clean this mess up, but I never seem to have the time. You sure that was a security guard from Ambion?"

"Yes."

"Damn! Here, put these sunglasses on. I'm gonna circle around and go back in. I wanna make sure we're not being followed."

He put them on. "Jesú, everything is dark."

"That's what they're for. Anyway, they hide your eyes, maybe that'll plant some doubt." Sean flipped the visor down, revealing a mirror. "Keep it down and watch to see if anyone is following us."

Startled by his appearance in the mirror, Richard could see Sean was right; he did look different, hopefully enough for those who did not know him well. He could see a blue car, a rusted red car, and a black SUV all reflected in the mirror. "There are three different cars. How will I know if someone is following?"

"Just tell me what they do and if it changes. I'm watching, too."

Sean pulled into the McDonald's lot again.

"They have all remained on the street," he said. "They were not following us."

"Don't bet on it." Sean pulled in behind the building and backed into a parking spot. "We're gonna wait a few and see what happens." He let the car idle.

"You've got some interesting scars there, Dick. You think they'll be able to identify you from them?"

He examined his arms and legs. In the past, he had not given them any thought. His clothes had covered him, leaving only the face, neck, and hands exposed. Most men he knew had more battle scars than he did. As his brother's most trusted general, he had often been in the thick of battle, but because of his skill, he had avoided the more serious injuries, but could not avoid all.

But now, he could see that most men had unblemished skin, and wore short-sleeved shirts. Some wore shorts, too. He had one scar that stood out on his thigh, going diagonally across where he had taken a blow from a battle-ax. Though it had seemed grave, he had not noticed when it happened, and it had quickly healed. His armor had protected him from serious injury.

He also had an ugly scar that ran from just above his right wrist through his elbow on the inside of his arm. Although he'd worn full armor in battle, he had decided to eliminate the plate that would have covered the backs of his arms, opting for mobility in the hand-to-hand combat. A soldier had slipped a broad sword past his shield, and the blade's edge had torn through his flesh before he was able to kill the man with his battle-ax. He had kept fighting, unaware of his injury until his squires had wrenched him from the battle. He'd lost a lot of blood and had nearly lost his life.

"It would be best for me not to show this much nakedness."

Sean gave a quick laugh. "Is that what you think? That we're naked? You ain't seen nuttin' yet, bro." He scanned the lot and put the car in drive. "I think it's safe now. Scan the streets as we go by just to make sure no one is waiting for us."

As they went through the first intersection, Richard thought he saw the black SUV pull away from the curb and follow them across.

"Yeah, I see him too," Sean said. "I'm gonna try something. You keep watching. If we lose him, keep an eye out for someone else. If we're being followed, they'll team us."

"I do not understand—team?"

"It means that another car may pick up when the first one drops out," Sean said.

Richard gulped. He had not considered they needed to be suspicious of more than one car.

They took a right at the next intersection. The SUV stayed with them. However, on the next right they took, it continued straight through. Sean pulled into a no parking zone and waited to turn the car around. Before he could do it, the SUV entered the street from the opposite direction and pulled in front, blocking them.

The SUV driver dashed out and ran to the passenger side. Sean drove onto the sidewalk and sped away as the guard reached for the door handle.

They took a right, a left, and then another left in rapid succession. "I think I've lost him. Keep watching."

Instead of going straight, Sean made extra turns. They didn't see any car staying with them long enough to make them think they were still being followed.

"Dick, I think we got lucky."

"I do not understand."

"I don't think that guy contacted anyone, and then he made a stupid mistake when he got out of his car. That's what allowed us to get away."

"Am I putting you at peril?"

"Naw, forget it. I can take care of myself. Anyway, we gotta get you outta those shorts," Sean said. "Clothes first, then we can go to the barber and then the library. That's going to take the most time."

They parked at a metered spot a block from the clothing store. "So what are you thinking of getting?" Sean asked as they walked in.

"You will have to guide me. I think it best if my appearance does not differ from most men today."

"Worry not my friend, these clothes are as ordinary as you can get."

After about forty minutes, Richard had added to his wardrobe a couple of pairs of khakis, a pair of black camo pants, shirts, a denim jacket, sunglasses, and a wallet, which Sean stuffed with several twenty-dollar bills.

Despite the heat, he chose to wear a black long-sleeved tee shirt and a pair of khakis when they left for the barber.

Sean walked around him. "You look good, man. Black is your color. You may not need the beard, I bet your own mother could not recognize you now."

"My mother would recognize me no matter what I did to disguise myself. She has a keen eye for faces," he said and then amended, "I mean did. She was alive before I was brought here."

"Were you very close to your parents?" Sean asked.

"No." He stopped walking, stunned by his own unconsidered response. He had worshipped his father. But had it been his desire to please his mother? He hardly knew his father. "My father was killed when I was eight, and I did not know him well. I got to know my mother afterwards. I admired and respected her greatly, but I never felt completely at ease in her presence, not even as an adult. I swore I would never do that to my children."

They got into the car and headed for the barber's.

"Did you have kids?"

"Kids?"

"Slang for children."

"Yes, and I do miss them terribly."

"How many? If I may ask," Sean said, turning off the ignition and then getting out of the car.

"Three. Two natural children before I married Anne, and then a son by her. But he died over a year ago."

"I'm sorry to hear about your son," Sean said. "I thought all children are natural—oh, you mean your wife wasn't their mother."

They entered the barbershop.

He thought the haircut suited him. It was shorter on the sides and back and the top was slicked back, held in place with some pomade. It did emphasize that his hair had receded some at the temples, but this gave him a more sophisticated appearance. In all, he was pleased with his appearance; even the day's worth of stubble did not seem as unkempt as it had before the haircut.

They had just left when Sean steered him into an alley. "I think I just saw that SUV pull into the lot.

"Perhaps I should not try to evade him."

"Don't be an idiot! Besides, if anything happened, Katarina would kill me." Sean pulled him away from the alley. "But you gave me an idea. Follow my lead. I'm gonna call you 'John,' and if you say anything, stick to mumbling something short, disguising your voice if you can."

He followed Sean to the SUV, getting to it as the driver got out. He had turned away from them.

"Hey!" Sean said. "You lookin' for somethin'?" He balled his hands into fists. Richard did the same.

"Yeah, I was supposed to meet a friend here. What's it to you?"

"I don't see nobody else here," Sean said. "You too ugly to be staying here." He leaned forward. "Ain't that right, Johnny?"

Richard growled and jabbed his fist into his palm.

The guard put his hands up, keys jangling in his fingers. "Okay, okay. I'll leave."

Sean grabbed the keys and threw them into the bushes at the edge of the lot. "Now you can go treasure hunting with your friend." He bared his teeth.

The guard ran for his keys while Richard and Sean sped away with as much acceleration as a ten-year-old Corolla would allow. "I think we're okay now. He had to have followed us from this morning."

"I believe he is still searching for his keys."

"Well Dick, you're one man I'd want on my team. You were real menacing."

"That is a skill I needed. It appears you know that skill as well."

"That's one thing my old man taught me."

"Old man?"

"Slang for dad, uh, father."

"Are you close to him?" Richard asked.

"I am now, but if you had asked me the same question ten years ago, I would've laughed. I have to say that for all the times I rebelled against him and thought he was a tyrant, he really cared what happened, and he was there as much as the U.S. Army allowed. We get along good now."

"Is he still a soldier?"

"Naw, he's retired. He lives in San Diego near the base where my sister is stationed." Sean's face lit up as he talked about his family. "She was the one to follow in Pop's footsteps. He wanted me to, but I wasn't interested."

"Although women and children performed tasks on the battlefield, there were very few women who led armies—those who came from wealth and power."

Sean put his hand on Richard's shoulder. "I've heard of Joan of Arc, but I had no idea there were any women in armies then."

"The poor women did not engage in battle. The men had them scavenge for arrows, light the cannons, and perform other tasks that were hazardous. They were expendable."

Sean clucked. "Well, my sister shouldn't have re-upped, uh, re-enlisted. She's got two kids and her husband's in the Navy. He's away at sea for months at a time. She should've thought about her kids. She could end up in Iraq or Afghanistan.

"I'm hungry. We'll get something quick and head for the library, okay?"

"Okay."

Sean explained what he intended to do, on their way to the library. Richard would have to help search through the newspaper microfiche.

Once in the library, Richard found the quantity of available books daunting. He'd never seen so many books in one place; this was even more glorious than the bookstore. He became aware of Sean standing next to him, speaking. "I did not hear what you said."

"You look like you're in another world. The microfiche is downstairs, let's go there and I'll show you how to use it."

Sean set him up in front of a fiche reader and selected newspapers for 1972. He showed him how to load the machine and how to scan through it to find the Obituary section.

"Okay, search for notices of male babies that died when they were born, up to one year old. When you see one with that description, write down all the information you can find. I'm going to do the same for 1977 and work backwards. Between us, we should come up with a name you can use. Remember, it doesn't matter what the baby's name was, only the age and sex is important.

"Why are we doing this?"

"There's a whole bunch of things that you need, such as a Social Security number and driver's license. You can't get those without a birth certificate, and without the proper ID, you can't do anything."

They pored through the records. At first, he was astonished at the number of people who lived to their seventies, eighties, and nineties and awestruck by one notice of a woman who died at one hundred and one. It took him twenty minutes before he found the first child of three and that was a girl. He began to think that they wouldn't find anyone. He continued searching, stunned by the low infant mortality of this time.

After two hours, Sean interrupted him. "We gotta go. I have to get ready for work. We can come back tomorrow if we have to."

"I am amazed at how few infants there were. So many infants died in my time that I thought we would find a name immediately."

When they got back to the apartment, they spread their notes out on the table.

"This is the best one." Sean circled the note: Eric Wilde, died June 27, 1977, age five years, six months.

"But there are two others who are named Richard, why not one of them?"

"Because, my friend, I think that Eric came from a family who didn't go to doctors. If we're lucky, he wasn't born in a hospital."

"Why is that important and why do you think they did not see a doctor?" Richard asked.

"Eric's records may be sketchy, or if we're lucky, non-existent—less for the authorities to trace."

"I understand why it's beneficial to not have records," he rubbed his temples, "but why do you think this is true of Eric?"

"According to the obit, Eric died of an appendicitis, which is very rare if you go to a hospital for treatment."

"What is appendicitis?"

"Um, it's when the appendix, a little unused part of the intestine, becomes infected and swells up. If it ruptures before the doctors can remove it, then the person will often die," Sean said.

"How do you know if your appendix is about to rupture?" Richard asked.

"As far as I know, it's very painful here and you run a high fever, and that's before it ruptures." Sean placed his hand near his hip. "It's worse after because fecal matter is released internally. Anyway, it acts as a poison. You can research it later for—"

Richard moaned.

"Dick! Don't tell me you think your appendix is going to rupture."

He shook his head, his voice raspy with emotion, "No, dear God, I think my son's did." He put his head in his hands.

TWELVE

"Hello." Katarina picked up her mobile on the fourth ring. She had just driven off campus and was on her way to the supermarket. It was late afternoon.

"May I please speak to Dr. Katarina Parvic?"

"Speaking, who is this?"

"You don't know me, but I work for your mobile phone company, and I think you ought to know that I've been asked to hand over your phone records to the VP of operations."

Katarina forced herself to take a deep breath. "Hold on a minute." The screen showed the caller's number was blocked.

She caught her breath and pulled over to the curb. "Who are you? How do you know me?"

"I can't give you my name," the woman said. "I only know your name and cell phone number, but I'm calling you because I was asked to hand over your phone records at work today."

"Were they subpoenaed?"

"No, and that's why I'm calling you. It's not official and I'm afraid of losing my job."

"Please let the authorities know." Katarina was livid. She sensed that this caller would not follow through, but she had to ask anyway. "Do you know who requested them?"

"Please," her voice cracked, "I can't afford to lose my job. I just wanted to tell you is all... so that you know this has happened."

The phone went dead. Katarina leaned her head against the backrest and was thankful that she had the foresight to have used a pay phone.

So Richard was right all along. He must've understood that Hosgrove had intended to send him back well after he had heard the words. She was further impressed with his intelligence.

Once Sean left for work, Richard could no longer stave off his feelings of depression. He told himself he should feel lucky to be alive at all, let alone in this time of miracles. Instead he despaired that he'd ever really fit into this culture, that he'd ever learn enough to be a useful member of society, or if he even wanted to.

And, the more he thought about his last few days in the fifteenth century, the more he realized he had been much too eager to go into battle. He'd ignored the advice to delay engaging Henry before all of his supporters could join the ranks. His eagerness had cost the lives of those loyal to him. His own spies had told him that both Lord Thomas Stanley and Sir William Stanley would betray him. Why had he not had an alternate plan? Contrary to what Sean had said about not beating himself up over the past, he couldn't stop himself from doing it now.

Though he did not want to revisit his son's death, he had to see what history thought. So he locked up his emotions and sat in front of Sean's computer, left on for him to use. He spread his notes next to the keyboard and went to the Google search site. It took a few attempts at selecting the right combination of key words, but he did find several references.

About the only point they agreed upon was the suddenness of Edward's death. Many disagreed with his own knowledge of Edward's general health. It was true his son was small for his age, but so had he been, and compared to his brothers and sisters, small still. While Richard thought his son had a few more sore throats and childhood fevers than other children, he did not think he had been sickly as the sites he found asserted.

Then there was the matter of when Edward had died. Some had listed the date as the last day of March, 1484, whereas others recorded the death as late as the ninth of April of that year.

Despite his feelings, a laugh—more like a bark—exploded from his throat. He would never forget when he had learned of his son leaving this sphere. On the fourth of April, a messenger had galloped into Nottingham Castle—exhausted from his journey on the network of fast horses—and collapsed at his feet, weeping. Stammering through his tears, the terrified man had told them that his beloved son had died two days before.

If he could have gone back with today's medicine and prevented his son's sudden death, then perhaps Anne would still be alive. His head spun with the illogic of his last conjecture. For him, these events had happened recently, not over five hundred years ago. He should be dead.

While seeking information on Edward, he came across a couple of sites that were dedicated to restoring his name and refuting the lies that were spread about him. He knew of those deceits. Before he took the crown, all of London was rife with rumors. They only became more virulent after Henry became King. An American site had a lengthy discussion regarding Shakespeare's play, which not only cast him in an evil light, but also deformed his body. He had no abnormalities that he knew, and could fight and win against the bravest of them. He stopped reading about the play in disgust; it was pure fiction.

He turned his attention to his wife. Of the little he could find about Anne, he learned historians today agreed with the doctors of his time—she had died of consumption, or tuberculosis as they now called it. At least the rumor flying around London that he had poisoned her was not given any credence. With a perverse kind of relief, he moved from reading about his history, to learning about TB.

The phone rang. Richard jumped and held his breath. Sean told him to let it ring, and that if he, Sean, were calling, to go ahead and pick it up. Richard waited for the machine to answer. He heard Katarina's voice after two rings and a short message. "Sean, it's me, Katarina. Please pick up if you are there... crap—crap—crap—crap—crap... I must speak to you, something's -"

He grabbed the phone. "Katarina! What is the matter?"

"Richard! Thank God, you answered. I'm sure that Hosgrove suspects something. I just learned that someone is looking into my phone records illegally. It has to be Hosgrove."

"I think I should go back. Can Hosgrove hurt you, Katarina?"

"No! You can't go back there. Something is very wrong, else why would he go after my phone records?"

"I do not mean Hosgrove, Katarina. I mean back to my time. I do not belong here."

"You'll die." Her voice rang with alarm.

"That would not be a bad thing."

"Don't say that," she cried. "Please don't do anything until I get there, okay."

"I will wait."

Katarina scanned the strip mall for Hosgrove's men. She felt their presence everywhere—in the parking lot by the supermarket, reflected in the discount clothing store window, and grabbing a smoke ten feet from where she was standing by the pay phone.

She convinced herself that she wasn't being paranoid. Someone was illegally accessing her phone records, and she put her money on Hosgrove.

She entered the supermarket to do her week's shopping, but found herself randomly throwing items into the cart instead. She gave up after selecting four items and drove home.

After changing into jeans, tee shirt and loafers, Katarina left her house. She was being followed. Instead of going toward Sean's apartment, she turned right on Powell and then right on Thirty-ninth. She zigzagged through the middle-class neighborhood, doubling back to Burnside. Just to be sure Hosgrove's men hadn't followed her to this point, she drove to Laurelhurst Park and pulled to the curb. No one pulled over when she did. She drove back to Burnside, crossed the Willamette and headed over to the Pearl District where she parked in a garage on Davis, two blocks from Sean's apartment.

Still, despite her precautions, she couldn't shake the feeling she had been followed. So she walked away from his apartment toward Powell's Books on Burnside. Even though it would mean she'd delay seeing Richard for a few more minutes, she entered the bookstore and bought a tour guide for him.

Convinced she was no longer being watched, she left the store and took a left on tenth. She continued to check for Hosgrove's men, and by the time she crossed Everett, Katarina could not see or sense anyone behind her.

Richard heard a knock at the door and checked through the peephole. He saw Katarina twisting her head, first left, then to her right, as if she expected someone to pounce on her.

As soon as he opened it, she slid inside and pushed the door shut, locking it. "You can't go back, that's certain death."

"I know," he said. "I have come five centuries into the future, but my heart is in the past. Now, instead of dying as I should have, I have also hurt more people."

"No." Her eyes filled with tears. "This is hurting me—you wanting to die. You're my friend, I don't want to lose you."

He was being pulled by two worlds, and he did not know how he could explain it. "Allow me to show you something." He walked back to the computer and displayed the information on tuberculosis. "Do you know why I am reading about that?"

"Do you think you have tuberculosis? You aren't feverish, and I haven't heard you coughing."

"I buried my wife five months ago. I believe that is what killed her. We called it consumption or the white plague, but it is the same disease." He turned his head away from her and pinched the bridge of his nose.

Her hands rested lightly on his shoulders. "No, I don't think you're afraid of getting TB. You've seen the web site; you know that we have tests. Even if you have an active case, you know that we can cure it. What's the real reason?"

He stood and faced Katarina. "I have been thinking of that final battle, and I knowingly risked the lives of everyone who was loyal to me. I went into battle knowing Lord Thomas and Sir William Stanley would betray me, so eager was I to fight. God help me, I now know I meant to die. Now—"

"Is that how you felt then or is that hindsight speaking?"

"Hindsight?"

"Did you feel that way before you saw the video?"

"Nay." He rubbed his temples. Why had he been so stubborn and acted against his most trusted generals? "Regardless, I may not have cared about my own life, but I should have cared about their lives. Their deaths are my doing."

"And your dying will make things better?" Katarina stared into his eyes.

"Not better, just make it as it was preordained." He stared back, challenging her.

"Preordained! What a load of—" Pausing, she breathed deeply and spoke in a measured tone. "I'm not going to help you to kill yourself, period."

"Do you think that I would be taking my own life by returning to accept my fate?" he asked.

She shook her head and frowned. "I don't know. I'm not sure I believe there is such a thing as fate. I think there are possibilities, and our choices and actions determine the outcome. Your being here hasn't affected our past, but it will change our future. I want you in this future." She set her jaw and squared her shoulders.

"I see that you mean to give me no quarter," he said. "If I agree and don't try to contact Hosgrove today, if I agree to wait, will you agree to help me go back if I should want to later?"

"I think you need to give yourself enough time to grieve, and that varies from person to person. You also have the shock of waking up five hundred years into the future. I think you're doing a remarkable job adapting to our culture and technology."

"There are certain losses that I will never get over."

"But there are some that you will," Katarina said. "Richard, it's normal to hold certain people forever in your heart, but the difference is whether or not you can deal with these losses.

Would you be willing to wait a month to see how you feel at that time? You can always change your mind if you don't go back."

He paced. "I don't know what to do. I do not belong here, and Sean may be in danger because of me."

"What do you mean? Did something happen?"

"Yes. We had stopped to get something to eat when I saw a guard from Ambion. I believe he saw me and followed us."

"Did Sean think so?" she asked.

"Yes."

"Is he concerned about himself?"

"No." He spun away from Katarina.

She stepped in front of him, making him come to a halt. She held both his hands. "I thought you wanted to escape from Hosgrove yesterday, and that's what you've done. Why did you go along with my scheme if you didn't want to live?"

He turned his face from hers and sat down on the couch. "I did want to escape yesterday. I am overwhelmed today. Your being here with me helps me more than you can know. And yet, I am afraid for you."

"Don't worry about me, I'm perfectly safe. Nothing is going to happen. I won't abandon you again. I'm sorry that I had to do it at all." Tears dampened her cheeks while she spoke.

He brushed the tears away with his thumb. "I will wait." As he made that promise to her, he at once thought that maybe instead of going back to die, he could go back to save his wife and his son.

"I'm glad you're willing to hold off on any action." She blew her nose into a wadded tissue. "Let's talk about something a little more cheerful, like food. I haven't eaten and I'm hungry, what about you?"

"Maybe, a little," he said, "but there is very little here to eat."

"Why don't I order a pizza and have it delivered?"

THIRTEEN

Stan beeped the other security team on his Nextel.

"We got Katarina. She's headed north on Northwest eleventh. We'll check back in fifteen minutes."

"I bet she leads us right to him," Joe said. He dropped back when the pickup between them turned down Couch Street."

"Yup. She's driving too crazy—like she's trying to make sure nobody follows her." Stan shook his head. "Amateur. Hey, did you catch that? She just took a left on Davis?"

"I'm way ahead of you." Joe accelerated to the corner and got there in time for them to see Katarina drive into a garage. He pulled to the curb. "I'll get into position to follow her car. You follow on foot."

Stan got out of the van. "I'm on it. I'll call you if I see anything."

Katarina walked out of the parking garage three minutes after Stan had taken a discreet position across from the garage's exit.

He followed her back toward Burnside, keeping at least half a block back until she ducked into Powell's. If he lost her now, he'd lose his job. He took a deep breath and moved to the exit— she'd have to leave at some point. He got to within a half a block when he spotted her leaving.

At first it was easy to follow her because of all the people around, but once she crossed Couch, the crowd had thinned, and he had to keep ducking behind parked cars and anything else that could hide his presence. *Man, she's nervous.* She checked over her shoulder before ducking into a doorway.

Stan called his partner on the radio. "Hey Joe, I know where she is. Pick me up on Everett and Tenth."

He waited near the corner, keeping the apartment in view. Joe pulled up in the van after a few minutes and Stan got in.

"The apartment building is around the corner." Stan pointed in its general direction. "We can park across the street."

Joe drove around the block, parked and set up the surveillance equipment while Stan called Hosgrove. "We're on Northwest Tenth facing Everett across from the apartment building Katarina entered. We don't know which apartment she's in, but we're scanning for her now."

"We're on our way. Don't do anything until we get there, even if you know which apartment she's in. I'll call Frank and have him meet up with us."

It was dark out by the time Hosgrove and Frank drove up. Stan let them into the back of the van and showed him what they had done so far.

"We found her. She's in the basement apartment with a man," Joe told Hosgrove when he arrived.

"Do you know who she's with?" Hosgrove asked.

"It sounds like Richard," Joe said. "I think I recognized his voice, and he does have that odd accent and way of speaking that I thought I heard at Ambion."

"The good news is," Stan said. "Katarina ordered a pizza about fifteen minutes ago. It should be here in five, ten minutes at most."

"Are you boys up to delivering a pizza?" Hosgrove asked.

They all laughed.

"Sir," Joe said, eying Hosgrove. "Are you interested in listening in?"

"Absolutely, I want to confirm it's him."

"Boy, these listening devices are incredible," Stan said while Joe turned the volume up. "Used to be the bug had to be in the room to listen in."

"Yeah, welcome to the age of wireless," Frank said.

They heard Katarina first. "… name on the obit?"

Then they heard Richard's voice. "Eric Wilde, he was a child of …"

Hosgrove signaled Joe to mute the sound. "That's him. Good job, lads. We should be watching for the pizza boy."

They cracked open the back door of the van and waited for the pizza delivery. About five minutes passed before an old rusted Hyundai screeched up to the curb, and a kid jumped out with a pizza box.

They reached him before he turned away from the car door.

"Oh-uh," the kid said, in a squeaky, startled voice.

"Who's the pizza for?" Hosgrove asked.

"Umm, Katarina."

Hosgrove reached for his wallet. "Let me pay for it. We were invited over for pizza. I thought it'd be fun if we delivered it, instead of you."

"Cool," the kid said. "That'll be 14.95."

"Here's twenty, keep the change," Hosgrove said.

"Thanks, pops." With that, the kid jumped in his Hyundai and quickly took off.

He handed the pizza to Stan and followed him into the building, patting the twenty-two tucked away in his jacket pocket. *At least I'll be able to bring Richard to heel, if these guys can't control him.*

FOURTEEN

Katarina heard a knock at the door.

"I hope it's the pizza, I'm starved." She stuffed some money into her jean's pocket, walked to the door and peered through the peephole. "Who is it?"

"Pizza!"

The door was wrenched from her as she opened it. The man on the other side rushed in and sent her staggering backward.

Frank and Joe rushed by the man who had pushed her. "Grab her, Stan," Joe called out. She tried to jump away from him, but he was fast and grabbed her wrist.

"Richard," she shouted. "Watch—"

A hand covered her mouth and twisted her head away from Richard. She saw Hosgrove steal into the room.

Katarina swung wildly at Stan.

Stan grabbed her by the shoulder and then pushed her against the wall. "Dr. Parvic, calm down, we aren't here to hurt anyone. Hosgrove hired us to find that guy over there." He kept his hand over her mouth.

She brought her knee up to Stan's gut, loosening his grip on her. Then she kicked his knee as hard as she could, before he could straighten up from the first blow, snagged the opened pizza box, and pushed the pepperoni pizza with extra cheese into his face. She turned to Richard.

To her horror Frank and Joe had ganged up on Richard. He held his own, even though Joe swung a club down on him. Richard grabbed its shaft and yanked it out of Joe's fist before it did any harm.

The room grew still and instead of focusing on Richard, Frank and Joe stared at Hosgrove. He stood at a right angle to

Richard, his right arm held out to his side aiming a small handgun at the man he'd saved at Bosworth. His eyes, now several shades darker than Katarina remembered them being, aligned along his arm.

"Don't shoot!" she called out.

When Hosgrove didn't move, she lunged for the gun, knocking him back. The gun fired.

She turned in time to see Richard drop to his knees and then fall to the floor, his left hand clutching at his upper chest.

"My God. You shot him," she cried, pushing away from Hosgrove. "How could you shoot him?" she sobbed.

"Idiot," Hosgrove yelled just before Stan pinned him to the wall. The gun clattered on the floor.

Stan shouted, "Somebody call nine-one-one."

"Oh man," Joe said. "I didn't know he had a gun." He pulled his cell phone out and made the emergency call.

She crawled over to Richard as he was trying to stand. "Don't move." She wrapped her arms around him and looked at Hosgrove and then to Stan. "Why?"

Bits of pizza still clung to Stan's eyebrows, nose, and chin, giving him a clownish appearance in a very unfunny situation.

Frank rubbed his bruised arm. "We thought we were just helping Hosgrove pick Richard up. He told us that you'd tricked him."

Richard's breathing was becoming labored. He gasped. "No... trick... I..."

They heard sirens. Joe ran out of the apartment to the street.

"Richard, the ambulance is here, and you are going to be taken to the hospital, do you understand?" She cradled him in her arms.

His voice was barely audible. "Aye."

She heard the clatter of equipment, pounding feet, and Joe shouting, "He's in there! He's been shot!"

A hand slipped between her and Richard. "You can let go, ma'am. We've got him." She pulled back to give the emergency technicians room to work.

They slid him onto the gurney and pulled it to its "up" position. She returned to his side and grasped his hand.

"You have to step aside, ma'am," the EMT closest to her said.

She pulled away. "Please, I must ride with him."

"You can ride in the front," the technician said. "You'll just be in my way back there."

"Don't... leave...," Richard said. He gasped for air.

"I'll be with you, I promise," she said. "But you have to trust them to take care of you."

One emergency technician tended to him, while the other drove. Katarina occupied the shotgun seat. The driver paged ahead to the hospital, all the while racing through downtown Portland, their sirens blaring. It took five minutes to get to Legacy Emanuel Hospital.

The hospital team was ready for Richard when they arrived and started processing him while they raced him into the emergency room. She ran with them, staying as close as she dared.

The bits and pieces of medical lingo that she understood nearly put her into shock. His blood pressure and pulse were dropping. "Get his blood type! Get his blood type!" someone shouted.

"Who's the surgeon on duty?" someone else called out.

"Rodriguez, I'll page her," said a nurse.

An aide walked up to her. "You must go into the waiting room. You can't stay here."

The aide led her away when they put a mask over his nose and mouth. "What's happening to him?"

"The doctor will tell you after they take care of him."

"Is he going to be all right?"

Oh God! Please don't let him die.

"The doctor will speak with you later." The aide patted her arm and walked away.

She watched the aide disappear down the corridor, and Katerina nearly crashed into a gray-haired man in a rumpled, navy suit when she turned around. "Oh sorry, I didn't see you."

He smiled. "That's okay, I need to speak to you now about the shooting."

She stared at him, not comprehending.

He showed her his badge. "I'm Lt. Seely. I'd like you to tell me what happened back there in that apartment."

"Hosgrove shot him. He was just sitting there. He wasn't armed," she said. "Where's Hosgrove?"

"We're questioning him now," the policeman said. "Take your time and tell me what happened, for the record. Give me as much detail as you can remember."

"Has he been arrested? How soon can he get out on bail?"

"I can't answer that," Seely said. "I need to ask you some questions. We can start with your name and your relationship to the victim." Seely flipped his pad open.

"Katarina Parvic, I'm a friend." Her eyes teared up and she turned her head away from the detective, crying. Friend sounded so hollow. He meant more to her than merely a friend. Seely's fingers brushed her arm.

"Ms. Parvic," he said. "I'm sorry, but I really must know what happened. Would some coffee help?"

She nodded.

Katarina detailed what she had witnessed. By the time she finished describing the events to Seely, she felt a little better. Of course, all that would change if he died. She felt sick, having thought the unthinkable.

At the end, Seely said, "Here's my card if you think of anything else. I'll need you to come to the station tomorrow to go over this again."

"Those other guys, the security guards that Hosgrove brought with him. They didn't do anything wrong. They didn't know what Hosgrove was up to, and I wouldn't be sitting here now telling you all this if it weren't for them," she said.

"I'll make sure that is part of the report. It was one of them who made the nine-one-one call, isn't it?" Seely asked.

"Yes." She paused. "Has anyone contacted Sean Collins? We were in his apartment, and this all happened while Sean was at work."

"I don't know; I didn't stay there long enough to find out. Why don't you give me a number where he can be reached, and I'll call him myself," Seely said.

An administrator came up to them when they had walked back to emergency. "I need to ask you a few questions about the patient."

"She'll provide you with the details," Seely said.

Before returning to the waiting area, she called Sean and asked if he had talked to Seely.

"Yes. Katarina, is he going to be all right?"

"I-I don't know. The doctors were grim when they took him into the operating room. I'm extremely worried."

"Call me as soon as you know anything. Please!" Sean said.

"Absolutely. I wouldn't dream of not letting you know. Oh, if you do call the hospital, ask for Eric Wilde. I took a chance that this is the name you've settled on. At least Richard believes you think it's the right one."

"Yeah, I do. Listen, I gotta run. I'll be waiting for your call." He disconnected.

The surgeon came out to the waiting area after another hour and sat down next to Katarina. "Doctor Parvic? I'm Nancy Rodriguez, Eric Wilde's surgeon." She smiled.

Relief flooded through her, but she still asked, "How is he? Is he going to be all right?"

"Yes, we stopped the bleeding and repaired the blood vessel. Eric lost a lot of blood, but he's stable now."

"I need to be with him when he regains consciousness. He's never been in a hospital before, and I know it will be frightening for him if he wakes up and everyone around him is a stranger. It's very important for his safety that I be there."

"I'm afraid that's impossible. You'll have to wait out here. I can't let you in the recovery room. Are you a relative?"

Her gut cramped. "Please, he could panic and hurt himself, especially if he doesn't see anyone he knows."

"I can't let you in there. But don't worry, he'll be too sedated to do anything like that," the surgeon said. "I do need to know, are you a relative?"

"Er, not exactly, but he has no one else. I explained all that to the administrator, Doctor Rodriguez."

"Do you know anything of his history, because we found a lesion on his lung."

"His wife died of TB about six months ago."

"That could explain the lesion; we'll have to run some tests," Rodriguez said. "He's going to be under for at least another two hours. You can get something to eat in the cafeteria if you want. Then come back here, and someone will get you when he's ready to be brought to the room."

Katarina was sure the extra adrenaline in her system combined with three cups of hot brown sludge that tried to pass for coffee would have kept her awake, but neither did. She was startled into wakefulness when she felt someone sitting beside her and heard the person clear her throat.

"Katarina?" the aide asked and then continued when she nodded. "Mr. Wilde is being taken out of recovery to room 322. The room is on the third floor. If you follow that corridor to the left, you'll find some elevators."

"Thanks." Katarina got up and found her way to the room, still stiff and groggy.

Richard was wheeled into the room on his bed about five minutes after she got there. She rushed to his side as soon as the orderly left. "Richard, it's me, Katarina." She touched his hand, and he curled his fingers around it.

His intelligent gray eyes were half-open and gazed at her. He was being fed oxygen through a clear plastic tube in his nose, and an IV dripped its medication into a needle taped to his forearm. Although it was not quite two days since he had shaved, his beard promised to be thick and black.

"I am glad you are here." His voice was barely a whisper.

Tears filled her eyes and spilled down her cheeks. "I was terrified you were going to die."

"Do not cry, Katarina. I am much too strong to kill that easily." He brushed her tears with his fingertips.

"I care for you." She held his hand against her cheek. "Even though we've only had a few days together, I feel like we are old friends. I would be devastated if I lost you."

"I am alive. I have recovered from worse."

"Promise me," she said. "You won't try to go back. Not any more."

FIFTEEN

From the day after Ambion's team brought Richard into the twenty-first century, Michael Fairchild had been searching for a way to send the medieval king back. He had tried to convince Hosgrove that it would be a foolish waste of money and resources, but now that the hospital had demanded the remains, Hosgrove had become unreasonable. He not only wanted Michael to return Richard, but wanted him to do it right away.

However, Michael had discovered he couldn't send a camera to the exact place and time, let alone several men. Leery he'd see himself through the camera; he set the coordinates for twenty meters above the point of entry for his first try. It seemed nothing happened when he powered on the device. The logs told him otherwise. The camera had been repelled. It had happened too fast for human observation. He next varied the geographical coordinates and determined the closest he could get was sixty meters out, and all that the camera recorded was a distorted field around the action—blurry gray figures moving about.

He next tried to determine how close in time he could hit the geographical location. The earliest time he could return to the scene was over an hour later. By then, the body had been stripped and was on its way to Leicester. The only way they could reverse it now would be to kill Richard first. Michael couldn't do that. Just the thought made him sick.

He wished he'd never proposed the project to Hosgrove. He hardly knew the man on a personal level. He had no idea if Hosgrove would be willing to murder in order to protect Ambion Technologies. Michael decided to call in sick. He wouldn't be party to murder. If he could clear his head, maybe he'd be able to come up with alternatives to sending Richard back to the past.

For now, he needed to get his mind off Richard and Ambion, so he thumbed through the paper, sports first, then the comics, and then he did the crossword puzzle before he buckled down to the news. The national news got worse and worse daily, compounded by the presidential election. The two main candidates faced off with attack and counterattack. Michael tuned them out. The international news held no solace. There was always a firefight, a civil war, famine, and overall world misery, take your pick. So he skipped to the local news, which, while sensational at times, was at least predictable, and sometimes even uplifting.

That's when he saw it.

Prominent Portland Businessman Arrested in Shooting
    by Staff Reporter
    Portland—Evan   Hosgrove,   a   prominent businessman who came out of retirement five years ago to start a new venture was arrested late last night for shooting a white male in his early- to mid-thirties, name withheld. The victim was rushed to Legacy Emanuel Hospital where he underwent emergency surgery. He is in stable condition.

    Hosgrove posted a $50,000 bond. He is scheduled to be arraigned in Superior Court on September 14.

At that moment he decided to dismantle the device before more harm could be done. He signed onto the Ambion Technologies server from his laptop and spent the next four hours changing the data and modifying the programming to render the equipment inoperative.

SIXTEEN

Richard's eyes snapped open, awakened by the sunlight hitting them through the open blind. He scanned the unfamiliar room. A soft beep broke the silence, and then he heard distant voices murmuring something unintelligible.

He slowly recalled what had happened, from the guards pushing past Katarina to the ensuing fight, to Hosgrove shooting him. He was surprised that such a small weapon could have rendered him helpless so quickly.

He turned his head away from the window and saw Katarina asleep on a cot, still in shadow. He remembered her holding his hand when he was brought into this room. He remembered his promise to her.

As he pieced together recent events, he became aware that it wasn't just the sun shining on his eyes that had caused him to awaken. Something was irritating his member. The cot creaked. "Katarina." His voice rasped.

She jerked in the cot and her eyes blinked open. "Richard, how do you feel?" She sat up and put her feet on the floor, gripping the edge of the cot.

"S-something is-is…" He could not contain his panic.

She rushed to his bed and pushed the call button. "What's wrong?"

"Something is piercing my member!"

Her frown was transformed into a broad smile. "The catheter?" She stifled a giggle. "It's used to dispose of urine."

"I don't understand."

"The nurse will explain it better, but this is often done after surgery, especially with the severity of your wound."

"I will take it out now." He reached under the sheet.

"Stop!" She put her hand on his arm. "You'll hurt yourself. While you were in surgery, they found a spot on your lung. They don't know what it is, but they want to test for tuberculosis."

"Am I infected?"

"Don't know, that's what the tests are for, to see if you are."

When he pushed up onto his elbows, pain squeezed his chest where the bullet had been. "Ah Katarina, could you..."

"Richard, lie back down before you pull your stitches out!" She gently pushed against his uninjured side.

He fell back against the pillow. "I did want to sit up."

"Here, all you have to do is push this button." She showed him how to adjust the bed's position and handed over the controls.

He experimented with raising and lowering the bed and stopped when he sat upright. "It seems if I can imagine a convenience, it will exist in this time."

"Maybe even a few you can't," she said.

"I would prefer to rid myself of the catheter. I do not like this convenience."

She laughed. "I'll see if I can find a nurse. Just don't try to get out of bed until someone is with you."

He pressed the bandage with his fingertips, testing the injury. Though there was some pain, it was mild compared to when the bullet pierced his flesh and to some of the injuries he'd had to endure in his old life.

Many minutes had gone by, but Katarina had not returned. He could bear that abomination no longer. Just when he reached under the sheet to remove it, she returned with a nurse.

The nurse gaped at him. "Stop! What are you doing?"

"This must be removed."

She put his chart down and folded her arms across her chest. "Please be patient, Mr. Wilde. We'll take care of it in a few minutes."

Dr. Rodriguez stopped by about an hour later. She brought dark sheets of paper with her and put them on the light panel.

"Mr. Wilde, these are the x-rays of your lungs." She swept her hand over it. "As you can see, you have this one small lesion. There are several things we will have to test for, in addition to tuberculosis. The nurse will be in shortly to give you a skin test. We'll be injecting a small amount of fluid into your forearm." She handed him some papers. "I'm going to leave this questionnaire for you to complete before we do the test.

"If you have no questions for me, Mr. Wilde, I must be off," Dr. Rodriguez said. "I will sign your release tomorrow if you continue to improve as you have and there are no infections from the wound."

After he nodded, the doctor left the room.

"Did I understand the surgeon? Did she just show me a picture of my lungs and bones?" He asked.

"Oh my God! Yes, of course, you wouldn't know about x-rays. I don't really know how it works, but it's something that I've grown up with and never gave it a second thought."

Richard left the hospital on a Thursday, just two days after he was shot. Katarina told him that Hosgrove paid for everything, and to expect a call from his lawyer.

"Why would he do that?" he asked.

"I'm not sure, Richard. It may be that he's trying to plea bargain, and his lawyer advised that if he paid for everything the charges might be reduced."

"I'm glad that it's not you who is paying," Richard said.

"You got that right," she said. "I doubt that I could afford this. Medical care may be very good today, but it's also extremely expensive. So how are you feeling? I'm surprised they let you out so soon."

"I've had worse and had to go fully armored into battle, Katarina. I do not need this sling."

"I think you should wear it until you get to my house. You can decide then."

While she drove him back to her house, he studied the instructions that he had to follow and the antibiotic prescription he had to fill. He didn't have an active case of tuberculosis, but he had tested positive. He needed no convincing to take a course of antibiotics to rid his system of this horrible disease.

"...Earth to Richard." She was waving her hand in front of his face.

He blinked. "I'm sorry, Katarina, I did not hear you."

"We've arrived, wait 'til I get around to your side before you get out of the car."

"It is not necessary," he said, getting out of the car.

She walked to the door. "Listen, let's get in the house. There's something I think you'll want to see."

Katarina handed Richard a piece of paper with the blanks filled in about Eric Wilde. "You're going to have to sign this, so we can fax in this order for your birth certificate."

He stared at the form. "If I get this birth certificate, will my name be Eric? Is there anyway it can be Richard?"

"You need this certificate to get all the other forms of identification you'll require here. Once you have it, you can officially change your name to anything you want. Just get this first," she said.

He was pulling at one of the tabs on the sling, but it was tied around a metal ring. "I am making this tighter instead of releasing it."

"Let me see." She bent her head close to the offending knot and picked at it. "Damn, this is tight. Oh wait, I've got it."

She was so close to him. Her faint lavender scent enveloped him. He took a deep breath, inhaling her perfume. "Come, my flower." He reached up and gently drew her face to his, and wrapped his other arm about her waist, coaxing her body to him.

She stepped back. "I'm sorry, Richard. I don't think this is a good idea."

He let go and searched her large, brown eyes. "Why? We are not strangers to each other. Do you not want me now?"

"It's not a matter of what I do or don't want. I do want you." She took another step back from Richard.

"Why are you pulling away from me?"

"I'm afraid."

"What are you afraid of, Katarina? Surely, not me."

"No, of course, not you! I'm afraid of my own feelings. I'm afraid that I might fall in love with you and that I might get hurt." She sat down.

He sat down opposite her and pinched the bridge of his nose. "Katarina, I do like you. I don't want to hurt you."

"But you will want children, will you not?"

"Yes, oh God, yes!"

"I'm too old." She covered her eyes with her hands and then peeked through her fingers. "I've made a huge mess, haven't I?"

"Perhaps a little mess." His mouth quirked up in that lopsided smile Anne had teased him about. "I see that there is more than the technology and subtleties of the language that I must learn."

"Friends?" Katarina stuck her hand out to him.

"Friends," he said, taking her hand in both of his.

"Why don't I make us some lunch while you complete filling out the form. Bring it into the kitchen so I can answer any questions you have."

"So, what do you want, Richard?" They were returning from grocery shopping after faxing the form off to the state.

"I want Anne and Edward here with me in this time."

"I would want the same thing in your place. But I don't know that it's possible to do," Katarina said, pulling into the driveway.

"It was possible to bring me here, why not them?" he asked.

"Richard," Katarina rested her hand on top of his, "there are more obstacles than the device being broken and Hosgrove."

"Obstacles?"

She sighed. "There's no good way to put it, but both your son and wife died from diseases. You wouldn't want to get them here only to have them die two minutes later, would you?"

He averted her gaze and bit his lip.

She turned off the ignition and got out of the car. "Help me bring in the groceries, okay?"

He winced when Katarina handed him two of the large grocery bags.

"Sorry," she said. "Let me take one of those bags."

"Why? I do not mind carrying both."

"Your wound, it's hurting you."

"This is really nothing to me." Physical pain was so much easier to bear. "But I thought that Anne and Edward could be cured today."

"Richard, as good as our medicine is, I doubt that anyone that close to death is curable," she said, walking into the house.

He followed her in and set the bags down on the kitchen counter. "We could pull them forward long before they died instead of just before they died."

"But history would change."

"Then change history!" He abruptly turned his back on Katarina.

He tensed when her hand brushed his back. "I'm really sorry, Richard," she said softly. "Think, if history changes then there is no guarantee that we'll even exist let alone go back like we have done. They picked the time very carefully, and had the tiniest of windows where they could get you and not affect things as we know it."

Damn them and their technology! Am I to go on bereft of my wife and son forever? I would be at peace now, but for Ambion. Now I shall get neither.

He gripped the edge of the sink to steady himself and took a few deep breaths. "If I can find a time where it is safe to bring them here, will you help me do it?"

"What do you mean by safe?"

"I would look for a time when history would not be affected, and they can be cured."

"Yes, but that means you are going to have to deal with Hosgrove. He meant to send you back, you know."

"I know." He frowned. Hosgrove may have been right. "Do you think he intended to send me back already dead?"

She folded the last bag from the groceries and faced him. "According to the police, he didn't intend to shoot you. He claims it's my fault that the gun went off."

He stared into her eyes and shook his head. "Do you believe that? Every time I carried an offensive weapon, I meant to use it."

"No, Richard, I don't. But I believe that he's convinced himself that he didn't mean to shoot you."

She put the bags away. "I didn't tell you, but I'm picking up my daughter and her fiancé at the airport Saturday. They're going to be staying here a few days before they visit their friends in San Francisco."

"Should I return to Sean's place?"

"You can't, he's going away on vacation for a couple of weeks, starting Saturday. But I have plenty of room for everyone. I assume that you don't want any more people to know your true identity."

"Yes."

"Well, I've got to check my email, and then I'll help steer you to some medical sites where you can do preliminary research on TB and appendicitis."

He followed her from the kitchen to the study where she powered on her computer. She gave a low whistle and printed something out. "Richard, I received an email from Michael Fairchild. It's printing now. I think you should read it, but you'd better sit down."

He remained standing when she handed him the printout.

Katarina,

I read the article in the paper and although no names were cited, I came to the conclusion that Hosgrove shot Richard. He had wanted me to send Richard back anyway, and when I read the article, I decided I couldn't do it. There was no way I'd be party to murder, as that's how I saw it. I destroyed the programming; the equipment won't work anymore.

Hosgrove will be receiving my letter of resignation Monday. By then he'll know that he can't send anything back in time. Richard is safe.

I'm sorry that we can't keep in touch in person, I always thought of you as a friend, but I'm already gone from the area.

You may use this email address to contact me. It's safe.

Mike

Richard felt his blood drain from his head. He dropped into the armchair, crushing the printout in his fist. He had knowingly chosen to live when he didn't give himself up to Hosgrove. He had hoped he could pull his family from death like Orpheus saving Eurydice. And like Orpheus, he had failed. He was now stuck in the twenty-first century. He gave a low moan and pinched the bridge of his nose, bending his head forward.

Katarina's hand was on his. He raised his head and saw her kneeling before him. Her eyes were wide with concern. "Richard, don't give up. I intend to keep in touch with Michael."

He took a deep breath and concentrated on modulating his voice. "He intentionally broke the device."

"People do change their minds," she said. "Besides, you need to find out if it's medically feasible."

"Perhaps you are right. This was the first time in a year and a half that my heart did not ache for them, so hopeful was I." He clenched his jaw and turned his head away from her. He let the crumpled email roll to the floor.

She picked up the paper and her laptop, and left the room.

Richard wept. He had lost his family. Again.

SEVENTEEN

Once Richard regained his composure, he found Katarina sitting at the breakfast bar in front of the computer. "Sean's computer could not be moved, and there were many wires that were connected to it. How are you able to use it unattached to anything?"

"I have a wireless network, and laptops are self-contained," she said. "Anyway, I need to show you how to use the Mac because it's a bit different from a PC. Grab a stool. I'm on a medical site now."

He sat next to her and she slid the computer to him. "One major difference is the mouse. You'll need to slide your finger over this pad." She demonstrated its use. "I'm sure you'll get the hang of it quickly. There are a lot of similarities," she said. "Do you feel any better? You appeared devastated before."

"I felt they had died a second time. I'm afraid to dare hope again."

"We have a little saying. 'Hope for the best, but expect the worst.'" She gave him a tremulous smile. "It's important to have hope."

"I'll try, but it is hard to do."

"I've sent an email back to Michael. Hopefully, he'll get back to me soon," she said.

He glanced up from the computer screen. "Do you know him well? Do you think he will help me get my family back?"

"I don't know. He's a casual friend and, in my opinion, a decent fellow. If he agrees to let you email him, then I'm sure it will mean that he is willing to help," she said. "But it's the medical stuff that is more worrisome at present. Let's see what we can find."

The best information on tuberculosis they could find on-line was an article from the Mayo clinic. It not only confirmed what he had learned at the hospital regarding his course of treatment, but also briefly talked about what happens if it's left untreated. The untreated results were dire, because not only are the lungs permanently damaged, but other organs can be affected as well, including the bones and the lymphatic system. His hopes for Anne diminished.

"I hope you see why you shouldn't drink anything alcoholic until you're off this medication, Richard. You could end up destroying your liver."

"I don't understand what is wrong with having ale or wine. I am going to be on it for at least the next six months."

"Ask the doctor to explain it to you tomorrow when you see her. But trust me, you want to avoid all things alcoholic until you're off the medication," she said.

The information on ruptured appendices was grim, but not as hopeless sounding as was the article on tuberculosis. He had reason to be optimistic. Both required a more informed opinion.

"Why don't you ask about Anne when you see the doctor tomorrow?" she said.

"How should I ask that question? I don't think that I can phrase it truthfully," he said.

"I don't suppose you can. Tell you what, I'll think about it over night, and you do the same. We should be able to come up with way to ask the question without sounding like a crazy person.

"Meanwhile, why don't we have dinner? There's a movie on TV tonight that I think you might enjoy," she said while closing down the iBook.

Richard found Katarina was making breakfast when he walked into the kitchen the next morning.

"Morning." She was beating the eggs for an omelet. The mushrooms and spices were already sautéing. "Sleep well?"

"Yes," he said. "That movie we watched, you said it was science fiction? How did they show us those things if they don't exist?"

"There's an entire industry that has evolved around this. Creature shops make some of those beings. The Death Star and the space ships are models, which through tricks of the camera, are made to appear real."

"It did divert me." He ran a hand over his three-day-old beard. "I would very much like to shave."

"You'd better wait until the anti-coagulant is out of your system. You wouldn't stop bleeding if you cut yourself."

"I still need to be able to ask the doctor about Anne without revealing my purpose," he said. "Have you thought of a way to do it? I haven't."

She served the omelets and sat down next to him. "Not yet."

They had been eating for a few minutes in silence, when she put her fork down. "Maybe the best thing to do is just ask how far advanced can the disease be before the medication would not be effective. Don't give her any explanation. If she asks you why you're asking, respond with 'just curious.'"

"Yes," he said. "I think it is better to keep it simple."

"Can you handle an answer that means Anne can't be saved? That the disease might be too far advanced for the medicine to work?"

He thought about those questions and understood that she expected this answer. Her eyes bore into him. "I don't know. It will be very hard for me now, but if I wait to ask, it will be all that much harder to hear."

She rested her hand on his. "If you want, I can be with you while the doctor examines you, and you ask your questions."

Richard was grim when they left the doctor's office.

"I'm so sorry," Katarina said. "I was afraid this was going to be the answer. Is there anything I can do?"

He shook his head. "No. I need to be alone for a while."

They were downtown in a busy parking lot. It was noisy and the sound bounced off the concrete.

"This isn't a very good place," she said. "Let's get in the car and I'll drive to the college. We'll be there in fifteen, twenty minutes. I need to pick up some things in my office. You'll be able to find some privacy there."

After Katarina parked the car, they walked to a footbridge that spanned a narrow lake. "My office is in that brick building behind us," she said. "Take as much time as you need. I'll be in my office—second floor, room two-eighteen.

He stood at the center of the bridge and stared at the water below. It was quiet; even the few students nearby were speaking in low voices. One crossed behind him and stopped.

"Hey man, you okay?"

Richard pasted on a smile. "Yes, but thank you for asking."

He left the bridge and walked down the steep embankment to the lake's edge. He worked his way along the bank to a position under the footbridge. Here, he'd be shielded from the curious and the touchingly concerned students.

He squatted down on his heels and stared at the water, swiping his hand through the leaves. His fingers knocked against some pebbles. He picked one up and skipped it across the water. It hopped three times before it sank, scattering a group of ducks that were placidly paddling along the surface. He ignored the ducks and sent another pebble skittering across the pond. It bounced off the water five times before sinking. *Forgive me, my love.* He picked up another, two hops; and another, again two hops. *I cannot save you.* He let fly with a fifth. It skipped but once. Richard scooped up a handful and slammed them into the lake.

The water splashed onto his sneakers. As the sun bounced off the quieting surface, he thought he could see Anne just beneath the surface. Then, she was gone in a blink.

"Beloved," he murmured, "it is with heavy heart that I must abandon my quest to bring you into this century. I will love you always, forever."

He climbed up the embankment and went to the building where Katarina's office was located.

He found her office, knocked softly and opened the door. She peered over her reading glasses when he entered. "I'm about done here, Richard. Give me two minutes and then we can go. Are you okay?"

"Aye." He wasn't, but he was determined to come to terms with his loss. He had failed to do so in the past, but then he'd lost all hope. If he could save Edward, he could bear anything.

She stuffed some papers in a slim leather briefcase, stood and grabbed her keys. "Let's go. Are you interested in lunch? I'm hungry."

"Where are we going?" Richard asked when Katarina steered the car away from her house. "I thought you were going to make lunch."

"Changed my mind." She turned left on Powell and crossed the Willamette river at the Ross Island Bridge. "I thought it would be a nice change to get out of Portland for the afternoon." She drove onto interstate five going south.

Soon they were moving faster than he'd ever had in his life. Once he got over his surprise, he found it exhilarating.

He looked out the passenger's window at the buildings whizzing by and then at Katarina. "I would like to learn how to drive. It appears that I am at a disadvantage by not knowing how to do it."

"We can start today if there's time."

She took the Lake Oswego exit and wound their way to the lake's shore. Soon, only the gated driveways bordering Summit Drive were visible from the road.

"I think this would be a good place for Edward," he said. "How should I arrange to get property here?"

"All it takes is money...a lot of money."

"How much?"

"Several million," she said. "Hosgrove lives here. He's the only one I know who can afford it."

"Jesú!" She had trapped him. This wasn't the first time a friend had betrayed him, but Katarina... "Do you intend to deliver me to my enemy?"

She swerved to the curb and turned off the ignition. Her face turned ashen. "Oh my God no, Richard! I'd never do that. He's at work—in Portland—not here." Tears spilled down her cheeks. She gripped the steering wheel with both hands and put her forehead against the top of the rim.

When he stroked her back, she shrank from him. "Katarina, forgive me, please. In the past, I was betrayed by many who I thought were my friends...allies...those whom I trusted. They had tried to kill me. I fear I've forgotten how to trust."

She hiccoughed and sat back, facing him. "Of course I forgive you. I'm sorry, too. I know your history, I should have guessed how this could appear."

The realization that he would have to learn how to trust affected him more than Katarina's misstep warranted. She was his only true friend now, and the possibility that he could drive her away was more than he could bear. "Mayhap we should go back to your house." He caressed her cheek, still damp.

Leaning her head into his hand, she wrapped her slender fingers around his. "I agree." She started the car and headed back to the highway.

"Forgive me for asking," she said, "but do you know when Edward died? I know that you weren't with him at the time."

"Aye, but why do you ask? Is it important?"

"Very. Our historical records are vague as to the date of Edward's death, so changing it won't affect history," she said.

"Would it be possible to bring him here before his appendix ruptures?" he asked. "Do I dare to hope? I could not bear to lose him again."

"Maybe it would be better to let me find out whether it can be done," she said. "Now it's a technical problem, and not so much of a medical one. Although, people still die in surgery, it's just much rarer if there is no rupture."

Richard pushed his half-eaten omelet to the side.

"I thought you were hungry." Katarina stacked the dirty dishes in the sink. "Are you up for a driving lesson?"

"Yes."

She drove to a closed factory. It had a large parking lot with few obstructions. She parked in the center, surrounded by a field of asphalt. The boarded-up building was at least a dozen parking rows from the car.

They traded places. "Before you do anything else," she said, "adjust the seat so you can reach everything comfortably."

His body thrilled to the car's vibrations the moment he turned the key in the ignition. It felt different here in the driver's seat than when he was a passenger. He released the parking brake and shifted the gear to drive. The car rolled forward before he touched the gas. When he did put his foot on the gas pedal, the car leapt forward with a jerk. He gripped the wheel hard and stepped on the brake, jerking it to a stop. "Uh..."

"It's okay, Richard. I should have warned you about stepping on the gas too hard. Try it again, only this time ease down on the pedal."

In short time he was able to control the speed with ease. He guided it between the painted lines, turning left and right as directed. He pulled to a stop and put the gear in park.

"You've been circling this lot for over half an hour," she said. "How do you feel?"

He stared at the clock in the dash, astonished. He was ready to swear he had been driving only a few minutes. "Wonderful—excited. Shall I drive to the house?"

"No, it's too soon," she said. "You have to learn how to handle the car in traffic—it's too heavy here and it would be dangerous."

"I'm anxious to do more."

"Tomorrow. I think my neighborhood will be perfect—it's quiet and lightly traveled."

He paid close attention to everything Katarina did on the way to her house. Before, when he had to assimilate so much, he had blocked out the sometimes frightening effects of so many cars whizzing by and being buffeted by the large trucks just by the force of the air around them.

When they got to the house, he followed her to the study. The answering machine flashed, signaling new messages. The first was from her daughter, confirming that she expected to arrive the next day; the second was for him.

EIGHTEEN

Richard grabbed a pen and tablet and then sat at the desk. He replayed the message and copied down the number. Katarina walked to the door.

"Don't go," he said. "I'd prefer it if you were with me while I call."

He got the firm's voice menu when he called. "I'm sorry. The offices are closed and will not reopen until nine thirty Monday morning. If this is an emergency, press one; if you wish to leave a message, press two." He hung up.

"Closed?" she asked.

He nodded.

"That'll give you the weekend to think about what you will say," she said. "Do you want to come with me when pick up my daughter and her fiancé at the airport? They're coming in at two."

"I would like that very much."

"Katarina," Richard said, stabbing the pancakes with his fork, "how well do you know Hosgrove?"

"Not very well. I only know him through the Richard III Society because of our mutual interest in you." Katarina shook her head and smiled. "That is such a strange thing to say—'our mutual interest in you.' Just a week ago, I would have said Richard III. But why do you ask?"

"Am I right in assuming that he is the money behind Ambion Technologies? He has a lot of power, does he not?"

"You're correct; money does equal power. We must find you a lawyer before we deal with Hosgrove."

"Is he above the law?"

"In this country, no one is supposed to be above the law. Our Constitution guarantees it," she said. "But realistically, money can enable him to bend the law. He will still have to account for what he's done, but he'll likely plea bargain down to a much-reduced charge."

"I think getting a lawyer is a very good idea. Do you have one I could use?" he asked.

"I do have a lawyer, but she's not the right kind. I used her for my will." Katarina poured herself another cup of coffee. "But I'll call her Monday and ask if she can recommend someone. She works for a large firm."

"Can you reach Hosgrove directly?"

"I think so, why?"

"There is that matter of bringing my son into this time and saving him. I want to have Hosgrove begin to work on it."

She put her fork down and frowned. "First, Hosgrove is the money, not the brains. Michael is the one who did the science and worked on the technology. It took nearly five years for him to get it to work well enough that you are here. And now he's made it so you can't go back. Second, I said that I would look into it…"

He put his fingers across her lips. "I know you want to help, but Edward is my son and my responsibility, not yours."

She wrapped her long, slender fingers around his. "Anything, Richard, I'll help in anyway I can. Just ask me. But what makes you think Hosgrove will help?"

"I am the one Hosgrove injured. What sort of punishment does he face?"

"Hmm, he could be facing months, if not years in prison. It will depend on how good his lawyer is in getting the charges reduced."

"I will offer a *quid pro quo*—my Edward for his freedom."

"But the police are already involved."

His shoulders sagged. "Is there nothing I can do?"

"I don't know. I'm not a lawyer." She shook her head. "I'm sure Hosgrove would be interested in having you speak with his lawyers."

"That is what I will do. It will be Hosgrove's decision."

"It still doesn't change the fact that Michael is gone."

"Was Michael the only one at Ambion who had the knowledge to reconstruct the device? I saw many desks there. I would think that out of all those people, there is someone who can rebuild it. Has Michael returned your email?"

"No, he hasn't. But aren't you entering the lion's den, to use a biblical reference?"

"What you say may be the truth. I am willing to risk it. As you have shown me, there are laws in this country and in this time that will allow redress. Michael did say that they cannot send anything back now. I will be safe for the present."

"All right." Katarina sighed. "Call Hosgrove Monday morning and set something up."

"Can I not call him today?" he asked.

"Aside from the fact that he usually turns his cell phone off on the weekends, aren't you being a bit rash? Wouldn't you be better off waiting to see if Michael will get back to you?"

"I do not wait well."

"Neither does Hosgrove. You might be better off waiting until after you've taken care of the lawyers. Plus, if we can believe Michael's email, Hosgrove won't know until Monday that he can't return you and that he's been put back five years worth of development."

"I don't want to wait five years to get Edward back. I will be nearly the age Ned was when he died."

She arched her eyebrows, giving her face a quizzical expression. "Forty is young and you're young. Who's to say you won't take after your mother. She lived to see her eightieth birthday."

"I did not know." His eyes widened. "There is one thing more that requires my understanding. What do you think is most important to Hosgrove?"

"I never thought one way or another about it. I'm not sure I understand where you are headed."

"I must get his cooperation," he said. "Perhaps my offer will not be enough. I need to understand him more to get what I want."

"Let me think about it," she said. "We don't have to leave for the airport until one, which should still give you some time for another driving lesson."

"Good. I would also like to see this Constitution of yours."

"Relax, you have to expect some setbacks." Katarina's hand rested on Richard's shoulder.

His second driving lesson had ended on a down note when he nearly crashed into a parked car because instead of applying the brakes, he had tried to stop it like he would have a horse.

"I didn't think driving was that hard. Why can I not get it right?"

"It isn't, but like any other skill, it takes practice," she said. "This was only the second time you've ever been behind the wheel. Don't be so hard on yourself."

"But there is so much that I must learn."

"And you will, Richard, you will." She checked her watch. "We need to go to the airport now."

They joined the crowd at the gate after parking in the short-term lot. After a few minutes, the passengers started trickling out past security. Some headed straight for baggage while others scanned the group of people with whom he waited.

Katarina started waving and called out, "Elaine, Elaine! Here, I'm over here."

She let go of his hand when a pretty young woman carrying a backpack over one shoulder ran to her. Elaine had an olive complexion and a broad, clear brow. In contrast to her mother's slender build, she seemed athletic, compact and muscular.

"Mom! It's so good to see you." Elaine embraced her mother and a beautiful smile lighted her heart-shaped face.

Katarina held her for a few seconds longer and then asked, "Where's Adam?"

"He's not coming, Mom. We split up."

"I'm so sorry. Did it just happen?" Katarina gave her another hug.

"Yes, a few days ago, but I didn't want to leave it on the answering machine."

"What happened?" They headed for the exit. Richard kept pace with them.

"I've been accepted to MIT, and he doesn't want to leave Chicago. I'll tell you all about it after we get home," Elaine said. "So who's your friend, Mom?"

"Oh sorry, I didn't mean to be rude. Richard is a friend who I met at Ambion. He's staying at my house temporarily." Katarina turned to him. "This is my daughter, Elaine."

Elaine stuck her hand out in greeting. "Nice to meet you, Richard."

"It is my pleasure." He drew her hand to his lips and lightly kissed the back of her hand.

She slowly pulled her hand away, her brown eyes showing surprise. "Yeah, likewise. Um, I don't have any other bags, we can go."

Richard rode in the back of the car when they left. Mother and daughter were chatting amicably, both heads nodding in unison. Elaine's hair refused to stay tucked into the knot at the base of her neck and instead formed a wispy brown halo around her head.

Elaine turned to him and pushed the hair away from her face. "How long have you known Mom?"

Katarina spoke before he could say anything. "Not that long, Elaine, he started there about a week ago. Anyway, we became friends and he didn't have anywhere to go for the Labor Day holiday, so I said he could stay with me. I hope you don't mind, honey."

"Mind? Of course not," Elaine said. She winked at him before facing to the front of the car.

After dinner, Richard joined Katarina and Elaine in the living room. He listened to them discussing Elaine's change of plans.

"So," Katarina said, "tell me about MIT. Are you still going to study linguistics?"

"Sort of. I want to combine linguistics with artificial intelligence and robotics and be able to use all I've learned. I applied to MIT and got accepted into their graduate program, with an emphasis on artificial intelligence. Adam didn't want to leave Chicago."

Seeing how close they were made his desire to have his wife and son with him all the more acute. He could not save Anne, but he had hope for Edward. He returned his attention to their conversation.

"Couldn't he practice law in Boston?" Katarina said.

"Yeah, but he thinks he's this close to being made a partner, and he doesn't want to have to start over again in a strange city." Elaine held her thumb and index finger an inch apart. "At first I thought he might be willing to follow me to Boston, but he told me just a week ago that he'd decided to stay in Chicago and if I wanted to be with him, I'd have to stay too."

Bereft of his wife and son, he thought Adam would soon regret putting career above someone he loved. Richard would have given everything to get Anne back, but that was to be denied him. He now accepted there was nothing he could do for her, but he couldn't shake his anger. He noticed that Katarina and Elaine were sitting shoulder-to-shoulder on the couch.

Feeling his arms empty, and longing for his own child, he wished Katarina would hug her daughter.

She put her arm around Elaine and gave her a hug. "I am so sorry, sweetheart. Are you okay with this?"

"Truthfully, I'm hurt that he couldn't be more supportive, but I'm glad I found out now rather than after we were married. That would have been worse."

Unable to get his thoughts off Anne, he bade them goodnight and retired to his room. He remembered the angry words he and Katarina had the night before. They had watched a

TV show that showed people who'd had their failing hearts replaced. Once he got over the shock that bad organs could now be replaced, he had questioned why this could not be done for Anne.

Katarina had told him that she didn't think Anne could be kept alive long enough to find a matching donor for all the organs that she might need. He had angrily and unfairly accused her of not wanting him to get his wife back.

His doctor had confirmed that not only would it be too late to do a transplant for someone that close to death even if a matching donor could be found in time, but the disease would be in the bones and lymphatic system and would still kill the affected person. Such a person would not be considered for transplant.

He picked up the copy of the constitution that Katarina had printed for him. "We the people of the United States..." *The people—no lords or bishops.*

The sun was high in the sky by the time Richard awakened. He couldn't remember the last time this had happened to him. He stretched, rolled to a sitting position, and slapped his chest. He wasn't quite so bony as he'd been just one week ago. He felt good, even a little optimistic about his future—a future that might include his son.

He put on the clothes he wore yesterday and went into the kitchen, hoping to find some hot coffee. Katarina was sitting at the breakfast bar reading the Sunday papers.

"Morning."

He poured the last of the coffee into a mug and sat next to her. "Good morning. Where is Elaine?"

"She went to the video store to get a movie for tonight. She should be back any minute."

"Is there anything to eat?" He'd gone to the refrigerator and stared blankly at its shelves.

She laughed. "There's enough food there to feed a small army. You can always have cold cereal, or bagels and cheese, or eggs. Take your pick.

"Elaine was asking about you last night after you left. I told her to ask you for the details."

"Does she keep her own counsel?" He selected a bagel and sat down.

"You can trust her, but you'll have to ask her not to repeat anything if you don't want her to."

"Ask who what?" Elaine asked, entering the room. "I've decided to go to Mt. Hood for a hike. Anyone want to come with?"

"I'll pass," Katarina said. "Richard, you might enjoy hiking. It'll get you into the country, and there are some really beautiful trails there."

"Say yes, Richard," Elaine said. "Please."

"I have yet to shower," he said. "I will be but a moment."

"You're gonna need a shower after. I wouldn't bother doing it before."

Once they were on the road, Elaine headed east on Interstate Eighty-four. "So, do all your friends call you Richard? That sounds so formal."

"Some people call me Dick, and I was called Dickon in my youth." He didn't want to tell her that lately he'd been called *Old Dick*. He hoped that wouldn't follow him to this time. "Are you called by another name?"

"My friends call me Lani. I like the sound of Dickon. I don't think I've ever heard anyone called that before." She pulled into the passing lane.

"I have not heard your mother call you Lani. Does she not use the familiar name?"

"Ha-ha, you're very funny. You speak even more formally than my Mom. No, she prefers to call everyone by their given names." She pulled back into the right lane. "Anyway, what do you mean, 'in your youth'? You said that like you are no longer young. If I had to guess your age, I would say no older than thirty-five, I bet you're younger."

"Aye— thirty-two. But that be middle age."

Elaine exited the highway onto Route 35. "No way, José is that middle age! My great-granddad is ninety-five and he's as sharp as a tack. He's even got a lady friend who's fifteen years his junior."

He gaped at her. "Jesú, ninety-five! Katarina never mentioned him to me."

"Yeah, he's my Dad's grandfather. He's this old Italian stonemason. That's where I get my sallow complexion and fat ass. It sure isn't from my Mom."

"You do yourself a disservice by your own description. You are quite comely," he said.

"Thank you. So, my Mom said to ask you where you're from. I'm asking."

He squirmed in the seat. "I will answer you truthfully, but you must first swear that you will not speak of this to anyone but Katarina."

"You're serious, aren't you?" she asked. "Mom was very mysterious when I asked her, and now you're creeping me out a little. I promise not to say anything."

"What is 'creeping me out'?"

"Now that's creeping me out. You're scaring me. A little, anyway." Elaine glanced over to him and then back to the road. "It won't take us long to get to Zigzag Trail. Why don't you wait 'til then to tell me? I get the feeling that this is going to take a lot longer than I expected."

"You mentioned you are going to be studying robotics. I did not want to interrupt you last night, but I'm interested in hearing about it."

"Sure, but I might not finish before we get to the trail. Feel free to interrupt me with any questions."

NINETEEN

Richard got out of the car and met up with Elaine at the head of the trail.

"This leads to a beautiful waterfall, but it's a bit of a climb," she said.

They entered the trail and followed the path.

"Here's some water, in case we get thirsty," she said, handing him a liter-sized bottle of water. "Do you mind carrying it?"

"I don't mind holding the water, but will we not find water at a waterfall?"

"Huh? I wouldn't drink untreated water unless I had to. Anyway, why don't you tell me about yourself? I'm listening."

"It is hard for me to know where to begin. I am not from your time. I am the result of that project your mother worked on. When I first got here, she had to translate your English to mine. My real birth date is the second of October, 1452."

She stopped abruptly and grabbed his arm, staring into his eyes. "Get outta town! You want me to believe you're over five-hundred years old?"

"What?"

"You're putting me on; you're saying you've been around for over five hundred years—that's impossible. Anyway, you just said you are thirty-two. Which is it?"

He studied Elaine and slowly shook his head. "I'm thirty-two, but I was born over five-hundred years ago. I was moved through time, I have not been around for five hundred and fifty-two years."

"And space," she said. "They had to move you through space as well, you know."

"This is a new continent."

"Oh no, it's much more than that. The entire solar system is hurtling through space. Earth is billions of miles from where it was. How the hell could it have been done? It's not possible."

"Billions? Jesu!" He gaped at her. "How can that be? The Earth does not move, it is the center of all creation."

"Uh-uh." Elaine stopped and drew in the dirt with a stick she picked up. "See, the Earth revolves around the sun, and the sun moves through the galaxy, and the galaxy moves through the universe at blindingly high speeds."

He was staggered. This was so different from what he had learned, and yet she seemed so sure. "How can you know that?"

"I'll show you when we get back home, but we can measure the speeds at which suns and planets are moving."

"Jesú," he whispered. "Yet I am here. I know who I am and where I came from."

"So, assuming you aren't hallucinating this, have you any knowledge of how it was done? I mean, wouldn't anyone notice if you suddenly disappeared?"

They resumed their walk. "I was told that a dead body was left in my place before I would have been killed on Redemore Plain on the twenty-second of August 1485."

Elaine backed away from him. "If mom hadn't been so dead serious when she told me to believe you—I'd be searching for the men in white coats."

"What?"

"Forget it. Why you and not someone else?"

"It's because of who I was." Richard frowned. "My brother was King Edward IV, and I was Duke of Gloucester until he died. My coronation was held on the seventh of July 1483. You may know me as Richard III."

"Okay, so you're my mom's favorite king—man! I'm gonna kill her if this is an elaborate joke."

He sighed. "You hear with your own ears my manner of speech and yet you question my veracity. Why would I make up something so outrageous?"

"Man," Elaine said, "did you understand half of what I've said?"

"Aye, perchance half."

They continued and after a steep section, reached the top of a rocky crest. The view opened up and the mountain's snowy cap was clearly visible. "How long will it take for us to get there?" he asked.

"Over an hour. But we can't drive to the top if that's what you mean." She turned back to the trail. "Let's keep going."

The path was now a gentle slope upward and led back into the wooded part of the foothill. It switched into the shade.

He'd meant to be witty when he replied that he maybe understood half of what she'd said, but it wasn't as far from the truth as he would have liked. He thought he was doing so well, but now it was apparent that Katarina, Hosgrove, and Michael had been easing him into the modern vernacular. "I have not been privy to your English, I am but learning. You have many more words than did exist in my time," he said. "Some are said differently and some have changed their meaning."

"Well, I'm not an expert like my Mom is, but I've studied linguistics. No wonder you're so quiet. And I thought it was because you were thinking profound thoughts. Who knew it was because you were trying to figure out the meaning of what was said."

He laughed.

"So, what word that reversed its meaning gave you the most pause?" she said.

"That would have to be 'corpse.' When I first got here, Hosgrove kept referring to the corpse they substituted for me. In my time, corpse referred to a living person, not a dead body as it does today. Katarina explained it to me as soon as she could, but it did provoke a sickening feeling."

The path curved to the left and opened to a small glade that faced a waterfall. They sat down on a broad sunlit rock facing the cataract. The top of the fall was about thirty feet over their heads. It was about two feet wide at the top, spreading out to meet a shallow pool at the bottom. The sunlight streaked through the pine canopy and reflected off the mist that permanently draped the bottom six feet of the shallow pool. The resulting rainbow appeared to be painted on the misted rocks.

Elaine took a small object out of her pants pocket and aimed it at the waterfall.

"What are you holding?"

"It's a camera. You just point and shoot, like this." She snapped a picture and then showed him the display. "Uh, close your mouth, you'll let all the flies in." She laughed. "Listen, why don't I get a photo of you standing in front of the rainbow?"

"I would like that."

"Okay, stand over there." She pointed to a sunny spot to the left of the fall.

He stood by the fall and waited for her to take the picture. In less than a minute she showed him the image. And he was smiling, something he could not sustain for the portraits he had commissioned. His appearance was grimmer than the originals in the posthumous copies he found on the Internet—sadder too.

"This is most amazing to me, Lani. Show me how to do it and I will take one of you."

"Okay, but first, I want to get one more shot of you. Stand sideways and focus on that holly on the other side of the pool."

He turned to the side and watched out of the corner of his eye while she backed away. She lurched to the side and fell to the ground with a thud.

"Ow!"

He ran to help her. "What happened?" He extended his hands to her.

"I twisted my ankle on that root. Help me over to the rock where we were sitting before."

He helped pull Elaine to her feet, supporting her while she hopped to the rock.

"Could you pick the camera up? I dropped it over there somewhere."

In the short time it took him to find the camera, Elaine had removed her right shoe and sock. He put the camera down and knelt down in front of her. "May I see your ankle?"

"Sure, I think I've sprained it. I did the exact same thing last winter when I stepped on a broken curb getting out of the car." She stuck her bare foot out at him.

He felt around the ankle as gently as he could. "It does not seem to be broken. It is starting to swell."

"It would help if I had something to wrap it with. Then I could limp back to the car."

He tore up his T-shirt and wrapped her ankle with the strips, hoping it would provide enough support until they could get to the car.

"That's a nasty scar on your arm. Were you badly injured?" she asked.

"It was nothing. I lost a little blood but I won the battle."

She gasped.

"Am I hurting you?"

"No, I'm okay." She wiggled her toes. "This helps, but I'm afraid I'm going to have to lean on you to get down the trail, though." She put on her shoe and loosely tied it.

With him acting as a crutch for her, they were able to slowly make their way back down. They stopped frequently so that she could sit down and put her foot up for a few minutes to rest it. He saw that she was in a fair amount of pain, but she did not complain. He was favorably impressed. Both to divert her, and to satisfy his curiosity, he asked her to expand on what she had told him about the robots. "Where would one use them?"

"Rescue, of course," she said. "It's probably because I just sprained my ankle that I'm thinking about it, but imagine a situation where it would be too dangerous for a human to enter, but there are people who are trapped. An appropriately designed robot could go in and save lives. I can even think of situations where they'd be better than people."

She went into more detail about the robots than his question had warranted. He reckoned she was doing it to keep her mind off the pain. The robot dissertation ceased at the rocky cliff. That section of the trail required nearly an hour for them to get down, where he had to support her full weight for a good portion of the descent. In total, it took just over two hours to get to the car. It had taken only forty-five minutes to climb to the waterfall.

He helped her to the car and she leaned back in the passenger seat, closing her eyes. "I don't know how the hell I'm going to drive. I can't put enough pressure on the foot, and I feel sick to my stomach from the pain. Do you know how to drive, by any chance?"

He gulped. "Your mother gave me two lessons. The first was in an empty parking lot and the second was in her neighborhood."

"Do you think you can drive us home if we don't go on the highway and we stick to the slower state and local roads?"

"I will try."

"Good. See that building over there across the parking lot? That's the first aid station. I want you to drive me across the lot so I can have this ankle checked."

The emergency technician rewrapped the sprained ankle with an Ace bandage. She refused any painkiller stronger than aspirin.

"I think I'm good to drive," she said.

He helped her to the car. Elaine grimaced when she pulled the car onto the road.

"Lani, you appear to be in pain still."

"Only a little. I'll be fine."

He could see her mouth relax and the tightness leave her eyes as she maneuvered the car onto the road. He resolved to attain this skill.

"I'm curious," she said. "What in this time are you most impressed with, and what do you find the most disappointing?"

He thought for a moment before answering, "I don't know. There is so much for me to take in. If I had to name but one thing, it would have to be your medicine. My wife and son would still be alive if we'd had the medicine you have."

"What happened?"

"They died of diseases that you can cure today. Anne died of tuberculosis nearly six months ago, and I think Edward died from a ruptured appendix almost a year before that."

"I'm so very sorry. You're still grieving, aren't you?" She reached over and squeezed his hand.

"Aye," he whispered and then cleared his throat. "But I hope to rescue Edward."

"How?"

"I need to work it out. I would like to know more about your robots."

"You first, what is most disappointing to you?"

"I think this is more bothersome than disappointing, but it is very noisy here. I sometimes cannot think with this noise in my head."

"Humph, I guess I'm used to the noise, I never noticed." Elaine shrugged and shifted slightly in the seat. "Okay, more on robots ..."

Elaine was whimpering by the time she pulled the car into the garage. Tears clung to her eyelashes.

"You should have told me you were in pain," Richard said. "I would have driven."

"Just help me get in the house. I was fine until the last five miles, and I didn't want to stop then."

Katarina came into the garage when he reached the driver's side. "What happened? I heard you come in, and it's much later than I expected."

"Lani sprained her ankle." He helped Elaine get out of the car. She grabbed onto his shoulders.

Katarina rushed to her. "What can I do? You are so pale."

"I just need to lie down and put my foot up. It was like this the last time I sprained it, but then I didn't have to hike down a trail. They gave me a prescription for a painkiller. Could you fill it?"

"Yes, but let's get you into the house first."

"Dickon can do that."

"Okay, I'll get my purse," Katarina said and ran into the house.

He wrapped his arm around her back and bent his knees to pick her up. "What are you doing? I'm much too heavy for..."

He had her in his arms before she finished. "You are not too heavy." He met Katarina at the door to the garage.

"I'll be back in a few minutes." Katarina left.

He carried Elaine to the couch. He found he was winded even after that short a distance. "Jesú, I am becoming soft," he said, panting a little.

"Sit down, I told you I was too heavy. I bet I weigh at least as much as you do, and I'm a couple of inches taller than you."

"I'm okay. Is there anything you need?"

"I feel better already just lying here with my foot up."

Katarina returned a short time later. "I hope you guys are hungry, I picked up dinner. We can watch the movie if you want."

"Mom, did you see what I got?" Elaine laughed.

"Yup, I was giggling all day thinking about it. I think you are in for a surprise, Richard."

When she did not elaborate, he said, "If you do not mind, I should like to shower first. I will be but five minutes."

He was part way up the stairs when he heard Elaine ask, "Is he for real?"

He found a plate for the pizza when he returned to the living room. He took a couple of slices and sat down in a chair next to the couch. "You are being mysterious about this movie. Do you think I will have a problem with it?"

"You might," Katarina said. "Just remember *Monty Python and the Holy Grail* is meant to be funny. It's one of our favorites."

The beginning of the movie was lost on him. When it started, he heard horse-like clip-clops, but there were no horses. Instead, he saw men in twelfth or thirteenth century-like garb pretending to be on horseback. He wondered where the horses were.

He stole a glance at Katarina and Elaine, who were together on the couch. Elaine was lying with her head on her mother's lap and her bandaged foot rested on a pillow. They were both laughing.

"What, ridden on a horse?" one of the characters said.

I was just wondering the same thing.

"Yes!" The man claiming to be Arthur said.

"You're using coconuts!" the man dressed like a guard said.

He wasn't getting the humor of the movie, but both women were laughing. He pasted a smile on his face when he noticed Katarina checking on him.

He was about to give up on the movie when a scene about the Black Death flashed on the screen. He stiffened, expecting to see the plague's horrors. Instead, the body said, "I'm getting better!" He was startled into laughter.

He couldn't believe he was laughing at the plague. And it was not polite laughter, but a full, deep down, wonderful laugh as the scene played out and the cart driver, the large man, and the body all argued as to the state of the body's health.

He enjoyed the peasants mocking King Arthur, despite that it was really against the monarchy in general. Reflecting on his own reign, he thought he had governed well and dispensed justice to rich and poor alike.

But it was the scene with the Black Knight where Arthur was hacking off his limbs one by one that caused him to laugh the hardest. How many battles had he fought in to see these grievous wounds where the knights continued to fight as if nothing had happened? He howled when the Black Knight said, "Tis but a scratch" after his left arm was separated from his body.

Elaine paused the DVD. "You know, Mom, when he wrapped my ankle on the trail, I noticed some scars and asked about them. Those weren't his exact words, but they may as well have been."

"Despite the scar's appearance, I was not seriously injured," he said. "I would have noticed if I had lost an arm."

They doubled over in laughter. "Stop it!" Elaine cried. "They were serious wounds. It had to have smarted."

He got it. He laughed until his cheeks were wet with tears. "It feels good to laugh."

She hit the play button and they watched the movie to the end.

"Well, Dickon, what did you think of this movie?" Elaine asked when the movie ended.

"It was blasphemous." He winked. "That is what people would have thought in my time. It has been too long since I have been able to laugh that freely, thank you." His tone grew serious. "The plague would sweep through the villages and cities. It was dreadful and feared, and yet I laughed when it was shown in the movie." He shook his head.

"It's what we call black humor. It's also called gallows humor, I'm sure you had that in your time," Katarina said.

"Yes, of course we did. I was too serious minded to laugh at the Church. Is there anything today that you will not laugh about?"

"Very little, and there are some unspeakable horrors that most won't joke about except in a very oblique way. But let's not spoil tonight with that. You'll have plenty of time to learn about those things," Katarina said. "It's getting late, and I'm tired. Elaine, would you like to be set up down here tonight so you don't have to negotiate the stairs?"

"Actually, no. I'd rather be in my own room, and I'd like to take a bath before I go to sleep," she said. "I feel a lot better. I'll manage."

"I'll help you up the stairs," he said.

"You aren't going to carry me."

"I was going to support you the way I did on the trail."

After helping Elaine get to her room, he found he was still chuckling over the movie and was in a much better mood than earlier. He picked up the remote and began scanning the channels to see what was on.

Suddenly an image flashed into his awareness that was so horrific that he stopped hitting the scan button. *This can't be real.* But as he listened to the voiceover he came to understand that the footage he saw was nightmarishly real. Horrified, he watched as skeletal bodies were shoved into ditches by large machines, and the people who were little more than walking skeletons being tortured and shot. It was over an hour before he was able to turn it off.

He sat for a while in the dimly lit room, numbed by what he had just seen. He finally went to bed a little after one in the morning and lay staring at the ceiling before falling into a fitful sleep. The smell of coffee awakened him. He found Katarina and Elaine eating when he walked into the kitchen.

"My god, Dickon, what happened? Are you feeling okay?"

"I watched TV last night after you went to bed. It was on something called The Holocaust," he said, sitting down at the breakfast counter. "I have seen some wicked acts and met evil people, but I had never seen it done to so many people all at once."

"That has to be one of the most inhumane acts of the twentieth century." Katarina winced and put a reassuring hand on his shoulder.

"Who would do those terrible things? Where were the good Christians who would stop them?"

"Before the war started, those who would stop them were powerless to do so," Katarina said. "I'm ashamed to say that the people who did it were Christians, who accepted Hitler's interpretation of the Church's teaching about Jews being Christ's killers."

"According to the Church, they did kill Christ."

"The church no longer preaches that. Can you honestly say the rumor about the Jews is any more true than the one that says you ordered your nephews' execution?" Katarina asked.

"Are you saying that the Cardinals and Bishops and the Pope are liars? Are they not God's voice?"

"I'm not saying they're liars. I'm saying they're human. And as humans, they are flawed and fallible. Thomas More wrote some terrible lies about you, and yet he was canonized by that same organization."

He'd read More's history of himself, and it was a cleverly written lie. "But the testament is the word of God. Is God's word corrupt?"

"I believe it's the word of God as written and interpreted by flawed human beings, and contains human errors as a result," Katarina said. "I understand that the Jews had been expelled from England two hundred years before your time. Did you even know anyone Jewish?"

"I knighted Edward Brampton, a Portuguese Jew who converted."

Katarina stopped drinking her coffee. "I had forgotten that. I read that you were the first British monarch to do so. My apologies."

"Apologies for what?" he asked.

"For assuming that you hated Jews because of what the Church had taught you."

"I do not hate them, but I do believe they should convert."

"You know, Jews do not try to convert people to their religion, and I think it's a matter of respect not to try to convert anyone to your set of beliefs."

"I will have to think about that." He took a mug out of the cabinet and poured himself some coffee. "It appears that I owe a Jew for my life today."

"Who?"

"Michael Fairchild."

"He isn't Jewish," Katarina said. "Why did you think so?"

"He has the mark of Abraham."

Both she and Elaine laughed.

Richard's brows knitted together. "I did not realize that this should be an object of mirth."

"No, it isn't," Katarina said. "Most newborn males are circumcised before they leave the hospital unless the parents request not to. But how did you know he'd been circumcised?"

"It was the morning you brought me back to Ambion, and Michael escorted me to the men's room when we took a break. I was at the urinal next to him and I happened to notice," he said. "Lani, how is your ankle?"

"Much better, thanks," she said. "You know, I've been thinking. I've got an extra plane ticket to San Francisco. Do you want to come with me? The plane's not until Saturday, so there's plenty of time to get the name changed on the ticket."

Richard's eyes widened at the prospect of actually being able to fly. "Yes, that is something I would very much like to do."

TWENTY

Hosgrove arrived at Ambion Technologies early Monday morning. He frowned, remembering the conversation with his lawyer, Harry Sullivan. He could still hear Harry saying that the DA was willing to deal, but only to an extent. "Your position in the community has worked to your advantage, as has your age. But unless Mr. Wilde agrees not to testify against you, I doubt you can avoid incarceration. We'll do the best we can to get you a reduced sentence in a low security prison."

For once he was glad he was seventy-eight.

Late last Friday he got a piece of good news regarding the body when he met with Ralph Sanders. Whether or not the family would accept records in lieu of remains was not his concern. His lawyer assured him the contract did not explicitly state he was obligated to return any remains, only records of how the body was disposed and proof there were no remains.

The one thing he wished to conceal for the present was the time travel aspect. While the records said displacement, they never explicitly made mention of temporal displacement. He was in the clear legally. And, it seemed, their ability to retrieve someone from the past would remain secret.

Still, he was disturbed about the hospital's insistence he return any remains. Had he overstepped his friendship with Sanders to the point where the hospital was negligent? He shrugged in annoyance, hoping this didn't lead to anyone snooping into Ambion's affairs.

He still wanted Richard, but when Harry glared at him when he suggested he contact Richard personally, Hosgrove realized that would be the wrong thing to do.

There must be something that I can offer Richard besides money so that he doesn't testify against me. And why the hell had he tried to escape?

Dumbfounded, he could think of nothing he'd said or done to have prompted this action. True, he was thinking of returning him to Bosworth, but how had that been telegraphed to Richard?

Didn't I go along with the scheming Katarina to allay any suspicions? Not that I wanted to, but—damn Katarina! How did she know how that prisoner line would work on me? She couldn't have known about Jack. He was never the same after he got out of POW camp.

And what was going on with Michael? He had been the most dedicated worker he ever knew, putting in long hours and often working through weekends to get the Quantum Displacement Engine working. It wasn't like Mike to have disappeared like this.

He needed Michael to take what they had already done and use it to develop something a little more commercially practical. He searched for the physicist when he got in at seven in the morning. He often found him there, hunched over the computer display even at this early an hour. Michael hadn't signed in, and he wasn't in the lab or his office. It was unreasonable for him to expect Mike to be keeping such long hours. Hosgrove signed onto his computer.

His secretary buzzed him at a quarter after eight and asked if he had anything that needed her attention before she settled into her routine.

"Yes, locate Michael Fairchild and have him come to my office immediately."

When Linda reported back ten minutes later that their physicist had not yet arrived at Ambion, Hosgrove requested she let him know the minute Michael signed in.

His buzzer sounded at ten-o-five. "Harry Sullivan is on the line."

"I'll take it. Thank you, Linda.

"Harry, what have you got for me?"

"At present the best deal I can work is six months in a minimum security prison and a year of probation doing community service. You will also have to pay a fine."

"Any chance of getting the sentence suspended?"

"I'm working on it," Harry said. "I wanted you to know what the worst case scenario is should I not be able to deal further. You do know that you have to plead guilty to aggravated assault. That's a felony."

He sucked in his breath. "Can't you get it reduced to a misdemeanor?" He was starting to sweat. He loosened his tie.

"Hosgrove, that is the reduced charge. The original charge was attempted murder. Your only real hope is for Mr. Wilde to agree not to testify against you."

"But I wasn't going to shoot anyone. Things got out of hand and that idiot Parvic jumped me. She's the reason the gun went off."

"So you've already told me. The fact is you were the one with the loaded gun, and it was your finger on the trigger," Harry said. "The problem is there were four witnesses who will testify to the fact that you shot him."

As the gravity of his situation sunk in, he strained to think of something for his lawyer to use. "I'm confident you will find a way to get it reduced still further."

"It would help if there were mitigating circumstances that caused you to carry a gun. Did he ever threaten you in any way?"

That was it! He'd almost forgotten what Richard had said when he was on the phone with Katarina. "Yes he did. Two days before I shot him, he threatened me over the phone. His tone was menacing when he said, 'I'll fucking kill you.' Those were his exact words. I had the gun with me because I felt threatened by him."

"Will you be available to meet with me later today in my office?" Harry asked.

"Yes, I can be there shortly after four."

"Good."

He hung up, encouraged by Harry's reaction.

Assuming Michael had come in by now, Hosgrove buzzed his secretary, asking for him.

"We've searched for him, but he isn't here, and he didn't sign in."

His throat constricted. "Not in?"

"No, Mr. Hosgrove. But the mail came, and there's a letter from him addressed to—"

He lurched out of his chair and dashed to the outer office. He was looming over her desk before she could finish.

"Where? Give it to me!" He tore the letter from her desk and ran back into his office. Slamming the door shut, he mangled the envelope open and pulled out a single sheet revealing a neatly printed letter of resignation, hand signed by Fairchild.

> *Due to a personal problem that I am forced to attend, I am tendering my two weeks notice as of the date of this letter, Friday, August 27, 2004. I will be taking my unused vacation allotment starting Monday, August 30, 2004.*
>
> *You have access to the complete project notes and test results, including my latest failure to find an appropriate time slot. My continual review of that time has affected my health. In addition, the equipment failed catastrophically. Temporal displacement is no longer possible.*

He tried to call Michael, surprised that he hadn't called in, but got a "no longer in service" message instead.

Hosgrove broke into a cold sweat. How could Michael do that to him? He tried scanning Michael's files to make sense of the complicated physics, but he was a miner turned businessman, not a physicist. He would need his engineering team in on this.

He turned his thoughts to who should be Michael Fairchild's replacement. He knew that Michael didn't invent the device, but instead, adapted an invention that had not passed development stage. He decided to have the device's original inventor found, and make an offer.

"Linda," he called to her through the open door. "Have Carole Weill come to my office."

"Yes sir."

At exactly five feet tall, honey blond hair, and a figure that leaned toward matronly, Carole Weill surprised everyone with her management acumen and technical abilities. Although she ran the engineering department with a soft hand, she was well respected. More often than not, she would be able to find ways of accomplishing the department's goals when no one else could.

He had hired her away from the local sales office of the computer company that supported Ambion. She was languishing there as an under-valued systems analyst. In addition to the skills she brought to Ambion, she belied the rumor that Hosgrove would not promote women into positions of authority.

"Sit down," he said when Carole entered his office. He wasted no time with preliminaries; after all, Carole ran the damn department that had developed the device under Michael's guidance. "I require two things from you. First, I need to know who invented the displacement device originally. Do you know who that is?"

"No sir, but I believe Dr. Fairchild knows. Why don't you ask him?"

"He's on a long overdue vacation at present. I need the information now and can't wait for Mike to return. How long do you think it'll take you to find out?"

"Without researching it first, I'd guess a day or two," she said.

"Please let me know the minute you know anything. Secondly, when I insisted that Mike take a few weeks off, he protested, saying that it had failed. I know you and your team worked very closely with him. You'll have to investigate this failure without his assistance for now."

"Mike didn't share all the science with us. It will take us longer without him, but I'm confident we'll be able to make it work again," Carole said.

"I want a status report by Monday with recommendations on what is required to restore it," he said.

"Monday is a holiday, sir. It's Labor Day."

"So it is. This Friday, then. That will be all."

He closed the door after she left his office.

He had just one more task to do before he met with Harry Sullivan. He called the detective agency he used and initiated a search for Michael Fairchild.

TWENTY-ONE

"Wow!" Elaine said. "You're much handsomer without a beard. What prompted you to grow one?"

"I didn't—"

Katarina entered the room at that moment. "Richard! I thought you had to wait until Wednesday. Did I hear wrong?"

"Wait for what?" Elaine asked.

"They gave him an anti-coagulant after the surgery. He was supposed to wait until this Wednesday to shave. Did I not remember correctly?" Katarina glared at him.

"I dislike beards. I don't see what difference two days will make."

"I suppose you would've if you'd cut yourself and bled to death on my bathroom floor."

"How should I bleed to death? I have never had any difficulty in healing from even the worst of wounds," he said.

"You are the most stubborn, willful, exasperating person I know, next to Hosgrove! We've gone over this before, Richard. What in 'it prevents your blood from clotting' did you not understand?"

"I did not cut myself." He rubbed his smooth chin. "Were you able to contact your lawyer?"

"Yes," Katarina said, her voice calmer. "She recommends Matthew Black, he's a full partner in the firm. Here's his number. You can use the phone in my study if you want some privacy."

"Thank you, Katarina. Have you received an email from Michael?"

"Not yet. Let me grab my Mac before you make your phone call. Also, I should give you the name of Hosgrove's lawyers. I'm sure Attorney Black will want that information."

"I believe you have given me it."

Elaine made a derisive snort.

He snapped his head around to the couch, where she occupied its length, keeping her ankle elevated. Her expression showed no malice. "Lani, is there a problem?"

"No-o-o, it's just that you should hear yourselves." Elaine laughed. "You both sound like you're in a business meeting instead of being home."

Richard stood. "Excuse me. I have some matters I must attend to." As he walked into the den, he overheard Katarina scolding Elaine. Not wanting to be interrupted, he brought Katarina's iBook out to her and returned to the study, closing the door behind him. This was one time where their presence would be too distracting.

Sitting at the desk, he found a pad of yellow, lined paper and a coffee mug that held an assortment of writing implements. He selected one and jotted down a few quick notes. It was good to not have to make every word perfect, or to have to form flawless sentences. He was no longer constrained to place every thought into a single sentence. It was liberating.

There was a knock at the door, and Katarina stuck her head in. "Richard, your birth certificate just arrived, and you need to sign for it. The FedEx guy is waiting at the front door."

Once he'd signed for the package, he returned to the study with the oversized envelope. "I don't see where this opens." He tugged at a flap that refused to yield.

"Just pull on this string to open it." She held the string for him to see. "I got an email from Michael. Prepare yourself, it's not good."

> *Katarina,*
>
> *Please do not contact me. It was a mistake for me to tell you how to reach me before. By the time you get this email, my account will be deactivated.*
>
> *I can't help Richard, I'm sorry. He can't go back, ever. It will kill him. Before we went back to his time, we tested objects by first sending them back a few days in time. They were*

vaporized within a second of going back. This may explain why it never properly worked as a displacement device, because it required that an object exist twice at the same time.

It was only through experimentation that we discovered that objects could exist for even a few significant seconds prior to their manufacture. That's why Richard can't go back to when he existed. It may vaporize him in both times.

Hosgrove will have my letter of resignation by the time you get this email. I have no intention of going back to Ambion Technologies. I don't want him to be able to find me and I'm afraid he will try to contact me through you. I think it's better that you don't know how to reach me.

If I ever feel it's safe to do so, I will contact you. Until then, I wish the best of luck to you and to Richard. I hope he can find a place for himself in today's world.

Mike

Richard gripped the edge of the desk to keep his hands from shaking. Tears stung his eyes. "I feel like Edward just died again."

Katarina stood and looped her arm about his shoulder. "Remember what you said, Richard? That Michael can't be the only one who knows the technology?"

He straightened up and wiped his eyes with the back of his hand. "What do you mean? If I try to go back, I will ruin what I did have."

"You may not be able to go back, but that doesn't mean that someone else can't do it for you."

"How will they know who my son is?"

"Michael didn't say that you couldn't view the photos. If Ambion Technologies can make it operational again, then the first thing they have to do is send a camera back to find Edward and photograph him."

"Do I dare hope?"

"I don't know what to say, Richard, when each setback is so personally devastating."

"I didn't care when it was only my own life that I risked, why can I not risk this?"

"Would it help if you thought of it this way? Edward *is dead*; you aren't risking him at all. It's your heart that you are putting on the line."

"I owe it to him to try." He renewed his resolve.

"What's this?" Katarina sat back down, pointing to the yellow pad where he had written his notes.

"I was trying to understand my adversaries." He ripped the sheet from the pad and crumpled it up. "It's not important."

"I disagree, may I see them?"

He placed the wadded paper ball into her upraised hand. "It's meaningless."

She smoothed his notes out and read them.

> *Evan Hosgrove –*
> *soldier, leader, responsible to his men, brave?*
> *businessman, wealthy, powerful, impulsive*
> *husband, father? grandfather? loved his wife*
> *age – 78, vital, aggressive*
> *What does he want? Why did he risk everything to get me*
> *here only to send me back?*

"Richard, I think you're right on the money regarding Evan. I can tell you he is a father and a grandfather, although I've never heard him talk about them." She glanced up from the paper. "I'm rather surprised at the brevity of your notes from what I saw of your formal writing from the fifteenth century. A single sentence could go on for pages."

"Your newspapers have taught me that I don't have to use every word I know to express my thoughts." He smiled to himself remembering those unwieldy sentences that could fill an ocean.

"If you took age off the list, you could be describing yourself. No wonder the two of you clash. You're too much alike. I may have a partial answer to these questions."

"I'm listening."

"Hosgrove was bending my ear after one of the Portland chapter meetings three or four years ago. He had too much to drink, and it loosened his tongue. Anyway, he called me an academic snob who never had to make it in the real world, and he was going to prove to us all that we needed to respect him for his historical knowledge, and not just for the cash he's given to the universities."

"Do you think his reputation is worth that much to him?" he asked.

"Could be," she said. "Tell me, does it bother you that your reputation is so foul? You are not the person that Shakespeare portrayed."

"It does bother me, but I don't think that I can do anything about it."

"You probably shouldn't. Let the various Ricardian societies take care of that. But, I bet that Hosgrove thought he could be accepted into academic society if he were to contribute a scholarly work."

"Thank you; I may be able to use it when I meet with him."

"Have you called Attorney Black yet?"

"Not yet. I'll do it now."

"We're going to have to go downtown after you've finished with this call. You need a picture ID so you can get the plane ticket, among other things."

"Maybe I should not leave. I do have to meet with Hosgrove."

"No," she said. "You need to have some fun. Anyway, this is a holiday weekend. Nobody else is going to be around, so you may as well go."

"I appreciate your help," Richard said.

He and Katarina had spent the entire afternoon at various local and state agencies where he got a picture ID he could use in lieu of a driver's license, and completed the paperwork necessary to legally change his name to Richard Gloucestre.

"I was glad to, Richard. What did you think of Matthew Black? Do you think he'll be able to serve your best interests when it comes to Evan Hosgrove?"

"He has a lot of confidence. And I have to believe he knows what he is doing."

They entered Katarina's house through the garage.

"Elaine, it's us," Katarina called out. They went to the living room and found her reclining on the couch, foot propped up on a cushion. And while her ankle was still swollen, it seemed to have lessened, and the color was better.

"How is your ankle?" He sat next to Elaine.

"Much better, thanks. Keeping my weight off it made all the difference." Elaine then called out to her mother, "Did you get the DVD I asked for?"

"Yes," Katarina said. "It's by the TV, but wait until after dinner to watch. I'm not interested in seeing it again."

Elaine faced him. "I wanted this one because the creature shop my friends work for made all the animatronics for this movie."

"What are animatronics?"

She paused, closing her eyes for a few seconds before answering. "The closest I can come to what you'd know are puppets. But hold that question until after the movie, then it will make a lot more sense to you."

Elaine removed the DVD from the player and put it back in its case. "So, what did you think of the critters?"

He continued to stare at the screen, now a solid blue. "I am awestruck," he said. "I thought they were real, not like puppets at all."

"That's because they're not puppets. I used the term earlier because it was the closest thing I could think of that you'd know about. That is really what animatronics is."

"You said your friends work for the company that makes these dinosaurs?" he asked.

"Uh-huh, maybe they can take you on a tour when we're there this weekend. Would you like that?"

"Yes."

"So, are you up for a virtual tour?" Elaine powered the iBook on. "This will give you an idea of it."

He nodded.

With a couple of clicks of the mouse, Elaine selected the studio tour once she was on the site. "Tony and Ali Califani work here. They took me on a tour a couple of years ago."

The menu allowed them to explore the different aspects of creating a creature, in this case, a dinosaur. As she clicked through the presentation, he saw the photos of how they went from a sketch, to a model, to the animatronics.

"If you had not told me they were dinosaurs, I'd have thought them to be dragons," he said. "How would they make a human body?"

"You'll have to ask my friends for the details. They don't have a lot on here for creating a person. I think more people are interested in seeing how the dinosaurs were made." She clicked on fabrication and found a photo of someone working on a human head.

Katarina joined them. "Interestingly, I heard Ambion Technologies considered building a body to substitute for you. They decided to use a cadaver instead."

"Was it easier to use a real body?" Elaine asked.

"I believe they decided a fabricated body wouldn't be convincing enough in real life," Katarina said.

"I don't understand," he said. "That head looks real to me."

"But you would know the difference if you touched and smelled a body from a creature shop creation," Katarina said.

"Is it possible to manufacture a body that can pass for a real one?" he asked.

"I don't know. What do you think, Elaine?"

"I don't know either. That's a question for the Califanis."

TWENTY-TWO

Monday afternoon Carole Weill met with her two principal engineers, John Reye and Philip Miller. John, a twenty-nine-year-old native of Hawaii, had a Ph.D. in Scientific Computing from Stanford. He also sported a ponytail that went halfway down his back. He had started his career with a football scholarship to UCLA. He'd begun and ended as a linebacker, when he blew out his knee during the third game he'd played in his freshman year.

Phil, a mature man in his forties, with close-cropped, salt-and-pepper hair, came up through the engineering ranks in the Aerospace industry. After getting a B.S. in Aeronautical Engineering at Rensselaer Polytechnic Institute, he'd joined the U.S. Air Force and became a fighter pilot. From there, he became a test pilot for Boeing and then took an engineering position, designing components of commercial jets. He'd been caught in one of the cyclical layoffs at the time Ambion was looking for someone with his type of background. He signed on four years ago and moved to Portland with his wife, three sons, and one dog.

Carole presented the situation as she knew it, and concluded with, "Hosgrove expects a report from us that will describe the steps necessary to fix the Quantum Displacement Engine—QDE. Unfortunately, Dr. Fairchild is unavailable at this time, and Hosgrove did not say when he would be. You all know how many hours Dr. Fairchild invested in this project. He is on a well-deserved, and necessary vacation.

"John, I want you to select two people to work with you to reconstruct the computer logs on this device. See if you can pinpoint just when things started going south. We know it worked Saturday, August twenty-first, when the last two objects were exchanged. I would start with the records from that day, but be prepared to go back if you can't find an event that explains the failures Dr. Fairchild has reported."

"That Saturday was several days ago," John said. "Can you give me a better fix on when the failures started?"

"Sorry, that's the best I can do for now." Carole turned to Phil. "I want you to work with the remaining team members and develop a plan of action that will detail how we expect to recover the QDE and make it operational. That should include a list of equipment and parts required and their associated costs."

She stepped forward and leaned on the table, making sure she had their attention. "Hosgrove also asked who the original inventor of the QDE is. I know Dr. Fairchild has that information, but I don't. Do either of you know who else does? I didn't find any patent information associated with it."

Both John and Phil shook their heads *no* and agreed to ask the rest of the team. "We may have to strip it to find the boiler plate. You know how they are sometimes hidden. Even the copier technician can't always find it on the copier," Phil said.

"Do you have to dismantle it anyway?" Carole asked.

"Probably," Phil said. "But let us know if you do find out before we have it stripped to it's frame—just in case."

"I'll be available if either of you needs my help. But in the meantime, I suggest we get started," Carole said. "I think we should reconvene Thursday morning at nine. Be prepared to give me your preliminary findings, so that I can complete the report to Hosgrove by Friday morning, as he requested."

They did have to remove about two-thirds of the QDE's components before they found the patent information. Phil's team did not find it until Tuesday afternoon, giving Carole but one day to locate the group that had invented it.

Once she traced the patent down, she discovered why she had not been able to find any information using her standard search techniques. Michael had renamed it from the original Quantum Trip, or Q-Trip as it was called in the science project.

Having the patent number proved to be significant, because she discovered that not only did one person invent it, but that it was invented by a high school senior eighteen years ago, and that the patent rights had expired.

When she searched for the inventor, Sarah Levine, the only information available showed that she had won the award. Regarding the original device, she learned that prior to Mike's modifications, it had never worked in a practical sense. The most it had ever transported across space were a few atoms, and they cancelled each other out within a few milliseconds of the transport.

It was late Tuesday night by the time Carole had collected these facts. She called Hosgrove when she arrived Wednesday morning at eight thirty. He was ready to see her then.

"So what have you got for me?" Hosgrove asked, inviting Carole to sit down and offering her coffee.

"I found the inventor of the QDE. The good news is, not only had one person invented it, but it was done as a result of a science project that won the Westinghouse award in 1986. The patent has since expired." Carole paused and took a sip of coffee. "According to the records it was invented by Sarah Levine. I tried to find out about her, but she hasn't done anything of note since then. Also, she may have married and not kept her maiden name."

"Excellent," Hosgrove said. "I should be able to trace her. Do you have the name of the high school?"

"Yes, it's that magnet school for science in New York City, Erasmus."

"How are you coming with recovering the QDE?"

"That's much more complicated," Carole said. "We have isolated when it started to fail, sometime on Wednesday afternoon, August twenty-fifth. A worm attacked the server, which in turn, affected the QDE's computer."

"Isn't everything backed up, not once, but several times?" Hosgrove asked. "I'm paying for a vault for the grandfather tape should everything else fail here."

"All the tapes here are corrupted, and the vault tape is missing," she said. "Did you remove it by any chance? The log shows that you signed it out."

All color drained from Hosgrove's face and then he turned a bright red. "I do not have the tape."

"Then someone forged your signature, and the guard wasn't paying attention."

Hosgrove sat quietly for a minute, staring at his coffee. "Continue with what you are doing. Why can't you reconstruct it from scratch? You've already done it once. Don't tell me all your notes are gone."

"We've all kept handwritten notes. I like to keep a bound notebook, but we each have our own methods. I'll check with my team and that information will be included in the report." She left Hosgrove's office.

Once she was back in her office, Carole called John and Philip in. "Hosgrove doesn't have the grandfather tape. He didn't say anything, but I'm wondering what part Mike had in this whole thing. Anyway, we're going to have to reconstruct it from our handwritten notes, our collective memories, and the original software. The hardware is the least of our concerns, although we do have to replace some of it, too."

John gave a low whistle when she finished speaking. "I wonder how successful we'll be without Mike. He never let us see the whole picture."

She stared sharply at John. "According to Hosgrove, Mike is on vacation. Do you know something that I don't know?"

"Mike just disappeared. I'd have thought that if he were going on vacation that he'd have said something."

"Well, I have to go by what Hosgrove told me. We'll have to assume he's coming back. Also, Hosgrove intends to hire the QDE's inventor, so maybe we won't need Mike, at least to start.

"I suggest we all get together to review our notes after I've submitted our report."

Hosgrove called the detective agency and got the partner he usually worked with, Ted Carter. "Hey listen, Ted. There's one more person I need you to find. She graduated from Erasmus High School in 1986. Her name then was Sarah Levine. She won this prestigious science award, the Westinghouse one. I'm thinking of offering her a position here if she's available, and I do not know her current address, or even if she got married and has a different name."

"I'm on it. Do you want me to contact her when we find her?"

"No, just give me the information. I'll have someone from Human Resources contact her."

Part Two

TWENTY-THREE

Richard sat at Katarina's desk, stunned. She had showed him what she earned and what housing, cars, food, and other things cost.

"In addition to that," Katarina had said. "We all pay taxes which can be more than a third of gross earnings."

And those weren't the only deductions, as it was left to the individual to pay for medical insurance. All these taxes and expenses appeared worse than the benevolences he had abolished in his first and only Parliament. He would not have been able to impose such taxes as these when he was king.

He was further impressed with Katarina's generosity, now that he saw how things measured up. He felt indebted to her. She was not wealthy, but she gave beyond what he would have expected from anyone. He needed to settle with Hosgrove.

"Are you ready to go?" Katarina asked, poking her head into the study.

Richard stood and straightened his tie. "I do not remember ever feeling this edgy going into battle."

"Remember, you can ask for clarification at any time. You don't have to accept what Hosgrove's lawyers say at face value," Katarina said. "I'm there for you."

"Thank you."

Elaine dropped them off at the attorney's office, promising to pick them up in a little over two hours—by noon. It was twenty minutes before the hour, and the meeting was to start promptly at ten.

They were ushered into Matthew Black's office as soon as they arrived. "Sit down," Matthew said, extending his hands to both Richard and Katarina. "I'm glad you could be here early."

He sat down next to Richard and spread his notes out. "I spoke with Hosgrove's attorneys, Eric, and this is the best deal they can offer short of suing."

Richard studied the notes, and was rather overwhelmed by the dollar amounts despite the crash course Katarina had just given him. "Am I correct in my assessment that Mr. Hosgrove will pay me $450,000? And this does not include the medical expenses which he is presently covering?"

"Yes and no, Eric. You will have to pay my fees out of the figure there, and any new medical expenses will come out of your pocket."

"You were unable to negotiate for Hosgrove to pay your fees?" When Richard had met with Attorney Black the week before, he was told that the standard attorney's fee, whether it went to court or was settled out of court, would be one third of the final settlement. They had discussed the possibility of Hosgrove paying the fee in addition to the settlement. This was disappointing.

"No, furthermore, this was the highest they would go without taking it to court. If you want more, you will have to chance a jury trial." He pulled at a spike of his short red hair.

Richard sat back. "Do you recommend that I accept this offer?"

"Yes, I do. Going to court is always risky. You could get substantially more than what they're offering, but you're risking more than the settlement. Not only could you get nothing but also there could be additional fees you may be liable for. Evan Hosgrove is popular in this community and finding a jury that would be sympathetic enough to your cause could be problematic. Furthermore, it could take months, if not years before a court date is set."

"Why would a court appearance take such a long time?" Richard arched an eyebrow.

"I know that Hosgrove's lawyers would want to delay the process, and the court calendar is full." Black leaned forward and placed his square, muscular hands on the table, palms down. "It's your call, but my advice is to accept this offer."

"Very well, but before I sign anything I want to meet with Mr. Hosgrove in private."

"In my presence?" Black's forehead wrinkled.

"No, just him and me."

"I don't know if he will agree to that."

He spread his hands on the table, palms down. "I believe he will agree. Four-hundred and fifty thousand may not seem like a lot of money to you, but I do not believe he would have agreed to that figure if he thought he could not lose more in court."

"Very well," Attorney Black said. "They should be in the conference room by now. Why don't we proceed?"

His secretary stopped them as they left the office. "Attorney Smithfield and Evan Hosgrove are in the West Conference Room."

"When did they get here?"

"Just a couple of minutes ago."

"Thank you," Black said. He led them to the conference room where they found Hosgrove pacing. His attorney, Smithfield, sat reclined in one of a dozen, high-backed, gray leather chairs.

Richard noted the room was set up to impress, much like the great halls in his and other nobles' castles. Money and power exuded from every inch of this spacious conference room. The massive slate conference table dominated the room, over which was a large multicolored-lighted glass sculpture. The sculpture gave the room an iridescent, otherworldly quality.

He was impressed.

"Please sit down," Black said as they filed in. Hosgrove sat down next to his attorney; Richard and Katarina took seats opposite. Black sat at the head of the table.

"Before we start, is there anything either of the parties would like to say?" Black asked, nodding at Richard.

"Mr. Wilde," Hosgrove said. "I would like to extend my apologies for the grievous harm and suffering I have caused you. I can assure you, it was an accident. It was not my intention to harm you in any way. Please accept my apology."

"It is accepted," he said, "but before I sign any papers, I should like to speak to you in private."

Hosgrove glanced at his lawyer, who said, "This is highly irregular. I would advise against it, Evan."

"If you feel uncomfortable meeting with him alone," Katarina said. "I'd be willing to be a silent witness to this discussion."

"Thanks for the offer, Katarina," Hosgrove said. "But I don't think it's necessary. Do you agree, Mr. Wilde?"

"I do." He asked Attorney Black where he and Hosgrove could get some privacy. Black took them to a small conference room opposite the reception area.

Richard closed the door behind him and turned toward the table. Hosgrove remained standing. They stood at an impasse, studying each other for a few seconds.

Hosgrove was the first to blink, "You are looking well, Richard."

"Sit down, please."

"I prefer to stand," Hosgrove said, not moving. "Speak, it's your dime."

Flustered by Hosgrove's brusqueness, he forgot the arguments he'd prepared, and instead blurted out, "I want my son."

Hosgrove sat down. "What?"

He stood opposite Hosgrove and placed his fists on the table, leaning toward him. "I have been denied the two most important people of my life, my wife and my son." He straightened up. "I would save both of them if I could, but it will only be possible for Edward."

"Sit down, Richard. Why are you bringing it up at this time, when we are here to talk about a settlement?"

"You have the technology I require." He continued to stand. "I need your help and I am prepared to offer you something you want in return. But I could not include any of this in the settlement." He selected a chair that was adjusted higher than the others and sat.

"All right. First explain how and why you think I can help you save your son."

"I was not at Middleham when Edward died and the date isn't precise in the historical records. I don't know for a certainty what he died of, but I have reason to believe his appendix ruptured, and he died of the resulting infection. I think he can be saved with today's medicine. All I'm asking of you is to apply the same technology you used to get me, to pull my son into this time."

"Hmm." Hosgrove ran his fingers through his white hair. "And why do you think I'd want to go to the expense to retrieve your son? What do I get out of it?"

"I would consider not testifying against you."

"Only consider?" Hosgrove asked. "You'll have to do better than that. I know that I can get the charges greatly reduced."

"I would not testify against you if you give me the resources to rescue my son."

"I can't promise that we'd be able to get your son. I can only promise to try. Would that satisfy?"

Richard pinched the bridge of his nose. "You pulled me into this century, why can't you get my son?"

"We've—ah—run into some technical difficulties."

"Can you overcome them?"

"Possibly," Hosgrove said. "The equipment failed a few days after we brought you here."

Richard knew what had happened from Michael's email, but he needed to see just how much Hosgrove was willing to divulge. "How did it fail?"

Hosgrove grimaced. "I don't know, but my engineers tell me that the programming is corrupted, and we can no longer go back."

"Can Dr. Fairchild repair it?" he asked.

"The major complication is that Dr. Fairchild has resigned, and he's key to getting it working again."

"Is Dr. Fairchild the only person who can get the equipment to work? I saw a lot of people at Ambion."

"We're examining the alternatives. My engineers are trying to reconstruct what they did. The problem is, much of the data in the computer was destroyed. I'm in the process of tracking down the original inventor, and we're trying to find Michael to see if I can persuade him to return."

His eyes widened at this news. It hadn't occurred to him that someone other than Michael Fairchild had created the device they'd used. "Do you know who invented it?"

"Yeah, it seems this high school girl did, some eighteen years ago. She won a prestigious science award for it, but she has since faded into obscurity. If I can track her down, I'm going to make her an offer."

"Do you think you will be able to find Michael?"

"Probably, but there is no guarantee that he'll return even if I do find him."

"I will not testify against you in exchange for trying to save my son," he said. "I also believe I have more to offer you."

"I'm listening." Hosgrove sat back.

"I can provide you with details about the fifteenth century, such as battles I fought and matters of government. Is this something that you would want?"

"Of course I want that information, but what good is it if I can't corroborate your data?"

"I would be able to tell you what to look for and where to search. I am fluent in Latin. I could provide reliable translations." What more could he offer? "In addition, I can help you persuade Dr. Fairchild to return to Ambion Technologies when you find him."

"Why do you think you can convince Michael when I can't?"

"I received an email from him explaining that he was afraid you would make him send me back and he could not bring himself to do it. I think my requesting he return should allay his fears."

Hosgrove nodded. "I will put my resources into getting your son here."

He suppressed a smile. There was still one more detail that he needed to work out. "How can I ensure that you do engage in this project and continue once the criminal charges are dropped?"

Hosgrove stared at him for a few heartbeats and then answered. "I'll hire you into a position—create one if necessary. That will give you access to Ambion, and me access to you."

"What function will I serve?" he asked. "I'm somewhat out of date on the technology."

Hosgrove laughed. "Don't worry, I'll figure something out. I also want you to speak to my lawyer, Harry Sullivan, that you are not going to testify against me."

He nodded. This might work out better than he had hoped. Being at Ambion daily was a risk, but it would also provide him with immediate access. Maybe he could even be part of that team.

"Gentleman's agreement then," Hosgrove said, extending his hand.

"Agreed." He shook Hosgrove's hand.

Instead of letting go, Hosgrove clasped his hand in both of his. "I meant it when I apologized to you earlier. I wasn't just saying that to meet a legal obligation. I'm very sorry for what I've done."

"And I meant it when I said that I accepted your apology. I forgive you, Mr. Hosgrove."

"Call me Evan." Hosgrove let go of Richard's hand. "What are you going to do about your name? I don't feel right calling you Eric, or even Mr. Wilde."

"I'm changing it to Richard Gloucestre. I submitted the papers last week."

"Have you received your Social Security Number yet?"

"What is that?"

Hosgrove wrote on the back of his business card and handed it to him. "There are two numbers here. The first one belongs to Sullivan and the other is for Cindy Becker, the Human Resources director at Ambion. I will let each know to expect your call later today. Will you be able to do that?"

"Yes."

"My number's on the other side; feel free to call me if you have any questions. It's time we rejoined the legal beagles. We have papers to sign and I have a check for you."

TWENTY-FOUR

When Elaine picked them up, Richard suggested they celebrate his "victory"—his treat. They chose a nouveau-cuisine café near the law offices. They were seated outdoors, in the restaurant's garden located on the side of the building.

"So you mean to tell me Hosgrove offered you a job?" Katarina asked, peering over a menu.

"Yes. You were right about his wanting to prove himself to academia, and I believe I can furnish sufficient information to satisfy him." He folded his menu before adding, "I am indebted to you, Katarina. I feel I can never adequately return the favor, but I would like to reimburse you for your expenses in my behalf."

"Ah, the keyword here is 'favor,'" Katarina said. "It's my gift. I'm sure you'll repay in kind someday, just not today."

"So what kind of job did you get, Dickon?" Elaine asked.

"I don't know," he said. "I'm supposed to call Cindy Becker at Ambion later today. I fear I don't have the knowledge needed for this century."

"Sweat it not," Elaine said. "It's just another example of OJT—on the job training."

"One thing you have going for you, is that you are a good listener," Katarina said. "I wonder where our waiter is."

He caught the waiter's attention a few minutes later. The young man couldn't have been more than twenty, a tall, gangly youth who seemed new at the job. At least he wrote their order down and didn't pretend to memorize it.

Both Katarina and Elaine excused themselves, leaving Richard alone. He tried to put his thoughts in order, but so much had occurred in such a short time. Would he ever be able to catch up?

Soon they returned to the table. Katarina spoke first. "I've noticed you like to watch both the Science and History Channels."

"There's a lot I need to learn. I never thought entertainment could be this educational."

"Didn't the Church deliver some of their teachings through morality plays?" Katarina asked.

"That was religious teachings, not science," Richard said. "The church suppressed science. They suppressed and persecuted those whose science did not agree with their beliefs."

Katarina put her hand on his. "You sound bitter."

He supposed he was. But that wasn't right. What had happened in the fifteenth century was his fault if anyone's. It was he who had believed most of the church's teachings. They may have been right about religion, but they could not have been more wrong about science. "I cannot reconcile what I now know to be true about what they taught. There is much that I am witnessing that has made a sham of much that I learned from the church." He frowned.

The waiter arrived with their orders. After he left, Katarina said, "Is that why you haven't gone to church?"

He realized with sudden force that he had been avoiding the church. Even after he'd lost Edward and Anne, he had kept his faith, even sought solace. Were things that different now?

"I don't know what to believe. The program on the Holocaust bothers me still. The worst of it is that I fear the church of my day would have thought those actions justified."

"I think this is a human condition, as horrible as that sounds." Elaine stared at her barely touched penne prima vera. "I've read there was cruelty to spare in your day. Why did you find it so shocking?"

"Perhaps it is because I see how much your medicine and technology have advanced that I equated it to a more enlightened philosophy." He took a bite of his chicken. "I was mistaken."

"You had me print a copy of our Constitution," Katarina said. "What do you think of it?"

"It's enlightened. Mayhap, that's why I am all the more disheartened by that program."

"I would encourage you to work it out, Richard. You need to come to terms with how you are going to handle your beliefs and the Church."

"Give him a break, Ma! Sheesh, he's been here, what, two weeks? He's already starting to sound like us—well, more than before. I'm sure he'll figure this out, too."

Katarina smiled.

He liked how Elaine wasn't afraid to stand up to her mother, even chide her, and that Katarina took it with good humor. How different it was from his day. If he succeeded in bringing his son here, would he, could he, have that kind of relationship with him? He hoped so.

"I don't see either of you celebrating mass. Is that done in this country or have all religious observances been abandoned?"

Elaine chuckled. "I'm afraid you've fallen in with the wrong crowd. Most people here do worship, and most people do believe in God."

He was shaken. He'd been so sure of his convictions then. He glanced at his companions, who were waiting for him to speak. He tried to make light of his turmoil. "Aye. 'Tis the story of my life, I am always associating with the wrong people."

Elaine drew her eyebrows together and then lightly slapped her cheek, laughing. "You almost got me, Dickon."

"Still," Katarina said, "the Church doesn't have the same power as they had in your time. They no longer have governmental powers."

The words—separation of church and state—leapt to his mind. He had considered the phrase interesting, but they now held personal meaning.

"I was devout, not only because it was expected of me, but because I truly believed. But so much was taken from me." He bowed his head and rubbed his temples. "Then I thought I was being punished, and if I prayed and was contrite, I would be forgiven."

Katarina put her hand on his arm and gave him a gentle squeeze. "Bad things happen all the time, not just to bad people. However, I don't believe you'll find peace within your heart if you don't come to terms about religion."

"Are you saying that I should go?" he asked.

"No, I'm saying it's your decision to make. But, you need to base this decision on the Church that exists today."

"I will consider it." He would consider it, but not today. As much as he needed to learn about the current Church, he did not feel ready.

"I forgot to mention," Elaine said, tapping her mother on the arm. "I can't go with you to the concert tonight. I've got too much to do, and I have to be at the airport early tomorrow."

"That's too bad, honey," Katarina said, frowning. "Would you like to go, Richard? It's a live performance by one of my favorite singers."

Although Richard no longer had servants attending him, he was ready before Katarina. But he didn't have to wait long for her to sweep by him. The crimson fabric added a warm glow to her fair skin. "You are very elegant, Katarina. The gown becomes you."

"Thank you. We should go."

They headed west, directly into the setting sun. The cloudless sky afforded no relief, and even as a passenger, Richard found it difficult to keep his eyes on the road. Finally, they turned and got behind a line of cars all headed for the concert.

She parked the car in a garage opposite the large concert hall. There appeared to Richard to be an endless line of people of all sizes, ages, and dress. "There must be hundreds of people here."

They found the end of the line and only had to wait a few minutes to reach an usher who showed them to their seats in the center balcony.

"I have to go to the ladies' room." Katarina put her program down. "Just hang onto the ticket stub so you can be shown back to the seat if you need to leave. I'll be back in a few minutes."

The seats fanned out from the stage, which was enclosed by a crimson-velvet curtain. Despite being in the balcony, the ceiling appeared to be another fifteen feet above him. He guessed the chamber could hold as many as a thousand people, and he guessed all the seats would be occupied.

Thus absorbed, he was startled by a tap on his shoulder followed by someone clearing his throat. "Er, I believe our seats are over there," the stranger said, pointing to Richard's right.

"Sorry." He stood, giving them room to pass. He had to back into his seat to let the woman by, as she was heavy with child. He stole a glance at the woman when he sat down. Her fair skin was radiant against her dark brown hair. She glowed.

Suddenly the house lights dimmed and then came up again. Many people were rushing to their seats, but Katarina was still not back. The house lights dimmed again, and this time he saw Katarina at the end of the row, working her way toward him.

"Ugh, there's always a line for the ladies' room. I hope you weren't wondering if I'd disappeared." Katarina sat down.

"Dr. Parvic," the man to his right said. "I didn't know you're a Norma Price fan."

Katarina leaned forward, peering at the man. "Steve! I haven't seen you since you graduated. My God, it must be seven or eight years."

The house lights went down again, and this time stayed dark.

"We'll catch up during intermission," Steve whispered and then sat back.

As soon as the applause died down, Norma Price hung a lute-like instrument around her neck and shoulder and started plucking at the strings. Then her beautiful contralto's voice rang out with the first song.

She continued singing and talking until the intermission, wrapping up the first set with "Amazing Grace," which she sung a cappella. Richard enjoyed every piece she did, but it was the last song that resonated with him the most.

Katarina and Steve picked up their conversation when the lights came up. They walked to the concession stand for beverages.

"So what have you been doing with yourself since you've graduated?"

"I want you to meet my wife, Ann. This is Dr. Parvic, I took linguistics from her when I was more academically inclined," Steve said.

Richards felt his face drain of blood on hearing her name. She bore no resemblance to his Anne, but it did take him back.

"Call me Katarina, please. So when are you due?" she asked.

"What time is it?" Ann laughed. "I wish. But it won't be for another two or three weeks. So, who's your friend?"

"Oh sorry, how rude of me. Ann, Steve, this is Richard. Steve was one of my students, what, eight years ago? Richard and I worked together at Ambion Technologies."

"Did you leave the university?" Steve asked.

"No, I was consulting on a special project. So what are you doing these days? I mean, besides having babies."

"Making money. I went into sales," Steve said. "In fact, Ambion is one of my accounts. So who are you working for, Richard?"

"John Fortas"

"Uh oh. What do you think of him?"

"I start working for him, Monday. I don't know him."

Steve drew close and spoke in a low voice, "I'd be real careful around him if I were you. I heard he's not playing with a full deck."

"I don't understand."

"Something happened in his previous job," Steve said. "I heard he threatened his boss. That company is also one of my accounts. It was supposed to be hush-hush, but word got around."

"Did he do more than threaten his superior?" he asked.

"I'm not really sure. It might be just some nasty rumor." Steve's eyes locked on him. "There was talk of a gun, but as I never heard anything further, I don't know how reliable my information was."

"Was anyone shot?" Richard pinched the bridge of his nose.

"I don't think so." Steve clapped his hand on Richard's shoulder. "It would have been on the news if anything like that had happened. Like I said, it was probably just a rumor."

"It is worrisome," Richard said.

"Yeah, I know what you mean, but hey, you're not going to be his boss are you?"

"No, he is going to be my boss."

"You'll probably be okay," Steve said. "But if it were me, I'd watch my back."

The house lights dimmed, signaling the start of the second half of the concert. They discarded their beverages and went back to their seats.

The second half of the concert continued much as the first half had. Price got a standing ovation after the last song in the program, with shouts of "encore, encore" echoing through the audience.

She smiled and held up her hand. "Thank you, thank you so much. You are all so beautiful. I think you all know this one by heart. Sing "Amazing Grace" with me, please."

At first, hers was the only voice, but she urged everyone to sing along. More and more voices joined in until the entire space rang melodically.

Richard and Katarina were returning to her house when she asked if he'd enjoyed the concert.

"Yes, very much. What was the instrument she played? It's somewhat like the gyterne, but I have not seen one like this before."

"Guitar."

"I would have troupes come to my castles and entertain my guests and us all the time."

"I read that you were quite a patron of the arts."

"We enjoyed our plays, dances, and songs. The advantage I had was they came to us. We did not have to go to them."

"But at what expense?"

"I didn't worry about the expense," Richard said and smiled. "It was never a problem."

"You have a beautiful voice." Katarina turned off the car radio. "If you remember the words to "Amazing Grace," I would love to hear you sing it now?"

"It will be my pleasure." He cleared his throat.

The miles flew by as his rich baritone filled the car.

Amazing grace! How sweet the sound
That saved a wretch like me!
I once was lost, but now am found;
Was blind, but now I see.
'Twas grace that...

TWENTY-FIVE

Friday at last! This was Richard's first Friday at Ambion. He had gotten his driver's license the previous day with only two small white-knuckle moments during the driving part of the test. Sean promised to help him buy a car this coming weekend.

He felt he should not continue to live at Katarina's house despite her protests. He didn't want to impose on their friendship.

His job at Ambion was proving to be a mixed blessing, one that he was determined to see through, at least until he retrieved his son. As far as he could tell, the only difference between this job and his stint as a dishwasher was the type of work. This was clean and did not leave him exhausted at the end of the day. But as far as the hierarchy at Ambion went, he was near the bottom.

He had learned that most of the people at Ambion had college degrees, whereas he'd just begun studying for his high school equivalency degree—GED. It chaffed him to realize that at eighteen, he had been a general in his brother's army, and now at thirty-two, he found he was a lowly clerk working for John Fortas, a man who resented him. John made it known that he had someone else in mind for the position when Hosgrove had assigned him there.

It was still early on Friday Morning and the ritual coffee break had yet to occur, when his manager asked to see him.

He sat opposite his boss, the desk separating them. When John didn't immediately say anything, he asked, "Is there a problem with anything I have done?"

"No, not at all. I have a new project for you to work on, and I wanted to review it with you," John said. "But the big guy just called me. He wants to see you sometime this morning and asked if you were available. Is there something between you and Hosgrove that I should know about?" John tugged at the knot of his tie.

Had Steve foretold what Fortas would do? Being shot once was quite enough. "Evan Hosgrove and I know each other from the Portland chapter of the Richard III Society—we share a mutual interest."

"And you just happened to be available when this job came up?"

"I was seeking a position, and he said that he would see if anything was available here." He and Hosgrove had prepared this story before he'd started.

"I see," John said, appearing more relaxed. "Stop in my office when you're done with Hosgrove, and I'll show you what I want."

"Good morning, Linda." Richard said. He had walked across the sound-absorbing rug to the secretary's desk.

"Oh!" Her head jerked back from the monitor. "You startled me. He's expecting you, just go in." She returned to her work.

He knocked on the door and entered the office. "You wanted to see me?"

Hosgrove peered over his reading glasses and removed them. "Come in. Close the door please and sit down.

"I want to thank you again for agreeing to be a reluctant witness. I can get the felony charges dropped if I plead guilty to a misdemeanor."

"Will you have to serve any prison time?"

"No, but I will have to do some community service," Hosgrove said. "I acted recklessly and I do have to pay for that."

"Have you been able to find Michael?"

"Not yet, he seems to have covered his trail pretty well. But we did find the inventor and offered her a job here. She's starting next Monday."

"I should like to meet her."

"I'm sure you would. But as with most of the others, keep your true identity to yourself. We need to see how she works out first."

"But, you said she invented the device. I don't understand."

"She hasn't touched it since she won the Westinghouse award for science when she was a senior in high school," Hosgrove said. "She was only seventeen at the time, and has done nothing notable for the past eighteen years."

He found this worrisome. "Will you be able to restore the device without Michael?"

"Don't worry until you have to. We'll find Michael, and the people here are very talented."

"I've learned that John Fortas had someone else in mind for the position I was hired to fill," he said.

"He told Cindy Becker the same. You'll just have to win him over, Richard. You've done it in the past and against much more hostility."

"The situations are not comparable. Then I was the one in the position of power. It was through my governance that I gained their support."

"That is something about you that has always amazed me. I've read of many instances where you dealt justice equitably. You earned their loyalty."

He felt pride and regret on hearing Hosgrove's words. "That is kind of you to say, but the proof of my folly lies with Bosworth."

"What do you mean?"

"I won their loyalty only to lead them to slaughter. I should have died that day, not them."

"Historically you did."

"Jesú! I am alive and I should not be," he whispered.

"Let me ask you something. Do you feel you don't deserve to be here, alive? That you shouldn't have survived?"

"Yes, it's my doing they died."

Hosgrove rubbed his temples. "I don't think there's a soldier, especially a commander such as yourself, who hasn't experienced these feelings." The blue eyes that stared back appeared haunted.

"Have you experienced this?"

"Yes." Hosgrove frowned. "I did for years."

"Do you no longer feel that way?"

"On good days. Mostly I don't. But sometimes...."

"It haunts me," Richard said. "I was eager for battle and led them into one I could not win."

"Is that hindsight, Richard?"

"What do you mean?"

"When you led them to that final battle, did you think you wouldn't win?"

He closed his eyes momentarily, remembering. "I suspected Lord Thomas Stanley and Sir William Stanley had joined up with Henry. But I thought I could get the advantage by surprise."

"You're trying to second-guess what you can't change. It happened to me; we call it survivor's guilt. Even people who were blameless victims have felt this way. I can get help for you."

"Did you get help?"

"Not right away," Hosgrove said. "I was a mess when I came home. I was lucky, though. My wife stuck by me. I ended up dragging her off to the wildest, remotest parts of the U.S., and mined for gold. I think I would have taken my own life if she hadn't been there."

"How did you get beyond it?"

"I finally went to a Veteran's hospital, and they sent me to a psychologist who straightened me out. But you shouldn't have to tough it out alone. Let me find someone who can help you."

"How will I tell him about a battle that happened over five-hundred years ago? Will he not think me mad?"

Hosgrove snorted. "That was an unfortunate choice of words. Psychologists deal with problems of the mind. That would be the last person you'd want thinking you're mad."

"It does appear that I will have to 'tough it out,' Evan."

"No, we'll figure something out. I know from my own experience that you would be wise to accept the help."

Richard stood. "Thank you. I should get back. Fortas has a new project he wants me to work on."

Richard opened the first of six replies to a request for a specialized computer equipment proposal. Each bidder responded to thirty-two points, detailing how they could or could not meet the requirements. The department making the request had ranked the responses. His task was to consolidate the bids onto a single matrix, incorporating it onto a spreadsheet.

He knew nothing about this application, yet he could see that John expected him to know it. He hoped Sean would be able to show him this weekend.

"Uh, Dick," a man spoke.

He swung his head toward the familiar voice and eyed Lou Kowalski. "What can I do for you?" Lou worked in another department across from Purchasing.

"A group of us are going to lunch," Lou said. "Wanna come with?"

He glanced at the pile of papers on his desk and hesitated.

"C'mon man, it'll be there when you get back. You gotta eat, right?"

He stood. "Right."

They walked out to the atrium where they met up with six others. "I told you I could talk him into coming," Lou said. "Dick, do you know everyone?"

"I don't believe we have met." He turned to the three new people. The woman in the group couldn't have been more than five-feet tall, with dark blond hair that fell to just below her chin. The older, gray-haired man was a little taller than he was and the younger man had to be a head taller.

"That's because Hosgrove doesn't let us out much," the petite woman said, laughing. "Hi, I'm Carole Weill, and these are my two partners in crime, John Reye and Philip Miller." She stuck her hand out to him.

"I started Monday," he said, shaking her hand. "I am Richard Gloucestre, Carole."

The tall man to her right held his hand out. "Name's John. Do you call yourself Richard?" John's hair was pulled back in a ponytail that disappeared behind the collar of his rugby shirt.

He shook John's hand. "You may call me Dick." An odd expression crossed John's face.

"And you may call me Phil," the older man said, smiling.

"Hey enough with the meet and greet," Lou said. "Who else is driving besides me, we'd better take two cars."

"I'll drive. I've got my soccer-mom car today." Carole retrieved her car keys. "Why don't you ride with us, Dick?"

"Okay," Lou said, heading off to his car. "We'll meet you at the restaurant. See you in a few."

Carole led Phil, John, and Richard to her Volvo wagon. "Why don't you ride up front with me, Dick?"

John and Phil got in the back and he sat up front. He didn't mind, but found it interesting how quickly Carole controlled everything. He noticed they were treating him differently than others at Ambion when first meeting him. It was as if they knew his true identity.

"Richard, I'll cut to the chase," Carole said. She exited the parking lot. "I almost didn't recognize you from when you were brought here, but we know who you are. That's why I had Lou ask you to come with us. We're part of the engineering team that works closely with Dr. Fairchild."

"Yeah man, you look a lot healthier than when you first arrived," John said, leaning forward. "Are you sure you want us to call you Dick? Isn't that a bit familiar?"

"I did not think 'Your Grace' would be appropriate," he said, keeping his voice flat.

Everyone laughed at his joke.

"Either Richard or Dick will do."

"So what are you doing working at Ambion?" Phil asked. "It's hard for me to imagine what you would do, actually."

"I have been put in the purchasing department, reporting to John Fortas. I don't much like this position, and Fortas doesn't much like me."

"Hosgrove can be such an idiot sometimes," Carole said. "I'll talk to him when we get back to see what I can do to get you into my department. Anyway, Fortas is a nut case. We need to get you out of there."

"But what can I do for you when I don't have the skills for even this low-level job?"

"Let me worry about that." Carole drove into the restaurant's parking lot.

Phil hung back, signaling that Richard should wait. Carole and John walked to the entrance. "Carole is the best manager I've ever had. If anybody can get you away from that prick, Fortas, she can."

"Why do you call Fortas by that name?"

"Because he's a power freak. He's got a spreadsheet for everything and forces us to jump through fiery hoops before we can purchase the equipment we know we need."

Richard laughed. "I got my first spreadsheet today, and I have no idea how it is supposed to work."

"Hey, you guys," John shouted from the door. "Are you going to spend the lunch hour in the parking lot, or are you going to come in and eat?"

"Coming," Phil said. They both walked to the restaurant. Phil continued in a quiet voice, "Your secret is safe with us. We've signed a legally binding document not to reveal anything about you."

After lunch, they all returned to Ambion. Again he rode with Carole, John, and Phil. This time he sat in the back with Phil, behind John.

"Richard," Carole said. "I think I know how we can get you into our group, but don't get mad at me. It would be doing something similar to what you are doing now in purchasing, but you'd be requisitioning the items instead of approving them."

"Does it involve spreadsheets?"

She chuckled. "I'm afraid it does. But we'll show you how to use them. It doesn't take a rocket scientist, believe me."

"I also need time to re-educate myself. I am five hundred years out of date."

"We'll be able to help you with that, too. I'll make sure I get to speak to Hosgrove this afternoon. Just sit tight."

He returned to his desk to find John Fortas seated there. The purchasing manager glowered at him. "Where have you been?"

"I do not understand. I went to lunch with Lou and a few other people."

"Well, you're late. You only get a forty-five-minute lunch. You have been gone for over an hour." John stood up and walked toward his office. He turned just before he got there and added, "I'm putting you on notice. One more infraction and you're outta here." He turned on his heels and disappeared into his office.

Richard shrugged. *Prick.*

He was so busy reviewing the bids and hand writing the matrix that he jumped when the phone rang. The phone displayed that the call was from Carole Weill. "Hello Carole."

"I've got good news. Why don't you come to my office?" she said. "Oh, and bring your personal things with you. You won't have to go back to purchasing. Hosgrove's given me the go-ahead."

When he hung up the phone, he discovered Fortas had returned to his desk, making the most of his five-foot-five-inch frame. He leaned into the desk. "I just got a call from Human Resources," Fortas said, his voice edgy. "I understand you want to transfer to Research."

"I understand I have." Richard stood and glared down into his eyes.

"Nobody transfers out of this department without my approval, buster. You don't have it." Fortas rose up on his toes and folded his arms across his chest; jaw jutting.

He stared at this officious little man. "It is done. I suggest you take it up with Hosgrove if you have any questions." He picked his jacket up and pushed past Fortas. He had no other personal effects to clutter Fortas' little kingdom.

"You'll be sorry, Mr. Gloucestre," Fortas said, drawing the sibilant ess out in Richard's name. "You'll find I'm not so easy to get around."

He quickly walked to Carole's office, trying to shake the bad feeling he had about Fortas. Steve's warning filled his mind.

"Richard, what happened?" Carole asked when he entered her office. "Close the door and sit down."

"Fortas tried to prevent me from transferring here."

"He can't do that. I got the okay from Hosgrove."

"That is what I told him."

"Speaking of Hosgrove, I need to ask you something that's been driving me crazy. Didn't Hosgrove shoot you?"

"Yes."

"Then, what's going on? Why isn't he in jail? And what are you doing within spitting distance of him? Or are you taking Machiavelli's advice to 'Keep your friends close and your enemies closer'?"

He grinned at the Machiavelli reference. "Hosgrove apologized to me and we settled out of court. I want to bring my son here, and I need Ambion to do it. Hosgrove agreed to help me."

"Okay, so you kissed and made up. That takes care of Hosgrove. But how can you bring your son without changing history, and why not your wife too?"

"My son died of what I now suspect was a ruptured appendix about a year and a half before Bosworth. There are no historical records saying exactly when he died, so I want to get him just before his appendix ruptures."

"That makes sense, but what about your wife?" Carole asked.

"She died of consumption, what you call tuberculosis, about a year after that. Not only was there a solar eclipse on the day she died, but medically, there is nothing that can be done for her."

"I am so sorry, Richard. Well, here's the deal. Ambion has got to start making money. We've got a year to come out with something that we can sell," she said. "We'll work on getting your son back, but it will be tangential to the main project of coming up with a product or system that can bring revenue in."

His heart sank. "Hosgrove did promise me—"

"We'll keep that promise. I just want you to know where Ambion's priorities lay. Anyway, the QDE's inventor is starting here Monday. You'll get to meet her, but don't tell her anything about yourself just yet."

"QDE?"

"The device that rescued you is called a Quantum Displacement Engine, or QDE for short," she said. "So, Richard, are you curious to see the lab and the equipment such as it is now?"

"Yes."

"You don't have to wear a suit and tie. Our dress code is a lot more casual than purchasing." Carole walked out of the office with him. "Don't lose hope. I'm optimistic that with Sarah joining us, we'll get it working again."

"Hope is really all I have," he said. "Is Sarah the inventor?"

"Hosgrove didn't tell you, huh? Yeah, her name's Sarah Gold. She's gotta be some kind of genius to have invented the QDE when she was just a teenager. I'm in awe. I can't wait for Mike to get back from vacation. I bet their working together will be quite exciting to see."

"Michael resigned," he said. "Part of my agreement with Hosgrove is to help convince him to come back."

Carole stopped walking and stared up at him. "Son of a bitch! He told us Michael was on vacation. So have you talked to him yet?"

"No, he's disappeared. Hosgrove has someone searching for him now."

"Well, good thing we all kept handwritten notes. We should be able to work with Sarah and get this puppy back on line." Carole opened the door to the lab.

"Puppy?"

"Yeah, it's a figure of speech. I meant the QDE," Carole said. "Anyway, it's not too impressive now. As you can see, it's in pieces. So, assuming we will be able to make it work again, you will want to be the one to retrieve your son, no doubt."

"I can't go back," he said. "Michael sent Dr. Parvic an email stating that I can't go back to my time because I would then exist twice and the consequences would be dire. He thinks that not only would I cease to exist now, but I would also cease to exist then."

TWENTY-SIX

"Cease to exist?" Carole asked. She twisted a few strands of her dark blond hair around her index finger. "What happens? Do you spontaneously combust?"

Richard stared at the ceiling, recalling the email. "Michael didn't say exactly what would happen, but that I could not be in a time twice because that would cause my destruction in both times."

"Well, it's getting late and I have to pick up my son at day care. Why don't we review this on Monday? So, Dick, do you have any plans for the weekend?"

"I will be looking for a car. I just got my driver's license."

"Congratulations, that's great. Monday, then."

Richard drove Katrina's car into Ambion's lot the following Monday.

"So," Katarina said, "excited about getting your first car?"

"Aye." He broke into a grin thinking of the white Jeep Grand Cherokee he'd purchased with a portion of the settlement money. He would complete the transaction after work, once he had proof of insurance and a cashier's check. "I had no idea that buying a car could be this complicated."

"Surely you had to deal with much more in your time?"

"Yes, but not for one item. I believe I provisioned an entire army without as much paperwork as this car."

"Very funny, Richard. Just make sure you have insurance and a cashier's check when I pick you up tonight. The dealer will take care of the rest. Do you think you'll need a ride to the bank or anything?"

He pulled to the front of the building, and turned the car over to Katarina. "I'm sure. I'd planned to take the bus." He entered the building and met up with Phil on the way to his desk in Research.

"Morning, Dick. Check in with Carole. She wants to see you."

He went directly to her office and tapped on the open door.

"Come in," Carole said. "Did you have a good weekend?"

"Yes, thank you. I hope you did as well."

"Um-hum. Okay. See these papers?" Carole pointed to a folder on her desk. "This is the inventory of all the different parts we used for the QDE. The items that aren't checked off need to be replaced."

The top sheet listed at least thirty items. Richard guessed there were about two hundred sheets in the stack. "Does every sheet have this many items?"

"Oh no, just the bit that's stapled together," Carole said, picking up the top few sheets. "The rest are the individual purchase orders for the equipment. We need to replace some of these items, the ones that got damaged or spent when we ran the QDE."

"Is that why it is in pieces in the lab?"

"Yup. Now for the bad news. I'll need a spreadsheet for all these parts that need to be replaced. I'll work with you on it, so you'll see how to do it. But first, I have a laptop for you."

They worked together until he felt comfortable with the application. It wasn't that different from requisitioning armaments and materials for some of the campaigns he had run, if you discounted the technology. Instead of ordering weapons and armor, he now ordered parts for the QDE. And while these parts were completely alien to anything he'd used in the past, still, they were just parts.

Phil came into the area shortly after lunch. "Are you ready to work in the lab?"

"Yes." He held the spreadsheet out to Phil. "Carole said that we will be able to get the missing information from the equipment?"

"Uh-huh, let's go to the lab, and I'll demonstrate," Phil said.

Phil showed him how the room was organized when they entered. What appeared to be a chaotic mess earlier was systematically organized by function. Unfortunately, the spreadsheet was sorted alphabetically by manufacturer and then by part number. He penciled a function column in the margin.

As they sorted through components at the back of the lab, Carole came in with Hosgrove and a woman whom Richard had not seen before. Where everyone else wore casual clothing, this woman had on a silky, plum-colored suit. The skirt graced the smooth curve of her hips and fell in a straight line to just below the knee. His eyes swept up past the jacket, its high collar brushing against the bottom of her auburn hair. Silver earrings dangled shyly, framing her long neck and contrasting with her milky complexion. When she smiled, he wanted it to be for him alone.

Jesú, she is beautiful. His pulse quickened.

"Phil, Richard, come here for a minute. I'd like you to meet Sarah Gold," Carole said.

He and Phil walked toward the lab's entrance. Carole said, "Sarah, this is Phil Miller, one of our principal engineers, and Richard Gloucestre. Richard just joined us last week."

"Nice to meet you, Sarah," Phil said, shaking her hand. "So you're the one responsible for this mess."

"Nice to meet you too, Phil. I guess I am, although it has grown some since I played with it." Sarah shook his hand and smiled. She turned slightly and extended her hand. "Pleased to meet you, Richard."

When he took her hand, breathed in the spice of her perfume and peered into her limpid violet eyes, he wanted this moment to last. It took him a second to find his voice. "It is my pleasure, Sarah."

Sarah smiled and blushed slightly before pulling her hand out of his.

"I can't wait to learn what you did to my initial design," she said. "It looks like quite a lot, if all these parts belong to it.

"A major piece of what we've done is in the software," Carole said. "A virus, ah, got past our firewall and, ah, attacked the server. We should go meet John Reye, the principal software engineer on this project."

He watched them walk out of the lab, but it was Sarah who held his full attention. He stood staring at the door for quite a few seconds after they were gone.

"Dick? What just happened there?" Phil asked. "I never saw anyone react like you did just now when you met Sarah."

Richard pinched the bridge of his nose and peered over his fingers at Phil. "I am not sure. Her eyes, did you see her eyes? They are violet."

"Hmm, hard to miss, that's a rare eye color. Well, c'mon, we're almost done with this inventory. We should have enough for you to put the spreadsheet together and for Carole to give to Fortas tomorrow."

Richard drove his Grand Cherokee into work Tuesday morning. Even this modest level of independence felt good.

"Hey Dick, wait up," John said. "Is that your Jeep?"

"Yes, I just got it yesterday." He pocketed his keys, waiting for John to catch up to him.

"Nice car! I bet it feels good."

"It does."

They walked into the building together. "So, do you have your own apartment yet?" John asked.

"No, why do you ask?"

"I saw you scanning the bulletin board yesterday. I was just going to put this notice up for a friend of mine who wants a housemate," John said. "He's got a place near here."

He took the number John tore off the sheet. "Thank you, I will give him a call tonight."

"You might get his answering machine. Anyway, tell him that I sent you, and let me know if you're going to see it."

Richard went to his desk.

He was adding the function column to the spreadsheet when Sarah entered. "Morning, Richard. Have you seen Phil or John?"

He felt the heat of her body when she approached and her distinctive spice aroma infused his senses. He was glad to be sitting behind a desk. "Good morning, Sarah. I have not seen Phil yet, but John should be here soon. We walked in together."

"Oh good, I'm anxious to get started," she said. "So, are you new to the area, too? I think I'm going to like Portland. It's so different from New York City."

He saw John walking toward them. "Will you have lunch with me?" he asked before John could steal her away from him.

"Hi Sarah," John said. "I'm glad you're here, I've got a lot to review with you. Let me get my notes."

"Excellent, I can't wait to get my hands on it again," she said, and then turned back to Richard, giving him a brilliant smile. "Lunch would be great. I'll come back here around noon."

He watched her leave and sat staring at the spot where she had stood just a few moments before. He forced himself to resume his task.

A couple of hours later, he took the printed version to Carole. "I believe this is complete." He placed it on her desk.

"Very good," she said, studying the document. "I see you've added a function column."

"Yes, that is how the components are sorted in the lab."

"That's going to be very useful for us, internally. But it's not something that Fortas needs to know. I'll show you how to set it up for him later after I've reviewed what you have here," she said. "How far along are you on getting your GED?"

"I just started the process. Dr. Parvic thinks I should be able to complete it in two months, and then I will be able to start the college-level courses."

"And what do you think, Richard? Now that you've seen what's required."

"I have more than the basic skills. My biggest concerns are my lack of knowledge in the sciences and your culture."

"Well, don't hesitate to ask me, John, or Phil, any questions in that regard. I, for one, want to see you find your place in this society," she said. "I'm curious, how did you manage to get a birth certificate and one with your own name?"

"I must legally change my name. It won't be official for another month or so. A friend of Dr. Parvic's helped me get a birth certificate."

Carole pointed past Richard through the doorway. "You have company. Sarah's standing by your desk. Stop back after lunch."

He went back to his desk.

"Hi Richard," Sarah said. "I saw you talking with your manager. Is this a good time, or do you want to postpone lunch 'til tomorrow?"

"I can go now. Where would you like to eat?"

"I can't take a lot of time, someplace fast."

Carole recommended a deli that was a five-minute drive from Ambion. Richard guided Sarah to his Jeep and held the door for her.

"Thanks," she said. "Nice car, it smells new."

"I just got it yesterday." He got behind the wheel and handed her the directions that Carole had scribbled down. His body tingled when his hand brushed Sarah's arm, and he noticed her face redden. He was thrilled to be this close to her, even if her only words were to tell him when to take a left or a right turn.

He parked the Jeep, and they entered the brightly lit deli. Immediately, odors from the pickles and breads and cold cuts made his mouth water. The sandwich counter ran half the length of the deli, with some tables to the side and more places to sit in the back. He got in line for the sandwiches while Sarah found an empty table.

"What is New York City like?" he asked once they were seated. "I have never been there."

"Crowded, hectic, and expensive. It's a fabulous city to live in if you have the money. It has so much to offer, but I didn't live in the city," Sarah said and then took a bite out of her Reuben.

"Where did you live?"

"Umph," she swallowed. "Syosset, Long Island. It's about thirty miles from Manhattan. It's not a bad place to live, but it was time for me to move."

"Why do you say that?"

"Personal reasons, but I had to sell my house after my divorce, and then when I got the opportunity to work on my invention, I jumped at the chance," she said. "So what about you, where are you from? You don't sound like you're from here."

He chewed on his turkey sandwich before answering. This was a question that came up frequently enough that he had a pat answer based on the origin of Eric's birth certificate. "I'm from this little remote community not too far from here. I did not have electricity or telephones."

"No kidding? I can't imagine not having a computer these days, let alone such basic conveniences. It must have been hell. So, are you married?"

"I was, my wife died."

"I'm very sorry, was it long ago?"

He cast his eyes down before answering, not wanting her to see his pain. "Yes, but it feels like it just happened."

"Well, that puts a whole new perspective on my divorce. He left me for another woman and I was furious," Sarah said. "But I think I'd rather that than what you went through."

"Do you have any children?"

"Two girls. They were devastated when he left. I can forgive him for what he did to me, but never for what he did to them."

"Please tell me about them."

"Emma's seven, she just started second grade, and Mary is five, but I won't be able to get her into Kindergarten until January." Her expression changed from a scowl when talking about her ex-husband, to a bright smile now that she was talking about her daughters. "Do you have any children?"

"I had a boy, but he died before my wife did."

She clasped her strong hand over his and squeezed. "I am so very sorry, Richard. I can't imagine what you have gone through, but it had to have been hell."

His heart beat faster when she touched him. He held her hand in both of his for as long as he dared. He didn't want to let go. "Thank you, Sarah."

"Oh, look at the time. I really have to get back. I wish we weren't ending lunch on such a downer." Sarah stood and picked up her tray.

It wasn't until he was driving back to Ambion that he risked speaking. He watched the road. "Sarah, I would like to take you to dinner sometime this week."

"I would like to see you, too, Richard. But I can't leave my girls alone in the house, and I don't know anyone who will babysit."

"I will take them to dinner as well."

"Oh, be still my heart. A man who not only wants to see me, but my children as well." Sarah laughed. "Yes, I'd like that a lot. How does Wednesday sound?"

"Wednesday sounds good. Tonight would sound better."

She laughed. "I'm afraid it'll have to wait a day."

TWENTY-SEVEN

On his drive home, Richard thought about Sarah and her children. When they had arrived back at Ambion, she had shown him a photo taken the year before of her and daughters. Mary, her five-year-old, was a pretty girl with a halo of black curly hair surrounding a tanned, round face. She had dark eyes. Emma had long, flame-red hair and a freckled, pale complexion. She reminded him a little of his son, Edward.

He missed her driveway, and had to go to the stop sign at the end of the block in order to turn around. He realized he could not remember one detail about the drive.

Ever since he'd lost Anne, he'd despaired of ever being so emotionally stirred. But all that had changed when he met Sarah. She didn't resemble Anne, and for that he felt grateful. He would be less apt to compare them. He knew that would be unfair, but would he be able to avoid doing so?

Children! He longed for his.

He parked the jeep in the driveway and went into the house. "Katarina," he said, "where are you?"

"In the living room."

He spotted her sitting in the armchair across from the sofa. She set the newspaper down on the glass and rosewood end table, while he sat down on the edge of the sofa.

"I met a woman at work yesterday," he said. "She's the one who invented the device that brought me into this time— Michael's replacement."

"So Hosgrove was able to find her, that's excellent." Katarina shifted in the chair and placed her reading glasses on top of the newspaper. "Does she know who you are?"

"I have been asked not to tell her, but…" He sighed.

"But what? And why can't you tell her?" she asked.

"According to Hosgrove, if she can't figure out how the device was modified, then she'll not stay with the company."

She grimaced. "That seems rather draconian. You'd think he'd want to do the opposite. But you were about to say something else."

He nodded. "I took her to lunch today, and I'm taking her and her two daughters to dinner tomorrow."

"What's her name? Is she a widow?"

"Sarah. She's divorced."

"Divorced?" Katarina arched an eyebrow. "Will that be a problem for you?"

He hadn't considered the implications. "I haven't given it much thought." It would not be the first time that he'd need papal dispensation. Although Anne had been a widow at sixteen, the issue there was one of affinity. Not only was Anne his first cousin, once removed, but also his brother George had married her sister, Isabel. No one today could be that closely related to him. One corner of his mouth quirked up.

Katarina cocked her head. "Did I say something funny?"

"Hmm? No, I was just thinking." His smile got broader as he reflected on the direction their conversation and his thoughts had taken. *Dispensation*. Was he thinking of marrying Sarah? He was strongly attracted to her, but in truth, they had only talked for a short time.

"So, what can you tell me about her children?"

"She showed me a photograph taken last year. Emma, her seven-year-old, takes after Sarah with her red hair and pale skin. I suppose Mary, her five-year-old, looks more like her father. She has black curly hair and darker skin tones."

"I'm really happy for you, Richard. I'm happy you've found someone to care about that way."

"I hope I'll continue to feel that way. I'm anxious to meet her children. I do miss mine a great deal."

"Not just Edward?"

"Of course not just Edward. I miss John and Katherine, but not with the same intensity. They didn't die on me. I know they are dead now, but it doesn't feel that way to me."

"What you did for them, that was quite unusual, even for today."

"They were my children, too. I hated it when some men would take advantage of women who were powerless, force themselves upon them and then not acknowledge their own children." The muscles in his jaw stiffened as he remembered cases he had judged. He also remembered with satisfaction how he'd find in favor of the woman, much to the chagrin of the more powerful man.

"I shouldn't have mentioned that. I've made you tense up. Let me massage your neck." Katarina walked behind the sofa. Her thumbs pressed into the nape of his neck as she kneaded the muscles along the collarbone. "You even gave John a title."

"Yes." He relaxed. "I made him Captain of Calais. I loved them, too." Even as he said that, he realized he favored Edward. Neither John nor Katherine complained. But he should have been less partial.

"What was going on with your niece, Elizabeth? There were many rumors that you meant to marry her."

He jumped up, his shoulders as tense as before. "Why are you bringing that up? You know it isn't true, or do I have to declare how I never intended to marry her to you as well?" He glared at her.

"Look...I'm sorry. You're right. I didn't mean it that way. All I can say is you're doing exactly the right thing with Sarah by taking her girls out, too."

Richard didn't need the alarm to get up the next morning. He was eager to take Sarah and her daughters out to dinner that evening.

He awakened several times during the night, and now, at 4:30 A.M., he felt it futile to go back to sleep. He threw on some sweats and went outside for a run.

When he first arrived in the twenty-first century, he was astounded by how people demanded so little of their bodies. He'd been a soldier and he'd had to ride hard while wearing fifty pounds of armor and wielding a battle-ax, his weapon of choice.

When he wasn't campaigning, he'd maintained his fitness through more pleasant diversions, such as dancing, hunting, and riding. He'd watched his brother—a magnificent man at six foot four—grow fat and dissolute. Richard would not allow it to happen to him.

So, at twenty of five, he dashed out of the house into the late September chill. He ran.

"Sarah," he said her name aloud, for the pleasure of its sound. His breath, visible under the streetlights, puffed out in white clouds.

Halfway through the run, it started to drizzle, a cold, penetrating rain. Every nerve in Richard's body vibrated with life. He reveled in it.

He returned to Katarina's house exhilarated, impatient to begin the day's activities.

While his laptop was booting up, Richard walked over to the control room for the QDE, hoping to find Sarah. He found John Reye in front of the QDE's monitor instead. "Good morning. Is Sarah here?"

John turned away from the computer. "Oh, hi Dick. I haven't seen her yet. I'll ask her to call you when she gets in."

"Thank you."

When he got back to his desk, he found that not only was the phone's message light on, but the login prompt was waiting for him to sign in. Electronic leashes, that's what Phil had called them. He had a momentary yearning for his no-tech world.

The message was from Linda, requesting that he come to Hosgrove's office at his earliest convenience. He signed onto his laptop before going down.

He walked in, closing the office door after Hosgrove signaled him to enter.

"Richard, sit down," Hosgrove said. "I have a name of a therapist for you. Someone who may be able to help you."

"Does he know of my peculiar situation?"

"No, but I've thought of a way you can speak about it. We always used code names in the army. Every service does it. So a battle that took place somewhere in Somalia, to use a recent example, could go under the code name Redemore."

"You are saying that I can use the real names that I am familiar with and just say they are code names?" Richard asked.

"Exactly. You don't even have to give any locations or time frames, just say it's still classified."

"And you think that I should speak to this person."

"I can only say that I wish I hadn't waited so long to go myself," Hosgrove said.

He stood and took the card from Hosgrove and put it in his pocket. "Thank you." He turned to leave.

"This survival guilt," Hosgrove said, "is a tough nut to crack. I never got over it, but at least now I can live with it."

"I will contact this therapist," he said. "But know you have helped me." He returned to his desk.

He saw he had another message when he got back to his desk, this one from Sarah. He located her in the control room, working with John, both hunkered over the screen, studying columns of numbers.

He cleared his throat. "Ah, Sarah, is this a bad time?"

She turned around and stepped toward him, a smile lighting her face. "John, excuse me for a minute, I'll be right back."

Richard spoke as soon as they were in the hallway. "Would you like to have lunch with me as well?"

Sarah tugged at her SUNY sweatshirt. "I can't. I'm gonna have to work through lunch, so I've brown-bagged it today."

That disappointed him, but at least he'd see her tonight. "Shall I pick you and your daughters up around six?"

"That sounds good," she said. "I really have to go. See you at six." Sarah returned to the screen and resumed poring over the numbers with John.

Richard was nervous about seeing Sarah, despite Katarina's assurances. And it was raining, not the nice gentle, spring rain that he loved to feel on his skin, but a penetrating, autumn rain that further darkened the sky.

Getting to Sarah's rented house near Laurelhurst Park was straightforward until he turned off Thirty-ninth onto Hassalo. Then he missed the turn onto Floral Park. He had to find a place to turn around, a tricky proposition because of the narrow-curved streets and heavy rain. Although not quite dusk, the dense clouds afforded little light on the tree-lined streets. He pulled into her driveway a few minutes after the hour.

In the seconds it took him to run up to her porch and ring the bell, the rain had soaked his hair and jacket.

"C'mon in, Richard," Sarah said, opening the door. "Let me get you a towel. I can't believe how hard it's raining."

Her auburn hair curled under her chin, stopping halfway to her shoulder. Small, silver earrings winked out through the curls. She turned before he was ready to stop gazing into her violet eyes.

He followed her to the back of the house, inhaling the scent of exotic spices he'd come to associate as hers.

"Excuse the boxes," she said. "I haven't had time to unpack everything."

She'd changed from her more casual work attire to a black cashmere sweater and light-gray wool slacks, emphasizing the curve of her hips. He shoved his hands in his pockets. It was still too soon to touch her.

They passed a modest room with a desk tucked into the far corner near a small window. Four tall, empty bookcases lined the back wall, waiting to receive the books that were packed in the boxes stacked in front. She handed him a small towel when they entered the kitchen.

He watched her two girls, while rubbing his hair with the towel. They sat unquietly at the kitchen table. Mary swung her feet back and forth under the table. Her sneaker glanced off her sister's calf.

"Ow," Emma cried. "Make her stop." She struck her hand out and grabbed her sister's knee.

"You're hurting me! Let go," Mary said.

"Behave, both of you!" Sarah rolled her eyes skyward. "Now I want you to say hello to this nice man. Richard, these are my daughters. Emma, the whiner, and Mary, the imp." She squeezed Mary's shoulder.

"Ma," Emma whined, "that's not fair. Mary kicked me."

"I'm sorry," Mary said into her chest. "I didn't mean to."

A smile spread on his lips. After five hundred years, children were still children.

"If you want to leave now after seeing this display, I won't blame you in the least."

He was dumbfounded that Sarah should even suggest this. "I would not dream of doing that." He turned to her daughters and bowed slightly, "The pleasure is all mine."

They giggled.

"Did you make a reservation for us?" Sarah asked.

"No, why do you ask?"

"I'm not sure I feel like going out in this weather. Would you be opposed to my making dinner? I have the fixings for a frittata."

"I will defer to your preference," he said. "I have never eaten a frittata. What is it?"

"It's basically an omelet with vegetables and cheese. But instead of folding it over in the frying pan, you stick it under the broiler until the cheese browns."

"It sounds quite good."

"Okay girls, you know the drill. Get the table ready. So Richard, why don't you take your jacket off and stay awhile? There're hooks over by the door where you can put it."

He put his jacket on the coat hook, and she started cooking. He felt a tug on the left cuff of his oxford shirt, and glanced down to see Mary staring up at him. Her curly, black hair framed her round face.

"How do you know Mommy?"

"We work at the same place. We met when she started, Monday."

Emma walked up to him on the right.

He realized just how much he missed having children present, now that Sarah's were so close.

Emma bent her head so that her long, red hair obscured her freckled face. "What do you do?" She spoke to her shoes.

He wondered how he could answer them honestly without giving himself away.

"Are you an inventor like Mommy?" asked Mary.

"Girls," Sarah said. "Stop bothering him and get the table ready."

"They are not bothering me. To answer your questions, Mary and Emma, I am not an inventor. I support people such as your mother by administering those details they do not have the time for."

"Or the inclination," Sarah said, winking at Richard. "Emma, Mary—I really need you to get the table set now."

"Okay," Emma said. She walked to a cabinet and pulled a drawer open. "Ma, where're the forks?"

"Emma! You're staring right at them."

"Oh—yeah."

He sat down at the table. "Do you have a lot of family back in New York?"

"Some, but it seems half have moved away. I guess it was my turn now," she said. "My mom's parents retired to Florida, and my dad's parents are in Arizona. My parents now live in Rochester, New York, but I don't think they'll stay there once they retire."

"Why do you think that?"

"Besides the rotten weather, I think they'll probably split most of their time between Florida and Arizona."

She put the frying pan under the broiler. "It'll be ready in a minute or two."

As soon as Sarah served the meal and sat down to join them, Emma asked, "Do you think Grandma and Grandpa will come here?"

"Oh, I'm sure they'll visit. I don't know if they will want to live here, though."

"Mom?" Mary said, tugging at Sarah's shirt. "Can I watch TV?"

"After you finish dinner, young lady." She turned toward Emma. "Have you done all your homework?"

"Mmm," Emma grunted.

"Is that a yes or a no?"

"Yes, Ma."

"Don't get smart with me. Have you done all your homework?"

"Yeah," Emma said, sighing. "Can I watch TV now? I'm full." She pushed her plate, food half-eaten, to the center of the table.

"Do you feel all right, Emma? You've hardly eaten your dinner."

Emma squirmed away from her mother's hand as Sarah reached for her forehead. "I'm okay, Ma. I don't want anymore. It's too spicy."

That complaint surprised him. He thought the dish was bland. But then, he thought most food he had in this century was uninteresting.

Mary pushed her cleaned plate away. "I'm done. Can I watch TV?"

"All right," Sarah said. "Do you want dessert? I have chocolate ice cream."

"Yeah, can we have it while we're watching TV?"

They left the room when Sarah nodded. She stood, fetched the ice cream scoop, and turned to him. "I bet you're sorry you didn't leave sooner. They really get cranky around this time, and I'm not much better."

This was the second time she'd made reference to his leaving. Was she sorry he came? "I'll leave if you want me to, but I am enjoying this time with you and your children. I miss my old life."

Sarah stared at him, mouth open. "Oh no! I didn't mean that. I want you to stay. I'm being an idiot."

He shook his head, relieved by Sarah's confession. "I think I am nervous as well."

She got the ice cream out of the freezer. "Would you like some dessert?"

"Ah, not right now, thank you," he said. "How do you like working at Ambion?"

"It's exciting but I'm a bit overwhelmed." She picked up two bowls. "Hold that thought, I'll be right back." On returning to the kitchen, she continued, "I never thought I'd get the chance to work on my project after I turned it over to Westinghouse eighteen years ago. So I'm thrilled to be working on it again."

"Why did you give it to Westinghouse?"

"That's how the science award works. I got money to go to college, and Westinghouse got my invention. It was a gamble on their part. In this case they lost, because they were never able to use it."

"But Ambion used it."

"I know," Sarah said, frowning. "I've been studying the project team's notes these past couple of days, but I don't yet see what they did. From what I can gather at this point, is that you can't make matter on the molecular level jump from one physical location to another. It destroys itself in the process."

"I don't understand."

"Have you studied quantum mechanics or read anything on the concepts?"

"No."

"Ah, then it's going to be a stretch for you, but I'll try to explain it as best I can in layman's terms. On the most basic level, it's the study of the state of a system at each point in its history. Now it gets really interesting when you examine things on the subatomic level."

"I'm afraid that I don't even have the knowledge for you to explain things to me in layman's terms. I don't know what subatomic is."

"Would you like to know?"

"Yes, but I don't want to impose. Instead of taking you out to dinner, you have made it, and now you are giving me a science lesson."

"Nonsense, I love doing this. Anyway, I need to get some paper and a pencil. I can't talk without drawing pictures. Be right back."

While Sarah drew her pictures and explained the basics of Quantum Mechanics, Richard found concentrating on the science difficult. Her closeness made his heart race. He longed to embrace her, to be intimate, but instead, he interrupted her discourse with questions. He wondered if she detected his ardor.

She put the pencil down and turned toward him. "So, Richard, is it as clear as mud now?"

He chanced brushing her jaw with his fingers. "I think I understood a good deal of what you told me. You are a very good teacher."

She wrapped her fingers around his, and pressed his palm against her cheek. "Thanks. But I need to put the girls to bed now. Excuse me."

He followed her into the living room where they were sprawled out on the floor watching the television. Sarah walked before them, blocking the screen. "Emma, Mary, time to go to bed. Turn off the TV now."

"Ah, Ma, it's only eight thirty." Emma wriggled to the side, craning her head around her mother.

"Never mind that. I want you to get ready now." Sarah held her hand out. "The remote, please."

"Will you at least read to us?"

"Oh honey, all our books are still packed. It will have to wait until tomorrow."

"Why don't I tell them a story, Sarah?"

"Oh, please, Ma, please," Mary said.

"That'd be wonderful! Thanks."

Richard waited in the living room while Sarah put her daughters to bed. He was glad for the chance to tell them a story and to be among children and with a woman who stirred him.

He sorely missed these pleasures since he'd lost his son and wife.

"Are you sure you want to do this?" Sarah asked from the archway.

"I'm quite sure." He followed her back to the bedroom. A small nightstand separated the twin beds, where Emma occupied the bed to the right, and her sister, Mary, the one to the left.

He cast about for a place to sit and saw a thick cushion by the still-empty dresser. He moved the cushion nearer the beds.

"Do you want a chair?" Sarah asked and then chewed on her thumbnail. "It'll only take me a minute to get one from the kitchen."

"The cushion will do me," he said and winked at her two girls tucked in under their quilts. He sat and crossed his legs. Sarah stood in the doorway watching.

"This is a story about a girl who would become the Queen of England, and her young man, who would be king. This happened a long, long time ago, when girls and women were made to marry men they didn't want or like, and men were made to marry to increase their family's power and wealth." He stopped himself from telling them that true to the mores of that time, the man was interested in the woman's inheritance and for the opportunity to weaken his older brother's power. Instead, he stretched the truth. "But it wasn't like that for this future Queen and King. They were in love and wanted each other very much."

"Once upon a time," Mary said, hugging her blanket. "I love fairy tales."

Emma rose up on an elbow. "Shut up, Mary!" She flopped back on her pillow and a puff of air escaped her lips. "What are their names?"

"We will call the girl, Anne, and the boy, Dickon."

Emma giggled. "King Dickon. That doesn't sound very royal."

Richard smiled. "Nor was he regal then. By today's standards, he was barely a man."

"Now you shut up, Emma! I want to hear the story."

He continued once they quieted.

"The story starts long before Dickon was king. Ned, the man who was king then, had promised Dickon that he could marry Anne—someday. He then sent Dickon out to do battle for him. When Dickon returned victorious, he learned Anne had been married to an enemy's son, Eduoard. Anne's father forced her to marry Eduoard because he, Ned, had gone against his scheme to ally England with France. King Ned could not keep his promise to Dickon."

"But you said Dickon and Anne got married?" Emma asked.

"They did, but not before they had to endure many hardships," Richard said. "Dickon was furious when he found out, but there was little he could do. He felt like he had lost his life and his soul. Anne was only fourteen years old."

"Fourteen is too young to get married," Emma said. "How old was Dickon?"

"It is now," he said. "They did not think it was too young back then. Dickon was eighteen.

"Two years later, Anne's husband tried to take the throne for himself. He was killed in battle, and Anne was left a penniless and childless widow."

"Was Anne in love with Eduoard?" Mary asked.

"She didn't love him, but she did not wish for him to die," Richard said. "Anne's sister, Isabel, was married to George, brother to both Dickon and King Ned. The sisters were very close to each other, and Isabel wanted to help Anne anyway she could. She convinced George to take Anne into their home.

"George had other plans for Anne, but he did not want to make his wife angry. He secretly plotted to separate Anne from his wife."

"Oh!" both girls cried together, and Mary added, "George is very mean!"

"But Isabel learned of her husband's scheming and knew every minute that passed in George's home was a danger to Anne. She could not remain there even that night.

"Isabel secretly met with Anne in the chapel and told her of the danger she was in. Together they worked out a plan that would keep Anne in London, but safe from George. 'But what will I do and how will Dickon find me if you don't know where I am?' she'd asked of Isabel.

"This was a great risk they both were taking, but the greater danger was for Anne to remain and let George seal her fate. 'Have faith, my little sister,' Isabel had replied. She hung a wooden cross about Anne's neck. 'Wait a week or more and then send this cross to me. I'll get word to Dickon.' They clasped each other tightly one last time, before Isabel returned to her chambers. She had her attending lady send one of the maids to meet Anne. Isabel did not know, nor did she want to know, who would help Anne or where she would be taken.

"The maid brought Anne some clothes fitting for someone of low class, and together they escaped to London. She was brought to an Inn where she was disguised as a cook's maid. No one at George's estate knew where Anne was. The maid who helped Anne escape did not return to the estate.

"She toiled for several weeks in the kitchens, despairing that she would ever see her Dickon again. These were not like the kitchens you know. She didn't have hot and cold running water, refrigerators, and stoves. The food was cooked in the fireplace, and the water had to be hauled from wells. It was very hard on Anne." Richard grew quiet for a moment.

"What happened next?" Emma asked.

"After Anne fled, Dickon came to the castle for her. George gave him a sly smile and said that she had disappeared. He didn't know where she was. 'You'll never find her,' he had said. Dickon did not believe his brother. This was not the first time he had lied.

"How much he'd changed since they were children. Then, George had been his friend and protector, though only three years older. What had happened to him? He was as different from that boy as lead from gold. But, this was not the time to dwell on the past. He pushed past George and glimpsed Isabel cowering by the door. 'I will search your castles. I will find Anne.' He raced to his horse and left."

"Did he find her?" Mary whispered.

"He did, but not until after he had wasted weeks searching all of George's estates and had returned to his brother's home still seeking his love. George was not around and Isabel was then able to speak to him privately. She told him about how Anne had escaped, and how she had paid a maid to hide her in London. 'I do not know precisely where she is, but I can tell you where to begin looking.' As proof, she handed Dickon the wooden cross she had given Anne and whispered what the messenger had said. It was west of Greyfriars.

"Even with this information, it took nearly another two weeks before he found the house Isabel had described. He could only hope Anne was there. He asked the owner if he had a new girl and described her—tall and stately with chestnut hair and fair skin. When the owner remained silent and only stared at his feet, Dickon promised a reward, but the owner looked at him with fear."

"Was she there?" Emma asked.

Richard nodded. "Dickon learned George had discovered his wife's scheme and contrived to have the daughter of a London innkeeper in his charge be the one to spirit Anne away. He gave the daughter money to ensure Anne would never be found and threatened that if she were, he'd ruin her father. After that, Anne was never left alone to get a message out, or so they thought.

"Anne wasn't in the house, but had gone to the market with the owner's son and daughter. Dickon watched for her, his heart racing. Soon, he spotted three people approaching from the distance, struggling with a load of food. He ran up to them calling her name. She stopped walking for a moment, as if in a dream, and then she dropped what she was carrying and tried to run to him, but she was bound at the waist to the owner's son. She fell down in a heap, and Dickon was on them in an instant, sawing at the rope with his dagger to free her, while Dickon's men held the boy. As soon as he had freed Anne, he picked her up and wrapped her in his arms."

"Oh, that sounds so romantic." Emma sighed. "Did she cry?"

Romantic! He supposed it was. He hadn't expected his fondness for his childhood friend to turn to love, but when he saw how resourceful she'd been, his heart had softened. To marry for power and property had been common, but to get love as part of the contract was a miracle.

He glanced up and noticed three pairs of eyes staring expectantly at him. He drew in his breath and relived the moment. His eyes caught Sarah's.

"It was very romantic, and they both cried," he said. "When he could control his breath and his eyes cleared, he stepped back to get a good look at her and almost did not recognize her. She was dirty, because she did not have access to the baths she was used to, her chestnut hair was shoved under a dirty rag, and the wisps that strayed out were greasy and darkened with soil. She had lost so much weight that her clothes hung on her. But her large, liquid brown eyes held him, and he saw his Anne in those eyes.

"Shocked at how thin she was, he was sure she had been mistreated, but she assured him she had not. She was unused to working such long, hard hours, and they were as kind to her as they were able. He nodded to the owner, telling him not to worry about George, that he would make sure no harm came to them. Finally, he put her on his horse and they rode away. She nestled into his arms."

Richard stood. "Goodnight, Mary and Emma."

"Did they get married? What happened next?" Emma asked.

"They did marry a few months later, but that's another story, for another day."

He turned around and saw Sarah standing in the doorway smiling with tears in her eyes.

"That's a wonderful story, Richard. And I'm such a sap for romance." She pulled the door behind her, leaving it slightly open. As they walked toward the living room, Sarah stopped by the study and looked in.

He pressed against her, chest to back. He put his hands on her shoulders and nuzzled his cheek to hers. "Why did you stop here?"

"It occurred to me as I saw those boxes, you wouldn't have told the story if I had unpacked them. I loved that story and the way you told it. I cried for joy when Dickon found Anne. Thank you."

He wished he could tell her more—tell her he was Dickon. Instead, he said, "Would you like me to help you unpack these books?"

TWENTY-EIGHT

Sarah held the last book to be shelved in both hands. "Thanks. I didn't know when I'd get to these books. They were a bit daunting."

Richard relieved her of the book and placed it on the shelf. He took both her hands in his, stroking them with his thumbs. "It's been a while since I have had these feelings for anyone besides my wife. You have awakened something in me."

"Kiss me," she whispered.

She pulled his head toward her mouth, and his entire body came alive when they kissed. She felt so different from Anne— her quiet depths where he'd lost himself. Sarah was alive with currents and eddies that resonated in him. He sensed her blood coursing through her veins, her pulse quickening, her body responding to his, unlike anything he had ever experienced. He held her close.

"I want to know you," he murmured. Her thick, auburn hair brushed against his cheek and tickled his nose.

"Me, too." She pulled back a few inches. "I swore I'd never get involved with anyone else when my ex dumped me. I'm afraid for my girls."

He longed to hold her, to kiss her, to know her intimately. When Anne had died, he'd shut himself off from the world for three days. At the end, when he had emerged, he'd had to resume the business of governing, and that meant finding another consort. But it was to provide an heir, not for love.

Somehow, Sarah had found his heart. He loved her, was in love with her. He gently pulled her to him.

"I swear I would never do anything to hurt you or your daughters."

"I believe you," she said, running her fingers over his eyebrows.

He cupped his hands behind her ears and pulled her face to his. Her kiss was soft. He felt her tongue briefly on his teeth, inviting him to explore her mouth. They kissed, harder, more eagerly.

Her eyes were open and her pupils expanded until all he could see was a purple rim around their blackness. *Sarah.* He let her name surround him as he surrounded her with his arms.

She took his hands in hers and held him away from her body. "Oh God! Please wait. I can't now."

"I'll wait." He swallowed and willed his heart to stop racing. "May I take you and your daughters out to dinner tomorrow night?"

"Yes, I'd like that. I'd like that very much."

"Good morning," Katarina said.

Richard poured a mug of coffee for himself and thought about Sarah. He was suddenly aware that Katarina had asked him something. He hadn't heard anything beyond her greeting. "I'm sorry, I wasn't listening."

She chuckled. "I said, I heard you singing in the shower. Things must have gone well last night."

He took a sip of his coffee. "They did."

"How come the suit and tie? I thought this department was more casual."

"It is," he said. "I was thinking of taking Sarah and her daughters to Morrison's. Maybe I'll be able to finish my dinner this time."

Katarina smiled. "So why are you taking her out to such a fancy restaurant?" She sipped her coffee.

"I haven't felt like this about a woman since Anne. I'm going to ask her to marry me."

Katarina choked on her coffee. "Richard! Aren't you being...a little...hasty?" She coughed.

He jumped to his feet and thumped Katarina on her back. "Are you all right?"

She held her hand up and nodded her head. "Yes, I'm fine. It's good that she wants to see you again so soon, but you hardly know each other."

"I know my heart, and I want a mother for Edward."

"Oh Richard, I don't know where to begin. There are so many reasons why you've got it all wrong. Will you hear me out, or won't it make any difference?"

"I'll listen," he said, sitting down. "But it might not make any difference."

"I haven't met the woman, but I know I'd never rush into a commitment as serious as that. Two or three days is not enough time, not even for you."

"I don't agree. I know we are right for each other."

She sighed. "Edward doesn't know his mother is dead. He might resent finding you with a complete stranger as your wife. At the same time, he must adjust to living in very strange times."

"He will have me and I have had to adapt. I'll be able to help him."

"You're determined, aren't you?"

He grinned. "Yes, I am."

"Okay, then play it smart. Give her a way so she doesn't have to refuse you, but can take the time she'll probably need to make this sort of decision."

"What would you have me say?"

"Instead of asking her to marry you, tell her what your intentions are. Ask her to tell you what her decision is when she is ready to make it. And then don't pressure her."

"I'll think about that."

"Also consider that you shouldn't wait too long before you tell her who you really are," she said. "So, what's Sarah like?"

"She has the most beautiful violet eyes."

"And?"

"And she is kind and very intelligent. I'm hopeful that she will be able to get the device to work even if Michael cannot be found."

"I hope so, too. But what does she look like? Or did you only see her eyes?"

Richard closed his own and smiled. "I think she is beautiful, but I don't know how to describe her."

"Well, can you start with some obvious things like her hair color, how tall she is, does she resemble Anne?"

"Sarah doesn't resemble Anne except for her fair skin. Anne had freckles, but Sarah doesn't. Anne hated her freckles, she saw them as flaws, but I adored them." He sighed. "Sarah has auburn hair. She's shorter than Anne—"

"How tall was Anne?"

He smiled, remembering how she'd slouch to make him appear taller. But she was a Neville. "About an inch taller than me."

"Wow," Katarina said. "I'd have thought she was a good deal shorter from the coronation illustration in the Rous roll. Sorry, I interrupted—you were saying about Sarah?"

"I think she's around five-foot five or six." He ran his fingers along the length of his nose. "Her nose is a little long, like mine, and I think she broke it. It has a bump right here, and it's a bit crooked." His fingers went to the bridge of his nose.

"Maybe she broke it playing some sport. Is she athletic?"

"Yes," he said. "I'm still getting used to seeing women in sports."

"She sounds very nice. I'd like to meet her."

"Can Richard tell us another story, Ma?" Emma asked.

"It's too late for that tonight. Some other time if that's all right with him."

"It would be my honor to," Richard said.

"Are you Dickon?" Mary asked, peeking around her mother.

His face grew hot. "Wha—"

"Mary! You are so stupid," Emma said, standing with her hands on her hips and feet spaced apart. "I bet it happened before TV even. Didn't it?"

He winked at Sarah and smiled. "Yes, it was before TV, even. That story took place over five hundred years ago."

"Honestly Mary, I don't know where you get your ideas from sometimes," Sarah said. "I'll be right back—make yourself comfortable."

He scanned the books they had put away the night before and found several books by Isaac Asimov. He picked one out at random and flipped through it. He was still standing by the bookcase when Sarah returned.

"Thank you so much for that lovely dinner. The food was wonderful," she said. "What're you reading?" Sarah scrunched down to read the book's title.

"I was just looking at this," he said, putting *The Genetic Code* back on the shelf. "There is something that I must ask you. Let us go into the kitchen to talk."

"Sure." She preceded him into the kitchen. "What's up?"

Faced with the opportunity to ask Sarah to be his wife, he suddenly felt unsure of himself. Katarina's cautionary words came back to him. "I have feelings for you that I thought I would never again have. I want to be with you forever."

He watched Sarah study him and then nibble on her index fingernail. He held his breath.

"I'm also feeling more for you than I would have expected. And the girls wouldn't stop talking about you all morning and then again when I picked them up this afternoon." She cocked her head and peered directly into his eyes. "I think you should breathe now."

His breath exploded out of him in a quick laugh. "Sarah, will you marry me?"

It was her turn to catch her breath. She let it out slowly. "We just met."

"I cannot stop thinking about you, Sarah. I want to be your husband and father to your children. I beg you to consider my plea."

"I feel more than I'd have expected," she said, frowning slightly. "But I need time. I can't answer you now. Will you wait and ask again? You might change your mind, you know."

"Take as much time as you need. I know my heart and I can't imagine anything that would cause me to change my mind."

Five weeks had elapsed since Richard was shot and he'd begun the medication regimen to rid the dormant tuberculosis from his system. The x-rays they took today showed the medication's efficacy. The lesion had shrunk. That he could see his lungs and bones without being cut into amazed him still. What the doctors of his day wouldn't have given for the tools available today.

As he headed for the door to leave, a stranger accosted him. "Dear God! You look so much like my brother. Who are you?"

He stared at a face that bore an uncanny resemblance to his own. "Richard, my name is Richard. I do not believe I know you."

"Tom Cleary. I'm sorry; it's just that you resemble Greg so much. We lost him two months ago. It's been especially hard on our Mom." Tom nodded toward a slender woman seated by the wall. She had her nose buried in a tissue.

"I am very sorry to hear that. You have my sincerest condolences," he said. "But what does it have to do with me?"

"Ah, probably nothing. It's just that the hospital can't seem to account for his remains to our satisfaction, and then when we saw you, we hoped that maybe the hospital had it wrong, that he had somehow recovered."

"I don't understand, Tom. Did you not bury your brother? You said it happened two months ago."

"No, see, that's the whole problem. Greg willed his body to science. He was in an auto accident, and when they said he was brain dead and there was nothing that could be done for him, we released his body. I know you can't possibly be him, but for a minute I had this wild hope they had made a mistake."

He stood awkwardly by Tom, wanting to leave, but not knowing quite how to gracefully exit. "I am not your brother, Tom."

"I know. Would you mind saying a couple of words to my Mom? You don't sound like my brother, and I think that will help ease her mind. I understand if you don't have the time."

"I'll be happy to speak to your mother," he said. "But I do have to leave immediately after."

Tom led him to the woman sitting on the bench. "Mother, this is Richard."

He sat down on the bench next to Tom's mother and held her hand in his. "I am very sorry for your loss, Mrs. Cleary." It took all his control not to call her "mother." "I, too, have lost a son, and it's the worst thing that has ever happened to me."

She studied Richard, making him uncomfortable. "Thank you. I am very sorry for your loss. May God be with you."

"Richard," Carole said, "I just got a call from Hosgrove's secretary. He wants both of us to meet with him as soon as possible. Can you do it now?"

He had just arrived at Ambion, having lost the entire morning to the hospital tests and was still a little shaken from his encounter with the Cleary's.

"I can go now, Carole. Do you know why he wants to see us?"

"Nope, Linda didn't say, and he didn't request that we bring anything in with us."

They walked down to Hosgrove's office together. Linda sent them in as soon as they got to her desk and closed the door behind them when they walked into the office.

"Carole, I have a confession to make," Hosgrove said. "I lied to you about Michael being on vacation. He actually quit."

Carole nodded.

"You aren't surprised are you?" Hosgrove shifted his gaze from Carole to Richard. "Well, I guess I should have asked you not to say anything. It's my fault. Anyway, we found him, and I'd like both of you to meet with him and get him to come back here."

"Where and when do you want us to go?" Carole asked.

"Amherst, Massachusetts. He got some kind of lab assistant position at the University of Massachusetts. I want both of you to leave Sunday afternoon to meet with him Monday, and then return here Monday."

"That would be very hard for me to do," Carole said. "I need to arrange for my husband to take my son to day care and pick him up. I don't know if I can do that today. Why don't you and Richard go? Why do you need me?"

"I think it would be better if I didn't go," Hosgrove said. "Richard, are you able to clear your schedule?"

"Yes, I'll be able to go whenever Carole is able."

"If that's all," Carole said, "I'll try to reach my husband now to see if I can arrange it."

Hosgrove nodded. "Richard, don't go just yet. I want to review some things with you."

He sat back down.

Hosgrove waited for Carole to shut the door before he began speaking. "As you know, we haven't been able to locate any documents to corroborate what you said regarding your nephews."

"I have told you what I know," he said. "I can't go back and recreate those documents."

"Is it at all possible that they didn't make it out of the country?"

"What do you mean?" His stomach formed a knot. Had his careful planning for their safety gone horribly awry, and he was not told? "I received their letters, they were genuine."

"First," Hosgrove sucked in his breath. "I have another question. Were they removed at the same time?"

"No. Prince Richard was brought to Baynard's Castle first where he was prepared for his journey to Portugal. Prince Edward followed two days later. He was destined for Ireland."

"So you know with certainty they got as far as Baynard."

"Aye." He had corresponded with his mother, for he could not have gotten them out of the country in secrecy without her help.

Why were they never heard from after Henry took the throne?

"One would have thought there'd have been more evidence that they had survived if you did get them out," Hosgrove said.

Hosgrove was reading his mind! "However, I continued to receive letters from them, signed in their hand."

"Were the letters specific?" Hosgrove asked. "Were there things in them that you could say had to be written at the time and not before?"

He swallowed. Had he allowed himself to be duped into thinking his orders had been faithfully carried out? "I am no longer sure." He stood and paced in front of Hosgrove. "Both Brampton and Tyrell swore the boys had been removed to safety. Now I must recreate the letters in my mind."

"Take whatever time you need." Hosgrove stepped in front of Richard, blocking him. "Will you please stop pacing?"

"Sorry." He sat.

"Consider also, that Richard may have been safely removed, but Edward wasn't."

"Why do you say that?" he asked.

"Tyrell was executed the sixth of May, 1502, for having supported De la Pole's claim to the throne. It was reported that Tyrell confessed to the Princes' murders just before he was executed."

"I don't believe that confession." He had trusted Tyrell and knew him to be honorable. Yet, could he have known something that made him confess to murder? "According to my intelligence, Richard was safely on his way to Portugal when Tyrell went for Edward."

Hosgrove nodded. "Which brings me to the Perkin Warbeck controversy."

"Perkin Warbeck?" He knit his brows. "This name is new to me."

"Supposedly, he was with Brampton in Portugal," Hosgrove said. "He claimed to be Richard. I'd like you to do some research on him. Henry got Warbeck to confess he was an imposter, but no one knows if his confession was true or if he was the younger prince."

That would be a relief—to find solid evidence that at least one nephew had survived.

Hosgrove stood. "One other thing before you go. According to Carole and the others on her team, Sarah made her breakthrough discovery this morning and figured out what Michael did. I still want Michael back, but it may not be as urgent as we initially thought."

He could barely contain his joy. *I will be able to save Edward and Sarah will be at my side.*

Richard heard footsteps and glanced up at Sarah, her face was pale and her expression drawn. "My God! Has anything happened?"

"No-o," Sarah said, her expression changed to neutral. "Is there anywhere we can talk privately?"

He scanned the area. His office mates, Phil and John were in the lab, but there was no telling when they would return. Carole was in her office, and he didn't feel right about asking her for it. "Perhaps we could get a conference room if you think it is necessary."

"It's necessary. But why don't we take a walk outside instead?"

"All right." He walked over to Sarah and stopped at the entrance to his shared office. "After you." He bowed slightly as Sarah walked out into the hallway.

Once they were outside, Sarah stopped by a small maple about twenty feet from the building. "I've been piecing Michael's work together with what Carole's team did, and I've come to an incredible conclusion," she said, averting her eyes.

He drew his breath in and then let it out in a puff. "Evan mentioned you made your discovery sometime this morning." The sun hung low in the sky, directly behind her. He squinted.

"I can't believe I'm saying this, but it's the only conclusion that makes sense." She moved to her right. "I think Michael made a time machine out of my invention."

"That is what I have been told."

"And they went into the past," she said. "They brought an important historical person alive into this century."

He nodded.

"And you are…are the result?" Sarah gazed at him; her eyes were bright.

"Yes," he whispered.

She rushed through her questions. "When? What happened? Which Richard are you? You are one of the Richards, yes?"

"I will tell you true, but you must promise not to tell anyone. Too many already know," Richard said.

"I promise," she said. "But I think I'd find out anyway. I figured out the hard part."

"So you did. You know me as Richard III."

Sarah's hand flew to her mouth and she started chewing on a cuticle still red from a recent attack. He reached for her hands to hold them in his, but she pulled away.

"Does who I am bother you?"

"Yes," she said. "You have to understand, I grew up on Shakespeare and according to him, Richard had his nephews …children…murdered so he could be king. If for no other reason than that, I have to consider my daughters."

He momentarily squeezed his eyes shut, rubbing his temples with the tips of his fingers. "I didn't need to murder them to be king. They were illegitimate and could not inherit the title. Even if they weren't, I would not murder children. Please believe me."

"I want to believe you. Can you prove it?"

"I can prove they were bastards, but I can't prove they weren't murdered. Can you not believe what your eyes are telling you, that I am not deformed? I can assure you that I do not resemble that piece of fiction in character any more than I resemble that physical description."

"You've read the play?"

"I forced myself to," he said. "It is the vilest of lies if it is about me. Else it is a piece of pure fiction where any resemblance to persons living or dead is purely coincidental."

Sarah laughed. "I'm glad you can joke about it. That story you told my girls—that was real, wasn't it? Mary knew. You are Dickon."

"Aye. I'd like you to call me Dickon, in private." He reached for her shoulder, but she backed away.

"You may not want me to once you hear what I came to tell you about myself. I'm Jewish and I know enough about the history of that time to know the lies the Church promoted about Jews."

He put his hand on the maple to steady himself, stunned by her revelation. "But you have a daughter named Mary?"

"Mary's a good Jewish name," Sarah said. "I named her after my great grandmother in our tradition of using the names of dead ancestors."

"Does that mean you are a descendant of the Blessed Virgin?" he asked.

"Not necessarily. It means that we at least have a common ancestor."

"Oh."

"Richard?" she asked. "Does it bother you?"

"Shortly after I got here I saw a program on the Holocaust, and I was appalled that anything like that could happen. It forced me to examine my beliefs." He shook his head in disbelief. "Are you religious?"

"No, not at all. Does that make any difference?" she asked.

"I don't know. I wondered."

"Were you, are you devout?"

"Everything is different today. I was devout, but I don't know what to think now. But, I am bothered. It is difficult to overcome a lifetime of teaching. I'm sorry."

"Me too," she said, there was a slight quaver in her voice. "Please don't let the girls know. They adore you."

"I'm very fond of them. They won't know."

"Thanks. Um, Richard? Oh God! This is so hard," she said, biting her nails again. "I do care for you, but I think you and I ought to cool it, at least until we can sort this out. Do you think you can, er, get beyond it?"

He stared into her eyes. They were bright with tears. "I want to, Sarah. Dear God, I want to," he whispered. "And you, can you get beyond that vile play?"

She looked at her watch. "Oh no! It's later than I thought. I've got to pick them up now." She left, running to her car.

He smashed the side of his fist against the tree trunk. "Nooooo!" he groaned.

TWENTY-NINE

Richard watched Sarah disappear around a curve in the sidewalk heading toward the parking lot. He ran after her. When she opened her Saturn's door, he called out, "Sarah, wait!" He couldn't lose her now. There had to be a way.

She turned toward him. Her face was pinched and gray.

When he got closer, he could see she was crying. "I am so very sorry. I'm hurting you and I don't know what to do." His own tears were hot in his eyes.

Sarah sniffled. "I know." She reached up and wiped his cheek with her thumb. "I assume you don't want to come over tonight after this."

"I have lost everyone whom I ever loved. I can't stand to lose you." He wrapped his fingers around her hand and held her palm against his cheek. "I do want to see you tonight if you will have me, if you will give me a chance."

"I don't know what to say." She sat behind the wheel. "I need some time to think. You say you can't prove you didn't murder your nephews. What am I to believe?"

"Your heart." His voice was a whisper. "You said you had feelings for me. Was that a lie?"

Sarah's head was bent down so that her voice was muffled. He knelt in order to hear her better and to see her face, now hidden below her thick, auburn hair.

"I do have these feelings, but I listened to my heart before. I refused to believe the evidence before my eyes and now what do I have?"

"Two beautiful healthy daughters. You are so lucky to have them. I would give anything to have my son."

"And what about your wife, Richard? In the play you poisoned her. Do I have to worry about that, too?"

He blinked. He had forgotten about that lie. "Anne died naturally. She had consumption. Of that there is proof. Please, let me come over tonight to show you what I can prove."

She shook her head. "Uh-uh, I think it best if you didn't come. I can't think with you around."

He turned his head away and swallowed. He felt his will leaving him. "May I see you tomorrow as we had planned?"

"I don't know," Sarah said. "Call me later tonight and we'll talk. I can't think right now, I'm too upset."

He took her hand and held it between his. "Please give me a chance. Do not lock me out."

"If you can show me that you didn't poison your wife and show me doubts about your nephews' murders, then I'll consider giving you that chance." She pulled her hand out of his. "How much is my being Jewish going to bother you?"

In trying to defend himself against the historical lies, he had pushed this from his mind. Now he had to think about it. Despite wanting to see her, he conceded she was right. They did need some time apart.

"I will call you tonight," he said, standing up. "You have my word."

Do I listen to my heart, or do I obey the church?

Richard pulled into the driveway to Katarina's house and turned the ignition off. He rested his head against the backrest and closed his eyes.

Dear God! How do I prove to her I am not the monster Shakespeare created?

When he opened his eyes he saw Katarina coming toward the car. He got out and met her in the driveway.

"Richard! What's wrong? Has anything happened to Sarah?"

"No." His throat constricted. "But I need your help."

"I was about to make some dinner. Why don't you tell me what's going on while I prepare it?"

He followed her into the kitchen and sat down at the breakfast bar. "She knows who I am. Only, the reputation she knows is the one from the Shakespearean play."

"How did Sarah find out? Did you tell her?"

"She deduced how the device was used, and she asked me which Richard I was. She is acquainted with the play and wants me to prove that I did not murder my nephews or my wife."

"I think there's enough evidence to prove your wife died of TB."

"I did say I could prove that, but I don't think I can prove anything about the princes."

"I know, that's something that has puzzled historians for centuries. And now that you're here to tell us what happened, we can't corroborate your story."

When he'd destroyed the letters, he had thought it was necessary. How could he have predicted he would ever need them? "She did say she would consider seeing me if I could show enough doubt about my nephews."

"That might not be as hard to do as you think."

He leaned forward. What did Katarina know?

"Do you know anything about Perkin Warbeck?"

He shook his head. "The name is one I would expect to find in Brugges, not England. Did he have a connection to the princes after Bosworth?"

Her smile broadened. "He may have been the younger prince. Many people were convinced he was, including King James."

He needed evidence to show Sarah that the boys survived him. "If he were Prince Richard, then why do people today believe I murdered my nephews?"

"Because Henry captured and extorted a confession from Perkin before executing him. In the confession, Perkin claimed his father was the burgess of Tournai and that when a youth he was put into Edward Brampton's service. According to the confession, Perkin traveled with Brampton and his wife by ship to Portugal."

"Jesú! I put Richard in Brampton's care and sent him to Portugal for his safety. This cannot be coincidence."

"It's circumstantial, though. Once Henry got this confession, he was able to execute Warbeck for treason."

"It's much more than I had before. I hope it is enough."

"When are you going to see her again? I have a couple of books I can lend her. I'll mark the places of interest."

"I need to call her. I had planned to see her tomorrow. Perhaps with this information I may yet."

"Well," Katarina said. "At least drop the books off, and then maybe she'll be more inclined to let you hang around for a while. Do you want me to speak to her when you call her tonight?"

"Yes." He sat staring at the kitchen counter, unblinking.

"There's more, isn't there?" She put the paring knife down next to the carrots and folded her arms across her chest.

"She is Jewish."

"And it bothers you?" She arched an eyebrow. "I thought you understood that diverse religious viewpoints are tolerated here. And I thought you were more tolerant than most of your time as well."

"It would not bother me if I did not want her to be my wife or the mother of my children."

"That's something that you and Sarah will have to work out," she said. "I'm afraid that will be much harder to resolve than the lies about your past."

A food timer buzzed.

"Dinner's ready." Katarina put the final touches on the salad and set up two places at the dining room table.

"In my day, the church did not tolerate a mixed marriage." Richard picked at his food.

"In order to be married by a priest," she said, "both parties had to be Catholic. But the church has changed its attitude toward Jews. Pope John Paul II has condemned anti-Semitism and has done more to promote the Jewish-Catholic relationship than any Pope in history."

He stared at Katarina, wide-eyed. "He did?"

"The church has changed," she said. "I thought you would have looked into it by now."

"Does the church now bless a mixed marriage?"

"No. Both of you have to figure out how to deal with it."

"Perhaps I can get her to convert." He reasoned that it would remove all objections the Church would have. "The only Jews I knew had converted."

Katarina sighed. "How willing would you be to convert to Judaism?"

The suggestion that he should convert insulted him. He started to speak, but stopped before a sound escaped. Wasn't that what he would ask Sarah to do? Would that be any less insulting to her? He stared at his untouched plate of pasta.

"It cuts both ways, doesn't it? I think you should try to get over your prejudice."

"What do you mean, prejudice? I'm not saying Jews are evil. Sarah is not religious. I would not be asking her to give up her beliefs."

"Richard! How dare you think that just because she doesn't follow traditional Jewish practices that her beliefs aren't valid or that she has none."

He glowered at Katarina. "She said she is not religious."

"What difference does that make?" She grimaced. "Don't confuse religion with belief."

"What kind of nonsense is that? They are the same."

"They absolutely are not. You know I don't follow any traditional religious teaching."

"So you have told me."

"But I do have my own belief system, it's just not part of any traditional religious order. And even though I'm Christian and I do believe in Christ, I wouldn't and didn't raise my child Catholic."

"Is your ex-husband Catholic?"

"Yes."

"Did you have a Catholic wedding."

"No."

He pinched the bridge of his nose. "I will think on it. We have not discussed this; she has only told me she is Jewish. I'm worried my reputation will do me in first."

"I'm sure she'll be able to tell fact from fiction."

He stood, pushing the chair away from the table. "I must call Sarah."

THIRTY

Late the next morning, Richard stood in front of the door to Sarah's home, his hand hovering over the doorbell. He gritted his teeth and pushed the button.

As soon as Sarah opened the door, Mary rushed past her mother, wrapped her arms around his hips and buried her face in his shirt. He gazed down at the mop of black, curly hair crowning the five-year-old, and felt her hot breath through his shirt when she said a muffled, "Hi."

He found himself grinning for the sheer pleasure of having a child hugging him; his heart ached for his own—Edward most. He bent down and hugged her back, his face inches from her hair, inhaling her child's scent. "Hi," he said back, wanting to say so much more, but unable to express his emotion.

He stood and Mary released her grip on him, but continued to stand next to him.

"Hello Sarah." He handed Sarah two reference books that dealt with the princes and Anne. "Thank you for allowing me to come over today."

She hugged the books to her chest. "Um, why don't you come into the kitchen with me. I was just going to make some lunch." She turned and walked to the back of the house. He followed her; Mary stuck to his side.

"Where is Emma?" he asked.

"I don't know, she was here a minute ago," Sarah said, putting the books down on the kitchen table. "Mary, go find Emma and play with her, I want to talk to Richard. I'll call when lunch is ready."

"Aw, Ma!" she said.

"You heard me, now go."

"Yes, Ma." Mary stomped off toward her bedroom.

Sarah sat and opened the top book to the first tagged section. "Sit down, please. I really enjoyed speaking with Katarina last night. She sounds like a very nice person."

He pulled a chair away from the table and sat down next to her. "I owe her much."

"I've also checked on the sites that she gave to me," she said. "I assume these references will further confirm what Katarina and the sites stated?"

"They will." He sat as close as he dared to her and felt the warmth of her body. "Please believe me, I would not murder my nephews or my wife."

She twisted in the chair and faced him. "I don't have to believe you about your wife, I'm convinced she died naturally. And I can see that Shakespeare also got it wrong about you having any deformities."

He braced himself, not expecting her to believe him. "Please believe me about my nephews. I was certain they were alive when I went to Bosworth."

"Why were you sure?" She knit her brows together, frowning.

He could do no more than tell her the truth, but he didn't think he would be able to prove any of it. "For my safety and their protection, I moved them secretly from the Royal Apartments to places where my enemies could not find them. I continued to receive letters from them until two months prior to Bosworth."

Sarah giggled and put her hand over her mouth quickly.

"Do you mock me?" He crossed his arms and squared his shoulders.

"No." She stroked his wrist. "I didn't mean to laugh. You reminded me of our witness protection program, and I found the connection funny."

He'd read about this in the newspapers. He laughed. "It appears that I was five-hundred years ahead of my time." He took her hands in his, and saw she had been biting her nails; the skin was ragged and red.

"What do you know about Perkin Warbeck?" she asked. "Katarina mentioned that he persuaded many important peers and Royals that he was the real deal, that he was Richard, the younger prince."

Would that he were Richard. How much will she believe without proof?

"I first heard of him yesterday," he said. "I know less about him than Katarina does."

"Have you seen the sketch of him?"

"No," he said. "I didn't know one existed."

"I printed off a version I found it on the Internet. It's not that good, but I think you'll be able to see what he looks like."

She stood. "Wait there. I'll be right back."

He prayed he could convince her he was not a murderer, not a monster. Perhaps the sketch of Warbeck would be enough for Sarah to believe they weren't murdered.

He rose from the table and waited in the doorway to the kitchen. He leaned against the jamb.

Sarah's voice drifted from the front of the house. "I want both of you to wait upstairs until I call you, is that clear? I have some private things that I need to discuss with Mr. Gloucestre."

"But Ma," Emma said.

"No buts, young lady. Have I ever tried to read your diary or listen in on your conversations with your friends when you didn't want me to?"

"No." Emma sniffed.

"Then, I expect the same from you. Both of you go upstairs now."

Their footsteps faded and Sarah entered the kitchen holding a sheet of paper, her face flushed. "This is supposed to be a sketch of Warbeck's portrait. The original didn't survive."

His stomach knotted when he looked at the printout. The person he saw resembled his brother and sister-in-law, but the eyes were too big and round. He stood frozen in the doorway, his hope fading. Her hand rested on his arm.

"It's not him, is it?"

"I don't think so. The eyes are wrong." He bit his lip to replace the emotional with physical pain.

Her breath warmed his cheek and she stroked his hair. "Seeing how much you wanted it to be your nephew goes a long way to convincing me that you believed you got them to safety."

He opened his eyes and saw her beautiful violet eyes fixed on him. He hugged her and she pressed into him.

"Do I have that chance?" he asked. "Will you allow me to see you?"

Sarah pulled away, nodding her head. "Do you want to come with us to the soccer fields today? I was just going to make some peanut butter and jelly sandwiches." She went to the refrigerator and got the food.

"Yes, I want very much to be with you and your daughters." He walked to the counter.

"I'm glad you do, because Emma had a fit when I told her that I asked you not to come over last night."

"Is Emma all right now, and how did Mary take it?"

"Mary's fine, she just shrugged and said okay. But Emma's a little gun-shy." She finished slathering the peanut butter on the bread and started on the jelly.

"What do you mean?" He put the two completed sandwiches on the table.

"When I figured out that my husband was cheating on me, I tried to protect my children from that fact, but Emma was old enough to understand some of what was going on."

"She thinks I'm cheating on you?"

"No, more like you're abandoning her. She was five when my ex decided to dump me. Until then, I hid our marital problems from the girls, hoping we'd work things out. I didn't want them hating their father."

"I'm sorry."

"It does help that you're here today and that you'll spend the rest of the day with us." She put the remaining sandwiches on the table. "But before I call them, we still need to talk about our religious differences. Just so you know, I don't have a problem with you not being Jewish."

He blinked. It had not occurred to him that his not being Jewish would be a consideration. As much as he wished she would convert, he now realized he couldn't ask her, nor did he have any hope that she would offer.

"The church imbued me with this aversion from infancy. Katarina suggested I learn about Judaism to overcome my prejudice."

"She is definitely giving you good advice," Sarah said. "I have a couple of books that I can loan you, but they aren't easy reading."

"In my day, in my world, I would never have met you. I would never have found myself in this position. I have no way to judge what I should do."

"You asked me to follow my heart, Richard. Isn't that good enough for you?"

Oh to be able to follow my heart! Why am I hesitating? Is my heart split between church and a woman?

"Will you help me to overcome thirty-two years of prejudice?"

"Before I can make any promises," she said. "There's one other thing that I must tell you, and then I'll call the girls in."

He gulped, now afraid of what the next surprise could be.

"I will not raise a child that I bear in any Christian faith. Is that going to affect your decision?"

"Jesú!" He glared at her. "What do you think? That I should abandon my beliefs and accept a child of mine be raised a Jew?" His head pounded.

He pulled away when she reached for his hands and turned his back to her. He stared out the kitchen window, clenching and unclenching his jaw.

"No!" she said. "I wouldn't ask anyone to stop believing. Please, that isn't what I meant."

He turned around and gazed into those eyes that had first captured him. They reflected an inner hurt. "What did you mean?"

"I think it's possible to raise children without any particular religious orientation. Then when they are adults, they can make their own decisions."

"There would be no Baptism?" His voice was a whisper.

"No Baptism, but also no Bar Mitzvah." She took his hands in hers and uncurled his fingers. "Is this something you can accept? Or should we end it now before we hurt each other more?"

"I need to think, and there is something else you need to know about me." He glimpsed her daughters pulling back from the doorway. "Your girls heard some of this, I just saw them hide behind the door."

"Oh God!" Sarah turned around. "Emma, Mary, where are you? Come in here."

Two heads peered around the doorjamb.

"Why didn't you wait upstairs until I called you?"

"I don't know," Emma said. Mary stood by her side, eyes wide.

"You heard us talking, didn't you?"

They nodded yes, bent their heads down and shuffled their feet for a few seconds.

"What did you hear?" Sarah asked.

"I don't know," Emma said.

"Are you going to be our new daddy?" Mary asked, staring up at him.

"Mary!" Sarah said.

He sat. "I don't know, Mary."

Mary walked over to him and tugged on the sleeve of his rugby shirt. "Do you love Mommy?" She cast her eyes down and her dark lashes stood out against her tanned cheeks.

"Yes, I do," he said.

She then favored him with a brilliant smile. "Can I sit on your lap?"

For an answer, he twirled her around and pulled her up on his lap. She leaned back and her head was just below his chin. He felt himself foolishly grinning.

"Now how is Richard going to eat his sandwich with you sitting on his lap like that, young lady?"

Giggling, Mary squirmed off his lap and sat down at her place.

Sarah got the milk out of the refrigerator and put it on the table. "Emma, stop moping and sit down."

They left for the soccer fields right after lunch.

While Sarah got Emma set up with one of the second grade soccer teams, Richard watched Mary play with a group of preschoolers. He heard Sarah speak before he saw her.

"I think Emma's all set. So what was it that you had to tell me about yourself?" She asked, searching his eyes.

"As you know, both my wife and son predeceased me. I do hope to—"

Sarah stepped back from him, her hand was over her mouth and her face was ashen. "You want them back!" She chewed on her thumbnail. "So that's why I was hired. It was to bring them here. Richard, how can you even be thinking about me in this way if you're planning to get your wife back?"

"Oh God, Sarah, no. I cannot get Anne. It is medically impossible to save her."

"Why is it impossible?"

"Her disease cannot be cured if she is brought here just before she actually died, and to bring her back when she can be cured, perhaps as much as a year earlier, would change history. At least that is what I have been told, and Hosgrove is unwilling to do that."

"Okay," Sarah said. "That makes some sense. So how come you can save your son?"

"There are two things that are working in his favor. I think his appendix ruptured, which can be cured at the last minute, and the actual date of his death is not recorded. We can probably get him before his appendix ruptures."

"Do you know when he died?" she asked.

"Not the exact hour," he said. "Anne and I were in Nottingham. We did not learn of his death until two days later."

"Your son wasn't with you?"

"He had a cold when Anne left Middleham to join me in London. Later, I needed him to represent me in the north while I set up the government in the Midlands." He swallowed hard in an effort to compose himself. "We thought he would outlive us both."

"I'm so sorry. I can't imagine what you must have gone through," she said. "Are you worried that I would interfere with your son's religious upbringing?"

"Yes."

"You needn't worry. I only meant it for any children that we might have if we resolve the other issues."

"In my time, it would have been considered heretical to raise a child outside the church," he said.

"That's why I'm putting all my cards on the table now. I need to protect my children, and I need to protect myself." She smiled at Mary who was playing nearby. "If you can overcome a lifetime of hate against my people, you will have my whole heart."

"Do you think I hate Jews?" he asked.

"Don't you?"

It is a miracle that I don't. The teachings were truly hateful.

"It's much more complex, but no, I don't."

"Explain," she said.

"I knew two or three converted Jews, one who fought alongside my brother, and who I knighted when I was king." Richard said. "I could not understand why, if these few could accept Christ, that the rest rejected Him."

"So, your objection to me isn't that I'm Jewish, but that I don't embrace the concept that Christ is the Messiah," she said. "Then, the hard thing for you to accept is that I will not raise a child as a Christian."

"Yes," he said. "Help me to overcome that."

"You have my word, I'll do what I can."

He wrapped his arms around her and they stood, her back against his chest.

THIRTY-ONE

Richard arrived at the airport two and a half hours early, got his seat assignment and went directly to the gate to wait for his flight. Carole had yet to arrive. The gate area was nearly empty so he had his choice of seats. He decided to work on the Sunday crossword puzzle while waiting to board.

He really enjoyed doing the crosswords, and it helped him learn Modern English faster than just through usage. Ever since he knew he could not return to the fifteenth century, he had worked at learning Modern English, and at his accent, flattening it out to sound more American. Then there was the issue of spelling the words. He came from a time before dictionaries and spelling standards. Plus, there were so many more words in the vernacular today, although some words he'd used were now obsolete.

What surprised him was how good he'd become at doing the puzzles. While his first attempts were pathetic, Katarina helped him to understand how they worked, and assured him, that his looking words up in the dictionary wasn't "cheating." She had laughed at the suggestion. He no longer needed to look up most words.

He finished the puzzle before he saw Carole running up to the gate. She arrived only a few minutes before they would start boarding.

"Hi, Richard," she said, a little out of breath. "Sorry I'm so late; I have all I can do to get out of the house with a two-year-old hanging onto me." She sat down next to him.

He clucked. "It must be difficult to leave such a young child, even if only for a day."

She nodded. "I'll manage. So, have you been waiting long?"

"I didn't notice."

"It's going to be a long flight," she said. "I hope you have something to read."

He nodded. Sarah had loaned him two books. One examined the German society that led up to the Holocaust and the role of ordinary Germans, and the other was a non-religious book about Judaism.

It would have been so much easier if he thought she would consider converting, but after her adamant refusal to raise a child of theirs as a Catholic, he knew he couldn't ask her to convert. He didn't know if he could accept his own child not being raised Catholic.

He'd always known who he was, sure of his philosophy, sure of his sense of right and wrong, devout. But now, everything was different. He was no longer sure. He squeezed his eyes shut.

"Richard, are you all right?" Carole asked.

He opened his eyes. "Yes, I was just thinking."

"They just announced the first rows for boarding. What's your seat assignment?"

He showed her his boarding pass. "Looks like you're three rows in front of me. We're up next."

He was glad to be seated next to someone he didn't know, and didn't have to speak to, at least for this, the longer leg of the journey. He would be able to read undisturbed.

He decided to start with the book on Judaism once he was settled in his seat next to the window.

He found the book interesting and was able to draw many parallels between what he knew as a Catholic and the tenets of Judaism. This should not have surprised him, as this was Christ's origin. But he was surprised. The Church had been utterly successful in its ability to demonize the Jews. According to the Church, Jews were not saved and were condemned to hell. But now, he'd have to accept that Sarah and her daughters were doomed to that fate. How could they be? Sarah was a good person, and Mary and Emma were innocent children.

Was it because he'd only known one converted Jew well that he'd allowed himself to be duped? At least he did not accept everything, or feel hatred toward the Jews.

There was really only one overriding issue for him. Could he reconcile himself to fathering a child who would not be raised Catholic? Not Jewish either, not anything. Would he be condemning his future children to eternal damnation?

They deplaned at Bradley International, a small, modern airport serving Hartford, Connecticut, and Springfield, Massachusetts. It was a relief to walk. He'd found sitting and reading for more than five hours in the cramped seats exhausting.

He followed Carole to the curb where they waited to be picked up by the shuttle for the rental car company. He could see his breath in the street lamp; it would be winter soon.

The secretary, Linda, had been unable to find them a place in Amherst. Instead, they were put in a hotel in Springfield, which was less than a half an hour north of the airport.

It was nearly eleven by the time they checked in. They decided to forego a late supper and meet early for breakfast before going to Amherst to meet with Michael.

He called Sarah as soon as he got into his room.

"Hello, Sarah," he said when she answered on the third ring. "I hope it is okay for me to call you this late."

"It's not late. It's only eight o'clock. So how was your flight?"

"I forgot about the time difference." He'd reset his watch when they landed in Connecticut, and that long, tiring flight made it feel late. "I was able to finish one of the books and started on the second."

"So what do you think?"

He could hear her voice tighten up.

"The books are helping me to better understand why you choose not to accept Christ is the Messiah. My larger issue is how do I want my own children to be raised. It never occurred to me that they should be raised as anything but Catholic, and now I have to accept they wouldn't be Christian."

"I understand the significance, else I would not have brought it up," she said. "You must be able to accept a non-religious upbringing. If you can't accept that, then it won't work."

"I will continue to think it through," he said.

"I'll help any way I can, Richard. I want this to work. I love you, you know."

His mind went blank. He wanted to see her and touch her, but they were three thousand miles apart. It sounded as though she were in the next room. His throat grew tight. "It must work."

"Would it help if we could map out a non-religious way to raise a child that will be acceptable to both of us?" she asked.

Dear God. Why can I not say yes?

"I will consider it."

"Is that the best you can do? Am I making a terrible mistake?" Her voice cracked at the end.

The Church taught that the Jews had a blood debt, were Christ's killers. He had believed this for thirty-two years, and it wasn't until he saw the program on the Holocaust that he had questioned beliefs he had held close. He had never expected to fall in love with a Jew, but he had. He had to reconcile his faith with his feelings for Sarah. He needed her and not just because she had the science and the knowledge to get his son. He needed her for himself.

"Richard? Are you still there? Am I making a mistake?"

His mouth went dry. "I can't lose you. Please, give me more time."

"Oh my God!" Carole said as she pulled into the small parking area off the interstate. It was still early, and both Richard and Carole were admiring the fall foliage as they drove north, when she saw a sign for a scenic overview.

They got out and stood by the railing, gazing out over a valley resplendent in the flaming reds, rusts, yellows, and touches of green, where the leaves had yet to turn. "Now I know why people go on these tours just to see the leaves. It's breathtaking."

"Does Michael know we are coming to see him?" Richard asked.

"He knows I am. I made sure he'd be available. But I can't wait to see his expression when he sees you." Carole smiled.

He remembered the last time he saw Michael. That was over a month ago. "Yes, that will be interesting. We should be on our way."

"Now that's the understatement of the year," she said.

They drove through Amherst and took a left onto North Pleasant when they got to the center. Amherst was a typical New England town, complete with a white wood-frame church on the corner, the bell in the steeple quiet. They continued onto the sprawling campus, whose high-rise buildings stuck out from the trees and farm fields beyond. After parking, they entered Michael's building a few minutes early. They waited for the people who were seeing Michael to leave before entering the lab.

Michael's back was toward them as they walked in. "Hello Michael," Carole said. "I hope it's all right if we're a little early."

"No pro—" Michael said, turning around. "Richard! I never thought I'd see you again." He closed the gap between them and pumped his hand. His face reddened and he was smiling broadly.

"Michael," he said. "It's good to see you, too."

"Can we talk freely here?" Carole asked.

"Let me get my jacket. I don't expect anyone for another hour, but you never know when someone will drop by."

Michael locked the door, and they followed him out of the building. "There's a coffee shop down the street. Why don't we go there?"

"I think you know why we're here, Mike," Carole said, matching her pace with his.

"Richard, I'm really surprised to see you after what happened. Are you okay with all this?"

"That is why I am here. I hope to encourage you with my presence as well as my words to come back to Ambion Technologies."

"Really," Michael said, arching an eyebrow. "And I thought Hosgrove had tried to kill you. Are you asking for my help to finish yourself off?"

He grabbed Michael by the elbow. "Christ no! I want to save my son." He stepped in front of Michael, and stared at the blond physicist who had saved his life, and now he hoped, would help to save his son's life.

"Your son? But I thought he'd died naturally." Michael shrugged. "Anyway, fill me in. You're obviously not afraid of Hosgrove."

Instead of having the coffee in the café, Carole suggested they go nearby to the town green where it would be more private. Coffees in hand, they ambled over to a cluster of stones near the far end.

"So what happened, Richard? The last I knew, Hosgrove had shot you. Were you badly injured?"

"I did not feel I was. However, I wasn't conscious for most of the first night. According to Katarina, I could have died while they were operating on me."

"No kidding? Where did he shoot you?"

He pointed to a spot just below the middle of his right collarbone. "It really did not bother me that much, but Katarina said my lung collapsed, and I almost bled to death. I think she overstated my peril."

"So Hosgrove is no longer trying to send you back," Michael said. "Explain to me how you think you can get your son, and why not your wife."

"It is because my son died from a ruptured appendix which is curable today. Unfortunately, Anne's tuberculosis was too far advanced at the time when a rescue would be feasible."

"So, Mike, has Richard persuaded you?" Carole asked.

"No. And you're not going to like what I'm about to tell you next, either." Michael took a sip from the Styrofoam cup. "In order to get your son, we will need a child's body to substitute for him. That's going to be damn near impossible to do."

His head spun and he staggered back. He would have overbalanced but for Michael grabbing his arm and steadying him.

"Maybe we should go over to those benches and sit down," Carole said.

"Is there any other way?" he asked once he was seated.

"Someone would notice if we substituted a sack of potatoes instead." Michael said. "Not only do we need a body, but it has to resemble him closely."

He put his head in his hands and moaned.

"Mike!" Carole said. "Are you being intentionally cruel, or are you just thoughtless?"

"What do you mean? It's the truth. We have to leave a body that closely resembles his son and is the same mass. That is the only way."

"He's right, Carole. That's what you did to get me, and now the family is asking questions. That's why Hosgrove wanted to send me back, is it not?"

"You got it. How did you figure that out?" Michael asked.

"I met up with the brother by chance. I bear a close resemblance to him."

"No shit! Well, there's no way in hell that I'm going back to Ambion without a guarantee that Hosgrove isn't going to still try to return you."

"How would we do that?" Carole asked. "Honestly, I wouldn't want to be part of that either. That would be murder."

"There will be no murder," Richard said. "Do you think Sarah would be part of it if she thought I would be killed?"

"Who's Sarah?" Michael sat down next to Richard. He leaned forward on his elbows and took a swig of coffee.

"Only the inventor of the QDE," Carole said, grinning. "It seems our boy here is head over heels with her and she with him."

"Is it that obvious?" Richard asked.

"Let me just say that if you both wore neon signs, it wouldn't be more apparent." Carole pitched her empty coffee cup into the trash container next to the bench.

"I'm happy for you, Richard." Michael gave him a sidelong stare. "But, I don't think there's any possibility that we could send you back. Hosgrove wanted me to find a way. I wasn't able to—not with you alive."

"Hosgrove and I have become friends. I doubt he will try to kill me now."

"Still, I'd be more comfortable knowing that the family isn't trying to recover the body," Michael said. "Boy, I'd love to meet this Sarah. I bet she's something."

"If I can learn that the family is no longer seeking his remains, would you consider it, Michael?" he asked.

"Yes, but not until the first of the year. I'm obligated to stay here until then."

"Do you want us to continue to contact you through the university?" Carole asked.

"You can," Michael said. "I've got to get back. Come with me and I'll give you my card. It has my email and crap like that on it." He rose and dumped his coffee cup into the trash.

Richard pulled a book out of his overnight bag before stashing it in the overhead bin.

"What're you reading?" Carole asked as they settled into their assigned seats on the plane out of Bradley.

He showed the book to Carole.

"*Hitler's Willing Executioners,*" she read the title and then gave a low whistle. "That's not light reading. Do you have a specific interest or are you just a glutton for history?"

"It's personal." He frowned.

"Sarah is Jewish, isn't she? Why is that a problem? There are lots of mixed marriages here."

"It's a problem for me." He pinched the bridge of his nose. "I never considered marrying or raising a child outside the Catholic faith."

"I take it Sarah doesn't want to convert, let alone raise her children Catholic."

"She has told me she won't. She was quite firm about it."

"I don't know if this will help you, but my brother married a Jew and we're Catholic."

"Do they have children?"

"A boy and a girl. They're being raised in the Jewish faith. My sister-in-law insisted."

"Does your brother have a problem with that?"

"Apparently not," Carole said. "My parents were really put out at first, but they've reconciled themselves to it. It does make for some family strife, though. Anyway, that's one problem that you won't have."

No, the strife is within myself.

"I've been thinking about this body business," Carole said. "Were any autopsies ever performed on the body?"

"I'm not sure what you are asking," Richard said, fastening the seat belt. "Are you using the French word for personal observation?"

"I didn't know that. No, it's come to mean an examination of the deceased in order to determine the cause of death. The body is cut open and the organs are examined."

Richard turned his head toward the window, feeling momentarily sickened that his son should be mutilated. "No, we would not defile the dead."

"It's not defiling. Sometimes that's the only way to know why someone died. But anyway, that's good. I have an idea."

THIRTY-TWO

The plane taxied for takeoff.

"What is this idea?" Richard asked. Could Carole have the solution he needed? Ever since Michael suggested they might not be able to get a child's body, he'd wondered if Hosgrove would abandon trying to retrieve Edward.

"I'm thinking that instead of a body, we buy a skeleton that's the right size and build it up replicate your son. That way, there won't be any family issues."

"I toured a creature shop when I went to San Francisco last month. When I first saw the bodies, I thought them real, but there was no odor. They used plastic for skin and bones. That would not suit our purposes."

"Well, it was a thought. You might want to research it."

Once the plane was airborne, Richard opened the second book, but found he couldn't concentrate. His thoughts turned instead to the body. Michael was right. What was he going to do? He needed a body to substitute for his son. As a father, he would never allow his son's body to be used this way. How could he in good conscience ask someone to do something he would not? That went against everything he was.

He put the headphones on and leaned back in the seat.

"Morning," Katarina said. "Coffee will be ready in a minute. When did you get back?"

Richard yawned. "After midnight. We were held up in Detroit because of thunderstorms." He got a mug out of the cabinet and leaned against the sink.

"That doesn't sound like much fun. So, do you think Michael will return?"

"I don't know. The earliest he can return to Ambion is January." He shrugged. "He insists that we guarantee Hosgrove no longer wants to retrieve the body."

"Why? Isn't the fact that you are working for Hosgrove enough?"

"He doesn't trust Hosgrove. I don't think I convinced him otherwise, and I'm not sure that I ever can."

The coffeepot stopped making its gurgling noises. Before the last splutter died, Richard poured some into his mug and sat down.

"What are these?" he asked. He held up two small envelopes. Each, he noted, had his name written on the front.

"I was wondering when you'd see them." Katarina was grinning. "Open them up. They're for you."

There was a card inside each. He pulled the first one out and found a drawing of a frowning cartoon character who was saying, *I was going to get a cake for your birthday, but...* He opened the card to the inside and read the rest, *I couldn't find a cake that would hold five hundred and fifty three candles. Happy late birthday.* It was signed — Katarina. He laughed.

He opened the next card. *Sorry I forgot your birthday,...but my memory doesn't go back that far.* Then a hand-written note that read, *I actually didn't know it was on Saturday until after you left for Amherst. Love, Sarah.* He sat there staring at the cards.

Katarina sat down next to him.

"I do not know what to say. I completely forgot about it. You saw Sarah?" he asked.

"We got together Sunday. I hope you're able to resolve these issues you have." She drank her coffee.

"I want to. It is not something that I gave any thought to in the past. Now it seems I must."

"Talk it over with her. She'll help you," Katarina said. "I have to get ready for class." She stood and put her mug in the sink.

"Thank you for remembering." He carefully put the cards back in their envelopes.

Richard took a bite from one of the sandwiches he and Sarah had bought for lunch. He glanced out the car window at the wind-blown picnic tables nearby.

"Thank you for the card. It was quite a surprise."

"You're welcome. It's nothing, and I have something else for you, too." She handed him a gift-wrapped package that was tucked behind the passenger seat. "Happy birthday, Richard. It was the second of October, wasn't it?"

"Yes." He stared at the package. "I-I don't know what to say. I am overwhelmed."

"Open it, don't worry about the paper. I hope you like what I got for you."

He tore the paper off the package and opened the box. "A chess set! How did you know that I play chess? Thank you." He leaned over and kissed her.

"I didn't know for sure. I guessed you might, since it was popular in your time, too."

"Do you play?"

"I used to. I was on my high school chess team. But it's been a few years since I've really played. My ex didn't, and then when the kids came along, I didn't have the time."

He put the set on the backseat and took his sandwich out, noticing Sarah had started on hers.

"I have been reading those books and thinking about them."

"You mentioned it when you called me."

"There were nearly no Jews in England in my time, but I did know a couple who converted, one who was a friend and fellow soldier. Most had been expelled nearly two-hundred years before."

"I did read about that." Sarah had stopped eating, and put her sandwich back in its wrapper.

"The church would have us believe Jews were evil."

"You don't think that now, do you?" She chewed on her thumbnail.

"I did not then, nor do I now."

"What do you think?" She arched an eyebrow.

"I no longer know." He scowled. As much as he wanted to ask her to convert, he knew he couldn't. She had to volunteer.

"I thought you told me over the phone that you are willing to put those teachings aside."

He turned his head and stared through the trees to a grassy patch. *Why am I so inflexible? Why am I not able to compromise, meet her halfway, as she is willing to do?* He felt her hand on his shoulder and turned back to see her studying him.

"I spoke in haste. I need your help to overcome what I was taught."

"I want to believe you. Of course I'll help. You mean a lot to me, and I won't give up on you that easily."

"You will take my word?"

"Yes, I can see you're struggling with this. I think you're having a harder time dealing with it than I did bringing myself to tell you."

He smiled. "Your fingernails tell a different story."

Sarah's face reddened at the same time that her hand jerked to her mouth.

He reached for and held both her hands in his, and this time she did not pull away from him. "Do you not know? I love that about you."

"My nervous habit? I don't even know I'm doing it half the time. What a silly thing to love. Why?"

"Because it is part of you." He let go of her hands and took a bite of his sandwich.

"My ex hated when I did it. He was forever on my case about it. And before that, my mom would be after me to stop." She spread her fingers out and stared at them.

"Has Carole talked to you about Michael Fairchild?" he asked.

"Um hmm, she didn't seem at all sure that he would return," she said.

"I don't think so, either. Do you need him in order to make the device work to get Edward?"

"I don't know. I need time to work on it," she said. "Regardless, the earliest Mike would come back is January. Isn't that right?"

"Yes, why do you ask?"

"Because, I should know by then." She glanced at her half-eaten sandwich and sighed.

"You seem worried. Is there something else I should know?"

She took his hands in hers and held them to her cheeks. "I've been thinking about Edward, and assuming that we can save him, I think you, uh, we, are going to have more problems than we bargained for."

"What do you mean?" An unbidden dread seized his heart. "Are you saying that I should not want to bring him here?"

"Oh God, no!" She took a gulp of air. "One reason that immediately springs to mind is that he doesn't know his mother is dead. Assuming we work the issues out, how well do you think he's going to accept me, let alone my children?"

"Sarah, I must try. I must have him if I can."

"Of course you should, and I'll do whatever I can to get him back. It's my job." She sighed. "Are we going to work through our issues?"

"I want to."

"Maybe you need to talk to someone else."

"Who?"

"I don't know. Maybe a counselor or a priest." She pointed to her watch. "I really should be heading back."

"I, too, must get back," he said. "May I see you tonight?"

"Will you speak to someone else about this?"

"Yes."

"Tonight then. I'll make dinner."

"Richard, come in," Katarina said. "What happened? Why the cloak and dagger?"

He entered Katarina's office on the university campus and closed the door behind him. "Cloak and dagger? I don't understand." He sat down.

"You're being secretive. You wouldn't tell me anything over the phone, and you're here in the middle of the afternoon instead of at work."

"I'm fairly sure I met the brother of the dead man who was substituted for me."

"When? What happened?"

"Last week, when I was leaving the hospital, I met a man who bears a close resemblance to me. We spoke for a few minutes, and I learned that the family doesn't know what happened to his brother's body."

"Why have you waited until now to tell me?" Katarina leaned forward on her elbows and put her chin in her hands.

"I received a call from their lawyer this afternoon. He requested I release my dental records for comparison. I don't know if I should."

"Why did you come here instead of calling me?"

"I am uneasy about speaking of this at Ambion."

"Is that because of Michael?" Katarina leaned back.

"He did have that effect on me." He slowly shook his head.

"I don't see any problem with releasing your dental records," Katarina said. "It will prove you're not the brother."

"Left or right," Sarah said, holding her fists out to Richard.

"Right."

She opened her right fist to reveal a black pawn. "You lose. Where were you this afternoon? I didn't see you around."

"I needed to see Katarina." He sat down and waited for Sarah to make the opening move.

"What about, if I may ask?"

"I got a call from the lawyer of the family whose body was substituted for mine, wanting my dental records to be released. I decided to talk to Katarina about it."

She moved the pawn to King three. "Why didn't you call her or ask me about it?"

"Hosgrove nearly sent me back to retrieve the body." He matched her move. "I didn't want him to know."

She frowned. "That's tantamount to murder. I can't believe Hosgrove would do anything like that!"

"He shot me after Michael warned me Hosgrove was looking into sending me back."

"Shot you?" She shifted her gaze from the board to him, her eyebrows knitted together. "B-but you're working for him. I would never have suspected anything like that."

"We've worked our differences out. I have information about my past and fifteenth century England that he wants, and he has the resources to get Edward."

"This certainly puts a different light on things," she said.

"I didn't feel safe discussing it at Ambion."

Sarah moved a piece. "Humph, I can see why. So why do they need your dental records? Do you have any?"

Richard moved a pawn. "I have a chart, x-rays, and a filling." He grinned. "I met the brother and he thought I was his brother."

"So they want evidence that you are not he?" She moved the king and rook together.

"Yes," he said, staring at the board. "What did you just do?"

"You mean my castling?"

"Is that a real move?"

"Yeah. Wow! You've never seen it?"

"No. The king is completely protected. What are the rules?"

They started the game anew after Sarah showed him both the King's and Queen's side castle, and when it could and couldn't be done.

"It appears that your heart is not in this game," he said, after castling.

"I can't get my mind off what you just told me."

"Are you concerned?"

"Of course I am," she said, chewing on the edge of her pinky.

"Do you think that Hosgrove would—"

"I don't know what to think, Richard. First you say that Hosgrove was going to return you to the battle where you would have been killed, and then, when he can't do that, he shoots you."

"He did settle with me, and he did apologize for what he had done."

"How well do you think you know him?"

"I have spent time with him nearly every weekday," he said. "We talk mostly about battles, but I feel I have come to know him… some. I wish I were more confident."

"Your battles?" she asked.

"Mostly mine. I do supply him with detail that is nowhere documented. But he has also told me about his battles, in Korea. We understand each other."

"Still, that wasn't very rational. Why did he think he had to return you, and why did he shoot you?"

"He claims he shot me by accident. Of that, I'm not sure. However, I thought the reason he wanted to return me had been nullified."

"But it isn't, is it? It's all about the body," she said.

"It does appear that the family is asking questions."

"So Michael is at U Mass in Amherst? I want to meet him."

"I think you should. I want my son and he has the key. Do you think you can do it without him?"

"I don't know at this point. He did something unique. He found a direction that I hadn't considered."

"I have faith in you," he said. "It took you less than a week to work out that Michael made a time machine out of your invention."

"I had help. I'll need more."

"Will Carole's team be sufficient?"

"I need more time to work on it," she said. "My parents don't live all that far from there. I'd be able to bring the girls to them, hop on a commuter flight and see Michael. That would work."

"May I go with you. Perhaps if Michael sees us together, he would be more willing to work with you."

"I'll be seeing my parents first. I'm not sure that's a good idea," she said. "We could meet up in Amherst."

THIRTY-THREE

It had been nearly a month since Richard learned that Sarah was Jewish. Because of her seemingly casual attitude toward religion, he had initially hoped she would consent to raise a child they might have as Catholic. But even though Sarah agreed to compromise, there was a point at which she had stopped. He didn't know how much longer they could continue ignoring their basic differences. He began to doubt they could find a middle ground.

He didn't want to stop seeing Sarah. Each day his feelings for her and her daughters deepened. They were becoming his family.

Nor could he avoid any contact with her, as they had to work together if he were to have any chance of getting Edward. And, therein lay the other problem—the job was boring. Without the requisite education and skills he needed for this time, he was relegated to the tasks that no one else wanted to do.

He heard someone approaching his desk as he settled in for the day and started up the laptop.

"Congratulations." Carole walked toward Richard. "I hear you got your High School Equivalency Diploma. Now you can concentrate on the Scholastic Aptitude Test. That's going to be a lot harder."

"So I see," he said. "I have been getting a lot of help with the studies. I think I'll be able to complete them in time for next fall."

"Have you decided what you are going to take?"

"I am planning to study business and economics."

"So, you're going to be our next Chief Executive Officer, eh?" She grinned. "I've been wanting to get you more involved with our processes. Now would be a good time to include you in our discussions and meetings. We need to find products that will keep this company a going concern."

"Thank you, I should like to be more productive."

"So, when are you and Sarah scheduled to see Michael?" She sat down in his guest chair.

"Next Monday."

"I'm surprised you haven't already gone. You were talking about it a couple of weeks ago."

"It took some planning to set up, and Michael wasn't available earlier," he said.

"Good luck. It would be good to have him back." Carole rose from the chair and turned to go to her office.

Phil rushed over. "Hey guys, did you hear the news?" His face was flushed.

"No, who'd we bomb?" Carole asked. She was smirking.

The room became silent as all heads turned toward her. He saw some heads pop up over cubicle partitions up and down the aisle.

"Jeeze Louise, I'm just kidding." Carole shook her head. "Did we bomb someone?" she asked in a small voice.

"No!" Phil said, laughing. "I just heard that Hosgrove fired Fortas this morning."

"All right," came a comment from someone behind a cubicle.

"Why now, and why did it take so long?" Carole asked.

"I don't know why it didn't happen sooner, but I guess Hosgrove had it when Fortas rejected our last purchase order request," Phil said.

"Well, it's about time," Carole said. "Every freaking time I'd put in for some equipment, that idiot would reject it for some stupid reason or other. At least now we won't have to keep going around him."

"Does this mean there are going to be no more spreadsheets?" Richard asked.

"Ha-ha-ha, no. That comes with the territory. You might not like them, but they are very useful tools." Carole headed for her office. "Well, that just made my day."

He checked his watch and realized he was a few minutes late for his meeting with Hosgrove. He left his desk and hurried to his daily chat.

He had come to enjoy these sessions when he and Evan were speaking soldier to soldier. The weapons and tactics were different, but the language transcended time, as did the feeling of camaraderie.

He dashed down the stairs and made the turn into Hosgrove's outer office. It was empty. He noticed the door to the inner office was closed. It was usually open if Linda had to leave the area for any reason. Something was wrong. He covered the distance between the hallway and Linda's desk in four long strides.

He saw her when he walked behind her desk. She was on the floor, face down, one arm stuck out, and the other tucked under her body. The chair was pushed away from the desk. He knelt down and tugged gently on her shoulder. "Linda?"

She groaned and stirred.

He helped her up and into a chair. "You're hurt!" His hand was sticky with her blood. "What happened?"

She touched the side of her head and winced. "Fortas—he's got a gun—he's with Hosgrove." She pointed to the closed office door. "Sarah's in there, too." Her voice squeaked.

His heart slammed against his ribs. He groaned. "I must get in there now. Are you able to call the police?"

She leaned forward and put her head in her hand. "Ye-es."

He ran to the door.

"D-don't try," Linda cried. "Let the police handle it." She picked up the phone.

He was desperate. He had to get in and save Sarah—save them both. *Oh God! Not Sarah!*

That Fortas had a gun made him all the more frantic. He'd faced much fiercer enemies in the past, but that was war, soldiering. Anne was never in the middle. At least Hosgrove was a fighter. If Hosgrove wasn't incapacitated, they'd be able to even the odds.

He caught his breath and tried the door. It was locked.

"Don't go in there. He'll kill you! I called 9-1-1. They'll be here in a couple of minutes."

He slammed the door near the latch with his heel. After the third kick, the door burst open revealing Hosgrove standing in front of his desk, his hands in the air.

Fortas had Sarah pinned to a chair on the left of Hosgrove's desk. His left hand was wrapped around her throat, and he held a gun in his right hand. It was jammed into her temple. Her eyes were wide and riveted on Richard.

He shouted, "Let her go!" He advanced toward them.

Fortas jerked his hand and Richard froze. "One more step and I'll blow your girlie's fucking brains out." He was past reason, his face blotchy red and lips white, pulled tightly against his teeth.

Sarah grabbed at his hand and coughed. Her eyes rolled back.

Richard fell back. His eyes darted to Hosgrove who made the slightest nod in the direction of a side table that held a small crystal globe resting on an onyx stand. He guessed the globe to be about three inches across.

Fortas waved the gun at Hosgrove and then at Richard. "One more move and I'll kill you both."

"Put the gun down," Hosgrove said, his voice controlled. "We can talk this out."

"Yeah?" Fortas screamed. "You're gonna hire me back like nothing happened?" He jammed the muzzle back into Sarah's temple.

She coughed. "You're choking me." Her voice was raspy.

"Shut the fuck up!" Fortas waved the gun around.

Richard saw Sarah's eyes bulge as her hands fell away from her throat. He had to act immediately. Fortas was choking her. The fear she could soon be dead curled through his gut.

He darted to the side table.

"Take me," he said. "Let her go." He rested his hand on the globe as Fortas moved the gun from Sarah's temple to aim it at him. She went limp and slid to the floor when Fortas released her throat. He steadied the gun with both hands.

Richard stood to the left of Hosgrove forcing John Fortas to wave the gun between them. He snatched the globe from its stand when Fortas aimed the gun at Evan.

Richard shouted, "Fortas." This caused Fortas to take his eyes off Hosgrove, allowing Hosgrove to jump Fortas.

He hurled the globe at Fortas. It struck him in the jaw at the instant the gun fired. The shot missed both Hosgrove and Richard. Instead, the bullet shattered the mirror behind the table, not half a foot from where Richard had been.

Fortas staggered.

Like a bull, Hosgrove charged the gunman. Richard dove at Fortas a second later and caught him in the ribs, knocking him back.

The handgun fell onto the rug, making a soft thud. Hosgrove snagged it and aimed at Fortas. "You move so much as a finger and I'll kill you."

"Fuck you!" Fortas lunged at Richard. "You'll have to kill him first."

Richard sidestepped his one-time manager and drove his fist into the side of Fortas's head, sending him to the carpet.

Hosgrove moved to the downed gunman. "I've got him." He jammed his knee into the small of Fortas' back. "Richard, get the packing tape out of my desk."

"You're breaking my back!" Fortas cried.

"I'll break more than your back if you don't stop struggling," Hosgrove said, his voice was cold and calm.

Once Fortas's wrists were taped, Richard scrambled to Sarah, unconscious where she had slid to the floor. He eased his arm under her shoulders and gathered her to him. "Sarah!" He brushed her cheek and moved his hand to her neck, feeling for a pulse.

"Richard, is Sarah okay?" Hosgrove said.

"She's alive." He examined her throat, now discolored from the chokehold Fortas had on her. "Sarah," he spoke her name like a prayer.

She groaned and then coughed. Her eyes opened.

There was a commotion at the door, and the uniforms ran in, guns drawn. "Police. Stay where you are, hands where we can see them."

He stared at the muzzle of a gun pointed directly at his head.

"Come away from her now, sir."

"Here's the guy you want," Hosgrove said, grabbing Fortas by his shirt and shoving him toward the police. "We'd all be dead if it weren't for him." He nodded toward Richard.

"Officer, it's all right. He didn't do this." Sarah coughed and put her hand to her throat.

"Do you need medical attention?" the police officer asked.

"No, I'm okay." She sat up and coughed.

Richard frowned. "Sarah, are you hurt?"

"I'm okay, really," she said. "My throat is a little sore. I'd like to stand up."

He helped her to her feet, and they stood together. He put his arms around her and she sank into him.

"Why were you here?" He spoke softly into her ear, his voice breaking on the last word.

"I was meeting with Evan. I-I -" She coughed and then grew quiet. He felt her press into his chest and tremble slightly.

He watched as the police cuffed and arrested Fortas and read him his rights. Fortas was working his jaw, head bent forward, taking inches from his short stature.

The globe that Richard had thrown at Fortas had not broken, but sat on the carpet as if it belonged there. Hosgrove was leaning against the desk, rubbing his arm.

"That was a nice bit of throwing, Richard," Hosgrove said, nodding at the crystal globe. "I could have used you in my unit."

He went to pick it up when the police officer interrupted him. "Was that used to disable Fortas?"

When Hosgrove nodded, the officer said, "We'll need it for evidence, sir."

"Sure," Hosgrove said. "I'd like it back when you're done with it."

They slipped it into an evidence bag.

"You risked your life for us," Richard said. "I do not know what to say."

"Bah. I'm an old man. I didn't want to see your lives wasted."

"Enough with this mutual admiration," the police officer said with a shake of his shaved head. "I'm going to need to take your statements, or do you want to come down to the precinct later when things are calmer?"

The three of them glanced at each other and nodded. "Now will be fine," Hosgrove said for them all. "Where's my secretary, Linda?" he asked.

"They took her to the hospital for observation. She has a slight concussion."

Relief washed over Richard as he pulled Sarah away from the center of the room and hugged her. "You mean everything to me," he whispered. "I have no life without you." A shiver ran down his spine.

She started to tremble. "Get a grip!" she muttered. Tears were streaming down her cheeks. "This is so stupid. Why am I crying?"

"Sarah, I thought I had lost you," he said. "You are not being stupid."

"I know." She coughed. "But nobody got hurt, and now I'm feeling scared." She coughed again.

"He did hurt you!"

"I'll be okay," she said and then went into a coughing spasm.

"You are going to the hospital," he said.

"But, I have to pick my girls up."

"I will pick them up." He turned his head and called to an officer. "Sarah has been hurt. She should go to the hospital."

One of the officers came over to where they were standing. "Where have you been hurt, Sarah?"

She took her hand away from her throat. "Fortas was choking me. My throat is bruised, Officer."

"I'll radio for an ambulance," the officer said. The marks Fortas' fingers had left on Sarah's throat were getting darker.

"My kids are at day care. I need to pick them up by five." Sarah coughed.

"I will pick them up," he repeated.

"Are you their father?"

He wanted to say yes, but that wasn't true. He whispered a "no," but it felt false, hollow. More than anything, he felt like their father. His bond was complete.

"You can't pick them up, sir. What are their names and where are they? We will bring them to you, Sarah," the policewoman said before radioing for the ambulance.

He headed for his car to follow Sarah to the hospital once the police left. He was worried about her and wondered if she could still be in danger. A wave of nausea swept through him. He threw up in the bushes lining the curb.

Richard waited for Sarah's examination to end when the social worker walked up to him with Emma and Mary. Mary ran up to him crying, "Mommy! Where's mommy?"

Emma hung back, standing halfway between him and the social worker.

He hugged Mary and held his other arm open for Emma. "Come here," he said softly. "Your mother is being examined by a doctor. She should be here soon."

Emma edged closer to him.

"Excuse me. I'm Jane Cameron, the social worker. You are...?"

"Richard Gloucestre. I am a close friend."

"Is Mommy gonna be okay?" Emma asked, her eyes downcast. She had moved closer to him, and he saw tears dribbling down her cheeks.

"Yes. The doctors are just making sure that she can go home tonight." He reached out and stroked her hair.

Sarah walked into the area, and both her daughters rushed to her. She was smiling but he saw the strain around her eyes.

"I guess my job is done," Jane said. "Nice to meet you Mr. Gloucestre." She nodded and left the area.

He walked up to Sarah and put his arm around her shoulder. "Are you all right?"

"Yes, I've only got some bruises. I'm fine."

"Let me take you home."

They picked up some Chinese takeout and then went to Sarah's home. As they sat down to eat, Richard knew with a certainty that he'd not experienced before—he belonged with them.

"I don't want to go to school tomorrow," Emma said, while staring at her nearly full dinner plate.

"What's wrong, honey?" Sarah asked. "Why aren't you eating your dinner?"

"Nothin', I don't feel well."

Sarah reached over to Emma and put her hand on her forehead. Emma frowned in obvious displeasure.

"You're not running a temperature. Where does it hurt?"

"I don't know."

"Emma," he said. "Are you afraid because of what happened today?"

She nodded and tears welled up in her eyes.

"Emmy is a scaredy-cat. Emmy is a scaredy-cat." Mary did a singsong.

"Ma! Make her stop," Emma wailed. She ran to her mother and buried her head into Sarah's shoulder, sobbing.

"No, she isn't." He narrowed his eyes at Mary. "I was afraid that something terrible would happen."

"You were?" Emma stopped crying as quickly as she started. She stared at him, her mouth still trembling, and her cheeks streaked with tears.

"Come here, Emma." He pushed his chair away from the table and waited.

Sarah nodded and coaxed her daughter toward him. Emma shuffled over to him, keeping her head down. He got a view of the crown of her carrot red hair. He put his hand on her back and rubbed it slowly. "Yes, I was afraid. I was more afraid than any battle I have been in."

She stared up at him, her brown eyes bloodshot from the tears. "You've been in battles? Were you wounded?"

"Yes, I've been in battles and I have been wounded."

Mary was now standing next to her sister, her brown eyes wide. "Weren't you afraid you would die?"

"I never thought I would die, Mary," he said. Although he'd written wills because that was always a real possibility, he had always thought of his men and the battle when fighting. Death wasn't something he had feared for himself. "Emma, why are you afraid to go to school tomorrow?"

"I'm scared that something else bad will happen."

"I won't tell you that something bad cannot take place, but being afraid that something might occur doesn't change what will happen. It only makes you afraid."

"But you said you were afraid today." Emma bowed her head.

"I was, but I no longer am. Now make your Mama happy and eat your dinner. You don't have a tummyache, do you?"

"No-o," Emma said to her feet.

The local news had just concluded and Ambion Technologies had figured prominently in it, which surprised Richard. He hadn't noticed any reporters, but he'd left for the hospital before they had arrived.

"Well, it seems we almost made the local news," Sarah said. "I'm glad our names have been withheld." She turned the TV off and joined him on the couch.

"I was so frightened for you. Thank God you aren't really hurt. I couldn't bear to lose you."

"I think that my passing out, because he was choking me, may have saved my life. It got me out of harm's way."

"How is your throat? I was really worried."

"I'm fine. It's only bruised. But you were right to have me check it out. It could have been serious." She ran the tips of her fingers down her neck. "Thanks for staying here tonight. I'm more shaken than I'd like to admit."

He put his hand over hers and caressed it. "Marry me. You mean everything to me."

"Does what just happened have anything to do with your asking me now?"

"I knew in that instant that you were the only thing that mattered to me. It was the same with Anne. I needed papal dispensation to marry Anne, and I got it shortly before we wed. I would have married her anyway, but it would have been much more difficult to arrange later."

"You do know it's not a good idea to have children by someone so closely related as Anne was?"

"What do you mean?"

"Have you come across anything about genetics?"

"I have heard the term, but I don't have an understanding."

"Okay, it's paper and pencil time," Sarah said, straightening her back and grabbing some writing material lying on the coffee table. She scribbled on the back of an envelope. "Mind you, this is not my area of expertise, so what I'm saying is highly simplified."

"I'm listening."

"The problem stems from the fact that you and Anne are cousins."

He listened as she explained about how the child gets half his traits from the mother and the other half from the father. If the two people aren't related, then the chance that each parent will pass on a deleterious trait is minimized. But in his and Anne's case, his mother's brother was Anne's grandfather. The odds of each of them passing on the same bad gene had dramatically increased.

"Are you saying that Edward has a genetic disease?" He shuddered. Edward had had more than his share of sore throats, but both Anne and he attributed that to normal childhood illnesses.

"Not necessarily. Your genes can be screened for certain diseases. If you're not a carrier, then the chance that he has one of them is the same as anybody."

"What if I am a carrier?" he asked.

"Then we would have to determine if Edward had specific symptoms and if he did, determine if there are treatments available," she said. "But aren't you jumping the gun?"

"I don't understand."

"Before we go down the path of doom and gloom, get yourself tested. Then we'll see if there's anything to worry about."

When she put the pencil down and leaned back, he wrapped his arms about her and spoke softly into her ear, "You still haven't said. Will you marry me?"

She sank into his arms. "Yes, my love. My answer is yes."

He stroked her hair and then brushed her eyebrows with his thumb. "When…how soon can we get married?"

"There's no rush. We can wait until after we get Edward. I think he'd want to be at your wedding, don't you?"

They kissed. She pressed her body into him, and he was instantly aroused. "I'm sorry, I do not mean to push you."

"You aren't pushing me. I want you," she said. "I've wanted you from the first."

"Jesú, we are not married."

"Now that surprises me," she said, pulling away from him slightly. "From what I've read, you were much less sexually inhibited than people today."

"It was what you would call a double standard. I had liaisons with women whom I would not marry. But with Anne, I waited."

"We are going to marry. I see no reason to wait Ri…?"

He put his fingers across her lips.

"Dickon. I want very much for you to call me Dickon, here, in private."

THIRTY-FOUR

Richard lay with Sarah in his arms, holding his breath to feel her heartbeat against his chest. He let it out slowly as she turned to face him in the darkened room. Her fingers traced his eyebrows to his jaw and then moved gently over his lips.

He held her hand and kissed the palm, inhaling her scent. "You make me feel light of heart. I am so very happy."

She leaned over and kissed him on the nose. "I'm thrilled to hear you say that," she whispered. "That's quite a change in your state of mind from when you lost your son and then your wife." Sighing, she rolled back down beside him.

He got up on his elbow and peered into her eyes deep in shadow. "Why are you bringing that up?" He stroked her hair.

"Because it really bothers me. It's almost like you were a shell, going through the motions. How did you do it? I don't know if I would have wanted to live if it had been me."

"I did want to die." His voice was barely audible.

"I am so sorry." Her hand brushed his cheek. She sat up. "How does one go on after losing a child? That would be my worst nightmare come true."

"Come here," he said, cupping his hand under her jaw and drawing her to him. "With your help, I hope to get him back." He was overcome with just how important she'd become to him.

"Mm, it's not a done deal." She nestled back into his arms, spoon fashion.

"I know. But I have you and I have hope for the future." He kissed her cheek. "I want Edward to be part of that future."

"H-how will you feel if I fail?" she asked.

"It will be very hard, but I have already lost him. I do know that it may not happen." He stoked her hair and whispered, "I won't blame you, beloved."

"The odds will be greatly improved if Dr. Fairchild will cooperate. At least he sounded excited to meet with me."

The nineteen-passenger commuter plane landed in Rochester, New York, a few minutes early. While the rest of the passengers rushed to the terminal, Mary and Emma stopped to gawk at the cockpit with its gauges covering every available surface. When the captain offered to show the girls what they did, Richard watched from the cabin. He couldn't fathom its complexity.

"And I thought driving a car was complicated," he said.

They walked toward the terminal building.

Sarah laughed. "Little did the pilot know he was giving you the tour, too." The wind gusted off the lake. She gasped. "I've forgotten how cold it gets here." She made sure the girls' parkas were zipped. The ground was wet and the stars weren't visible because of the cloud overcast. It started to snow.

Emma and Mary burst into a run as they exited the secure area. "Grandma! Grandpa!" they yelled together and ran up to a smiling gray-haired couple waving at them.

"Hi Mom, Dad," Sarah said, hugging them after they straightened up from greeting their grandchildren. "I'd like you to meet Richard Gloucestre."

"Hello, hello," her father said. "Sarah's told us about you. I'm Ira Levine, and this is my bride, Beth."

"I've got a piece of news for you," Sarah said, smiling broadly. "We're engaged."

"Isn't that rather sudden?" Beth asked.

They headed for the baggage area.

"Not as sudden as you and Dad," Sarah said, and then turned toward Richard. "Mom and Dad were engaged a week after they met." She turned back to her parents. "Isn't that right?"

"Yes," Ira said. "So-o, what took you so long to pop the question, Dick?"

"I did not want to rush her."

"Yeah, and he waited until our third date in as many days."

"Such restraint," her mother said. "Your father asked me at the end of our first date."

"And you said yes right away, didn't you, Ma?"

"Um-hmm, but I didn't have children. It was just me."

"That's why I waited until now," Sarah said. "And you can put that skepticism I see in your eyes back in the closet—I know what I'm doing. I'm sure."

They arrived in the baggage area and waited for the belt to move and disgorge its load.

"Then, I'm very happy for you," her mother said, hugging Sarah.

"Congratulations." Her father shook Richard's hand, and slapped him on the back. "You will take good care of my daughter."

"That is my intention, Mr. Levine."

"Never mind with that Mr. Stuff. You're family now. Call me Dad, or if you're not comfortable with that, Ira will do."

"I didn't mean to give you a hard time, Dick." Her mother hugged him and then got on her tiptoes to kiss him. She was a good four inches shorter than Sarah. "And you can call me Mom or Ma or Beth, or anything else, but not late for lunch." She grinned.

He returned the hug. "Excuse me," he said, and turned quickly around, overwhelmed by their acceptance of him and the feelings of family, which he'd always longed for.

"Are you all right?" Sarah asked, coming to his side.

"Aye." He cleared his throat. "I am more than all right. Let's not keep them waiting." He gave Sarah a quick hug and they rejoined her parents.

"It was beautiful here last month." Richard drove onto the U Mass campus. The leaves had fallen and the vista was mostly brown, broken only with the dark greens of the pines. At least the morning sun was streaking through the cloud breaks.

"Yeah, I know," Sarah said. "It's typical New England weather."

Richard led the way to the lab where they found Michael waiting for them. "Hello Michael, allow me to introduce you to Sarah Gold."

"I'm honored," Michael said, after the ritual handshakes. "I don't expect anyone to come around today, but you never know. Why don't you sit over there while I lock the door?" He pointed to a beat-up table surrounded by chrome and orange-plastic chairs.

He walked over to the table and sat down. "Sarah, I'm absolutely thrilled to meet you. How did you come to invent something this complicated when you were in high school?"

"I don't know. Just lucky, I guess."

"We don't have time to go into the history, Michael," Richard said. "We are here for a very specific reason. And that is to recover your work so that I can save my son."

"Aren't you afraid that Hosgrove still wants to send you back?" Michael asked. "And there's still the issue of the body."

"The body is not your concern," he said. "I am no longer in danger of being sent back."

"Michael," Sarah said. "Richard and I are getting married. Do you think I'd risk losing him?"

"Congratulations! I'm really happy for you both. Okay, so we're not talking murder anymore, but I was affected when I went back with the team to get you. I won't do it."

"We are not asking you to do that. We're asking you for your help in working through the issues Sarah and Carole's team are encountering in trying to recreate the work you have destroyed."

Sarah put her hand on Richard's arm. "You were very thorough."

"I had to be. I couldn't take the chance anyone on Carole's team could get it working."

"I will have my son, with or without your help."

"Are you that good, Sarah?" Michael asked. "You'll be able to figure out what I've done?"

Richard spoke first. "She is that good. Sarah did not need a week to work out that you created a time machine."

Michael sounded a low whistle. "And I wouldn't have been able to create it if you hadn't invented the device in the first place. Well then, you don't need me. Why are you wasting your time here?"

"We wouldn't be here if we thought that," he said. "If you will not return to Ambion Technologies, please consider collaborating with Sarah on a consultative basis."

"And if I don't?"

"Then spend some time with Sarah now to answer questions she has about the work that you have done."

Michael nodded.

"I'm curious," she said. "What made you think that you could modify this device to go back in time instead of its intended purpose?"

Michael's eyes lit up. "It all started with my graduate research. I was seeking for a way to transfer matter from one point in space to another. In researching the literature, I came across your work and soon realized that its inherent flaw was that matter couldn't exist in two places at the same time. That got me to thinking that the transfer would have to occur at a time other than now."

"I was of the mind that according to the principles of Quantum Mechanics, matter does exist in two places at once. That's the principle I used for Q-Trip."

"Not quite, Sarah. And anyway, that's only on a subatomic level."

"And I was trying to accomplish it on a macro-level," Sarah said. "But why the past? Why not the future?"

"Because the future doesn't exist, yet."

"Explain," she said.

"It gets down to the basic physical laws. No matter what, you still have to have a zero sum change in mass and energy. That's why…"

Richard watched as Sarah and Michael focused on the device and the research that they both had done independently. Within five minutes of their exchange, Michael had retrieved his notebooks and a piece of blank paper on which they were now busily writing. His hopes soared.

"But now you see what my dilemma is," Michael said after an hour of intense discussion. "It's not the science, it's how it affects the lives of the people we touch."

"I can't agree with you. If we didn't do the science, we would still be in caves hunting and gathering," she said. "No matter what the science, it's going to affect lives. Whether it's for good or evil depends on how it's used. Anyway, the toothpaste is out of the tube, so to speak."

"Michael," Richard said, "consider the ignorance I had to live under five hundred years ago and weigh that against Sarah's and my request for your cooperation."

"There is something else that I must tell you." Michael stared down at his hands that were spread in front of him. "I didn't want to mention it, but I think I've suffered some nerve and joint damage from having traveled into the past, even for the few seconds that I did."

"I-I do not understand," he said.

"I've lost sensation in the tips of my fingers, and my feet get numb a lot of the time. It's gotten a lot worse in the colder weather. And I'm feeling pain in my knees and wrists, mostly. I don't have arthritis and the doctors can't find any causes, but I'm definitely having these problems."

"I'm sorry to hear that," Sarah said. "So it's best not to send a live person back, even for a few seconds. But what if we could send a robot back to get Edward, would you help us then?"

"I'll have to think about it, but I will let you make a copy of my notes. Will that help?"

"Absolutely."

Michael retrieved two additional notebooks for a total of six lab books. Each was packed with Michael's hand-written notes. His writing ranged from tightly cramped script to large scrawling block print. "There's a commercial copy place on North Pleasant Street. We can go now."

They left the lab and walked to the copy center.

Richard stopped Michael just as they were about to enter the copy center. "Sarah, I need to talk to Michael, will you..."

"Of course," she said, opening the door. "It'll probably take me ten, fifteen minutes to work out how I want them to bind the copies."

"Michael," Richard said after the door closed behind Sarah. "I can see you are having some difficulty walking today. Why didn't you say anything when I was here with Carole?"

"I felt really good then and thought that my initial reaction was all in my head. When you were here, it had just started getting cold, and it didn't hit me right away."

"How do you know your nerves have been damaged?"

"I've had some tests which prove that they are damaged. But the doctors can't find any disease or anything else that might cause it. I need to talk to the others who went back with me."

"Why have you not done so?"

"They were temporary help. Hosgrove hired them for that purpose only. I don't know how to reach any of them."

"I will speak to Evan."

"Thank you, Richard. I've been afraid to."

"That didn't take long," she said, rejoining them. "They'll have the notes copied and bound in a couple of hours. I'm glad they weren't backed up with other work."

"So, uh, Richard," Michael said. "How long would it have taken your Monks to copy those notes?" He laughed.

"You have just made my point. Every time you suppress science, you repress progress."

"I don't entirely agree. Not everything is progress," Michael said.

They went to a restaurant that Michael suggested. The unpromising brick façade belied the exquisite aromas that enveloped them as soon as they entered. The kitchen opened to the seating area, treating the patrons to the smells and sounds of hamburgers sizzling on a charcoal grill, soup pots bubbling on the stove, and fresh bread baking in the ovens. They sat in a booth toward the front and placed their orders.

"I've been thinking about where we can get a robot that is sophisticated enough to do this job," Sarah said. "I bet we can hook up with a team at MIT's Media Lab. They could always use grant and project money."

Michael put his water glass down. "That's a good idea. You're right about them being the place to start. They are quite advanced in that field."

"I know someone who's there now working in that area." Richard was amazed he could contribute to this arcane discussion.

"You do?" Sarah asked. "How? I thought you just got here." She laughed.

"Katarina's daughter, Elaine, is getting her doctorate at MIT. She is working in the Media Lab on robots."

"Did you meet her?" she asked.

"Yes, she was visiting her mother prior to starting the fall semester. I asked her a lot of questions about the robots, and I think they are perfect for this task."

"What makes you think that?" Michael asked.

"She described in detail how they might be used to rescue people who are trapped somewhere. The difference is," Richard said, "it is not 'somewhere,' but a specific time."

"Portabella with pesto and mozzarella?" the server asked.

"That's mine," Sarah said.

Both Michael and Richard had ordered the same, a bacon burger with fries. The waitress set them up and left.

"Mm," Richard said, taking a bite out of his burger. "What are you having?" he asked, nodding toward her dish.

"It's a grilled portabella mushroom. Do you want a taste?" She cut off a wedge and speared it with her fork, handing it to him. "Here, try it."

He put the morsel in his mouth and then handed the fork back to her. "It's different."

Sarah frowned and Michael laughed.

"So, have you set a date?" Michael asked.

"We haven't as yet. I would do it tomorrow, but Sarah wants to wait."

Michael laughed. "You already act like you're married. Why wait?"

"I have my reasons," Sarah said. "Besides, what's the rush?"

"Anyway, I wish you the best, really. You deserve it."

"Thank you, Michael," Richard said. "Will you return to Ambion in January if we might be able to retrieve Edward using a robot?"

"I'll think about it. Maybe, yes," Michael said. "I still want to talk to the team members that went in with me."

"You have my word. I'll speak with Evan. I do have one question. Why are you having these problems and I am not?"

"You never existed in two places at the same time. The body did until you were pulled forward, but he was already dead."

"How far is Boston and MIT from here? It is in Massachusetts, is it not?" Richard asked.

"A couple of hours by car, I think," Michael said. "Then you probably need to add thirty to forty minutes to get to MIT. Are you thinking of going there, today?"

"The thought did cross my mind."

"Richard, we have to return to Rochester tonight. Dad can't take another day off to babysit, and Mom was unable to take any time this week at all."

"You have kids, Sarah?" Michael asked.

"Um hmm, two girls. Mary is five and Emma is seven, going on thirty."

"Surely we can get a flight to Rochester from Boston tonight," Richard said.

"Then, we had better start making some phone calls," Sarah said.

"Idiot!" Sarah shouted at a Jetta running the light. She jammed on the brakes as it sailed in front of them. "Asshole," she muttered.

Richard gulped. He was glad Sarah had insisted she drive.

"I can't believe you were able to pull this off, Dickon," she said, maneuvering the rented Taurus through the streets of Cambridge. "It's a good thing that Katarina had Elaine's number at the Media Lab. That's really nice of her to see us at the last minute like this."

They parked in a garage three blocks from the Media Lab, a low-rise, angular building, clad in light-gray granite, whose windows ran its length. It could not be accessed directly from the street, but instead the front of the building opened to a small quadrangle with lawn, shrubs, and walkways. They signed in and were directed to Robotics.

"Hello Elaine," he said. She sat on a stool in the center of the mechanical men. The large room was strewn with robots, parts of robots, and researchers who seemed to all be following independent activities.

A three-foot-high robot spun around. Its shaggy eyebrows shot up to the top of its metallic head a second before the rubbery lips moved. "Hello," it said in a sultry feminine voice. "Who are you? I don't believe we've met."

He gasped and took a step back. Sarah laughed and put her hand on his arm.

"I'm Sarah," she said with a little bow. "And this is Richard."

"Hello Sarah, hello Richard," the robot said. "I am Elaine and this is Lani. We work together."

"Hi," Lani said. "I talked to my mother after we spoke, so I know basically why you are here." She shook their hands. "So what do you think of Elaine? They gave her my name just to confuse everyone."

She led them to an office area that contained a small, round table. They sat down at the table while Elaine positioned itself next to Lani. "Elaine, go back to your station and wait for me there."

The robot wheeled around and went back to where they'd first found it.

"It's good to see you, Dickon, and to meet you, Sarah," Lani said. "So speak. I understand you have a plane to catch."

THIRTY-FIVE

"It is really strange. Before I was brought to this time, I would never have dreamt that man could accomplish so much. I would have thought so many things were impossible," Richard said. He was meeting with Evan Hosgrove and recapped what he had learned from his visits in Massachusetts. "Then, after seeing what you have and what you can do, I thought everything was possible."

"But now you know better?" Hosgrove asked.

"I thought all I had to do was convince Michael to return, or divulge to Sarah what he had done to get me. Either way, I'd have my Edward. It would just be a matter of time."

"Nothing is ever simple, is it?" Hosgrove leaned back in his chair and placed his hands behind his head.

"No, it's not simple. At this point, we can't go into the past as you did for me, and we cannot in good conscience send a person back for Edward," he said. "In addition, we cannot use a child's body where there are relatives who are concerned about the remains."

"You just reminded me, Richard, I've heard from the hospital. The family has not dropped their investigation."

"How will that affect us?"

"I'm not sure," Hosgrove said. "Legally, there is a firewall between the hospital and us. But still, it could prove to be quite uncomfortable if they are able to trace its use to this company."

"Is there anything we should do?" he asked.

"We are monitoring developments. Other than that, no."

"I met his mother and brother."

"You did?" Hosgrove stared at him. "When? Where?"

"I met them last month when I had those tests at the hospital."

Hosgrove ran his fingers through his shock of white hair. "I had hoped that you trusted me more and would have told me before now."

"Evan, I am sorry."

"Apology accepted. Besides, I think I would feel the same if our positions were reversed." Hosgrove leaned forward. "So, what do you see as the major sticking points?"

"After speaking with Michael, I thought it would be creating a mechanical man, ah... robot, that could rescue Edward."

"What made you think otherwise?"

"You had to see what they are doing at MIT with robots today. If we can transport the robot back, then there is no need for a living person to risk his health."

"Are you sure Michael suffered some permanent damage from having gone into the past?" Hosgrove asked. "He was only in the past for fifteen or twenty seconds, tops."

"I believe he is convinced. He's had medical tests, and they do show that he has both nerve and joint damage. Yet they cannot find a medical cause."

"Humph, I wonder what is going on."

"That is why it is very important that not only do we provide Michael with the contact information, but we should speak to them as well. We must know if it is just Michael."

"I'll have Linda give you the names of the people we used. But you still haven't said what you think the sticking point is."

"It's still the body." He pinched the bridge of his nose. "I liked Carole's idea of buying a skeleton and building it up to replicate Edward, but..."

"But where does one get a skeleton of a child?"

"Exactly. Assuming that can be done, how can it realistically be made so that it not only fools those who view it, but also those who prepare it for burial?" Richard stood and paced in front of Hosgrove's desk.

Hosgrove rose and walked around to face him, putting his hand on Richard's arm. "Stop! You're wearing out the carpet. Let's move on for now. We'll address this later."

"But if we can't solve this, then is there any point in doing the rest?"

"Richard, you do realize that our main goal is to create a marketable product. All this other work will move us in that direction." Hosgrove sat down in one of the guest chairs and waved his hand in the direction of the other.

"Sarah thinks she may be able to make the device work the way she originally intended." He sat down.

"Really! Now that's something we could sell." Hosgrove sat up, his eyes alight. "How long have you known about that?"

"What do you mean, Evan? She worked it out from her conversation with Michael. Apparently, it was something he said that made her think of a way to make it work."

"How long will she need to be sure?"

"I don't know. It's too soon to say."

"Okay Richard. I really liked the way you took charge on this trip and established a way to get around Michael's objection about going into the past. I want you to prepare a detailed report on what needs to be done to retrieve your son. Prepare a separate report that details what Sarah needs to make her device work to transport matter from one place to another."

Richard nodded.

"Do you think you can have them ready by Friday?"

"Yes." He stood to leave.

"Friday, then." Hosgrove stood and walked out of the office with him. "Linda, I want you to give Richard the information on Carter Services. He needs to contact the team we engaged last August."

Richard and Sarah stood in her parent's backyard, watching her girls play in the snow. "So, how do you like being Project Director?" she asked.

"It's a start."

"Dickon! What do you mean, start? Most people don't get to that level, ever."

"I like being in control, and for the first time since I got here, I feel I am in command of my destiny."

"It's good that Hosgrove had the courage to put you in that position after such a short time."

"We understand each other, commander to commander," he said. "Although the technologies are not comparable, the processes are remarkably similar."

"And you are a leader." Sarah squeezed his arm. "My mind boggles when I think of how much you've accomplished in such a short timeframe."

It struck him that while he had accomplished much, he also owed his position and good fortune to many kind and generous people. "I had to. But I didn't do it alone. Thank you."

"For what?"

"For staying, for not giving up on me. For risking your heart."

She laughed. "I refused to fail. I might just be more stubborn than you." Sarah took her mitten off and lightly traced his eyebrows and then his lips with her fingertips. "Do you think we'll be able to persuade Michael to return to Ambion now that he's talked to Carter's team?" she asked.

"I am more optimistic than I was before," he said. "I'm encouraged that he agreed to meet with me Monday."

"Daddy! Daddy! Look at me," Mary squealed as she spun down the snowy hill on her plastic disc-sled.

"He's not our father," Emma shouted. She was standing at the bottom of the hill facing the porch. "I've told you that a hundred times."

"I don't care, I'll call him Daddy if I want." Mary got off the sled before it stopped and ran up to Richard.

"One down, and one to go," Sarah said.

He smiled. "I haven't felt this happy in…"

"Five hundred years." She finished for him.

He knelt down and caught Mary as she dashed full tilt into him. "You tell your sister that I don't have to be her real father for her to call me Daddy and that I love both of you as much as I would my own children."

Mary gave him a quick hug and ran back to her sister. He stood and rested his arm across Sarah's back.

"Dinner's ready, people," her father called from the back porch. "Come and get it before we throw it away."

Sarah laughed. "He always says that. C'mon girls," she called, waving them in. "Are you ready to eat yourself into a turkey coma?"

"Is there that much food?"

"I'm sure it doesn't compare to those epic feasts that you'd have, but there's way more than all of us can eat."

Emma and Mary caught up with them, and they went inside.

Michael agreed to meet with Richard in New York City. It was the Monday after Thanksgiving and his first time in this city.

Sarah insisted they start at Grand Central Station. It was as grand as its name implied. He had never seen such a large public space in this time that was as beautiful. Gleaming brass rails displayed the light tan, marble walls to advantage. His eyes were drawn to the magnificent ceiling, which spanned the great hall in a spectacular, smooth curve, unencumbered by arches. The ceiling itself was a soft, sea green in which the sky's constellations were depicted in gold. This was surely a cathedral fitting for this century.

They took the shuttle to Times Square and Richard got on the A Train, while Sarah and her daughters waited for the C Train for the Natural History Museum.

"Don't forget," Sarah had said. "You'll need to take the A Train back downtown only as far as 145th Street, and change for the local C Train to Eighty-first Street."

He stepped into the subway car and the doors shut. The train was packed. He grabbed onto the nearest pole as it lurched uptown under the streets of Manhattan. He gazed around at the crush of humanity: people reading, sleeping, talking to their neighbor, and those staring blankly straight ahead.

He got off at 168th Street, and exited the subway across from Columbia Presbyterian where he was meeting Michael. He waited for the physicist near the entrance to the hospital.

"Hi, Richard," Michael said. "I see you found it okay."

"Michael, hello. How are you feeling?"

They shook hands.

"Actually, better than before. I don't know why at the moment, but I'm about to find out," he said. "Listen, thanks for asking. I appreciate it. But you're not here to learn of my health."

"It's not the purpose for my meeting with you here, but I'm not insensitive to what happened in my behalf," Richard said. "Have you talked to the team that went back with you?"

"Yes." Michael grimaced. "It seems that I'm the only one who thinks he's been affected. Except for Jesse. He may have some hearing loss, but he's not sure that's the reason. He said that it runs in his family."

Richard nodded; he had also talked with each member, and had received the same information.

"Before you tell me if you're going to return to Ambion, you need to know that I have been made project director."

"Hey, that's great, congratulations," Michael said. "So if I were to come back, you'd be my boss, eh?"

"Yes."

"But you're not a scientist, how...?"

"I am not doing the work of the scientists. I am making it possible for the scientists and engineers to do their jobs," he said. "Will you be returning to Ambion?"

"Not in January. I decided to finish my year at U Mass." Michael's fists were jammed inside his jacket pocket. "You're using robots?"

"That's the plan. We are negotiating with the Media Lab at MIT."

Michael's eyes widened when Richard mentioned the Media Lab. "So you were able to connect with Katarina's daughter?"

"Yes."

"I might be available in the summer."

He leaned back against the building and stuck his hands in his coat pockets. "Michael, even in my time, we were able to write letters to let people know of such decisions. Why was it necessary to meet face to face?"

"It's because of this." Michael pulled out a small, clear plastic object from his right pocket. "Give this to Sarah. She'll know what it's for."

He took it from Michael and read the label on which was written — *Ambion V5.00.04b R23.8.* "What is it?"

"That's the backup tape that was in the vault. I couldn't bring myself to destroy it." Michael put his hand on Richard's shoulder. They were eye to eye. "I thought I was saving you from being killed."

"I believe you did, Michael." Richard put the tape in his pocket. "Will you consult with Sarah over the phone should she require anything further from you?"

"Yes, absolutely," Michael said. "Uh, I gotta go, my appointment's in five minutes. I hope you're successful."

"And I do hope that the damage you suffered is not permanent. Perhaps you will join us in the summer."

"Maybe. I'll keep in touch." Michael walked into the hospital.

Perhaps for reassurance, or maybe to confirm he wasn't dreaming, he closed his hand around the tape, now securely in his pocket. He crossed the street and took the subway back downtown to the Museum of Natural History.

The subway stop seemed part of the museum. The tiles decorating the stop ranged from bas-reliefs of strange creatures to displays of the stars and planets.

He ran up the stairs and faced a park-like area. Tens of children assembled around the museum entrance a hundred yards in front and down a gentle slope. Richard estimated they were a year or two younger than Edward would have been. He prayed he'd see Edward taking in these sights.

He tried to place his son here in his mind, but could not. A dread seized him that he could not shake. *Is this a bad omen? Will I be denied my child?*

Blindly, he walked toward the glass façade, through the crowd of children, and pushed the revolving door to enter the museum. He was directed down a flight of stairs to the ticket counter.

He bought a ticket and found Sarah, Emma and Mary standing in front of a very large, lumpy rock. He showed his ticket to the guard and was waved through. Sarah's back was to him. Her luxuriant auburn hair stuck out at odd angles as she removed her hat.

"Sarah, did you just get inside? I thought I left you more than an hour ago?"

"Oh hi. Yes. It took longer for the C train, and then the girls wanted to walk around the park for a while. We bought some roasted chestnuts, but couldn't bring them in." She ran her fingers through her hair. "How'd it go with Michael?"

He stepped close to her, holding the tape in his palm. "Here, Michael said you would know what to do with it."

Sarah studied it for a few seconds, reading the label. "Is this a backup tape? I thought he destroyed them."

Mary tugged at his sleeve. "I wanna see the dinosaurs."

He stroked her hair. "We will soon, Mary. I need to talk with your Mama.

"He did destroy the others. This was in a vault."

"I wondered about that." Sarah put the tape in her pocketbook. "I take it he's not coming back. Are you going to do anything about his stealing this tape?"

"He's not coming back in January. He took the tape to keep me from being sent back to Redemore Plain. Sarah, he took a chance and trusted me. I'm not going to do anything."

He felt her shudder. "What is wrong?"

"Then we'd never have met. I will have to thank him the next time we speak," she said. "I hope this tape will be sufficient."

"So tell me about dinosaurs." He took Mary's hand. "Come on, Emma."

This was the hardest decision Richard had ever made. He was elated when they returned after Thanksgiving with the missing backup tape. He was sure that it would take no more than a few days for Sarah to be able to send a camera into the past.

But, they were unable to sustain the tiny cameras for more than a few milliseconds. Without Michael's direct help, it could takes months or longer to get back to the point where a rescue attempt was possible.

As much as it pained him, Richard knew he would have to make his son's retrieval the lower priority project. He went to the conference room early for the meeting he had set up with Carole, John, Phil, and Sarah. Carole was seated at the table when he walked in.

"Hi Boss," she said. "How are you progressing with finding a boy's skeleton?"

"I found a company that can provide the skeletons, but that isn't why I called this meeting."

"I know. I can read the writing on the wall, too. But you're not going to give up, are you?"

"No, never!" He sat down at the head of the table.

"So, have you given any thought as to who is going to convert the skeleton into a body that perfectly resembles your son?" Carole swiveled around in her seat to face him.

"I know some people who work for a creature shop, a couple. They want to move back to Portland to start their own business."

"That sounds like a plan, Richard."

The last three participants entered the conference room. He rose and faced the group. Everyone appeared grim. "My understanding is you are able to return to the past, but for such a short time, that a second is an eternity. You also can't send in anything larger than the smallest of cameras."

"That's correct," John said.

"We couldn't have done that without getting that tape from Michael," Sarah said. "It'd help a lot if you could get him to come here, even for a couple of months."

"Why were you able to get me and now you cannot retrieve a fly?"

Both Phil and Sarah started speaking at the same time. Phil bowed his head slightly. "Go ahead, Sarah."

"The Earth isn't at the same place in space now. We're billions of miles from where it was five hundred and twenty-two years ago. We're having a lot of trouble locking into the exact site."

"We had the same problem with you, Richard," Carole said. "But Mike figured it out. The solution never made it to the vault."

"Can you solve it without Michael?" Richard asked.

"I'm no longer sure," Sarah said. "Michael's notes aren't complete. I've called him, but he insists he gave us everything."

"Then Michael is still the key." He pinched the bridge of his nose. *Had Michael changed his mind?*

"I pressed him for more detail," Sarah said. "But it's hard to do over the phone. At this point I don't know if he's holding out on us or not."

His hope to see his son this year vanished. And if the company could not turn a profit, he'd never see his son again.

"Sarah, you told me that you think you have solved the problem with the original purpose of your device."

"I believe I have," she said. "I'll get into more detail later, but I think if I can figure out what the correct time interval should be between the present and the future, I can transport objects from point A to a receiving device at point B."

"Why are you able to transport to the future and not to the past?" he asked.

"Because the time interval is so small that for all practical purposes, the geographical points haven't shifted."

"You originally estimated that you could produce the first working model in less than a year. Is that still the case?" he asked.

"I'm not exactly sure. I think that if Q-trip is the primary focus, and we all work on it…"

"I think if we all concentrated on it, there's a good chance we could do it in six months or less," John said.

"Then, make that your priority. You have until June to create a working model. I will try to convince Michael to join us in June."

"In that case, we had better get started," Carole said. "We have just under six months to create a working prototype before Mike can possibly get here."

They all stood to leave the conference room.

"Sarah, wait. Close the door, please."

She closed the conference room door and returned to the table. "Dickon, this has to be very hard. I'm surprised… um, actually, I'm not surprised."

"You're not?"

"As king, you acted in the best interest of the many, and not always to your own benefit. Why should you change now? That was brilliant of Hosgrove to put you in charge."

"We should not wait until after Edward is here to get married."

"You're afraid we won't be able to get him, aren't you?" she asked.

"Aye," he whispered, taking her hands in his. "I need to move on. If we can't get him, then so be it. I won't give up, but I can't let it interfere with the rest of my life."

"Then, let's pick a date."

THIRTY-SIX

Richard and Sarah agreed on the day they would get married—the tenth of April. Finally, in a little over three months, they would be man and wife. Sarah wanted to wait until after she produced a working Q-Trip prototype, but he was anxious to marry sooner. She agreed to this date with the caveat that they would have to return to Portland after only a one- or two-day honeymoon, and they needed to combine it with business.

Michael agreed to meet with them again, and for the first time, Richard felt he was getting Michael's full cooperation.

It was now the time to contact the Califanis, Elaine's friends who he'd met in San Francisco and who both worked in the animatronics industry. He went to his office to phone Elaine for her friends' telephone number. Elaine was neither at the Media Lab, nor at home. Frustrated, he left a message at both numbers.

He shook his head, realizing he'd become spoiled by an age where instant communication was possible nearly everywhere in the world. In his past life, when messages sometimes took months to be returned, he'd had no choice but to wait. Then, in a effort to reduce the long wait times, especially with national concerns, both he and his brother had set up a network of fresh horses and messengers.

If only he had had this technology then. Maybe all those friends, all those people loyal to him, would not have died at Redemore. But that was nonsense, for hadn't he gone into battle knowing the Stanleys were likely to betray him?

Despite his sessions with the therapist, he still felt haunted by his fatal decision to fight at Bosworth over five hundred years ago. He wondered if he could ever forgive himself.

His vision blurred and instead of the office he saw the last moments of the battle of Bosworth. Henry had been in reach. If only he'd gotten to him before Stanley's army reached him. But he didn't and the resulting slaughter of his friends and supporters had been his doing. He feared he would dishonor those who died for him if he rid himself of the memory.

"A penny for your thoughts." Sarah leaned in from the doorway, her hand on the doorjamb.

"Come in, I was—"

"You have that look, Dickon." She closed the door and sat down by his desk.

"What do you mean?"

"Sometimes, it seems like you are reliving something terrible. It's in your eyes, your entire being. You get this stony expression. It's like some things won't stay buried."

"Jesú," he whispered. "I must talk, but not here."

"I'll get my coat and meet you at the car."

He waited until she was out of sight before he stood. He pulled his camelhair coat off the hook and carelessly put it on over his jacket. He didn't bother buttoning it.

He marched to the car, nodded to several people whose paths he crossed, but did not really notice who anyone was.

The therapist Evan had recommended provided limited help, but he was constrained by his inability to fully disclose all the facts, and who he really was.

The only good thing was Sarah, and even she didn't banish his black thoughts. He leaned against the hood of the car and watched her approach.

"Hi again." She reached up and pulled at his collar. One side was folded under at the shoulder.

He pulled his keys out and felt her hand on his.

"I'm driving," she said. "I don't think you should."

He was about to protest, but saw she was determined. He got in on the passenger's side while Sarah got behind the wheel.

She drove to the small park where they liked to share an occasional lunch. Because the sky was overcast and the temperature had dropped to below freezing, they had the park to themselves.

"Do you want to walk?" she asked, parking the car.

"Yes," he said. He couldn't stand to sit any longer. It would be easier to say what was on his mind if he didn't have to see her face or her eyes. It wasn't even about her, so why was he finding this so difficult?

She looped her arm around his waist as they started walking. The wind was blowing slightly, not bothersome yet, but carrying with it a hint of snow. A few brown oak leaves danced in front of them.

He put his hand on her shoulder and briefly hugged her. "You're right. I keep reliving that last day on Redemore Plain. I went into battle knowing I could die, knowing the odds had turned against me. But my friends, all those men who were loyal, did not deserve my fate. It is my doing they died that day."

"Is it?"

"What do you mean? I led them into battle, Sarah. They went in on my orders and by my command."

"But what were the alternatives? Would the outcome have been any different by more than a few days if you hadn't attacked? Wasn't Henry the aggressor?"

"Yes, he was." He stopped and took Sarah's gloved hands in his and pulled them to his chest. "I have been replaying that last day in my mind over a thousand times. It was I who was eager for battle. I was the one they followed."

"But if you hadn't gone into battle, you were doomed, weren't you? It seems to me that battle may have been the only alternative that offered a chance for your side."

"I suspected the Stanleys would change sides and they did," he said. "They gave Henry the strength he needed and robbed me. I should have delayed once I was sure of their treachery."

"So your choice was to show strength and fight, or weakness and back down. If you had backed down, would the outcome have been any different except for the exact date?"

"My advisors thought I should wait for more troops to come to my aid."

"But wouldn't that have given Henry time to solidify his position? And couldn't that have resulted in more deaths?"

"There is no way of knowing, Sarah."

"You can't second-guess what might have been. Right or wrong, you made the best decision you could with the information you had."

"I suppose so." He hugged her. "This has helped me more than you can imagine."

"Are you sure? You still seem to be haunted. You're not just saying it, are you?"

"No, you have helped me. I couldn't be candid with the therapist, and I didn't allow for the possibility there may have been nothing that I could have done that would have substantially changed what happened." He let go and took a step back. "But for all that, Henry was a coward. He hid behind his men."

"Henry castled."

Richard stood in the kitchen doorway watching Sarah tell the girls they were going to marry. He knew he was grinning like a fool, but he was giddy.

Earlier, he'd talked to Elaine and learned his project was moving forward a little ahead of schedule. She thought they would be ready to start testing the robots at Ambion Technologies in June. He had reason to hope that by summer's end, he'd not only have a wife and two daughters he loved as his own, but also, with Sarah's science and some luck, his son.

Emma's eyes widened as Sarah delivered the news. Mary jumped up squealing, "Daddy!" and ran into him, hugging him around his hips. "See, I told you he wouldn't leave us."

Emma's face crumpled.

"Honey, what's wrong?" Sarah asked.

Emma hiccoughed and sniffed. "N-nothing."

"You thought I was going to leave, didn't you, Emma?" he asked. He walked over to the table where she was seated, still holding Mary's hand. "As long as your Mama will have me, I am not going to leave. You have my solemn promise."

Emma nodded and hiccoughed a couple of times more. A few tears rolled down her cheeks. Sarah gave her a glass of water.

"Mary, I want to talk to your sister," he said, letting go of her hand. He pulled a chair next to Emma and sat down, his eyes never leaving her face.

"I would like it very much if you would call me Papa or Daddy, but only if you want to." He dabbed her tears.

"Why don't we go out to dinner to celebrate?" Sarah asked. "Anyway, I don't feel like cooking."

"I don't wanna go out," Emma said, a smile rapidly replacing her tears. "Can we have pizza?" She put her small hand on his and stared at him wide-eyed. "Promise you won't go away?"

"I promise." He placed his free hand over hers and looked deeply into her eyes. "I will always be loyal to you, your sister, and your mother. Loyalty binds me."

The color rose in her cheeks and she turned her head away. "Oh."

While Sarah called the order in, his cell phone rang and he walked into the living room while he answered. "Hello, this is Richard."

"Hey, Richard, how're you doing? This is Tony Califani. Lani said you wanted to talk to me."

"I need someone with your and Alison's abilities in creating a realistic body. I thought of both of you because of what you showed me when Lani and I visited you." He paced in front of the couch.

"When do you need it?" Tony asked.

"I'm planning on starting in June. Lani said you and Alison were thinking of starting your own company, and I don't want to contract this out."

"That sounds perfect," Tony said. "Alison is due in February. That would give us time to set things up."

"I would want you to do the work at Ambion Technologies. I need to keep it inside the company." He sat down.

"That could work. Listen, let me give you our phone number and let's set something up. Can you meet with us here?"

"I can arrange to come down," he said.

April 10, 2005
Home of Ira and Beth Levine
Rochester, New York

Richard had not been able to eat on this day—his wedding day. Sarah's parents had offered their home for the ceremony and for the reception after. Richard had paid for the airline tickets for her grandparents, her brother and his wife. It struck him how like this small affair was to his first wedding at Westminster Abbey.

"I have to hand it to you, Richard. I never thought that I'd see my sister marry again," Sam said. "She kept it to herself, but I know her ex really did a number on her."

Sarah had called Sam her kid brother. He was only five years younger than she was, but took after her father and had already begun losing his red hair. Although taller than him, Sam was still shy of an even six feet tall. But what struck Richard most about Sam was that, like his soon to be father-in-law, he felt immediately comfortable with him. While people were, in general, amicable, he was finding it difficult to form strong friendships, especially with the men of this century. He had so little in common with anyone here.

He was grateful to Sam for agreeing to be best man. He had no one, especially since the ceremony was being held at her parents' house in Rochester, New York. He'd met her brother and his wife during the Thanksgiving holiday.

That he could marry for love a second time was something he had not thought possible. Indeed, that outcome in his time was unlikely to ever happen. He had liked her parents and hoped to have the opportunity to come to love them. It would not be difficult—they were so generous and accepting of him.

"I love Sarah more than you can imagine, Sam. I hope to make her very happy."

"Trust me, you have. Well, are you ready to take your vows?"

They walked into the living room and the ceremony began. He had wanted something more elaborate, but was dissuaded because of time constraints, and Sarah's work took up most, if not all of her time. She had suggested they reaffirm their vows when they were not so busy.

The City Court Judge, a thin, serious man in his late forties, stood with his back to the fireplace. Richard and Sam stood to the right. Sarah's father led his bride to them, stepping in time to Handel's *Water Music*, playing softly in the background.

She was radiant in a pale violet suit that mirrored her eyes. She wore small heels for the occasion.

Sarah came abreast of him, and they stood facing the Judge. He began. "We are gathered here this Sunday, the tenth of April, two thousand and five to unite this man, Richard Gloucestre, and this woman, Sarah Levine Gold, in the bonds of holy matrimony by the authority invested in me by the State of New York."

The rite continued. They each swore to love, honor and be true to each other for the rest of their lives, exchanging rings when the Judge said it was time. Sarah had wanted to use the wedding ring from her first marriage as it had been passed down to her from her great-grandmother. He had wanted it to be from him. He had tried to get her an elaborate ruby and diamond encrusted band, but Sarah preferred a tri-colored-gold band, pointing out the nature of her work wouldn't allow her to wear something that delicate. She got him a matching ring.

Sarah's parents took care of Emma and Mary while they honeymooned in New York City for two days. Evan Hosgrove's wedding present was a suite for two nights at the St. Regis Hotel.

There was a bottle of Cristal Champagne waiting for them in their suite.

"Hosgrove has really outdone himself," Sarah said, reading the note. "I can't believe this suite. I don't want to know what it costs. This is really an extravagant gift."

"I suspect this is inconsequential compared to the money Q-trip is going to make for the company," he said. He took a napkin off the tray and draped it over the cork.

"I'm thrilled I was able to spec out the prototype before we left. I wouldn't have been able to enjoy myself otherwise. I know it didn't seem like much, but getting that paperclip to move across the lab like we did was huge."

He popped the cork and poured them each a glass. "To my beautiful bride." He took a drink.

"And to my handsome groom." Sarah sipped the champagne and set her glass down.

He put his glass down next to hers and embraced his bride. "You are everything to me," he whispered in her ear. They kissed passionately, the champagne quickly forgotten.

"Lessee," Sarah said as they got off the Acela Express in Boston. "You've been here what, eight months, and already you've experienced planes, trains, automobiles, ferries, and subways."

He grinned. "So, what's left?"

"Hah! You're even starting to sound like a Noo Yawker." She laughed. "Um, I guess submarines and rockets. Most people don't get to travel in either of those."

They fought their way off the platform through the icy April rain to the tunnels. "Ugh, I'm glad we don't have to walk outside," Sarah said as they ducked through the doorway leading down to the covered walk.

Once they were in the station, they found the car rental company. Within a half-hour of their Boston arrival, Sarah was driving to the Media Lab.

The human Elaine was expecting them, and as soon as they got there, she took them to where the work was being done on the project.

"I understand congratulations are in order," Elaine said. "There are your robots. What do you think?"

"Thanks," Sarah said. "Can you demonstrate how they work?"

"Sure." Elaine sat down at a control booth and slipped on a headset. "I can give it voice commands through this mike, as well as manipulate it with this joy stick." She pointed to a device that was shaped like half a steering wheel.

"I see that no wires are connected to it," Sarah said.

"That's the beauty of it. Everything is done remotely," Elaine said. "Also, there's a lot of programming built into it so if communication is lost, they can behave autonomously and complete the mission. We still have to test it when it goes through time. All bets are off until then."

"They don't appear to be human," Richard said. "I'm worried that will be too frightening for Edward."

"That's where the Califani's come in. They'll be able to make these suckers look human enough."

"They must be able to create a body that will not only closely resemble Edward," he said. "But will deceive the people who prepare the body for burial and display. It has to be convincing."

"You'll have to work with them," Sarah said. "You're the only one who'll be able to judge. Are you going to be all right with that?"

He knew he was risking a lot, and at this point, he wasn't sure if they would be able to get his son. The QDE had been put on hold to develop the Q-Trip to ensure Ambion's profitability. He might have to reconstruct Edward from memory and then have to bury him again. His only hope was he'd be able to convince Michael to join them in the summer, and then that he'd be able to reconstruct what he had done before.

Materializing inside Edward's bedchamber posed a special hazard. Someone might emerge inside a wall—certain to die.

"I understand," he said. "But this is the only way."

"If anyone can do it, they can," Elaine said. "I was talking to Alison the other day, and she's already going stir crazy. She can't wait to dig into this project. They're both very excited about it."

"Please show us how these robots work," Sarah said.

Elaine moved a robot behind a wall and then spent the next half-hour putting it through its paces. They saw what it saw on the monitors, receiving images from the attached cameras.

"We probably won't know if the robot will perform as demonstrated until we try it at Ambion. Being separated from the controls over time is a lot different from being separated by a physical wall."

"Our first priority will be to devise tests for them," Sarah said. "To do that, we have to get one more team member."

"Who's that?"

"Michael Fairchild," he said. "We're going to see him after we leave here."

"I can be available the beginning of June," Elaine said. "Will you be ready for me by then?"

Sarah shrugged. "We'll let you know, Elaine."

"Call me Lani. All my friends do."

"Do you think you will be able to recreate the QDE now that Michael has agreed to consult with you?" Richard asked once they were back in the car and on their way to Amherst to see him.

Sarah steered the car onto the Mass Turnpike. "I want to say yes, but I can't. I feel like I'm missing something obvious. We need him, if only for the summer."

The rain turned to snow as they headed into the Berkshires. He tensed as the visibility lessened. Sarah was noticeably nervous at the wheel, keeping to the right lane.

"Do you need to pull over?"

"No, I'm okay," she said. "I just need to take it slow."

"I'll drive if you want."

"Listen, I've had over fifteen years experience driving in these conditions, and you've had what, three months? I don't think so."

He turned his head away from Sarah. That stung. *It matters not that she is right.*

"I'm sorry, Dickon. I didn't mean it that way."

"I know," he said. "You're correct. I don't have enough experience with driving in these conditions."

She relaxed her shoulders and her expression softened. "Your test results were a piece of good news, eh? At least you won't have to worry about Edward having some of the more serious genetic diseases."

"I didn't realize how much that was preying on my mind until after I got the results back. I'm greatly relieved."

"I'm curious," she said. "How did you get to be such a great father when your own father pretty much abandoned you?"

"What do you mean abandoned? He was killed when I was seven. I hardly call that abandonment."

"But before that, how much did you see him? You've told me that you hardly knew him."

"I don't remember that much about my father. Even though Ned was my brother and only ten years my senior, he was more a father to me," he said. "I vowed never to neglect my children."

"And you didn't," Sarah said, her voice soft. "Not even the two you fathered before you married."

"There was no stigma attached to natural children then. Legally, they couldn't inherit title. I wasn't the only father who acknowledged these children. Your ex had no compunction about abandoning his daughters."

Sarah sighed. "You're right, of course. And I'm thrilled to no end how you've managed to win Emma over. She's tough."

"Methinks we have a lot in common," he said. "I want to adopt Emma and Mary as my own."

THIRTY-SEVEN

July Fourth

"Hey man," Sean said. "Gimme five." He held up his open palm to Richard. "I see you still won't wear shorts."

Richard noted everyone else had shorts on, including Sarah. He'd expressed his dismay at her near nakedness when she retorted that he and Anne had stripped to the waist in front of a thousand of his closest friends for his coronation. He relented, but still chose casual slacks for the barbecue.

"Sean," Richard said, slapping his palm. "It's good to see you."

"So why'd you sneak off and get married, man? I was looking forward to being at your wedding."

"Don't worry," Sarah said. "We're going to have a big party later. You have to come to that."

"I'm looking forward to it." Sean grinned. "Anyway, I've got some good news, too. I'm getting married next May. Rita's floating around here somewhere. I'd like you to meet her."

"Ah, I see the three of you connected," Katarina said. "I'm glad you could come. Richard, do me a favor, please. See Michael over there by himself? I tried to get him to mingle, but failed. Do you think you can convince him to join in?"

"I'll try."

Michael stood by the garden shed, the one spot isolated from the rest of the people who were mingling around, forming and reforming clusters of two, three, and four people. A few younger children were playing badminton where a net was set up in the yard. A group of older children were shooting hoops in the driveway.

He was one of only four other people at the picnic that Michael was at all friendly with. And even at that, he kept his distance. It concerned him that he knew so little about the man on whom he would depend to save his son.

"Hello, Michael," Richard said as he walked up to the shed. "You look like you are lost in thought."

"Hmm?" Michael said. He drank some of his beer, but his expression revealed nothing. "I suppose I was."

"Sarah tells me she really enjoys working with you. She feels that your being here has helped to save almost half a year of the development time."

"Your wife is great to work with, Richard. I've never had the pleasure of collaborating with someone with as quick a mind as she has." Michael's face gained some animation as he spoke.

It gladdened him to see Michael smile and to hear how he felt about working with Sarah. He didn't know how much of Michael's work depended on his state of mind, but from his own experience, he knew it made a difference. "She thinks you'll be able to send cameras back by the end of this month."

"That's our target," Michael said. "Listen, I'm not much for these barbecues, so if you'll excuse me, I'll be on my way."

"I don't believe you have ever met my friend, Sean. He's the one who helped me escape Hosgrove's grasp in the beginning. Please join us and stay at least a few more minutes."

"I know Katarina put you up to this." Michael laughed. "Really, I've got to get going. I only dropped by to say hello. I'll see you at Ambion." Michael cut across the yard to his car, waving to Katarina.

He rejoined his wife, who was now chatting with Elaine and John. "It seems that instead of getting Michael to join us, I just chased him away."

"He's like that," John said. "He's always kept to himself. I think the only person he ever really talked to socially was Hosgrove. Now he avoids him."

"Michael had mentioned he will be returning to Amherst the middle of September," he said.

Sarah nodded. "We should be all set by then. We may even be able to do without Mike earlier than that."

"Sarah's right," John said. "Plus, I'm not too keen on him having access to the server. He did destroy the original programming. And it's taken us these past eight or nine months to recover well enough to send a camera back."

Richard and Sarah put their arms around each other. "I think his actions come under the law of unintended consequences," she said.

Jesú, it's him. He's so thin. Someone is coming toward him, a woman. Anne?

The video ended much too soon, and yet it seemed an eternity. His son was clearly visible in the courtyard of Middleham. The camera was focused on Edward, so he didn't see the face of the woman who approached at the end of the twenty-second video. He realized she couldn't have been Anne. While he thought he recognized the gown, Anne was with him in Nottingham when Edward died.

"Are you okay?" Sarah asked. He had asked her to be with him while he watched this first video. Her hand rested on his shoulder. "You haven't moved for the past five minutes."

He covered her hand with his. "Yes," he whispered. "I thought I'd never see him again."

"You didn't think we'd be able to pull this off, did you?"

"I was afraid to hope." He stood and hugged her tightly. "I never told you this, but I would see something or hear something and think that I must tell Edward about it. I feel like I've been saving things for him."

"And now you'll have the chance to. I've come to love him because of all you have told me about him. I'm scared that he won't accept me," she said. "This is an excellent video of your son. We'll be able to figure out his mass and height from it."

"Don't be afraid. He's a really wonderful child. I'm sure he'll accept you. He'll just need some time." Richard smiled. "Would it be possible for me to have a photograph of Anne?"

"I thought she was with you in Nottingham, and not with Edward in Middleham"

"Yes."

"I think we should wait until after we get Edward. If we had to change the equipment's calibration just to get a photo of Anne, we could be delayed days if not weeks. I don't want to chance it, I'm sorry."

Richard walked into a darkened house. It was after midnight. He poured a shot of Blanton's bourbon and brought it into the study. He didn't bother turning a light on when he sat down, taking a sip of his drink. *They were so close!*

With Michael returning to Ambion, they were able to send a camera back to the fifteenth century and film Edward outside, before he got sick. But they were unable to send a camera back to Edward's chamber without it destroying itself within a couple of seconds. In addition, the computer simulations consistently showed the robot materializing partly inside a stone wall.

He heard footsteps and saw Sarah silhouetted in the doorway. She entered the study.

"Dickon, I'm so sorry."

"You did warn me."

She walked behind him and stroked his hair. "Both Mike and I are willing to keep trying, but it's your decision. I'm not sure Mike agrees, but I think we have a fifty-fifty chance of making this work."

"That's what he said." He put his glass down and took his wife's hand, pulling her from behind him. "I also saw Tony Califani. They are having a lot of technical problems with the human skin."

"How bad?"

"It would not take a minute to realize it wasn't real. I now understand why they used a real body for me."

"What did Tony say his odds are for success?"

"About the same, fifty-fifty."

"What are you going to do?"

He sighed, what should he do? What could he do? "I think I'll give it another month, and if there are no breakthroughs, I will have to let it go until the technology catches up and then try again."

August 22nd

Richard was quite concerned as he made his way to the executive conference room. He had just received a call from Linda asking him to meet with Evan and some key people working on the project to get Edward.

It was just last week when Sarah and Michael found the clue they needed to stabilize a camera for more than three seconds inside Edward's chamber. That still left the problem with the body, but they were a step closer.

Something has gone horribly wrong.

He turned down the corridor for the conference room, braced for bad news. Through the glass, he saw all the principal people. Hosgrove was at the head of the table; Sarah, Carole, and John were standing to the right with their backs to him. And Elaine, Michael, Alison, Tony, and Phil were on the opposite side of the table. He set his jaw and walked in.

"Happy one year anniversary, Richard," they all said, more or less in unison.

Stunned, he gasped in surprise. Despite the extra hours everyone had put in, he'd witnessed many setbacks regarding the body, and fixing on the time and position, that he'd been sure it could only be bad news. He should have known by their dedication that they'd not just give up, that they'd continue to work at it until he stopped them.

"I had forgotten it was today."

"Actually, it was yesterday," Carole said. "But today is the closest workday we had."

"And we have some good news for you," Alison said. "Stop by our lab later and we'll show you." They were beaming.

He was staggered; he'd expected the worst. "Thank you for remembering. This has been an amazing year for me. It is not something I could ever have imagined before."

"No, I don't think you could have," Hosgrove said. He put his hand on Richard's back and steered him to the corridor. "It seems you're very close to getting Edward here."

"Yes." He slowed his breathing, feeling somewhat dizzy. "Now I have reason to hope."

"Excellent. I'm going to need you to turn your attention back to Q-Trip fairly quickly. We have started to get inquiries on it. At present, how much time can you focus on Q-Trip?"

"I'll have to consult with the Califanis about the body, but that will not require all of my time. It will be good to divert my thoughts."

"We can't wait any longer to tell them about Edward," Richard said.

"We may as well get it over with." Sarah frowned. "I hate having to tell them that not only are they going to have a ten-year-old brother, but he may hate them because they're Jewish. Well, go ahead, call them in."

"Why do you assume he hates Jews?" he asked.

"Don't you think it likely?"

"I don't know what to think," he said. "I didn't teach him to, nor did Anne. He may have learned that from the church, but that has yet to be established."

"Did you ever talk about it with him?" she asked.

"No."

"Best guess then, do you think if he were being indoctrinated against a people, would he have talked to you about it?" she asked.

"We never discussed it. It had no importance, then." He took Sarah's hand in his and gave it a slight squeeze. "He may be indifferent, I just don't know."

"Hmm, so even if he were hearing those things, it may not have meant that much," she said. "Well, call the girls in, we still need to prepare them, just in case."

"Emma, Mary, come in here," Richard said. "There's something your mother and I need to tell you."

The girls came into the living room and sat down on the couch on either side of Sarah. He sat in a chair to the right of the couch.

"Your mother and I have been working on something that is very important to me." He leaned forward on his elbows.

"And to me, as well," Sarah said. She wrapped her arms around her girls and gave them each a squeeze.

"I have a son that we never told you about until now because we didn't know if he could be brought here. Now we think we can."

"What's his name?" Mary asked.

"How old is he?" Emma asked.

"His name is Edward and he's ten; he'll be eleven in December."

"Why didn't you think you could bring him here?" Emma asked.

"It's very complicated, but he's in a place that's quite different from what you know," Richard said. "He doesn't know anything about the world or things like TV. He also has been taught some very bad things."

Both Emma and Mary gaped nervously at their mother. It was Emma who spoke up.

"Will he be mean to us?"

"I don't know. I'll do everything I can to prevent that. Before I tell you about my son, there is something I must tell you about me. You both must promise not to tell anyone about this."

Emma gulped and nodded while Mary just smiled, her attention wandering.

"Girls, this is serious," Sarah said. "I want to hear both of you promise to keep this secret."

"I promise," Emma said.

Mary smiled and nodded.

"Mary," Sarah said. "What do you say?"

"Me too, I promise."

"Do you remember that story I've told you about Anne and Dickon?" he asked.

Mary nodded and Emma's eyes grew wide.

"You are Dickon!" Emma said.

"I am."

"I told you so, I told you so," Mary said.

"What happened to Anne?" Emma asked.

"She got sick and died. But we had a son and your mother has been working very hard to bring him into this time."

Mary clapped her hands. "We're gonna have a brother."

"If we're successful," Sarah said. "There is a chance that it won't work, but you need to be prepared either way. Do you understand?"

They both nodded, instantly quieting down.

"Both of you are going to have to help him," she said. "He's going to be very confused, and he has never met anyone who is Jewish."

"He has been taught by priests to fear Jews," he said. "We are all going to have to help him overcome this fear."

"Why does he fear us?" Emma asked.

"That's part of the bad things that he's been taught," he said.

"Were you taught the same thing, Daddy?" Mary asked.

"Yes, but I don't think that way anymore. I love you and your Mama with all my heart. I want my son to feel the same way. He will need all of us to help him to do that."

THIRTY-EIGHT

Early September, 2005

"Do you want to watch, Richard?" Michael asked.

"Aye." He reached for Sarah's hand. Now that the moment was here, his heart was pounding. *Dear God, let him survive, let him be all right.* He momentarily squeezed his eyes tightly shut.

"Come, we'll watch together." Sarah pulled gently at his hand.

Michael led them to a bank of monitors situated in a darkened room. The only lighting was the exit sign and the glow from the monitors, currently all blue screens. "I have to be at the QDE's controls. Yyou should be fine here." Michael left the room and went to the chamber where the time travel actually took place, one floor directly below.

He paced. "I should be with Michael for my son."

"No, you shouldn't," Sarah said. She stepped in front of him and grasped his hands. "You have to let them do their jobs, just as you so wisely did these past few months. I'm more qualified to be in the chamber, but I'm too emotionally close to make good decisions."

They sat behind John and Carole who were manning the monitors; one connected to two cameras set in the robot-like eyes, and two for independent cameras to aid Elaine in directing the robot.

The cameras' screens came alive. They watched the scene play out, as they had a dozen times before in rehearsal. Elaine was the primary operator, and Phil was connected to the secondary controls as a hot standby, ready to take over the second the primary ceased to operate.

Michael turned the robot on, and Elaine tested it by picking up the body for the last time. In his darkened room, Edward would mistake the robed robot for a servant. It worked flawlessly as she directed it to scoop up Edward's replacement.

Everyone gave a thumbs-up, and Michael activated the QDE. The quantum corridor opened up like an iris, and they stared into a darkened tunnel where light and shadow swirled inwardly. The second of April 1484 lay at the end of the tunnel. The robot slipped into the fifteenth century and Edward's chamber.

They picked the moment carefully, weeding through the videos until they could be absolutely sure there would be no disruption of their activity. Edward complained he wasn't feeling well and had gone to his chamber early the night before.

An hour before dawn, the last attendant vacated the chamber, leaving Edward alone. The team had less than five minutes to do the swap before the attendant returned with the doctor. In actuality, they had thirty seconds before the equipment would fail, and no rescue was possible.

His condition had worsened throughout the night. At the time the robot entered, he was in terrible pain. All this Richard had watched countless times already. It was hard to see his son in so much pain. But now he could hope his son could be saved. And, he was alive.

Sarah squeezed his hand.

The monitors fuzzed out momentarily as the cameras and the robot shared centuries and moved through time down the corridor. The robot reached the singularity that was the fifteenth century, and the monitor displayed the chamber glowing an eerie green from the night-vision optics.

'Jesú.' He watched his son writhe on his bed.

The robot placed the dummy on the floor near the foot of the bed. It then twisted sideways and scooped a squirming fevered boy into its flesh-like, covered steel arms. It started to roll back to the corridor and the twenty-first century.

He held his breath and prayed. Twelve seconds had elapsed.

Both he and Sarah rose together and stood directly behind John and Carole at the monitor panel, shivering in the warm room.

The monitors flickered and then went solid blue. The signal was lost.

"Shit!" Elaine's voice punctuated the silence over the speaker.

"Nothing's happening," Phil said. "No! Michael you—."

Richard spun on his heel and bolted for the door—Sarah followed. They ran down the stairs and into the chamber. The only two people in the chamber were Elaine and Phil.

"Michael went in," Phil said, his voice cracked. "We lost communication and when the robot didn't come back through, Michael ran in before I could stop him."

Richard jumped for the corridor. Phil grabbed his jacket and yanked him back. "You can't! You'll cease to exist and so will the Richard that's there now."

They stared at the spot where the robot had first exited, and where Michael had disappeared. The swirling lights and shadows coalesced when a slight, blond-haired man of Richard's height fell forward. Edward was cradled in his arms.

When Richard reached for Michael, his face and the backs of his hands burned. He pulled Michael and his son free of the QDE.

Phil and Elaine grasped the tag end of the robot's robe that had been tangled up in Michael's feet. It took the two of them to pull the robot back into the twenty-first century. It had been sharing centuries for a total of sixty-three seconds. The robot crumbled into small bits of steel, cloth, and plastic as it emerged.

The QDE stopped operating. No one had shut it down. No one needed to.

Richard cradled his son in his arms and felt him burning up. Michael did not rise, but lay on the floor, shaking.

"Someone bring Michael to the ambulance," Richard said, lifting Edward to carry him to the private ambulance they had waiting for him.

"Mike, can you walk?" Phil asked.

"L-let him g-go," Michael stammered. "I'll be—"

Richard ran out with his son in his arms. Sarah was by his side. "I'll follow you to the hospital," she said, and ran for the car while he stopped at the waiting gurney.

The paramedics took Edward and wheeled him down the loading dock's ramp once they secured him to the gurney. Richard kept pace with them.

The lead EMT jumped into the back of the ambulance and pulled the gurney into place as her partner pushed. Richard climbed into the back, and the second paramedic got behind the wheel.

"You have to go up front, Mr. Gloucestre. We can't allow you back here," she said.

"I must stay here with him. Work around me," he said. "This is what I'm paying for."

Edward's eyes fluttered open. He saw their naked panic. "Edward, it is Papa."

"Papa?"

"Do you trust me?"

"Aye," Edward said. He moved in the gurney and cried out.

Two loud blasts from the siren pierced the cabin. Edward's eyes went wide with fear. There were two more blasts and the ambulance picked up speed.

"You must listen to me. Everything you see and hear will be strange." He cupped his hand on Edward's face and stroked his cheek. "I swear; you will not be harmed. Let this woman touch you and see your stomach. She knows what she's doing."

"Aye, Papa."

"I think it's his appendix." He looked at the emergency medical technician who was hovering close to his elbow. He scuttled to the side and kept stroking Edward's cheek.

She crouched next to the cot and pressed gently on Edward's abdomen and groin. He screamed out when she pressed the spot directly above the appendix.

The siren blasted again and the ambulance swayed around a corner. Both Richard and the technician had to grab onto a handhold to keep from being thrown against the opposite wall.

"Owie - owie, I know, sweetheart. You'll be all better soon." She nodded at Richard. "You're right, it's appendicitis. I'd bet my salary on it. He'll be okay."

The ambulance slowed and pulled into the hospital's emergency entrance. Edward cried out in pain as they rolled the gurney into the hospital's entry. Richard ran alongside, keeping his hand on his son.

"Papa? Am I dead?"

"No! Why do you think that?"

"I feel very strange."

"You will be asleep for a while. I will be with you when you awake."

"Yes, Papa."

Richard stood aside and the medical team wheeled Edward to surgery. An aide walked up to him. "Sir, are you his father?"

"Yes."

"Please go to the admitting desk so they can get all the necessary information." She pointed to a glassed-in area to the right of the emergency room.

"Dickon, I'm sure Edward will be okay," Sarah said, chewing on a cuticle. "We got him before his appendix ruptured, didn't we?" She sat down next to him in the waiting room.

"I think so. I don't know."

"This hospital has a very good reputation. I'm sure everything will be fine," she said.

"Oh God! Sarah, I can't lose him now. That would be unbearable." He squeezed his eyes shut and buried his head in his hands. Sarah stroked the back of his head. He reached for her hand and held it against his cheek. "I know I could still lose him. I want him so much that I didn't want to face this possibility. But I must."

"I don't know how you're able to bear up. I'd be a basket case by now," she said. "Your hands and face are red. Did it happen when you pulled Michael and Edward from the QDE's interface?"

He examined his hands. "Yes, I felt a slight burning sensation. Michael was right. I really can't go back."

"Speaking of Michael, I want to find out how he's doing. I didn't like how he looked when we ran out. Will you be all right for a few minutes? I can't get a signal in here."

"Jesú! I do want to know."

He tried to calm himself after Sarah left. It was so hard to wait, to not be in the center of the action. Ever since his first command, he'd been in the thick of things, and now he was just an observer.

Sarah returned about five minutes later. "I spoke to Elaine, they called nine-one-one right after we left. He's here."

"Do you know where?"

"Yes, I stopped at the desk. He's in intensive care." She sat down.

"Do you know if he'll recover?" he asked. "God, I hope so. I owe him so much."

"We'll see him once Edward is in recovery. We'll have time then," she said. "How long has he been in surgery?"

"More than an hour."

"We shouldn't have too much longer to wait. Did he speak to you? Did he recognize you?"

"Aye, he was very frightened by what he was experiencing," he said. "But I was able to reassure him and tell him that he would see and hear many strange things and not to be afraid."

"That's good," she said. "I'm sure it will really help him."

"Mr. and Mrs. Gloucestre?"

"Yes," Richard said. He and Sarah stood. "How is Edward, doctor?"

"I'm Dr. Mark Benson, your son's surgeon. He'll be in recovery for about two hours. I have to warn you. There's been a slight complication. His appendix ruptured before we could operate."

The blood drained from Richard's head. He sat with a thud.

"Is he going to be all right, Doctor?" Sarah asked.

"We think so, but it means we'll want to keep him here at least two days if not three. We need to make sure there's no infection."

"How soon can I see him?" Richard asked.

"Check in with the administrator over there, and she'll let you know his room assignment once he's ready to be moved," Benson said. "Do you have any questions?"

"What is your prognosis, Doctor?" Sarah asked.

"Very good," Benson said. "There's always a risk with surgery, but I think you can relax. Will one of you be staying with him?"

"I will," Richard said.

"Good. You can arrange that with the head nurse once he's in his room. If there are no questions, I'll be on my way."

They both shook their heads no.

"Are you all right?" Sarah asked.

"That was a shock. I thought we got him before it ruptured."

"It had to have just happened. The doctor didn't seem overly concerned."

"Would he tell us?"

"I think so. If Edward were in more danger, I think Benson would have wanted to prepare us for the worst."

That eased his mind some.

"Feel better?"

"Yes."

"Let's go see Mike," Sarah said.

Richard and Sarah put the disposable gowns on over their street clothes before they entered the intensive care room that kept the blond physicist alive. There were many tubes and wires attached to various points on Michael's slight body, now swallowed up in the large hospital bed.

The oxygen fed through a clear tube that ran from inside his nose to the outlet on the wall in a loosely draped loop. Medication and nutrient sacks were hung on poles attached to other tubes, while they dripped measured drops through needles embedded in veins in Michael's hand.

Sensors were taped onto his chest, head and arm that were connected to wires plugged into equipment for monitoring his vital signs. Richard could see the bag for collecting urine hanging off the bottom bed rail. The sheet covered the catheter tube.

"He seems so frail," Sarah whispered. She entered the room.

Richard nodded, threading his way to the bed, holding her hand tightly in his.

Michael's blue eyes flicked open, and his lips moved as if to speak. Richard stepped closer and bent his head. "Michael?"

"Is your son okay?" Michael asked, his voice barely audible and strained.

"He's in recovery. The doctor says he's going to be all right."

Michael closed his eyes, and his lips formed a slight smile.

"And you, Michael, are you going to recover?" he asked.

"I don't think so," Michael said, his voice a little stronger. "The doctors haven't said, but I was in that chamber too long."

"Why did you go in?" Sarah asked, stepping closer to the bed. "Why didn't you let Phil or Elaine go in like you rehearsed?"

"I couldn't wait. It would have been too late. History would have changed."

"But you were in for so long." Sarah frowned. "Surely you could have picked Edward up and gotten out of there in ten or fifteen seconds."

A spasm shook Michael's body. He groaned. "The dummy body was on the floor—I had to put it on the bed."

"Should we come back later?" Richard asked.

"No, stay, it will soon pass." Michael swallowed. "It took only ten seconds to put the dummy on the bed. I thought I had enough time still. I tried to push the robot carrying Edward into this century, but I wasn't strong enough. I could only move it a few inches before I started to feel the effects."

"Is that when you lifted my son off the robot?"

"Yes, but by now twenty seconds had elapsed, and I was too weakened to do more than fall forward with him in my arms. I still wouldn't have made it completely through if you hadn't grabbed me, Richard."

"You told me that I could not go back to when I existed in the fifteenth century, because I would annihilate myself in both existences."

"Yes," Michael said.

"I would not have made it to the fifteenth century. Just grabbing you at the entry point caused my hands and face to burn slightly. I think the destruction started."

"I am very tired," Michael said, closing his eyes.

Richard and Sarah walked out together. Sarah spoke after they removed the disposable gowns. "We need to contact his family. I know he has a sister."

"But where does she live?" he asked. "Has he told you?"

She chewed on a cuticle while staring past Richard, her violet eyes appeared unfocused. "Uh-uh. You can see him tomorrow and ask him."

"I'll do that. Edward will be able to meet him, too. I think Michael will like that."

"Let's talk to the nurses here. Maybe they can tell us something about Michael's condition and give us his doctor's name."

Once Edward was out of recovery, Sarah prepared to go home.

"I'll come back with some clothes for both of you tomorrow," she said. "That way he can meet me, before the girls take over."

He drew her to him and then lightly kissed her. They walked to the elevators and waited in silence. His wife glanced at him when it arrived, and she slipped into the empty car. "I'll see you later."

He went to Edward's room.

Secure with the knowledge that his son would soon arrive, his thoughts turned to a recent conversation he'd had with Evan Hosgrove. Hosgrove had given him additional responsibilities, to the point where he was practically running the company. He had been called in for a meeting three days before the rescue.

"I am very pleased with your progress here, Richard," Hosgrove had said. "I'm going to be retiring soon." He went on to explain that with all the newly acquired information, he was planning on lecturing at various Ricardian Society meetings. He then added, "You have earned my trust and demonstrated your leadership through managing the Q-trip project. I'm naming you acting President."

Richard smiled to himself. He wasn't king, or even President of the United States, but maybe leading a commercial enterprise would be a satisfying position.

An orderly rolled Edward in. The equipment was hooked up to the bed. Though Edward's eyes were still closed, they were moving rapidly under the lids.

"Edward?" He touched his forehead. It was cool, no fever.

"Your son?" the orderly asked.

"Yes. I thought he would be awake."

"The anesthetic does that a lot of times. They wouldn't have sent him here if he hadn't come out of it, but he musta fell asleep right away." The orderly finished connecting the equipment and left the room.

He sat by the bed and studied his son, barely believing that he was actually here, alive. He brushed Edward's cheek with his fingertips, feeling the warmth of the child's skin. His own tears were hot in his eyes.

Edward slowly opened his eyes.

"Papa?"

"Yes Edward, I am here."

"When did you return? I haith missed you." Edward reached out, and he felt his son's warm hand in his.

Before he could respond, Edward had closed his eyes and his breathing had slowed. He was asleep.

Richard had arranged for a cot in the room, but stayed in the chair instead, not wanting to be out of Edward's sight for when he woke up. He gazed at his son, nearly lost in the large hospital bed.

It had been two and a half years since he was able to see his boy, now lying before him. He was the image of his mother, down to the fair skin and the stripe of freckles across his nose.

He dozed off in the cushioned chair by the side of the bed while watching his son sleep.

"Papa?"

It was early in the morning when he was jolted awake by Edward's clear voice.

"Yes, Edward, I am right here by your side." He peered lovingly into his son's large brown eyes and caressed his cheek.

"There is some manner of thing pricking my member."

"Are you ready to meet your sisters?" Richard asked. He'd spent the entire two days in the hospital with Edward. During that time, Sarah had visited, which gave Edward a somewhat more gradual introduction to his new family.

He knew his son had not fully recovered from learning that his mother was dead, or fully comprehended that he was living in a different century, or that history recorded he had died before his mother did. Admittedly, he still had difficulty reckoning with the time schisms.

But he could see Edward was doing his best to please him, and he hoped that would be enough to carry his son, at least for the first few days.

"Yes, Papa." Edward stood by the bed, dressed in the jeans and sweatshirt that Sarah had bought for him. He was only four and a half feet tall, which was small for a ten-year-old.

The doctors had assured him that Edward would catch up on his growth now that he would no longer have the chronic sore throats from infected tonsils. His fear that his son had something seriously genetically wrong was not realized.

Sarah led Emma and Mary into the room. She and her daughters stopped in front of Edward. Emma and Mary were on either side of her.

"Hello Edward," Sarah said. "It is so good to see you again. I hope you are eager to leave this hospital."

"Yes, Madame."

The girls giggled.

"Emma, Mary, what did I tell you earlier?" Sarah asked sharply. "I want you to apologize to Edward for laughing."

"I'm sorry," Emma said. She was still clinging to her mother.

"Me too," Mary said, smiling broadly. She hugged him. At four years his junior, she was about a head shorter than he. "My name is Mary."

Richard and Sarah held their breath watching Edward's reaction to Mary. They had told Edward to expect Mary to be forward and for Emma to be shy. He was pleased to see his son smile and return Mary's hug after a brief hesitation.

"I am Edward," he said, letting go of Mary.

"Emma, don't be so shy," Sarah said. "Say hello to your brother."

"Hello," Emma said. She let go of her mother and stepped toward him, still hesitating.

"It is my honor to meet you," Edward said, bowing slightly.

His new family stood before Richard, now complete, with his son from the past. He would never forget this moment. He would never forget this time.

Author's Notes

FATE OF THE PRINCES: No one knows what happened to Edward IV's sons, Edward V and Richard of York, after they were found illegitimate and could not inherit the throne. There is no contemporary account that reports their status after September of 1483, except *Titulus Regius* by implication. There, Edward's children were referred to in the present tense. *Titulus Regius* was issued by Richard III's first and only parliament of January, 1484.

Although there were rumors that the princes were dead by the fall of 1483, Henry Tudor never declared that Richard III had murdered them or had them murdered. I believe it would have been in Henry's interest to prove the boys dead, since he had all copies of *Titulus Regius* destroyed (or so he thought, but one survived), because he wanted to marry Edward IV's daughter, Elizabeth, and needed her to be legitimate. If she were a bastard, then any of Henry and Elizabeth's children would not have been eligible to inherit his title—King. By destroying *Titulus Regius*, Henry legitimized all Edward IV's children, and the princes would have had stronger claims to the throne than Henry.

Perkin Warbeck claimed to be Edward IV's younger son, Richard of York. He successfully convinced many European Royals of this, including the King of Scotland, James IV, who arranged the marriage of Lady Katherine Gordon, daughter of the Earl of Huntly. In July, 1497, Warbeck was the focus of a rebellion, which Henry Tudor crushed. Warbeck sought sanctuary but eventually surrendered to Henry, and was imprisoned in the Tower. On November 23, 1499, Henry had Warbeck executed after extracting a confession in which Warbeck stated he was an imposter.

HASTINGS: In Edward IV's deathbed-will, Richard was named protector to Prince Edward because the prince was twelve at the time and still a minor. Once Edward IV died, Queen Elizabeth failed to notify Richard. Instead, Hastings sent a message to Richard, letting him know he was now protector and to speed to London. The message reached Richard about one week after his brother Edward's death, on April 9, 1483. Richard did not speed to London as Hastings had urged, but went to York around April 20th to pledge his loyalty to Prince Edward, before proceeding south to London.

The council meeting of June 13, 1483, started normally, but at some point Richard left. He returned about thirty minutes later, enraged, accusing Lords Hastings and Stanley, and Bishops Rotherham and Morton of treason. A scuffle ensued where Richard's guards subdued the accused. The Bishops were put in Tower cells, and Lord Stanley was held in special detention in his own lodgings. Hastings was beheaded that day.

Richard's actions against Hastings have always puzzled me, especially as it appears Hastings was denied due process. Throughout his life, Richard was known as a fair arbiter. In his capacity as a judge in civil and criminal cases, he often found in favor of the commoner over the nobility when the evidence supported the commoner's case. His practice of blind justice was in contrast to the norm of the day. One of his first decrees as king was to reform bail and juror qualifications. He wrote, "The law shall cease to be an instrument of oppression and extortion."

In his keynote address at the 2008 annual meeting of the American Branch of the Richard III Society, Dr. Peter A. Hancock theorized about what happened in that thirty-minute break. In his forthcoming book, *Richard III and the Murder in the Tower,* Peter Hancock posits that Richard met with William Catesby, attorney to Hastings, who revealed Edward IV's precontract with Eleanor Butler, which Bishop Stillington confirmed. This information is used here with permission.

LEFT-HANDED: There is nothing in contemporary records that states Richard was left-handed. My speculation is based on Richard III's portrait in the National Portrait Gallery (London), where he is fingering his right hand with his left, suggesting to me that his left was dominant. This and all other portraits of Richard were painted posthumously.

RICHARD'S ACCENT: Early Modern English emerged right around the time Richard III was born (October 2, 1452) and was spoken up to 1650 or so, when the more recognizable Modern English became the vernacular. In the fifteenth century, English was probably spoken the way they spelled the words. This was before dictionaries codified spelling, so the spelling was often phonetic. The dialect in certain isolated pockets of Appalachia is thought to be as close to sixteenth century English as we can hear today.

RICHARD'S VOICE: There is no record of what his voice was like. I imagined it to be deep and resonant.

TREASON: Unlike what Shakespeare would have us believe, Richard went against the advice of his generals and did not run from the battle. Lord Thomas Stanley, Constable of England, and Sir William Stanley kept their armies (armies that were pledged to Richard) back from the fight. Richard held Thomas Stanley's son, Lord Strange, hostage and threatened his execution if Lord Stanley went against him. Lord Stanley replied that he had other sons (his stepson was Henry Tudor) and refused to commit. In the end, Lord Strange was not executed, and Stanley's army killed Richard. Contemporary accounts record that Richard fought "manfully" in the thickest of battle, and when he fell, his last words were shouts of "Treason!"

Bibliography:

CLARKE, PETER D. "English Royal Marriages and the Papal Penitentiary in the Fifteenth Century." *English Historical Review (Oxford University)*, Vol. CXX, no. 488 (2005).

FIELDS, BERTRAM. *Royal Blood: Richard III and the Mystery of the Princes*. New York: Regan Books, 1998.

FLANDRIN, JEAN-LOUIS AND MONTANARI, MASSIMO, eds., (English edition by Albert Sonnenfeld). *Food: A Culinary History from Antiquity to the Present*. New York: Columbia University Press, 1999.

KENDALL, PAUL MURRAY. *Richard the Third*. New York: W. W. Norton & Company, Inc., 1955.

MANCINUS, DOMINICUS. *The Usurpation of Richard the Third*. Translated by C. A. J. Armstrong. London: Oxford University Press, 1936.

MCGEE, TIMOTHY J., RIGG, A. G. AND KLAUSNER, DAVID N., eds., *Singing Early Music: The Pronunciation of European Languages in the Late Middle Ages and Renaissance*. Bloomington: Indiana University Press, 1996.

PRONAY, NICHOLAS AND COX, JOHN. *The Crowland Chronicle Continuations: 1459-1486*. London: Alan Sutton Publishing for Richard III and Yorkist History Trust, 1986.

WROE, ANN. *The Perfect Prince: The Mystery of Perkin Warbeck and His Quest for the Throne of England*. New York: Random House, 2003.

Online references

AUDIO FILES FROM THE AMERICAN FRONT PORCH
DIGITAL LIBRARY
(http://ils.unc.edu/afporch/audio/audio.html#).

THE NEW ENGLAND CHAPTER OF THE RICHARD III
SOCIETY, American Branch, http://www.r3ne.org/

THE RICHARD III SOCIETY, AMERICAN BRANCH,
http://www.r3.org/welcome.html

THE RICHARD III SOCIETY,
http://www.richardiii.net/begin.htm

THE SOCIETY OF FRIENDS OF KING RICHARD III,
http://www.silverboar.org/

The Unromantic Richard III,
http://unromanticrichardiii.blogspot.com/

Author's website, http://www.joanszechtman.com/

The Story Continues...

Coming in 2010: *Loyalty Binds Me.* Richard's story continues when he returns to England with his new wife, her children, and his son. He intends to say a last goodbye to Anne Neville, his queen and his son's mother, now interred in Westminster Abbey. Upon arriving in London, he is arrested for the murder of his nephews.

Coming in 2011: *Strange Times.* In studying what happened to his loyal supporters after he was defeated at Bosworth, Richard learns that his closest friend, Francis Lovel, may have died of starvation, trapped in an underground vault at Minster Lovel Hall. Richard is determined to change Lovel's fate.

Visit the author's website at: http://www.joanszechtman.com/ for announcements, discussion group, photos, and more.

For book sales and discounts on bulk orders contact Collected Stories Bookstore:
Web: www.collectedstoriesbookstore.com
Email: bassetpublishing@collectedstoriesbookstore.com
Phone: 1-203-874-0115